THE
LAST
CITY

THE AHLEMON SAGA ⚙ BOOK ONE

CASEY McGINTY

"If there's a book you really want to read but it hasn't been written yet, then you must write it."

—TONI MORRISON

Paperback ISBN 978-0-9979832-0-3
eBook ISBN 978-0-9979832-1-0

Dedicated to my mother

JOAN DOUGLAS MCGINTY

Your indomitable spirit still inspires me.

acknowledgments

with love and gratitude

To my wife Lori. For sending me to my first Room To Write retreat and for your steady encouragement to write simply because it is food for my soul. Thank you for doing life with me.

To my children: Emily, Zachary, and Caeleigh. For the joyful memories of bedtime stories and for your enduring excitement as I processed my ideas with you . . . for six years.

To Charlotte Rains Dixon, my writing coach. Your cheerleading and guidance turned an insecure draftsman into a writer. Charlotte can be found at www.wordstrumpet.com.

To Laura Valentine, the caretaker of Penuel Ridge Retreat Center. Your thoughtful care always leads me to care for my own soul.

To Penuel Ridge Retreat Center. For giving me real rest and room in my spirit to write. Seekers can find Penuel Ridge at www.penuelridge.org.

To all my Beta readers. For your positive energy and thoughtful input.

To my early readers: John Thompson, Crystal Bryant, and MariLynn Ross. I can't believe you actually read through that early draft and *still* encouraged me.

To Renee Chavez, my copy editor. For polishing my manuscript, for your invaluable production guidance, and for being my first fan.

To my dear friends who have walked me through fear and insecurity.

To my outstanding production team:

Cover Design Roy Roper / www.wideyedesign.net
Typesetting Design Mandi Cofer / www.thetinytypesetter.com
Proofreading Kevin Harvey
Diagrams Ray Taylor
Photograph Stewart Doka

pronunciations

Names of the colonists are spelled with an *h*. A sharp ear would notice a slight *huh* sound when pronounced by native Ahlemoni speakers. For Earth speakers, the *h* is silent. *Thorin* is pronounced TOR-in. *Mhara* is pronounced MARR-uh.

Ahlemon – a•la•MAWN
Alto Mair – al•to MAY•or
Alto Raun – al•to rawn
Gheno Ra – jen•no raw
Leevee – LEE•vee
Matan – muh•TAWN
Meken – MEK•en
Rakaan – ruh•KAWN
Rhaji – RAW•gee

prologue

Eight hours before Push

A lone figure stood shadowlike on the observation deck high atop the city's central tower, the humid ocean air whipping at his metallic skin. As he had countless times before, he wished that he could feel it.

"Atticus," a voice spoke from the darkness behind him. "The Push is expected today. Everything is ready. Rakaan requests your permission to proceed."

Every night for almost a thousand years Atticus had stood in this place, knowing that this moment would come, but not knowing when . . . until now. *How did we come to this?* The question lingered in his mind for a few seconds, a long time for someone with his processing capabilities; then he dismissed it. It didn't matter; it would not alter his course. Instead, he was struck with the significance of the moment, and how a single word could hold so much power over the future of a planet, perhaps even the galaxy. He cocked his head and said, "Proceed."

Then he returned to contemplate the causality between this particular moment and the word *proceed*, and how the two marked the beginning of the end for the human race.

1

1

Over the Rocky Mountains

His head resting against a window frame on a Boeing 737, Kane McKennon gazed through a clear sky at the snow-capped mountain range below. From the vantage point of an airliner flying at thirty-five thousand feet, he was always amazed at how much uninhabited land there was on the earth. *What overpopulation problem?* he thought. *Space isn't the problem. Keeping the masses happy is the problem.*

Yawning, he brushed a lock of dark hair behind his ear and scratched at his beard, which was deliberately trimmed to a seventy-two-hour shadow. He closed his eyes and nestled in to the corner nook between his seat and the cabin wall. Two minutes later, he was wide-eyed, staring blankly at the seat back in front of him. Sleep had been elusive for days, his thoughts continually drawn to the one thing he wished he could stop thinking about . . . Leslie. Ever since she'd left him, a week ago, her *I'm-breaking-up-with-you* note had run in a continuous loop in his brain as he repeatedly tried to solve an unsolvable puzzle.

Kane,

It's not working. You live in solo survival mode. I'm not some problem to be solved, and I don't need constant rescue. You make a good hero, but not a good life partner. I really do care about you, but I need someone who wants to be in a two-way relationship. I'm sorry, Kane.

Good-bye.
Leslie

But there was no secret code. There was no hidden solution. There was only pain. And Kane simply didn't know how to deal with it. Awash with an emotional ache he couldn't identify, he gritted his teeth and pressed the back of his head into the headrest. He could still feel her warm body, smell her perfume, and hear her laugh. *I'm such an idiot. What the hell's wrong with me?* Unbidden, memories of other personal failures floated like a swarm of ghosts into his consciousness. He winced and groaned out loud.

"Are you OK?" his row mate asked.

"Yeah," Kane said, embarrassed but quickly composing himself. "I just realized I forgot something," he lied.

"You didn't leave the oven on, I hope."

"No, nothing like that. I think I left the car running."

The man's eyebrows rose; then a smile crossed his face as he realized that Kane was watching for his reaction. "Good one."

"Sorry. I couldn't help myself." Kane faked a smile.

Having made eye contact now, the man said, "You know, I didn't want to bother you when you sat down, but you're Kane McKennon, aren't you?"

"That I am." Kane knew what was coming.

"I watch your show, *Surviving.* It's a good one. I love the survival programs; they're such an interesting blend of brain and brawn. Guess I fantasize about having more brawn . . . and rugged good looks." He extended his hand. "I'm James Manassa."

Kane looked him over. He was tall and lanky, probably in his forties, dark hair, well groomed. Kane took his hand. His grip was confident. "And what do you do, Mr. Manassa?"

"I'm a doctor, a surgeon. But I'm a student of everything, much like you, Mr. McKennon. Your work is very multidisciplinary."

"Call me Kane. Yeah, I'm always looking for anything to help me become better at what I do."

"So, are you filming an episode in the Canadian wilderness?"

"Actually, no. My friends think I'm a workaholic, so they bought me a fishing trip for my fortieth birthday. I'm on my way to meet up with a couple of them at a lodge outside of Vancouver. How about you?"

"I'm returning home from a Doctors Without Borders symposium. I was on a panel discussing critical care without electricity."

"That's gotta be some challenging work. Sounds like you're already a survival guy."

"Oh, no," he said, shaking his head. "Not really. I'm just a typical doctor with a busy practice in Vancouver who likes a little adventure once in a while."

"Any doctor doing work like that is not typical. You're doing a great service."

"Thank you." Then, sheepishly, the doctor ventured, "I wonder . . . would you mind walking me through one of your spontaneous survival exercises? That is, if you feel like talking. If you'd rather not, I totally understand; just say the word and I'll shut up and go back to reading."

"No, I'm good." Kane was still getting used to the public recognition from having his own TV show. The forced conversations with total strangers could often be awkward, but he was intrigued by Dr. James Manassa. "We need a scenario."

The doctor was prepared. "What if we had to make an emergency landing in these mountains?"

"OK." Kane looked out his window. "First, it'd be a miracle if any of us survived a landing down there."

5

"Say we did, I'd really like to hear what you would do."

Kane didn't respond immediately, already considering the scenario.

"Evaluation, right?" Dr. Manassa jumped in. "Three things: people, conditions, and resources."

"That's right." Kane smiled, pleased that someone was paying attention to his show. While TV was mostly about entertainment, he really wanted his show to be practical as well.

"Does it matter where we start?"

"Depends on the urgency of the situation," Kane replied. "In this case, we can start with the people."

"So . . . ," Dr. Manassa looked around the cabin, "what do we have here?"

Without so much as a glance at the passengers, Kane launched into a verbal analysis. "This 737 has 138 seats. Eighteen are empty, so that leaves 120 passengers. Add the pilot, copilot, and three flight attendants and there are 125 people on board. The demographics are almost evenly male and female. There are two college soccer teams traveling together, a men's and a women's, and they're planning one hell of a party when they get home—they both won their recent matches. We've got the usual solo travelers; I'd say half business, half personal. There are six couples, two that are elderly, no children or infants, and a couple of older teens. The woman in 1A is brown haired, single, probably mid-forties, and wearing a beige blouse and black slacks. I could describe the rest of the passengers and tell you what seats they're in, but it's irrelevant, although you might suggest a sedative to the guy in 13C; he's terrified of flying. My takeaway? It's unusual for such a large, randomly assembled group to be so focused in its demographic; this one is made up of mostly younger adults, and they're healthier than average. As a group, they should do better than normal in the colder conditions. But a younger group is more disposed to leadership tensions, especially under stress."

Dr. Manassa stared, awestruck. "How did you do that?"

"I boarded last and walked the entire plane before I took my seat. It's a habit from my military days—the evaluation thing follows me everywhere. And I have a photographic memory." Uncomfortable with the doctor's stare, Kane scratched at his beard and added, "Don't be too impressed, doc. It's a blessing and a curse."

"I can see the blessing. What's the curse?"

"I can't seem to shut it off."

"The gift that won't stop giving, huh?"

"Something like that."

"Well, that was amazing."

Kane nodded, acknowledging the compliment. But Dr. Manassa's comment had set him thinking . . . how his so-called *gift* might be spoiling his relationships.

"So, conditions," the doctor said. (If he had noticed Kane's mental distraction, he ignored it.)

Kane looked out his window. "It's late winter, but there's some clear valleys, which means snowmelt—"

A brilliant flash of light filled the sky, turning Kane's vision to a wash of pure yellow. There was a collective gasp in the plane as he recoiled. He felt the doctor's hand fumbling for the armrest, where it found Kane's forearm and squeezed desperately.

"Kane, are you blinded?"

"Yeah. Are you?"

"Yes. Did an engine explode?" The doctor's fear was evident in his voice.

"No. We'd feel it." Kane was alarmed, but he was already analyzing the situation.

"Thank God." Dr. Manassa relaxed his grip. "The flash has bleached our retinas, but it should pass shortly. Close your eyes for a minute or two; then open and close them slowly."

Kane closed his eyes and listened. The plane sounded and felt normal. From the distressed voices, he gathered that only those looking out a window on his side of the plane were blinded. Many of the passengers were asking questions, wondering what had happened. Nearby, a flight attendant was trying her best to calm a woman who was particularly upset.

"My vision's clear enough," the doctor said. "I'm going to see if I can help." He slipped out of his seat.

Opening and closing his eyes methodically, Kane fixed his blurred gaze on someone sitting across the aisle. A red-haired girl came into focus. She was staring back at him with a *what-are-you-looking-at?* glare. He pointed to his eyes and mouthed, "Sorry."

Turning back to the window, he looked for the source of the flash. His first thought was an atomic detonation, but there was no sign of a blast, at least not on the ground. Looking up, he searched, and almost missed it; there was a subtle distortion in the sky. He blinked a few times, wondering if his eyes were still adjusting, but then he overheard the man directly in front of him pointing out the anomaly to his travel companion.

A patch of sky rippled, like water from a stone thrown into a pond. In a perfect circle, concentric rings pulsed outward, in slow, repeating cycles. The wave grew and appeared to be moving toward them, but because of its transparency, it was difficult to discern how far away it was. Kane first thought it was some kind of thermal wave, generated by the source of the flash. But it didn't fit the logic; a flash of that magnitude had to have come from a blast that would have sent waves out in all directions. Instead, what he was seeing was a focused beam of energy . . . and it was on a direct intercept path with their plane. Since they were traveling at over five hundred miles per hour, he didn't think it was coincidence. Apparently, neither did their pilots. Kane felt his body lift as the plane abruptly dropped altitude; they were taking evasive action. But the wave moved with them, tracking their plane like a heat-seeking missile.

A man yelled, "It's gonna hit us!"

While most of the passengers looked to see what he was talking about, several panicked and tried to move to empty seats on the other side of the plane, hoping that would somehow protect them from the impact. Tempers quickly flared as people jostled one another.

"Everyone, please stay in your seats," a flustered flight attendant entreated over the speaker system. "Please return to your seats and fasten your seat belts."

Dr. Manassa had already returned to his, apparently deciding it was time to tend to his own safety. In the midst of the rising chaos, Kane caught the words of a distraught female sitting in the seat behind him.

"I don't want to die," she whimpered.

How quickly a situation can go from totally normal to life threatening, he thought. And he knew that there was absolutely nothing he could do about this one. He was not a religious man, but as was his habit in times like these, he uttered a prayer. "God, we could use a little help." Then, willing his body to relax, he watched the wave approach.

Passengers screamed.

"Now," he breathed, as it struck the plane.

Silence.

Literal and complete silence.

The screams, the whirring of the jet engines, the whoosh of the air vent blowing; all sound was gone. Kane thought to jiggle his ears, but his hand didn't move. He willed it to move; it still didn't respond. He tried to look at his hand and discovered that his head and eyes were locked in place; he could only see what was directly in his line of sight, framed within the windowpane. Then it struck him that the plane wasn't moving . . . but it wasn't falling . . . it was frozen in midair. It was as if someone had taken a photo of an instant in time, and he was trapped in it. His brain was working: he could see, he could think, he was aware, but he wasn't in any pain. *Am I dead?*

There was another flash of light, this time coming from behind them, followed by movement in his window—the ripples of a second energy wave rolling over the plane. The sky and the earth completely disappeared and his window turned black. Then he stopped breathing. He couldn't even hear it in his head. He tensed, waiting for the pain of suffocation to start, but it never came. He was still self-aware, but there was nothing, no sensation at all.

A terrible thought struck him; maybe his mind was trapped in a body that didn't work. He recalled a horrific scene in a spy thriller where the antagonist suspended a guy in a dark, liquid-filled tank, fitted with a special breathing mask, and removed all stimulation to his five senses. He quickly went crazy, imprisoned in a living nightmare. A wave of intense anxiety flooded Kane's system, and his heart rate jumped dramatically.

Stop! he yelled inside his head. *Stop!* Calling on years of training and high-stress experience, he forced the fear fantasies out of his mind and willed himself to calm down.

To his relief, a thin, white line streaked horizontally across the black of his window. They were moving; the plane was moving. Or were they? It was the oddest sensation: more like everything outside the plane was moving instead of . . . instead of what? A second white line appeared, then another, and then a pair. Before long, a mass of white lines streamed across his window. That's when it struck him.

Space. We're in space. And those are stars streaming by.

As the wonder of this dawned on him, Kane's thoughts began to drift and slow down; he was being pulled into a slow-motion, dreamlike state. He considered fighting it, but it felt so peaceful. *So, heaven is on the edge of the universe, and God's taking us there in an airplane? I should have known—God is a Trekkie.* Letting his internal guards down, he fell into himself, like falling into an endlessly thick down comforter. He just *was*, and he was at peace.

Time and self-awareness were lost to him. If he slept, he didn't remember dreaming. When he woke, he fully expected to see the familiar morning sun pushing through the window blinds in his bedroom. He groaned with disappointment when he recognized the white lines streaming across the blackened window. As he became more alert, he realized that the stars were diminishing in number and they were slowing down. Then, suddenly, the scene distorted and rippled as another energy wave struck.

The stars and black of space disappeared and were replaced by a light-blue daytime sky with a canopy of white clouds underneath. Everything was still frozen in place—the plane suspended in midair, his body still immovable, his eyes locked on the window—all encompassed by the eerie silence. Then he heard it . . . his heartbeat . . . and his breathing. It came as no surprise to him when a fourth energy wave appeared in the sky. He guessed rightly what would happen next as the wave washed over the plane.

Everything came back to life in an instant; his senses were assailed with the roar of the engines, the air blowing from the vent onto his forehead, and the screams of passengers who had not reconciled the nightmare from which they were waking. Groans and crying filled the cabin. Someone vomited. Kane was dizzy and had a splitting headache.

"Doc, are you OK?" he asked, checking on the doctor. Dr. Manassa's forehead was beaded with sweat.

"Terrible headache," he said groggily. "That . . . was . . . awful." The doctor looked dazed until he squinted and his eyes focused on something behind Kane. "My God, what is that?"

Turning to look out his window, Kane found a sleek, wingless, silver aircraft hovering just beyond the wingtip of their plane. In all his years of ultrasecret military life, he had never seen or heard of anything like it.

"This isn't heaven," he whispered to no one in particular. "And we sure as hell aren't in Kansas anymore."

2

Day 1
1300 hours
An unidentified sky

Seconds later, four of the strange aircraft hovered outside Kane's window, and from the alarmed reactions of passengers, there were more of the same on the other side of the plane. Already traumatized by their nightmare, some passengers trembled uncontrollably, some hugged their knees to their chests, and others erupted into light hysterics. A fight broke out, including a clumsy exchange of blows.

Kane asked the doctor to let him out, and he moved into the aisle. When he stood erect, vertigo washed over him and he had to grip a seat in each hand to steady himself. After taking a moment to recover, he whistled shrilly, a skill for which he had gained some notoriety in the military. He had to whistle three times to get everyone's attention.

"Everyone. Calm down. Calm down," he said, in a commanding but soothing voice. "Eyes on me, please. Eyes on me."

Looking around the cabin, Kane made eye contact with those who were visibly struggling with their composure. As his gaze moved from face to face, he said confidently, "Nobody's injured. The plane is stable. And we're not under attack. We're OK." He paused, then added, "Now, take a slow deep breath with me." He led his fellow passengers in a couple of slow inhalations and exhalations.

With the exception of an occasional sniffle, a quiet fell over the plane. The flight attendants looked at Kane with gratitude. He leaned over to look out a window.

The alien aircraft were slightly longer than a fighter jet and sleek, resembling a slim, elongated arrowhead. They were covered in a shiny, chrome-like metal and had no distinct wings and no sign of a propulsion system. With no windows, not even at the cockpit, Kane assumed they were unmanned. They were definitely sci-fi movie material. While the military had dreamed of advanced hovering aircraft, these were beyond existing Earth technology. But he did see something that looked familiar—their formation and movement.

"These are escorts," he announced to the cabin.

"Escorts?" a woman asked, fear in her voice. "Who are they and where are they taking us?"

This sparked a flurry of questions, and the noise level in the cabin quickly escalated. Kane whistled again and the cabin quieted.

"I promise you, the best way to handle this is to stay calm. The answers will come. In the meantime, we need to work together, not against each other. Besides, I don't think we're in imminent danger."

"How would *you* know?" a well-dressed businessman yelled from the front.

"I'm ex-military," Kane replied. "Special Forces. I recognize these movements, and they're not aggressive. Again, let's stay calm and work together. Can we do that?" He nodded, then waited for the passengers to nod with him.

"Good," he said finally. "Now, how about we let our flight attendants bring us some drinks . . . and some aspirin." He bobbed his head at the attendants, and they moved into action. Kane remained standing, like a shepherd reassuring his flock.

A fifth ship appeared at the left wing of the 737 and then moved forward to the front of their plane and out of sight. It came back into view a few moments later, then veered to the left and dropped back. The same ship returned to the front of their plane and again veered to the left, only this time the aircraft just behind it also veered left. Both ships dropped back and repeated the maneuver, moving forward and veering to the left. Just then, the cabin speakers crackled and the pilot addressed the passengers for the first time since the blinding flash of light.

"Attention, passengers. This is your captain, John Tygert. Sorry I haven't spoken to you sooner, but we've been busy up here. I can't begin to explain what has happened to us. But I can tell you that our plane is operating normally with the exception that we have absolutely no communications. And, as you can see, some very unusual aircraft now accompanies us on either side. They do not appear hostile and, based on their movements, I believe they're trying to get us to follow them. I have no idea of our location or bearing, so I'm going to follow their lead. Try to remain calm. We are not in any obvious danger at this time. If you need assistance, please ask a flight attendant for help. I'll keep you posted. Flight attendants, report as able. Captain out."

The plane banked to the left, following the lead alien ship, and the other escort ships moved with them. The flight attendants were pros, doing their job as if everything was normal. The routine activity in the cabin soon helped to settle everyone's nerves.

As Kane was about to take his seat, he noticed the red-haired girl, the one he had been staring at when his eyesight readjusted. She was traveling alone, and it looked like she was crying and trying to hide it. She reminded him of his younger sister, Madeline, and his big brother instinct kicked in. He whispered to the woman sitting in the aisle seat on the same row as the girl and the woman moved to a seat on another row. Kane took her place, an empty center seat between him and the girl.

"Are you OK?" he asked.

"What do *you* think?" she said, sniffling and refusing to look at him.

"Yeah, stupid question."

"Sorry. I'm a bit shook up."

"That's understandable. My name is Kane."

She didn't answer.

"Sorry I was staring at you earlier. I was trying to get my eyes to adjust after that flash, and you just happened to be my focal point."

"So, you're not some weirdo?"

"Some of my friends think so."

This caught her attention and she looked at him, wiping the tears from her cheeks. "I'm Charly."

"Nice to meet you, Charly. So, where were you headed . . . before our little detour?"

A pained look fell over her face. "To visit . . . family in Vancouver . . . for an anniversary." She shifted toward the window, her body language all but shutting down the conversation.

Kane didn't want to leave her alone. "Do you mind if I sit here?"

"Fine." She didn't turn.

He settled into his new seat. If nothing else, he thought his presence might give her some reassurance.

Dr. Manassa touched him on the shoulder, looking in on him and Charly. Kane assured him they were fine, and the doctor moved on. Kane watched as the doctor knelt in the aisle next to a lady who was hyperventilating and engaged her in a conversation. Within a minute, she was doing breathing exercises right along with the doctor.

"I'm scared," Charly said suddenly.

Kane turned his attention to her and answered, "Me too."

She looked him over. "You don't look like the type to get scared."

"Everyone gets scared. The difference between people is what they do with their fear." He glanced at the alien ships.

Charly looked out the window and turned back, "So, what do you do with it?"

Kane had a little speech about fear that he used to give to new recruits; it came to mind and he went with it. "I look it in the eye and ask why it's there. Most of the time, the fear is imagined. If it's imagined, I push it out of my mind. If it's a real threat, I consider what I can do about it. If there is something I can do, I start doing it. If there is nothing I can do, I try to accept what is."

She looked at him like he was crazy. "I don't think I can do that."

"You'd be surprised what you can do; it just takes some practice."

"How do you practice something like that?"

Kane thought for a moment. "What are you afraid of right now?"

"Bad things happening to us."

"Like what?"

"Scary aliens. Pain. Dying. Being alone."

"So, let's look at them. Are any of those things happening to you right now?"

"No. But they might."

"OK, but does that make them real or imagined?"

"Imagined . . . right now. But they could become real."

"But why worry about them now if they're not true now?"

Charly didn't have an answer.

"What's true now?" he continued.

"You mean . . . like . . . you and I are talking?"

"Yeah, what else?"

"We're flying in a plane and these spaceship things are flying around us."

"Right. Are you in pain, or alone, or dead?"

"No. But pain and alone are relative."

Kane was surprised at her response. "How old are you?"

"Seventeen."

"Pretty insightful for someone so young."

"Wasn't my choice."

Kane knew there was a story behind her words but decided to continue with his lesson. "Anything else?"

"We're not on Earth?"

"I think . . . that's true."

"So, *why* shouldn't I be afraid?"

Kane had asked himself the same question earlier.

"I suspect we've been brought here deliberately," he said, "probably at considerable effort. That would mean there's a purpose to this. Looking at the collective pieces so far, my gut says they mean us no harm."

"You really think so?"

"Yeah, I really think so."

She leaned back in her seat, wrapping her arms around herself.

Kane settled into his seat and closed his eyes; there was no telling when he might get another chance to rest.

"How do you know all this stuff anyway?"

He turned his head and looked at Charly with a serious face. "I read comic books."

She smiled. "You are a jerk."

Kane grinned back. "Yeah, I know." Then he shifted to a serious tone. "Charly, I believe I'm right about what's happening here. Trust me for now?"

"Yes," she said, visibly trying to accept his assurance.

The plane flew straight and level for another few minutes with no break in the cloud bank. Finally, the captain addressed the passengers over the intercom again.

"This is your captain. The aircraft are descending and we're going to follow. I want to thank you for staying calm. I hear that everyone's doing great. Keep up the good teamwork. Speak to you soon."

The passengers pressed together to see out the windows as the plane descended into the cloud bank. The white fog quickly gave way, revealing a dark-blue, choppy ocean far below, stretching to the horizon in all directions.

The plane banked left and Kane saw a small island in the distance. As they drew closer, he decided it was a man-made structure; perfectly round and several miles in diameter, it was a city-sized building sitting in the middle of an ocean.

"Is that where we're going?" Charly asked.

"Looks that way."

Kane marveled at the engineering required to construct a structure this size, particularly in the ocean waters; it had to be sitting on massive pylons or an island. As the 737 flew directly over the structure, he saw that it was composed of two sections, an outer ring and an inner circle. The outer ring was easily a mile thick, flat roofed, and covered in sand and a mature growth of coastal shrubbery and trees. The inner circle was clear of vegetation and was slightly domed, tinted, and translucent, with broad structural latticework barely visible underneath. The design suggested a vast open space below. *A giant skylight?* But it had to be three miles in diameter, an unthinkable span for a latticed structure. In the very center, a cylindrical tower extended high above the roof, the top section of a skyscraper towering well over a thousand feet.

Having completed the flyover, they began to circle the fortresslike building. Its outer wall was a dull grey, easily five hundred feet tall, sheer, and smooth except for the large, hangar-like doors at the base, dispersed regularly every half mile or so. Waves splashed against a ledge, the width of a single-lane road, encircling the building just above the water line. With the exception of the domed skylight, the entire structure was severely tarnished and weathered; it looked ancient and desolate.

It struck Kane that there was no place to land their plane. While the roof was certainly large enough, the outer ring was covered in trees, and the domed skylight was not an option. But as they rounded the building, their landing solution presented itself;

a runway-width platform was slowly extending out from a hangar, the open hangar door easily large enough for their plane to pass through. Drawing closer, he realized that the runway wasn't sliding out from the building via some hydraulic system; it was being constructed by—

"Robots," Charly said.

Indeed, unmanned machines in various shapes and sizes were in a flurry of activity on and around the runway. Flatbed, wheeled vehicles rolled out of the hangar, carrying stacks of large metal plates. At the leading edge of the runway, two barges with hydraulic arms lifted pylons from their decks and set them upright in the water. Two other barges lifted I-beams and aligned them between the pylons. A crew of spiderlike robots scampered up and down the pylons and I-beams, fastening them together to create a structural frame. Another dozen mechanical arms on treads set the metal plates on the I-beams, and the spider robots made the attachments. They worked methodically and amazingly fast; the runway was rapidly taking shape.

While the construction robots were fascinating, Kane's attention was drawn to a dozen robots scattered about the runway, directing the work. Encased in a smooth, silver metallic skin, they were humanoid in form, no male or female distinctions, jointed limbs, a mouth and jaw, eyes and nose, and a semblance of earlobes. Then his eyes fell on a single humanoid robot that stood just outside the hangar door, observing the overall construction activity; he was gold plated.

For Kane, a key question in his mind had just been answered. If these robots were designed in the image of their creators, then the inhabitants of this planet were human. This was welcome news. He looked over the passengers; if they had come to this same realization, it was subconscious. Glued to the windows, they were relatively relaxed and talking, more curious than alarmed at the scene below.

Their plane veered away from the building and they began a tight, circular holding pattern over the water, waiting for the robots to finish assembling the runway. Kane noted that a lone alien aircraft still led them while all the other escort ships had disappeared.

"We really gonna land on that thing?" Charly asked, tightening her grip on the arm of her seat.

"No problem," he said, concealing his own concern.

On their second pass, Kane found the departed escort ships were now hovering over the water at the leading edge of the runway. *Odd,* he thought; they were facing away from the construction, looking out and over the ocean water. Slipping from his seat, Kane moved to where he could see out a window on the other side of the plane. Sure enough, in the distance, just below the horizon, a number of objects in the water were moving in a line and toward the building. They appeared to be gliding over and under the surface of the water, like large sea animals rather than submarines. Whatever they were, even at this distance he could tell they were big, far bigger than Earth whales. He returned to his seat next to Charly.

"Everything OK?" she asked.

"Yeah," he said. But he knew an impending conflict when he saw one—a timer was ticking down.

Several circles later, their plane moved into a wider arc. As the captain addressed them, Kane saw half a dozen escort ships leave the runway and collectively move in the direction of the incoming water creatures.

"This is our final approach," the captain announced. "We're going to land. Everyone in your seats with seat belts on *now*—that's an order. Make sure anything loose is tucked up under your seat or in the seat pocket. I'm confident we can land on this runway, but I doubt it will be smooth. Remember: your seat cushion is a flotation device, just in case we end up in the water. Attendants, take a seat near the emergency exits. I will see all of you shortly, on the ground. Captain out."

Seconds after the captain signed off, a girl at the back of the plane let out a bloodcurdling scream. Kane and Charly twisted around and found her, wide-eyed and speechless, frantically pointing out her window. Charly gasped. Kane followed their gaze, and goose bumps rose on his arms. Like a skyscraper rising out of the sea, a gargantuan serpent towered a thousand feet, swaying in the sky. Kane immediately realized his mistake; what he thought was a herd of whales traveling in a line turned out to be this single serpentine creature undulating through the water. Great splashes erupted a mile behind its head as the monster flicked its tail. Reminiscent of a Chinese parade dragon, huge scales in varying shades of emerald green covered its thick, snake-like body, an occasional wispy fin fluttering on its sides. It roared as the alien escort ships hovered around its head. Even from this distance Kane could make out multiple rows of razor-sharp teeth framing a mouth that could easily hold an entire football field. Massive beyond anything he had ever imagined for a living creature, it was both terrifying and elegant.

The serpent faced off with the escort ships, which now fired bluish beams of light, striking just below its head. *Laser weapons*, Kane thought. But they were not inflicting any real harm. Irritated, the monster flung itself toward the ships, and they whipped themselves back, narrowly avoiding a collision. As they continued to fire, the serpent shook its head and then launched forward into the water and disappeared.

Kane heard the whir of the plane's landing gear deploying and felt it jolt into place. Low to the water, they were about to land.

"Sit back in your seat," he instructed Charly.

Her entire body tensed and started to tremble. She turned her head and reached out a hand toward Kane. "Please," she entreated. He wrapped his hand around hers.

Just outside his window, Kane saw giant inflated bags bulging out from under the sides of the runway. The wheels of the plane hit the metal planking, and the runway sank ten feet. With the sudden drop, the passengers were lifted off their seats, their bodies straining against their seat belts. Then they were thrown down into their seats as the plane bounced back up. On the second touchdown, the runway sank again, but this time the plane tilted to the left. Passengers screamed. The captain masterfully righted the plane by the next touchdown, where the balloon supports disappeared and the runway firmed up. Kane and Charly lurched forward and grunted as the engines reversed thrust and wing flaps moved into position. Even with the aggressive braking, the wall of the building was approaching fast; they would need more runway.

"KAAANE!" Charly yelled, her frantic voice rising in pitch as she dragged out his name. Following her gaze, he saw the serpent's head gliding over the water, coming in at an angle from their side of the plane; it would reach the runway behind them in a matter of seconds.

The alien ships had moved low and were firing a barrage of laser blasts directly at the serpent's head. The creature slowed and looked as if it were going to dive back under the water, but in a surprisingly quick movement, it jerked its head upward and struck a ship that had come too close. The ship crumpled and slid down the serpent's scaly hide and into the water. Shaking its head in triumph, the monster opened its cavernous mouth and emitted a roar that drowned out the jet engines and the passengers' screams. Then the serpent pushed ahead, a great wave of water welling up in its forward path. The plane shook as the wave struck the runway behind them.

Suddenly, the sunlight disappeared—they had entered the hangar. The wheel brakes locked and the plane lurched hard. Skidding and with tires screeching, the plane rotated slightly and finally came to a stop several hundred feet inside the hangar. Looking back through the open hangar door, Kane and Charly watched the wave roll toward them, twisting and snapping the runway in a series of breaks.

Then, to Kane's astonishment, the wave abruptly stopped surging a dozen yards out from the building, and the short length of runway that remained settled back down to level and then collapsed into the ocean, leaving only a very small swell of water to slosh into the hangar. The wave now rose in a sheer vertical wall of water, pressed against an invisible barrier that extended as far as he could see in either direction. A transparent film vibrated against the wave, extending into the air above it . . . *A force field*, Kane thought.

Unaware of the barrier, the serpent crashed headfirst into the force field at full momentum, generating a concussive wave that shook the building and their plane. With the impact, the force field turned an opaque white, and long fingers of spark-like static jumped into the air. Kane couldn't imagine anything withstanding such a massive blow, but the field held. The serpent roared in frustration and threw itself against the force field, only to meet with the same result. Kane lost sight of the monster, the hangar door blocking his view as it slowly closed from above and finally struck the floor with a clanging thud.

Engulfed in darkness, the passengers sat speechless amid the whir of the idling plane engines and the muted bellows of the sea serpent outside. Then, in a surreal moment, the cabin lights came on, the familiar chime sounded, and the unfasten-seat-belts sign illuminated.

3

The cockpit door opened, and the captain entered the main cabin. He addressed the passengers. "Sorry for that landing, folks. But considering the circumstances, I'm happy we made it in one piece."

"Bravo, Captain," an older man called out, and the passengers joined him in applauding.

The captain nodded and waved for them to quiet down.

"Thank you," he said in a deep Southern accent. "And, thanks to my copilot, Sam Williams. He's shutting down the engines to conserve our fuel in case we need it later. From the light of our forward headlamps, we can see that we're in a very large hangar. There's no sign of the robots." He loosened his tie, then added, "It's gonna get a bit stuffy in here, but I'd rather not open the doors just yet."

"Captain," a man sitting next to him interjected, "I have an international business to run, and I need to return immediately. I could be

25

losing millions." With sculptured dark hair, a tailored business suit, and a diamond-studded Rolex, the man appeared sincere.

Several passengers snickered. The captain leaned toward the businessman for a more personal communication. Kane strained to overhear the interaction.

"What's your name, sir?" the captain asked.

"Marshall Drummond," the man responded.

"Well, Mr. Drummond, I hate to say it, but I'm thinking we're a long ways away from your business. Are you a leader in your company, Mr. Drummond?"

"Yes, of course, I'm the founder and CEO."

"Well, I could sure use some leadership help right now. Can you help me keep these people calm and collected while we figure out how to get home?"

"Yes, I can do that."

"Thank you, Mr. Drummond." The captain turned and faced the larger group. He paused. Kane could see he was trying to gather his thoughts.

"I don't know who, or what, has brought us here," he began, "but they've gone to a lot of trouble to make sure we made it into this hangar safely. That's a good sign. Now, I need you to do two things. First, I want each of you to choose a buddy. You will be responsible to keep track of your buddy. Second, I want all of us to stay together as a group. Got that? Buddy up and stay together. Now, choose your buddy."

Charly tugged on Kane's shirtsleeve. "Will you be my buddy?" she asked.

"Yes, ma'am."

Evaluating the captain, Kane watched him ask the flight attendant a question. She pointed to Kane. When the captain made eye contact with him, the captain nodded his thanks. Kane nodded back.

Slightly taller than Kane, the captain was slim and fit, with close-cropped brown hair, and looked to be in his late thirties.

Based on his cowboy boots and particular Southern drawl, Kane pegged him as a Texan. Even in emergency command mode, he was relatively relaxed; Kane felt certain that he had active military experience.

Suddenly, ceiling lights came to life in the hangar and the passengers pressed to the windows. Flickering irregularly like old fluorescent tube bulbs, the overhead lighting was limited to a corridor the width of a two-lane highway, which ran in a straight line to the back of the hangar. On either side of the corridor, the light faded into darkness, the side walls of the massive empty hangar beyond visibility. The floor appeared to be covered in a thick layer of dust, recently trampled by the construction robots in a swath that followed the lighted corridor. Next to the hangar door and aligned side by side against the outer wall, the construction robots stood like statues, watching the plane.

"That's creepy," Charly said.

"He's coming!" a woman yelled from the back.

The golden robot approached them. Stopping beside the plane, just ahead of its wingtip, he stood, looking deeper into the hangar.

Following his gaze, Kane saw a small, flatbed vehicle moving toward them, a red light rotating around its outer edge. As it drew closer, he realized it was floating several feet off the ground, with no visible means of support or propulsion. *A hover platform*. It stopped between the plane and the golden robot. White light erupted upward from the platform, forming a column around seven feet tall. The column then swirled rapidly, distorted, and finally evolved into a recognizable image.

Standing on the platform now was a holographic image of a man dressed in loose-fitting white pants, white slippers, and a white, long-sleeved mock turtleneck. He had sparse white hair, wrinkled skin, and a gaunt frame. Facing the plane, he started to speak, but no one could hear him. Captain Tygert opened the front hatch of the plane and Kane caught the tail end of a statement from the holographic man . . . in an unfamiliar language. The man spoke again and Kane recognized the final words; he had repeated his prior statement. There was a pause, and then the man continued, this time in what was clearly a different language from the first. He then repeated that sentence and paused, waiting for a response.

Looking around the cabin, the captain asked, "Does anyone understand what he's saying?"

Dr. Manassa spoke up, "I think he's trying to find a language we understand. The last one sounded Asian, possibly a Chinese dialect. And curiously, the first one was very similar to ancient Hebrew."

"Are you a linguist?" the captain asked.

"I'm a doctor. But I've done some language study; I do a lot of international work. And I was raised Jewish, so—"

"What did he say?" several of the passengers asked in unison.

"I think he—"

"Please speak to me in your native language," the holographic man interjected suddenly—in English.

"Yes, that's what I thought he said," the doctor announced.

The captain shouted from the open door, "We speak English."

The hologram flickered and continued in English. "Do you understand me?"

"Yes!" the passengers shouted.

The holographic man smiled. "Welcome," he said. "Welcome to Ahlemon, our planet. I am Science Master Geno Ra, also known as the Professor. Do not be afraid; we mean you no harm. You are here as our honored guests."

"Wow! We won a free vacation to Fantasy Island and didn't even know it!" someone blurted out.

The passengers laughed, even Kane. With the tension broken, people started talking excitedly with one another.

The holographic professor spoke good English but with an accent that had a European flavor. Kane wondered at the odds of any dialect of English being an indigenous language on another planet. He over-heard Dr. Manassa speculating on that very topic with another pas-senger, suggesting that they must have paid prior visits to Earth to gather information.

The Professor continued: "You are in the city we call Alto Raun. Translated into your language, it would be known as the City of Hope. It was the last city—"

He was interrupted by the muted roar of the sea serpent outside the hangar door, followed by a deep thudding sound. The overhead lights went out and the image of the Professor froze as if on pause. After a couple of seconds, the lights returned. Then the image flick-ered and the Professor reshaped with a serious look on his face.

"You are in grave danger," he announced. "You must move deeper into the hangar, away from the exterior door. You must move imme-diately. Follow the Mekens."

A second muted thud echoed outside. The lights went out again and the hologram completely disappeared. This time neither the lights nor the Professor returned. A floodlight illuminated the area in front of the golden robot, radiating from his chest.

"You must move your aircraft or exit it immediately," the golden robot said. "You are in grave danger. The Leviathan has broken through our shield and is continuing its attack. Everyone needs to move much deeper into the hangar."

A bone-crushing thud sounded at the hangar door and shook the plane. The serpent's roar followed, thunderous, just outside. All the robots came to life, illuminating the entire area around the plane with floodlights.

"Exit the plane!" Captain Tygert ordered. "Open the emergency exits and launch the slides."

In the center of the plane, Kane opened the emergency door near-est him. As the inflatable slides activated, he yelled, "Everyone out!"

A monstrous bellow was followed by another blow to the hangar door. The door was heavily reinforced, clearly designed for extreme external conditions, but Kane knew it would be no match for the massive serpent. In a frantic rush to the exits, people started piling on top of each other.

"Single file!" the captain shouted.

Kane saw a giant of a man at the back of the plane start picking passengers up and setting them aside to undo the logjam. Kane had to wrestle a few people apart to avoid his own pileup. Out of the corner of his eye, he caught a glimpse of Charly arguing with an elderly man; she was trying to get him to go out the emergency exit first. The old man prevailed, moving Charly ahead of him. Kane called to her, but she was already speeding down the slide.

"Anyone else?" the captain called out when the plane looked empty. Kane and the remaining flight crew did a quick check of their areas, and each shouted, "Clear." Another blow from the serpent rattled the plane, and the hangar door gave a metallic creaking sound, forewarning that it was about to give way.

"Go!" the captain ordered, and they all jumped onto the slides.

Kane hit the floor running. A cloud of dust floated in the air, kicked up by the stampede of humans. Best he could see, the passengers were scattered but appeared to be moving in the right direction. He didn't see Charly, but she had left the plane well ahead of him. The next blow from the serpent brought the screech of tearing metal as one end of the hangar door crumpled inward. Sea air and sunlight rushed into the hangar along with a foul stench. Kane stopped to look. There was no way the serpent could get its head into the hangar, but it could still do some damage; a gushing wave of water would tumble anyone in its path.

A number of passengers lagged behind. Kane was about to go back to assist them when a robot buzzed by his shoulder. Twice as tall as Kane and rolling on a chassis with six wheels, it had the upper torso of an oversized human and four long mechanical arms and hands. Several more of the same robot passed him, all heading toward the passengers. When a robot reached a straggler, it would lift the unsuspecting person carefully and set him or her on the edge of its chassis, then move to pick up another passenger.

The serpent gave a deafening roar followed by its final blow. The hangar door tore away from the wall and tumbled to the floor with a concussive crash that knocked Kane off his feet and toppled several of the passenger-toting robots. Looking through the open doorway, Kane saw the inside of the serpent's cavernous mouth. It was lined with rows of closely set sharp teeth, each taller than a grown man. As he was getting to his feet, the serpent's tongue lashed out of its mouth and into the hangar until it touched the plane's landing gear. Feeling its prey, the tongue wrapped itself around the tail of the plane and then dragged the entire 737 out the hangar door. Giant jaws closed, crushing the plane midsection like tinfoil. The serpent shook its head and the forward half of the plane flew out and into the ocean.

Like an anteater attacking an anthill, the creature just needed an opening to reach its prey. The serpent's tongue lashed out again, extending deeper into the hangar and missing Kane by only a dozen feet. The vibration of it caused him to stumble and fall. At least fifty feet wide and half as thick, the tongue narrowed to a snakelike, two-pronged whip at the tip. Kane gagged from the acrid smell of sulphur and rotted meat. The tongue stopped and then pulled back in a sweeping arc away from Kane, catching any stragglers in its path. The terrorized screams of several passengers reverberated in the hangar until they disappeared into the serpent's mouth.

Pushing himself to his feet, Kane looked ahead, frantically searching the passengers until he spotted Charly. He broke into a run. She saw him and yelled something he couldn't hear. He waved for her to move deeper into the hangar. As her eyes widened in horror, he didn't even have time to look around before the serpent's tongue struck him in the back and swept him off his feet. He tried to pull away, but found his entire back side glued to the massive tongue by some sticky substance. Near the tongue's leading edge, he watched helplessly as it carried him directly toward Charly. She stood frozen with terror until a silver robot scooped her up in its arms and carried her out of harm's way. The tongue finally reached its limit and started to curl back. Kane's last sight of any human was the agonized look on Charly's face as she watched the serpent pull him away.

Helpless and flat on his back, Kane watched the ceiling light fixtures float by in slow motion. Dust particles hung frozen in mid-air, reflected in the floodlights. It was a phenomenon he had experienced only a couple of times in his life, the first when he was in a car wreck as a teen, and the second when he stormed a nest of terrorists in a crazed rush to rescue some of his men. Each of those times, he knew he was at death's door. This time, he was certain that death had finally caught up with him. Closing his eyes, he searched for a pleasant memory. His sister Madeline came to mind. She was laughing, sitting across the table from him in their favorite pastry shop, a white frosting mustache on her upper lip. He held this image of his sister in his mind; he would carry it into his death. Sensing the bright sunlight through his closed eyelids, he received its warmth as a farewell kiss from the sun just before being swallowed by the serpent. He relaxed his body, accepting the end.

But death did not come. The sunlight remained, warming his face. Somewhere behind him, the serpent screamed in a high-pitched, agonized tone. Deafeningly loud to anyone else, it sounded muted and distant to Kane. Cracking his eyelids, he saw the hangar ceiling, sun streaming in from the open hangar door just beyond his line of sight. The serpent's wails stopped abruptly, and Kane was left with the sound of his own breathing. He became vaguely aware of a silver robot standing next to him, cutting him away from the sticky tongue with a laser. Another robot joined the first and, within a minute, they were helping him down to the floor, chunks of serpent tongue still attached to his hair and clothes. The robots carefully burned the remaining residue from his back, then moved on to assist another survivor. He stood alone, wobbly and disoriented.

Charly slammed into Kane and he grunted. Wrapping her arms around his midsection, she buried her head in his chest. He returned her hug, and they held each other as her presence pulled him the rest of the way out of his death trance.

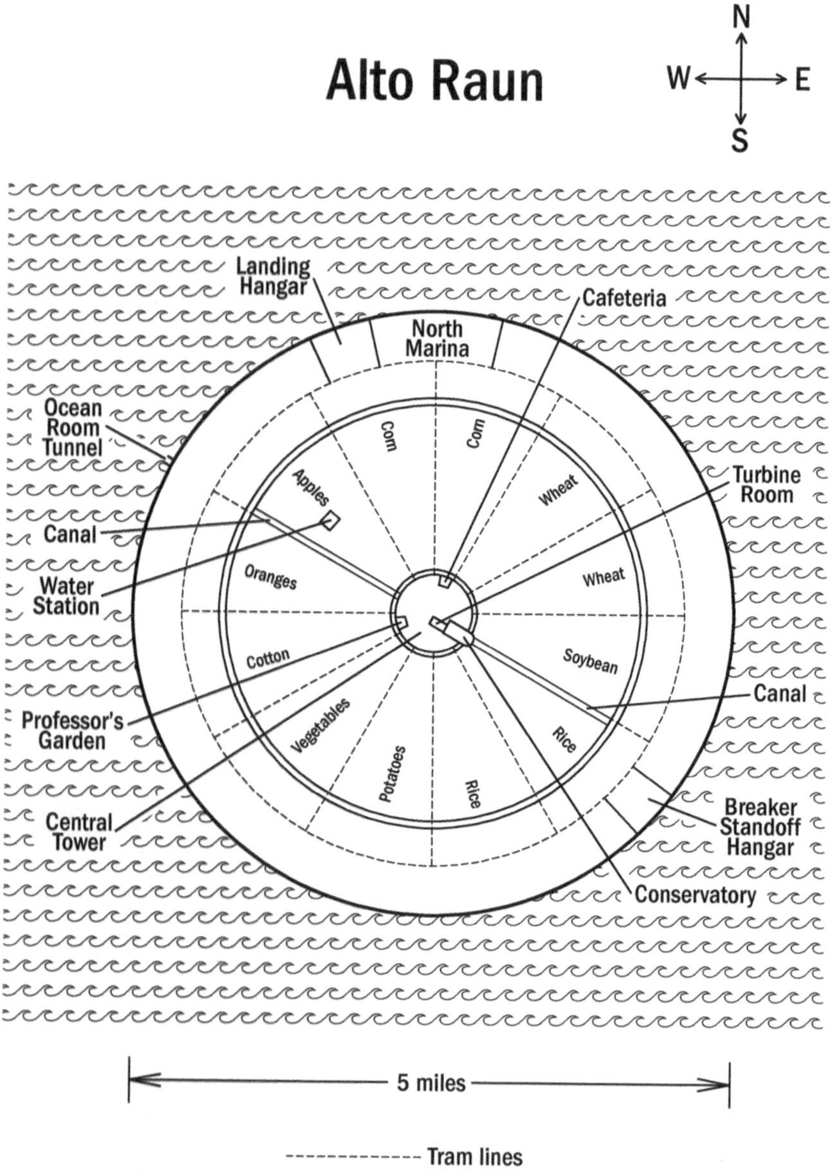

Alto Raun

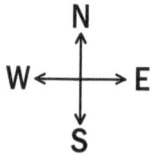

Landing Hangar

North Marina

Cafeteria

Ocean Room Tunnel

Corn

Corn

Apples

Wheat

Turbine Room

Canal

Oranges

Wheat

Water Station

Cotton

Soybean

Canal

Professor's Garden

Vegetables

Rice

Breaker Standoff Hangar

Central Tower

Potatoes

Rice

Conservatory

|← ———————————— 5 miles ———————————— →|

- - - - - - - - - - Tram lines

4

"What happened?" Kane finally asked.

Charly pointed. A translucent force field vibrated in place of the hangar door. "It cut off the end of its tongue," she explained, wincing.

Beyond the force field was the open sea; all signs of the runway and the serpent were gone. The force field flickered abruptly, then disappeared. A humid, tropical ocean breeze washed into the hangar and over Kane. He breathed deeply of the fresh air.

"You OK?" Captain Tygert asked, coming to his side.

"Looks like I can take a lickin' and keep on tickin'."

The captain smiled. "Glad you're still with us." He turned to Charly. "You OK, young lady?"

"Yes, sir."

The captain noticed a group of robots forming at the wall

35

next to the hangar door. Leaving Kane and Charly, he marched toward the gathered robots, bellowing, "Who's in charge? I want some answers!"

Kane and Charly followed him. Hidden inside the cluster of robots, they found the golden robot facing the wall, frozen in place.

"What happened here?" the captain asked.

A silver robot responded. "The Director generated a remote polarity field, and it has depleted his internal power supply."

Kane moved around the circle to get a better look and discovered that one of the robot's gold fingers was plugged into a receptacle in a control panel on the wall. This robot had saved his life.

"Is he dead?" Charly asked, the same question that was in Kane's mind.

"No," the robot said. "His power supply can be restored at the central tower."

"This is an outrage." Marshall Drummond, the business tycoon, had joined them, his expensive suit marred with dust from at least one good tumble to the floor. "Clearly, you were not sufficiently prepared. And your shield . . . thing wasn't strong enough. I hold you personally respon—"

The silver robot cut him off. "The resistance of an atomic polarity field increases in direct proportion to the energy of the opposing force. In simple terms, it absorbs the opposing energy and converts it into its own. Thus, the Leviathan's attacks would always be sufficiently countered by the nature of the field itself. The Leviathan did not break through the field due to our lack of preparation. The field failed for some reason as yet unknown to us."

Marshall's face turned red and he glared at the robot. Kane made a mental note to keep an eye on Marshall.

A self-propelled flatbed vehicle pressed its way through the crowd. Several silver robots disconnected the golden robot from the control panel and carefully laid him on his back on the flatbed; then they moved away toward the back of the hangar.

Before the throng could disperse, Captain Tygert confronted the silver robot. "Who's in charge?"

"In the absence of the Director, I am in charge."

"And who are you?"

"I am the supervisor."

Turning from the captain, the supervisor addressed the gathered robots in a series of mechanical tones, giving them instructions in a robotic language. The robots withdrew and separated into two groups. The supervisor started to join them but the captain blocked his way. Kane stood with him.

"I want some answers," the captain said.

"The Professor will explain everything to you when we return to the central tower."

"Why can't you tell me?"

"I am not programmed to receive you. It is the role of the Professor to receive you."

"Then I demand to see him immediately."

"The mobile imaging platform is not functional at this time. You will need to speak to the Professor in the central tower. I will take you there as soon as we have secured our perimeter. It will not take long." The supervisor stepped around him and joined the work teams.

The captain turned to Kane and shook his head, visibly frustrated by the brush-off.

"We're gonna have to let this one play out, Captain."

"Yeah . . . it's not like I can call his boss."

"Captain," Sam, the copilot, yelled from deeper in the hangar.

Tygert waved back, then turned back to Kane. "Can you gather these folks and bring them back to the group?"

"Sure. We've got it. You go."

Captain Tygert went and joined his crew. Kane looked at Charly and asked, "How 'bout we work together?" She nodded her agreement.

As the two of them looked for stragglers, Kane also watched the silver robots. Their structural design was impeccable, their movements fluid, very much like a human. One team carved up the serpent's tongue into large chunks and pushed them into the sea, while the other team built a makeshift hangar door with the same metal plates they had used to construct the runway. He could tell they were stronger than a human man, and he decided he would not want to face one in hand-to-hand combat. Other than when following an occasional command barked by the supervisor in their robotic language, all the robots appeared to be making autonomous decisions, even the non-humanoid ones. *How do they distinguish the supervisor from the other silver robots?* Kane wondered. But when he looked closely, he found that the backlight of their eyes varied in color—the supervisor had white eyes, the disposal crew had blue eyes, and the assembly crew had green eyes. *The eye color denotes function.*

Just then, the power returned and the lights flickered overhead, illuminating the corridor to the back of the hangar. Leading a small group of stragglers, Kane and Charly joined the others deeper in the hangar.

The passengers were not in good shape. Dusty, tearstained cheeks marked almost every face. Several small groups had formed, holding each other for comfort. Others wandered aimlessly, looking dazed. A woman had collapsed to the floor in her grief, sobbing in the arms of a stranger who was trying to console her. Some had started brushing the dust off one another's clothes and hair. The sight reminded Kane of a post–bomb-attack scene.

Kane and Charly found Captain Tygert with his flight crew; they were counting heads.

"How many did we lose?" Kane asked.

"We think twenty, maybe twenty-one," Sam said, wiping sweat and dust from his eyes. "But we need to confirm." Holding the plane's manifest, he did his best to call the passengers to attention and perform a roll call.

"They were here just minutes ago," a distraught young flight attendant said to no one in particular. I can still see their faces. Now . . . just like that . . . they're gone." She looked to each of her crewmates, tears welling in her eyes. "Those people, our plane, our luggage . . . it's all gone. Everything is gone."

An older flight attendant took the young attendant in her arms, and the girl burst into quiet sobs.

The captain regarded the grieving passengers with a pained expression; then he looked pointedly at each member of his flight crew. "We're going to keep everyone together," he said firmly. "We're gonna do our best to keep them safe. And we're gonna find this professor guy and get some answers."

A faint humming sound began to resonate in the hangar and slowly grew louder. "What is that?" the captain asked.

"It's them." Charly pointed.

The robots had stopped working and were assembled at the hangar door. Standing shoulder to shoulder, they gazed out to the open sea. All traces of the serpent's tongue were gone, and the replacement door was leaning against the wall ready to be moved into place. They had started in unison, but their humming had evolved into varied tones. Discordant at first, the tones modulated, finally finding a harmonious blend.

"They're singing," Charly said.

Kane looked over the passengers. They had calmed, mesmerized by the robotic chorus.

The robot song peaked in volume and held there, slowly undulating through several chordal changes over the course of a minute or so. Then the volume gradually faded and the harmonies fell away until finally they returned to a unison note, followed by an abrupt, synchronized ending.

The robots immediately dispersed into two groups. One began moving the makeshift hangar door into place, and the other, led by the supervisor, approached the passengers. He passed by the captain without so much as a glance. Outraged, Captain Tygert ran to head off the supervisor. The entire entourage of robots stopped when the captain confronted him.

"Wait a minute! You haven't given us any information. Twenty-one of our people have died. Where are you taking us, and how do I know we'll be safe?"

"We are taking you to the central tower. I assure you, it is safe there. The Professor will answer your questions."

"We need food and water, medical supplies, and bathroom facilities."

"We have prepared food and drink, and other resources and accommodations designed for humans at the central tower. Will you follow us?" The supervisor waited for a response. The captain looked over the passengers, stopping at Kane. Kane nodded, confirming that they didn't have a choice.

"OK," the captain said.

Without another word, the supervisor started toward the back of the hangar. The captain waved the passengers forward and reminded them to buddy up. Everyone fell into step behind the robots.

"A robot of few words," the captain said, coming alongside Kane. "What do you make of all this?"

Kane ran a hand through his disheveled, dusty hair and brushed it off on his pants. "I feel like I'm livin' in a Japanese sci-fi movie."

"More like a horror flick. Problem is, it's real. And I'm feeling out of control here. Not the way I like to roll."

"Captain," Kane said, getting his attention. "With the exception of the serpent attack, our coming here is not an accident, which is neither comforting nor cause for concern, but my gut says these robots are not a threat. We just need to stay together, remain alert, and let this thing play out."

"I agree." He looked Kane up and down. "You're military, aren't you?"

"I was. You too. Your landing on that floating runway was masterful. Where did you learn to fly?"

"Thanks. I flew from a carrier doing combat flights in the invasion of Iraq. What about you?"

"I joined just before the Gulf War and did special missions over the next twenty years. I left a couple years ago and went into consultant work; survival training."

"Sounds like the perfect guy to have on our plane."

"I'll help however I can. But"—Kane gave him a casual salute—"you're the captain."

The captain smiled. "Call me Tygert." Then he left to check on the passengers.

———

Since starting their march to the back of the hangar, Kane had noticed that Charly kept glancing over at him, as if there was something she wanted to say.

"What?" he finally asked.

"Nothing," she said.

"No, out with it."

She stopped walking and put a hand to her mouth. Kane could tell she was struggling with her emotions. He stopped beside her.

"What is it, Charly?"

Turning her face away. "It's . . . nothing."

"Tell me."

She glanced back at him, tearing up. "As I watched that monster drag you away . . . all I could think about was my parents waving good-bye." The tears started running down her cheeks.

Gently, Kane asked, "What happened?"

"They pulled out of the driveway . . ." She dropped her head and scrunched her shoulders.

"And?"

"They never came back. They died in a car wreck." Her tears turned into a sob. Kane took her in his arms.

41

"I'm so sorry, Charly. So sorry."

A minute later, she pulled away. "Yeah, well," she said, wiping at the tears with her shirtsleeve. "It's OK. I live with my grandparents now." She sniffled. "I was on my way to Vancouver to see my other grandparents . . . and visit my parents' graves. This weekend will be a year."

Kane was silent, reminded of his own painful story.

Charly looked up at him questioningly.

"Well, you need to know something about me," he said.

"What?"

"I'm pretty hard to get rid of."

Her face brightened. "I can see that." Then she grabbed his arm and pulled him forward to catch up with the others.

As they walked, Kane thought about his response to Charly. He was generally uncomfortable around teens, probably because he'd skipped being a teenager himself. His father had left when he was ten, and they'd never heard from him again. His mom had worked various part-time jobs and suffered from depression. He'd had no choice but to jump from childhood straight to adulthood, managing school, part-time jobs, and taking care of his mom and sister. The one ray of sunlight in that season of his life was his little sister, Maddie. She'd adored her big brother and he'd done everything he could to allow her to be a typical teenager. And now, here was Charly. Kane got a knot in his stomach, thinking that any attachment to her was probably going to hurt before this crazy adventure was over.

It was a half-mile walk to the back wall of the hangar. The robots led the passengers through a garage-sized doorway into a subway-like tunnel that ran left to right. Dimly lit, the tunnel was divided into a wide walkway on one side and a track of some kind on the other. Once they were all in the tunnel, the robots and passengers stopped and waited, the lights flickering overhead. The hard, smooth walkway was recently cleaned, obvious from the contrasting cobwebs and dust on the wall and ceiling. It was clear to Kane that a pathway had been prepared just for them, and he was willing to bet that the building around them suffered from a severe lack of maintenance. Shortly, a headlight appeared in the tunnel to their right and a tram silently glided down the track. Reminding Kane of the terminal trams at the Chicago airport, it was composed of six lighted passenger compartments, each with seating and hand poles. As soon as it came to a stop, double doors automatically opened on each of the tram compartments.

The supervisor and a dozen silver robots boarded, two in each compartment. The rest of the robots stepped aside on the walkway, making way for the humans. Spreading out, the passengers divided themselves among the six compartments. Once they were aboard, the doors closed and the tram silently eased forward into the dark tunnel ahead, the remaining robots watching them leave.

Inside the tram, the silver robots moved through the compartments, distributing water in canteen-like bottles. There was little conversation as the passengers received the water gratefully, parched from the dusty air. Lines formed outside of bathroom stalls in the back corner of each compartment.

At a T-intersection, the tram followed a curve to the right taking them into another dark tunnel and deeper into the complex. Half a mile later, the tram exited the tunnel into a wash of bright sunlight. Kane took in the sight through squinted eyes. It was rare for him to feel a sense of awe, but he felt it now: the tram had entered an enormous biosphere. Filtered through a translucent sunroof high above, sunlight filled the entire core of the vast building. At least a mile and a half ahead of them, at the center of the city, stood a massive cylindrical skyscraper, tapering slightly every two hundred feet or so; it reached to the roof and beyond, its polished silver surface reflecting rays of sunlight.

Immediately outside the tunnel, the tram passed through a green, manicured lawn crisscrossed with walkways. The lawn ran along the base of the building they had just exited, stretching left to right as far as he could see. After crossing the lawn, the tram entered a cornfield . . . at least, that's what it looked like to Kane. Walls of tall, green stalks stood on either side of the tram. Tipped with yellow corn peeking through leafy husks, it reminded Kane of central Indiana just before harvesttime. The cornfield extended all the way to the base of the tower ahead.

Looking back, he saw that the outer building rose five hundred feet in a sheer metallic wall to the sunroof. Encircling the entire city, it was deeply tarnished and dotted with dark, open spaces, probably once covered with glass. It looked as though it had housed a mix of offices and living apartments.

Kane immediately noted the juxtaposition—a building long abandoned, set against a manicured lawn and a cornfield ready for harvest. Doing some quick calculations in his head, he estimated that the entire structure was about the same land area as the island of Manhattan; it could house and sustain a lot of people . . . a lot of people who were nowhere to be seen. *What's going on here?*

Coming out of the cornfield, the tram veered to the left. To its right lay another parklike lawn, encircling the base of the tower. The tram came to a stop where the corn transitioned into what looked like a field of wheat. Beyond the gold of the wheat, Kane could see a green, leafy crop. *Beans?* He wondered how Earth crops had come to be grown here. The various fields were planted in precise, pie-sliced sections emanating from the tower.

The robots filed off the tram and waited at the base of the tower. Exiting the tram, the passengers meandered over the lawn, gawking at their surroundings. The air was slightly humid, but not unpleasant, and the aroma of the crops was carried to them on a light breeze.

The supervisor addressed the crowd. He pointed to a set of doors at the base of the tower. "These are your living quarters." Two silver robots opened the doors. "Inside, you will find food and drink, bath facilities, clothing, and sleeping quarters. Now, please choose no more than five representatives to accompany me to see the Professor. The rest of you will remain here."

In stark contrast to the outer ring of the city, the tower was well maintained; it even looked accommodating. As the passengers started making their way to the entry doors, Captain Tygert sprinted ahead and waved them to a halt. Complaints rippled through the crowd; they were hungry and tired.

Tygert held up his forefinger. "Give me just one more minute." He waved Sam over, and together they entered the tower. True to his word, they returned a minute later and announced that it was clear.

As the passengers streamed into their new quarters, Tygert pulled Kane and Sam aside and told them that he wanted to call an ad hoc council meeting to discuss the situation and choose their representatives to meet with the Professor. Then he motioned for the supervisor and told him he would return shortly with his representatives.

Inside was a cafeteria-style dining room with rectangular tables and chairs, more than enough to seat all the passengers. The room was pristine white, even the furnishings. Sunlight streamed through large panoramic windows facing onto the lawn. In the middle of the back wall was an open hallway leading to two floors of living quarters. At the far end of the cafeteria, a crew of silver robots moved in and out of an adjoining kitchen, delivering flasks of water and trays of what looked like fruit and vegetables, bread, and some kind of protein patty. Watching the others dig into the food, Kane felt his stomach growl; he really had no idea how long it had been since they had last eaten.

The captain selected his council and invited them to a table. It was a larger group than Kane would have chosen. He understood the captain's desire to get a wide range of perspectives, and he knew it would help with group buy-in when decisions were made, but decision making could get unwieldy. The council included Tygert; Kane; Sam, the copilot; Dr. Manassa; Marshall, the business tycoon; Shannon, the senior flight attendant; Arthur and Joanie, the elderly couple who had helped Charly out of the plane; Javier and Leslie, the captains of the two soccer teams; and a young couple named Ham and Jenn. Ham was the big guy who had helped the passengers exit the back of the plane. He was really big—NFL lineman big. Jenn stood in stark contrast to her husband; she was petite, wearing a conservative dress, with her long brown hair pulled back into a ponytail. Not wanting to leave Kane's side, Charly joined them.

The silver robots brought them several trays of food and there was a short period of silence as they ate together. The fruit and vegetables were tasty and crisp, the bread freshly baked and hearty, and the protein patty flavorful.

Tygert opened the discussion. "Thank you for your willingness to help. We need to see to the needs and safety of the passengers first. We've got food, water, bathrooms, and a place to sleep. And I understand there is clean clothing in the rooms. As for safety, the robots seem concerned enough about our well-being; I don't think they're a threat. Thoughts?"

Marshall practically exploded. "Captain, we've been kidnapped, lives have been lost, and our treatment has been inexcusable. Not to mention that my business was at a critical juncture and it's probably losing millions without my guidance. I want to know who's responsible and . . ."

Inwardly, Kane cringed. He knew the captain had invited Marshall to the table to keep an eye on him, but it came at a cost. To Kane's relief, Arthur, the elder council member, deftly stepped in when Marshall paused to take a breath. "You're quite right, young man; we have a lot of serious questions that need to be answered. But in my experience, things are rarely all that we see on the surface. I have a sense that we've been invited into a desperate situation and we may feel differently about our abduction once we hear the full story."

"I don't disagree," Dr. Manassa interjected. "But we know nothing about these robots or this place. And I'm uncomfortable with the thought of any of us splitting away from the group. For all we know, this Professor could be a trap."

In deference to the captain's leadership, Kane raised his hand, indicating that he'd like to respond. Tygert nodded for him to speak. Kane turned and faced the doctor.

"You could be right about the Professor," he said. "And I support your caution. But these robots have gone to a lot of trouble to make sure we safely reached this very place. All the signs indicate that we've been brought here with great deliberateness and, I suspect, for a specific purpose. I believe the failure of their shield, and the serpent attack, was as much a surprise to them as it was to us. From what I've seen so far, the robots are protective of humans by nature and they are serving a higher purpose . . . one which we are all keen to discover. I believe a mystery is unfolding here, not a trap, and we have some kind of role to play. But in case I'm wrong, I suggest we send no more than two or three to meet with the Professor."

Everyone agreed, and after a brief discussion—and despite Marshall's insistence that he be included in the group going to see the Professor—they decided to send Captain Tygert, Dr. Manassa, and Kane. Sam and Shannon would be the designated leaders in their absence. Standing on a chair, the captain called the passengers to attention and informed them of the plan.

Charly was not happy, reminding Kane that buddies stayed together. He could see that she was anxious about him leaving, and he fumbled with a response. Standing nearby and overhearing them, Jenn, Ham's wife, came to his rescue.

"Charly, right?" she asked in a sweet voice. Wearing a yellow sundress that favored her petite, hourglass figure, Jenn looked the epitome of girly.

"Yeah," Charly replied, not taking her eyes off Kane.

"I'm Jenn. You seem to be handling all of this really well. I was wondering if you might help me with some hospitality—you know: try to help everyone feel a little more at home."

Charly turned and stared at her with a *you've-got-to-be-kidding* look. "Hospitality isn't really my thing."

"It's the little things that make a difference." Jenn was extremely sweet mannered, but genuine.

"Why me?"

"Why not you?"

After a pause, Charly shrugged. "Yeah, I guess so."

Kane gave Jenn a grateful look, then put his hand on Charly's shoulder. "Thanks for helping. I'll be back as soon as I can."

"You better. I can't protect you when we're apart."

5

The supervisor led Tygert, Kane, and Dr. Manassa around the tower until they came to a garden. Set in the base of the tower, a short, white picket fence stood in stark contrast to the polished silver siding. They entered the garden through a vine-covered arbor and found an assortment of manicured shrubs and colorful flowers, natural light bathing them through a unique skylight system. The walls on each side of the garden were covered in a dark-green, climbing vine. A square toolshed made of ancient, grey wooden slats was nestled in the far left corner. The entire back wall was painted in an ornate, Asian-style mural. Following a moss-covered path inset with stones, the supervisor led them to the center of the mural and waved his hand across an unseen sensor. A small panel opened in the wall, revealing a touchpad and a circular receptacle. He inserted the tip of his right forefinger into the receptacle, and a door-sized section of the mural depressed into the wall and slid to the left.

They stepped into a small, rectangular room with no furniture and a polished metal door opposite the one they had just entered. The supervisor inserted his fingertip into another receptacle on the far wall and the door closed behind them. Immediately, a wall of red light formed on one end of the room and began moving toward them.

"Do not be alarmed," the robot said. "We must be scanned before we can enter this section of the tower. The scan is harmless."

Kane felt nothing as the light swept over his body. When it had scanned the entire room, the overhead lighting dimmed and the inner door slid open. Beyond was a brightly lit, sterile white hallway, thirty feet long, with another polished metal door at the far end. Once the group had entered the hallway, the door slid closed behind them. The lighting in the hall changed to a greenish hue, and Kane felt a wave of warmth wash over him. The supervisor led them down the hall.

"More scanning?" the doctor asked.

"Yes. This scan is confirming that you are the same entities that were in the prior room."

"And if we weren't?"

"A defensive mechanism would be activated. If the intruder tried to continue down the hall, the defensive measures would increase in intensity, ultimately incinerating anything in the hallway."

"Why the heat then?" Tygert asked.

"It is decontaminating the surface of your body."

"And it leaves you feeling so minty fresh," Tygert said sarcastically. Kane smiled. Dr. Manassa did not.

The supervisor opened the far door and they entered an elevator. The elevator ride was long, and there were no floor indicators. Kane felt unusual shiftings; he was certain that the elevator moved horizontally as well as vertically. When they finally stopped, the elevator doors opened into a large penthouse located on the exterior of the tower.

The far wall was one big panoramic window, revealing a light-blue sky with thin, wispy clouds outside. Entering the room, Kane noted that the hardwood floor was newly polished, dotted with several area rugs. There was an oval conference table on one side of the room with a dozen chairs around it. On the other end of the room was a sitting area with a large sofa, lounge chairs, end tables, and a coffee table. In the center of the room was a square dais rising two feet from the floor. The inner wall was dark wood paneling with no visible doors other than the elevator. They were hundreds of feet above the sunroof, which extended for miles in every direction. Kane stood several paces back from the window.

"Impressive," Dr. Manassa said, pressing his hands to the glass.

The captain joined the doctor at the window and whistled. "Quite a feat of engineering."

"There's a wide variety of crops," the doctor said. "And they all look very familiar. I wonder if they brought them here from Earth." He gave Kane a curious look and waved for him to join them. Kane moved cautiously to the window—he was afraid of heights. It had been a challenge during his military service and had only intensified with age. A deeply held secret, he knew how to manage it, but it always required a very deliberate exercise of mental willpower.

"The Professor will join you in a moment," the supervisor said. "I am returning to your comrades to assist with their settlement." And before they could say a word, he entered the elevator and was gone.

As the three men exchanged concerned glances, a panel on the inner wall slid open and, to Kane's surprise, the golden robot walked into the room. He stopped next to the dais, where a square column of light erupted toward the ceiling, swirled, and formed into a holographic image of the Professor in his all-white outfit. This time, he was leaning on a cane. Seeing him close up, Kane suspected that the Professor could easily be a hundred years old.

The golden robot spoke first. "We are very sorry for the loss of your people and your aircraft. While we expected the appearance of the leviathan, we did not anticipate the failure of our defensive shield. I deeply regret that we were not better prepared."

"You saved my life . . . and many others," Kane responded. "Thank you." Tygert and the doctor nodded.

"I was just performing my duty. I regret that I could not intervene sooner."

"What is your duty?" the doctor asked.

"Our primary duty is to serve and preserve human life."

"So, why didn't you destroy the serpent before it reached the runway?" Kane asked.

"We are programmed to preserve all life forms. We did not want to destroy the leviathan; we simply wanted to delay its progress until you were safely in the hangar and we could engage the city's external polarity shields. Unfortunately, a shield coupling exploded, sending a chain reaction back through the power network, severing several links to the city's central power source. The shields have not been used in a long time, and we suspect that—"

"You know," Tygert interrupted, "I really don't care what happened or why. We wouldn't be having this conversation if you hadn't kidnapped us in the first place. Why have you brought us here?"

As if that was his cue, the hologram of the Professor flickered and spoke. "Yes, you are due an explanation. Since we are now in my personal quarters, I can only surmise that my introduction upon your arrival was disrupted and the Director has brought you here. I am sorry for the delay. I hope there has not been a problem."

The captain exploded. "A *problem*?! Everything has been a problem. Against our will, we've been taken from our own planet, we've lost our plane, and twenty-one of our people are dead. Where the hell are we, and why have you brought us here?"

The hologram flickered, and the Professor spoke with genuine sadness. "I am very sorry to hear this, truly sorry."

Kane wondered where the Professor actually was; for all Kane knew, he could be in the next room—or on the other side of the planet.

"I can only hope," the Professor continued, "that you will have some empathy for our desperate actions when you hear the circumstances that have led us to bring you here. You are on the planet Ahlemon, the fourth in our solar system. I am Science Master Gheno Ra, commonly referred to as the Professor. The golden robot is the Director, the senior authority in my absence."

"In your absence?" Kane asked. "Where are you?"

"I am no longer living. The image you are speaking with is an interactive hologram of me responding in dialogue with you through an advanced communications processor in our central computer. I am also linked to the Director, who supplements the processor for real-time responses."

"How long have you been . . . not living?" the doctor asked.

"Two thousand, twenty-eight years and seventy-four days, based on our solar calendar, which is only slightly shorter than your Earth year."

The doctor gasped. Kane tensed. This added a whole new level of uncertainty to the reasons behind their abduction.

"Yes, a long time, longer than we expected. But we are very pleased that you are finally here."

"What do you mean, 'you are finally here'? Were you expecting us?" Tygert asked.

"Yes and no. Please sit down and allow me to tell you our story; you cannot understand without hearing what has led to this moment."

The Director motioned Kane, Tygert, and Dr. Manassa to the lounge area, where they sat on the sofa. The robot then went to the inner wall of the room, where a panel slid to one side, revealing a small kitchen. He returned with a tray of glasses and two clear flasks, one containing water and the other an orange-colored drink.

"Two thousand twenty-eight years ago our race died off. I was the last surviving human on Ahlemon. Prior to this, our planet had reached what we considered a mature state of civilization. We had achieved unified world governance and a stable world peace.

With this stability we were able to fully devote our collective resources to various cultural and scientific advancements. We had cured most terminal illnesses. To manage for population growth, we collectively chose to institute reproduction management, and people were allowed to die comfortably of natural causes without life-prolonging intervention. We shifted our resources away from military and medical development and focused on other sciences and new technologies.

"Our first advancement was in robotics, leading to the development of the Mekens. They are a sophisticated amalgamation of mechanical, biological, computer, and materials engineering. The Director is a Class 5 Meken, the pinnacle of our robotic program, the most advanced in every aspect of design. The Supervisor, identified by white eyes, is a class 4 Meken. He is identical to his Class 3 brethren with the exception of his advanced programming. Class 3 Mekens are the Sentries and the Builders. The Sentries are blue-eyed and designed to protect, and the Builders are green-eyed and designed for engineering. The remaining autonomous robots, including most of our aircraft and submersibles, are Class 2 Mekens. All Mekens have a capacity for independent judgment, decision making, and learning, but the Director exceeds them all. I must say, while the human mind and body are the ultimate creative masterpiece, the Director comes close, which is now affirmed by the fact that he has completed the unfinished pieces of our research and, through a relentless quest, has discovered you and brought you to Ahlemon."

The Professor turned toward the Director and bowed. "My congratulations to you, Director, on your achievements and success."

Tygert fidgeted, while Kane and the doctor were more tolerant of the pleasantries.

The Professor turned back to his guests. "There were numerous other fields we explored that brought wondrous discoveries, but in particular, we became obsessed with the search for human life beyond our planet. As you may have experienced in your own culture, when a person becomes inwardly fulfilled, they begin to look outward for greater purpose. And so it was with the entire human race on Ahlemon: we looked outward in hopes of finding a sister humanoid race in the universe and the origins of our existence. Our search led us to advancements in subatomic physics, from which we developed polarity fields, like the one used to block the leviathan, and our suspension technology, which is partly responsible for your travel to our planet."

Restless, Tygert stood up and started to pace behind the sofa. The doctor leaned forward in rapt attention. Kane was relaxed, absorbing the information.

"Then came our most monumental discovery. We confirmed the existence of other humanoid life in the universe and, simultaneously, discovered a means by which to reach it." The Professor paused, then asked, "Are you familiar with animals that have an innate instinct to find their way home, even over great distances?"

"Yes, homing pigeons do this on Earth," the doctor said. "It has never been explained."

"Well, such a link exists between humans. Through an accidental observation in a suspension experiment, one of our physicists identified a unique resonance that existed between our planet and another planet. In short, the resonance was a link between humanoid life forms. To our amazement, it reaches across astronomical distances, connecting with other human life resonances."

"And was that planet Earth?" the doctor asked.

"No, it was another."

"So there are a number of planets in the universe with human life?" the doctor asked.

"Yes," the Director answered. "There are numerous planets with humanoid life, each one at various stages of development."

"At various stages of development," the doctor echoed, visibly excited. "So they are all evolving out of their own ecosystem?"

"Not exactly," the Director said. "Your question is rooted in your theories of biological evolution. While there is always a subtle evolution to biological systems, the independent planetary humanoid communities we have discovered are evolving as civilizations, not so much biologically, as you suggest. While we have not studied these communities, based on our brief contact, it would appear that each humanoid group was planted there."

Dr. Manassa stood up, lifting his hands in amazement. "Do you realize what you're saying? The ramifications to our theories of the origins of human life? Our assumptions? How many worlds have you found with human life?"

"Nineteen. Earth was the nineteenth."

"Unbelievable," Tygert said, clearly struggling to accept what he was hearing. Kane sat with his arms crossed, quietly taking it all in.

"Nineteen" the doctor said, in awe. "And are we the first you have brought here?"

"No. We have brought humans to Ahlemon from three other planets."

"And what happened to them?"

"They were safely returned to their home planets."

At this point, in an obvious effort to regain control of the conversation, the Professor turned his attention to the doctor. "Sir," he began, "you sound like a man of scholarship. What is your background?"

"I'm Dr. James Manassa, medical doctor, surgeon, and a student of various disciplines."

"Dr. Manassa, I am pleased to meet you, and I would very much like to engage in a lengthy discussion with you about each of our worlds. But for now, I really need to convey the simple elements of our story so you can fully understand why you are here. I beg your patience and assure you that we will address all of your questions in time."

"Yes, of course," the doctor said as he sat back down.

"This human resonance between planets is potent but extremely subtle, and very difficult to identify. The resonance revealed itself only when a condensed suspension beam accidentally crossed the path of the resonance, outside of our planetary atmosphere, and at a precise calibration. At first discovery, we did not know what we had found. Once identified, we further experimented with varying attenuations of the suspension beam and a most amazing thing happened. For lack of a better description, a fourth dimension was revealed. We discovered a portal—a hallway, if you will—that connected the two resonant planets across the interstellar distance. In Earth vernacular, we found a wormhole. It was as if the portal had been deliberately hidden, waiting for the exact interaction of technology and resonance to reveal the doorway. I must say, in a lifetime of research, it never ceased to amaze me how one discovery is often a prerequisite to the next, as if there is a predetermined sequence for ongoing scientific revelation. But I diverge; that is a philosophical discussion we can enjoy another time."

Tygert refilled drinks for everyone and returned to take a seat on the sofa.

"We were on the verge of launching our first unmanned, interstellar expedition to the resonant planet when a catastrophic event struck Ahlemon. Our sun generated a solar storm that emitted an abberant ionic particle. We were aware of the storm when it occurred, and we even detected the existence of the new ionic particles soon after they struck our planet. But it would be several years before we realized their devastating affect on our way of life. To our horror, we discovered that the DNA of all humanoid life on Ahlemon had mutated, rendering the next generation sterile; humans could no longer reproduce. All land-based mammalian life was similarly affected. Aquatic mammals, all non-mammals, plant life, and aquatic life were not rendered sterile from the ionic particles.

"With this discovery a countdown commenced, and we began a race for our very existence. We immediately discontinued all nonessential programs, including our interstellar expedition, and focused all our resources on medical and biological research. We explored every conceivable idea to restore our mutated DNA. I was a middle-aged physicist when the sterility was discovered, and I devoted the rest of my life to finding a solution.

"Since aquatic life was unaffected, we built underwater habitats in an attempt to shield us from the effects of the ionic storm and potentially reverse the mutation. We never fully determined if it was the DNA of the aquatic life or the water itself that served as a protection from the aberrant particles. But it didn't matter; the underwater habitats failed. We built shielded and self-contained environments underground in hopes of deflecting the ionic particles, halting the mutation, and giving us a place to cultivate a restored DNA; they failed as well. We even built a special installation on our moon, to no avail.

"Simply put, we were too late. The few years of unfettered exposure to the ionic radiation had caused irreparable damage. Despite all our advancements, we could not re-create a pure human DNA strand, and we faced a stark conclusion—in order to save our race, we needed two things: a pure human DNA strand, and we had to wait until the ionic effects of the solar storm had fully receded. Alas, there were no pure human DNA strands left on our planet. And we estimated that the ionic storm would last almost a hundred years beyond our longest projected life expectancy."

Tygert stood and began pacing again. Dr. Manassa was nodding his head as if he suspected where this was going. Kane waited patiently, storing the information for evaluation after he knew the full story. The Professor continued.

"Upon reaching this conclusion, we focused our worldwide resources on two courses of action. The first included the building of this city, Alto Raun, our City of Hope. It is an enclosed community with a fully self-sufficient ecosystem. Not only was it the last city on Ahlemon to host human life; it was designed to be a place for a future iteration of our race to regenerate and grow. Which leads me to our second action . . . our final hope for averting total extinction. We devised a plan to bring a clean humanoid DNA to our planet to restore our race after the ionic particles dissipated."

"Astounding," Dr. Manassa whispered. "And we are your clean DNA."

"Yes."

The Professor paused to allow this to sink in.

"What do you intend to do with us?" Tygert said defensively, his fists clenching. Kane stood up, ready to restrain the captain or fend off a counterresponse from the Director.

The Professor seemed prepared for this reaction, and he spoke in a calming tone. "Do not be afraid; we will not harm you in any way. And, rest assured: we will not force you to do anything against your will. You must willingly choose to help us. It is our way."

"Willingly? So why were we so *un*willingly taken from our planet?" the captain retorted.

"Your abduction was my decision," the Director said. "I regret the method, but I felt that I had no other choice."

Tygert looked to Kane and Dr. Manassa. "You really OK with this?"

"Captain," the doctor said. "It's not like they need to dissect us to get our DNA; they could pull it out of a strand of our hair. I believe them. I think we should hear the rest of their story."

Tygert relaxed a bit and shook his head as they all sat back down.

Dr. Manassa addressed the Professor. "I'm puzzled, though. If your people died off so long ago, then what is left to regenerate with our DNA?"

"Ah yes. My earlier choice of words was not entirely accurate; I was being overly dramatic. I was the last living human on Ahlemon, and it certainly felt dramatic at the time. In any case, we did not die off *exactly*. There were two components to our final plan. One was to bring a compatible human DNA to our planet. The second . . . well . . . let me back up a bit. I mentioned the suspension technology that we had developed. It is an astounding technology, with multiple applications. One is for interstellar travel. Another is the suspension of activity at the atomic level." He paused, clearly excited about what he was about to say. "Deep underneath this city, there is a chamber holding one hundred and twenty Ahlemoni humans in a state of suspended animation. We refer to them as the Colony."

Kane glanced at his colleagues. While the doctor looked dumbfounded, the captain jumped in.

"Do you mean to tell us," Tygert said, "that there are people who have been frozen for two thousand years, and you plan to bring them back to life and restore them with our DNA?"

"Yes. But not frozen—suspended. In your interstellar travel to our planet, you were suspended for a very short period of time. The suspension slows all activity at a subatomic level to virtually zero, suspending aging and bodily activity, and without any decay."

"Will they be aware of the passage of time?" the doctor asked.

"Technically, no. However, we do not really know the possible effects of such a long suspension. Were you aware of the time it took to travel through space to reach our planet?"

"No," they all said together.

"Director, how long were they in deep suspension during their interstellar travel?"

"Four Earth hours."

"Four hours to travel how far?" Tygert asked.

"One hundred thirty-seven light-years."

Tygert whistled. "I've got to know how that works."

"It is an extremely complex process," the Professor said. "I'm sure the Director would be happy to discuss it with you another time."

Dr. Manassa continued with his questions. "So, if you just needed a pure DNA strand, why didn't you just extract samples from our planet? Why did you need to bring a hundred humans across the galaxy to restore your DNA?"

"Based on our best modeling, isolated DNA manipulation is not an optimal restoration solution. Our greatest hope for successful

DNA regeneration is through mixing of the races via the actual reproduction process. The offspring should have a fully regenerated DNA."

Tygert started to squirm. Kane looked from him to the doctor,
who seemed more at ease. The Professor continued:

"Thus, we needed to bring you here. While reproduction could
happen through artificial insemination, we hoped that the two
races would actually—"

The red in Tygert's face was half anger and half embarrassment.
"You mean you brought us here to mate with your two-thousand-
year-old kids?"

This time, the doctor stood up and put his hand on Tygert's
shoulder. "Captain, imagine it. What desperate lengths would you
go to if you were faced with the extinction of all human life on
Earth? While it pushes our cultural norms, this makes total sense."

"Yeah, well, why didn't they just ask us for help?" Tygert asked.

"That was my decision," the Director responded. "Allow me to
explain. We did not have the luxury of introducing Ahlemon to your
planet as humans; we could only appear in our robotic form. Our
analysis of your media and history led us to believe that Earth humans
would not respond well to the discovery of other human life in the
universe, particularly a small, post-apocalyptic colony under the over-
sight of robots. There are extreme ramifications to a humanoid system
when they unexpectedly discover that there is other advanced intel-
ligent life in the universe. I was deeply concerned about the possible
adverse impact to your entire world culture if we revealed ourselves
to Earth. So I determined it would be better to bring you here first,
without an introduction. I knew that doing so carried a risk of your
rejecting our request for help. I hoped that after meeting the Professor
and the colonists and hearing our story, congenial relations would
develop between the races on a small scale, after which you could
both determine the proper course, if any, for the introduction of
Ahlemon to the people of Earth."

"Captain, you have to admit, that makes sense," the doctor said.

"Yeah, but it doesn't mean I have to like it."

"Again," the Director said, "I am deeply sorry for the trauma and loss that I have caused."

Tygert eased up a bit. "Can you can get us back to Earth without our plane?"

"Yes."

All three men visibly relaxed at this news. There was a short silence in the room as this sank in.

"Will you help us?" the Professor finally asked.

"Do we have a choice?" Kane asked.

"Yes. It is your choice. When we set this course two thousand years ago, we determined that we would not force another human to help us against their will. If you choose not to help us, we will return you to Earth. In such a case, we will cease any further interaction with your planet and the Director will resume his search for another compatible humanoid race."

"Fair enough," Tygert said.

"No, it's not," the doctor said firmly. "We must help them. We can't just leave these people. This is a turning point for Earth, for all humanity; a momentous opportunity has been placed in our hands. Besides, if they took us back to Earth and left without a trace, nobody would believe our story; the whole world would think we were crazy. I would go crazy knowing that we had missed such an opportunity—"

"Hold your horses, doc," the captain interrupted. "I didn't say we were leaving them. But we can't decide for everyone. Each person will have to make their own choice." Then he turned to the Professor. "We should return to our people to explain the situation. Besides, we need some rest. After that, I guess we should meet your colonists. Where are they?"

The Director responded. "They are in the suspension chamber deep underneath—"

He stopped midsentence and stood silent, as if listening for something. The Professor's holographic image shut down.

"What's wrong?" Kane asked.

"We are under attack."

"The serpent is back?"

"No, it is not the leviathan."

"What is it?"

"The Breakers are attacking the city."

6

"Breakers?" the three men asked in unison.

"The Breakers are Mekens who have broken from their original program mandates. They no longer serve the purposes intended by our creators."

"You mean they're rogue robots?" Tygert asked.

"In a manner of speaking. In addition to our function and logic programs, some Class 2 and all Class 3 and higher Mekens have an empathic program. This program was designed to empathize with human emotions so we could better serve our creators. But it was an untested enhancement in Meken robotics at the time of the Colony's suspension. After hundreds of years with no humans to serve, the program started evolving on its own. After a thousand years, a group of Mekens collectivized and declared their independence. They would no longer perform their functions to preserve the Colony or the city, nor would they assist in our ongoing search for a compatible human race. Ultimately, they became a liability to our mission and we asked them to leave the city."

"You exiled them?" Tygert asked, his voice rising.

"They agreed to leave."

"My God," the doctor breathed. "Evolving sentient robots . . . and they live how long?"

"With proper maintenance, indefinitely."

"Are our people in danger?" Tygert asked, moving toward the elevator. The others followed.

"Not at this time. The attack is confined to the hangar in which you entered the city." The Director tapped a code into the control panel to recall the elevator.

"How do you know this?"

"All Mekens are connected to a satellite-based wireless communications network, potentially allowing communication between Mekens almost anywhere on the planet. Our Meken aircraft also have video surveillance capabilities that are transmitted to the central computer. At this time, our submersibles and aircraft are monitoring several Breaker submersibles just outside the hangar where you entered the city. The Breakers are using lasers and explosives at the weakened hangar door, attempting to gain entry."

"What about the supervisor . . . or the Mekens at the cafeteria . . . can you communicate with them?" Kane asked.

The Director paused. "No. They are not responding."

Kane and Tygert exchanged concerned glances.

"Where the hell is that elevator?" Tygert said.

The Director inserted his fingertip into the receptacle in the control panel. Moments later he announced, "It is not responding to my instructions. This elevator has been disabled."

"Damn it!" Tygert said. "We never should've left."

"Is there another way down?" Kane asked.

"Yes." The Director turned and headed toward the wall to their left. The three men followed. To their surprise, there was another hidden door in the wall paneling. The robot led them through the door, down a short hallway, into a bedroom, and into a walk-in closet. At the back of the closet, he opened a small access panel on the wall and tapped a code onto the touch screen. The closet paneling slid to the left, revealing an elevator compartment. "This was the Professor's private elevator."

It was a tight squeeze, but they all managed to fit.

"Are you at war with the Breakers?" Kane asked, as the elevator started to move.

"No. We have had very little contact with them in the thousand years since they left the city. They live in a city complex on the mainland. But we know that they monitor our activity."

"Do you monitor their activity?"

"No. We lost almost half the Meken population to the Breaker exodus. With our reduced numbers we have not had the resources to monitor them."

"Have they attacked the city before?"

"No."

"So why would they attack now?" the doctor asked.

"Us," Kane said, answering the question.

The elevator jolted as it shifted from a horizontal movement to a vertical descent.

"You may be correct," the Director said. "Three times we have brought humans to our planet, but, in each instance, we only brought a single pair, a male and female. This is the first time we have brought a large group of humans to Ahlemon, and this time, with a very high probability of waking the Colony. It is logical to conclude that your arrival, and the imminent regeneration of the Colonists, has precipitated the Breaker attack."

"But why wouldn't they want to revive the Colony?" the doctor asked.

"Conquer and retain," Kane said.

67

"I do not understand your response," the Director said.

"Powermongers do two things: they conquer and retain. If their power is threatened, they'll do anything to retain it. I've seen it before. If these Breakers have spent the last thousand years developing their own robotic culture, I would bet that someone in the Breaker camp doesn't like the idea that humans could be restored to power."

Tygert banged a fist on the elevator wall.

The elevator opened into the back of the toolshed in the far corner of the garden at the base of the tower. Kane took the lead, motioning for everyone to wait and remain quiet. Kneeling to the side of the shed door, he reached for a nearby shovel and used it to slowly push the door open.

Three laser beams silently penetrated the wooden door at chest height and narrowly missed the doctor.

"Hit the ground!" Kane commanded.

All four of them—robot and humans—fell to the floor as laser beams crisscrossed the air above them. As soon as the laser fire stopped, the Director launched himself with surprising speed at the wooden shed door, smashing it to pieces. Kane saw him fire his laser at unseen combatants, then run out of sight. Instinctively, Kane leapt out of the shed with his shovel. Rolling behind a bush, he brought the shovel up for a shield. A laser beam pierced the shovel blade and passed within centimeters of his ear. He dropped flat on the ground.

Before Kane could think about what to do next, the Director called out, "It is safe now. The Breakers are terminated."

Tygert and Dr. Manassa emerged from the shed and helped Kane to his feet; then they followed the Director to locate the three dead Breakers.

"Ugly fellows," the doctor said, after seeing the rogue robots.

The Breakers' silver finish was deeply tarnished, and they bore rough symbols painted in dark colors on their heads, chests, arms, or legs. They also wore an odd assortment of accessories—rough-hewn metallic medallions and fabric sashes. *An effort to establish their individualism*, Kane thought. Each Breaker had a single hole, surrounded by laser burn, at almost the exact same spot on its chest.

"Nice shootin'," Tygert said.

"I calculated their positions based on the trajectories of the laser fire in the shed," the Director responded flatly. "With the element of surprise, I determined that I could strike them before they could develop a coordinated response." He turned to Kane. "Mr. Kane, while your action was illogical and unnecessary, I can assure you that your distraction mitigated my own vulnerability and allowed me to locate and terminate the third Breaker without coming under his direct fire. Thank you."

"It was pretty crazy," Tygert said, giving Kane a curious look.

"Yeah, I know." Kane looked closely at the hole in his shovel blade. "It just happens with me. I quit apologizing for that kind of thing a long time ago."

Tygert smiled and shook his head while Kane silently said his prayer of thanks.

As soon as they were out of the garden, they broke into a jog around the base of the tower, the Director and Kane sharing the lead. Approaching the cafeteria, Kane felt his adrenaline spike— broken glass littered the walkway ahead. He motioned for the others to wait, then dropped to a crouch and moved along the wall under the windowsill until he reached the broken glass. He waited, listening for any activity inside. It was eerily quiet. Easing himself up, he peeked into the cafeteria. It was empty.

"Sam! Charly! Anybody!" he called. "Anybody here?" Plates of food were half-eaten, and some were spilled on the floor. A dark, liquid pool spread across the table just inside the broken window. Kane groaned, thinking the worst. He knocked away some glass, climbed onto the sill, and dropped into the cafeteria. He dipped his finger into the liquid and was relieved to find it was a thick, dark oil of some kind. Looking around, he spotted another small, dark pool on the floor between the table and the window. Another line of dark wet spots led out of the cafeteria.

Just then, the others entered through the cafeteria doors. The doctor came and knelt beside Kane.

"There's blood on the floor here," he said. "But it appears to be isolated to this spot." He pointed a few feet away and added, "That trail over there is the oil, I think."

The Director examined the pool of oil on the table.

"Let's search the area," Kane said.

The doctor and the Director went to the kitchen while Kane and Tygert investigated the living quarters. The facility was larger than Kane realized, containing close to a hundred rooms spread over two floors. They checked every one, including the bath facilities and closets. A few of the bed covers were thrown back, but most of them were untouched. Water was still running in a sink in one bathroom. Ten minutes later they gathered back at the cafeteria.

"Nobody in the living quarters," Kane said. "They didn't have time to settle in."

"There's nothing in the kitchen," the doctor reported. "And we checked the immediate area outside. The oil trail leads away to the right, around the tower." He walked to the broken window. "But *this* is interesting. There are divots in the grass and scratches on the walkway . . . something heavy was thrown *out* of the cafeteria."

"A high-intensity Meken laser was fired from outside the cafeteria, striking another Meken and killing him," the Director said. "The fluid on this table is unique to the core processor of a Meken; he would not have survived the loss of this much core fluid."

"How do you know he was shot by a laser from outside?" Kane asked.

"If you look at the inside wall of the cafeteria directly opposite the broken window, you will find a precision hole with a reddish burn circle surrounding it. This is from a high-intensity laser that passed directly through the Meken and into the wall. The laser was fired from outside the window."

"But the glass is broken outward," the doctor said.

"A struggle took place inside the cafeteria involving a human and more than one Meken. There are no human-based laser weapons outside of the armory vault, so a human could not have fired the laser. Thus, we can conclude that a Meken was thrown out the window and that same Meken shot the terminated Meken."

"Nice deduction," the doctor said.

"Would a Meken kill another Meken?" Tygert asked.

"No."

"But a Breaker would," Kane said. "Do you think they killed the supervisor?"

"I cannot tell from the evidence. Other than myself, he would pose their greatest threat. But, depending on the Breaker's intentions, the supervisor could also be very valuable to them."

Tygert was already moving toward the exit. "Let's see if we can tell which way they went." The others followed and they spread out to search the lawn for tracks.

"Over here," the doctor called from the right, moments later.

"And here," Kane shouted from the left.

Heavy tracks led away in opposite directions. The passengers had been split into two groups.

Tygert was pacing now, running his hands through his hair. Kane knew the captain's frustration . . . and guilt; it was a terrible feeling to leave your men and then lose them to enemy hands. "Captain, I want you to know that I've agreed with every one of your decisions," he said, trying to offer some reassurance. "The good news, the passengers are still alive."

Tygert stopped pacing and looked at him with deep concern. "We're at an extreme disadvantage."

Kane considered their situation. This was not the first time he had heard such words. But he had been trained to handle extreme disadvantage. A familiar indignation started to burn within him. "Captain, we may be playing on their game board, but think about it: these guys have never actually played against an opponent. And they have just messed with the wrong guys."

The Director interjected. "I have developed a hypothesis for the Breakers' intentions. If we can determine where they exited the greenway, I believe that I can draw some probable conclusions."

They decided to split up and follow the tracks in each direction, committing to return to the cafeteria to report rather than continue an independent pursuit of the Breakers.

Kane and the Director's trail ended at a dock on a canal.

"They have taken a canal barge," the Director said. "This is unfortunate."

"Why?"

"I cannot tell which direction they went."

Perfectly straight, the canal water ran from the outer ring of the city, through the farmland, and into a large indoor park at the base of the tower. Looking through three stories of glass window, Kane saw several acres of a lush park with trees, gardens, lawns, and walkways.

"The conservatory," the Director said, identifying the indoor park. "The canal runs through the center of the conservatory. Footbridges connect the two halves." There was no sign of the Breakers or passengers in any direction.

They returned to the lawn outside the cafeteria and found that Tygert and the doctor were already there.

"We went about a quarter of the way around the tower and the trail entered an apple orchard," Tygert reported. "We didn't see anyone."

"One group is going to the Colony," the Director announced. "The other is either exiting the city or going to the central computer."

"How do you know?" Kane asked.

"The surface entry to the suspension chamber and the Colony is in the middle of the apple orchard. The canal leads to the exterior of the city or, alternately, the surface entry to the central computer, which is located behind the conservatory."

"Critical systems," Tygert said.

"Perhaps," the doctor said. "But the Breakers could have destroyed those long ago. Instead, they've kidnapped a hundred passengers. I would suggest that their interest is in the humans, and they're trying to take them out of the city, maybe gathering the colonists on the way."

"I agree with the doctor's evaluation," the Director said.

"What about your defensive resources?" Kane asked. "Weapons, combat robots?"

"They are limited. All Class 2 and higher Mekens have laser capabilities. Sentries and builders have internal lasers they can fire from the palm of their right hand and they are programmed for hand-to-hand combat. A number of the Class 1 Mekens, the maintenance class, have lasers that could be used defensively, provided they are given instruction. Our aircraft and submersibles have laser functionality. And there are laser stations around the perimeter of the city, but they are not operational due to lack of maintenance."

"OK," Kane said. "First, we need to keep the Breakers from leaving the city with the passengers. Mobilize your forces outside the city—aircraft, boats, subs, whatever you've got. They must keep the Breakers away from the city exits. Use lethal force if necessary."

"They may resist."

"Of course they will," Tygert said.

"I am referring to the Mekens."

"What? Why?"

"We have never employed offensive force against another Meken."

Tygert looked appalled. "When the Cowboys don't play offense, they always lose."

"Director," Kane said. "The Breakers are now a direct threat to the survival of the colonists . . . and the passengers; the use of force against the Breakers, even lethal force, should be an acceptable course of action. Will the Mekens accept this?"

The Director did not immediately respond. "Yes," he finally said. "I have sent the command."

"Thank you. Now, do you have surveillance cameras in the city?"

"They are no longer functional."

"Then we need to set a watch at every exit from the city. Can you do that?"

The Director paused and sent a message. Seconds later he said, "It is done."

Tygert waved his hands, "Wait—can the Breakers access your wireless communications?"

"No. They are blocked from our network."

"Could they hack in?"

"No. I change the access algorithms daily."

"What about the supervisor? Could they—"

The sound of quick, heavy footfalls interrupted him. Tygert, Kane, and the doctor spun around just as a company of silver robots appeared around the bend of the tower, running in formation.

"Director?" Tygert's voice rose in pitch as he spoke the Director's name.

"They are sentries. I summoned them to join us here."

Approximately sixty blue-eyed, silver Meken sentries stopped in front of the Director. Three stepped forward, each presenting a bulky handheld weapon.

"Guns?" the doctor asked.

"Portable, handheld laser weapons designed for use by humans," the Director said. "They will fire five hundred bursts at half power, strong enough to disable a Breaker if struck in a critical area. A sustained, full-power discharge could slowly cut through a Breaker's skeletal structure, but it would drain the weapon's power supply much more quickly."

Dr. Manassa held his gun awkwardly while Kane and Tygert carefully tested their weapons' weight and feel. The Director gave them a brief lesson in its operation and then he left them to speak with the sentries. The three men moved further out on the lawn and each took practice shots at ears of corn on the nearby stalks. To everyone's surprise, the doctor was the first to hit his target. Provided their aim was true, the guns were extremely accurate.

After several minutes of target practice, they turned and found the Meken sentries standing in a single line formation, shoulder to shoulder, the Director moving down their line as if doing an inspection. He stopped in front of each one and opened a small panel on its upper left chest. Then he touched the tip of his fore-finger to a contact point inside the panel. The connection lasted ten seconds and then he moved to the next sentry and repeated the procedure. After moving down most of the line, he returned to a particular sentry and reconnected. This time the sentry convulsed and became rigid. Several minutes later, the sentry relaxed and the Director disconnected.

The Director rejoined Kane, Tygert, and the doctor.

"What was that all about?" Tygert asked.

"I have just created Supervisor 3, to replace Supervisor 1, who was taken by the Breakers."

"Just like that? No special order? No waiting a couple weeks for delivery?"

"Sentries and builders are identical in construction to a supervi-sor but do not have the advanced programming. I have upgraded his programming and given him my own experiential files and access authorities. He will accompany a team to the canal, where he can access the central computer if necessary. I will accompany the other team to the suspension chamber."

"I'm curious," the doctor said. "You were very specific. Why did you pick that particular sentry?"

"I assessed their empathic program, looking for one that reso-nated most with my own. I chose him because he is . . . unique."

"Director, you called this one Supervisor 3—to replace Supervisor 1. So, where is Supervisor 2?" Kane asked.

Tygert and the doctor exchanged glances; they'd missed that nuance in the prior exchange.

"Supervisor 2 is a Breaker."

"Is he the leader of the Breakers?"

"No. Atticus is their leader."

"Who is Atticus?"

"Atticus is my twin."

The three men looked at the Director, stunned. "You're not the only Director?" the doctor asked.

"No. I am Director 1, the primary of two directors. I have a twin, my secondary; he has taken the name of Atticus. There is also a secondary supervisor. Due to the critical nature of the Meken mission, our creators felt that it was necessary to build this redundancy into their plan."

"They were your backup," Tygert said.

"Yes. The secondary units are identical to the primary units with one exception; the secondary was designed to defer to the primary, unless the primary was incapacitated. Both of the secondary units led the Breaker revolt."

"So there are a couple of bad-guy robots who know everything you do," Tygert said.

"Not exactly. They have been disconnected from the central computer, the Meken network, and all of our activities since their departure. There is also a question as to the long-term degradation of their programming corruption."

"We can't underestimate these guys," Kane said. "They're already doing things you didn't expect. And now they have your supervisor. What does he mean to them?"

"Access to the Colony or the central computer core requires a series of unique identification codes. Those identification codes are changed daily. Only the supervisor and I know those codes. The Breakers will try to extract them from the supervisor."

"That doesn't sound pleasant," Tygert said.

"He would not experience pain, if that is what you refer to, Captain. And he will not divulge the codes under any circumstances. They will have to link directly to his core processor and forcibly extract the codes."

"Is that possible?" Kane asked.

"Atticus could do this."

Tygert shook his head. "Is there anything else that might be good for us to know before we run off half-cocked? Are there ninja robots? Giant mutant attack rats?"

"There are no such robots or creatures, Captain. Unfortunately, I cannot download my knowledge database to you. What is it that you would like to know?" the Director asked matter-of-factly.

"Never mind," Tygert sighed. "This is obviously a fly-by-the-seat-of-your-pants field trip."

"We have to assume they've taken the supervisor with them and they're going to get the codes," Kane said.

"Then we best get going," Tygert answered.

"Doctor," the Director said. "I would like for you to accompany me to the Colony. I am concerned about the condition of the colonists after such a long suspension. If they are awakened, your expertise could be invaluable."

"Of course. I'll do what I can."

Kane looked to Tygert and said, "Your call."

"I'll take the central computer with the new super, and you go with the doc and the Director."

Kane nodded.

Tygert extended his hand. "Let's go get our people back."

Kane shook his hand. "Will do. Good luck, Captain."

They divided the sentries evenly between the two teams. As Kane and his team started into a jog, he wondered which group of Breakers had Charly. Then he was immediately struck by a memory filled with unresolved guilt and sadness.

He swore under his breath, "I will not fail this time."

7

Day 1
1730 hours
Central tower, Alto Raun

Charly's heart pounded as she was herded with the rest of the passengers onto the lawn outside the cafeteria. A band of robots waved guns, growled, and shoved her and the others along. The marauders were silver, but grimy, painted with graffiti-like symbols and adorned with garish accessories. From the corner of her eye, she saw the food service robots carry their dead comrade out the cafeteria doors under heavy guard.

A shiny silver robot with a burgundy tattoo emblazoned on the left side of his face stood on a park bench, overseeing the assembly of the passengers, his long burgundy cape waving in the breeze. Charly recognized him as the one that had killed the cafeteria robot. When all the passengers were gathered, he addressed them in a commanding tone.

"Humans! Give me your attention. If you disobey or try to

escape, you will be terminated." He paused, looking over the crowd. "I repeat," he said louder, "if you disobey or try to escape, you will be terminated." Then he pointed to select passengers and the painted robots proceeded to pull them from the group. A robot grabbed Charly's arm.

"Don't touch me," she reacted, jerking away. The robot seized her upper arm in a painful grip, and she yelped as it pulled her forward. She and the other selectees were assembled into a separate group, divided into pairs, and the pairs were then formed into a line. Rogue robots surrounded them.

"Follow your group leader," the caped robot commanded. "Obedience will serve you well."

The leader of Charly's group barked an unintelligible command, and they started into a march. She glanced back to see the other group of passengers move away in the opposite direction, also under guard. Her anxiety was rising, and she desperately wished Kane were here. She looked around for a familiar face and recognized Arthur in her group, a couple of rows back. Joanie, his wife, wasn't with him. Arthur caught her looking at him and gave her a reassuring smile.

"Faster!" the lead robot shouted.

Forced into a jog, Charly tried to check on Arthur, worried about him keeping up with the pace. But she stumbled when they moved from the sidewalk onto the grass. Focusing her attention forward, her thoughts went to her grandparents. A wave of regret washed through her as she remembered how poorly she had treated them in recent months. For the first time, it struck her that her parents' deaths had been hard for them as well. She longed to tell them how much she loved them.

There was jostling beside her. She turned and found Arthur at her side; he had moved up through the line, the passengers behind them adjusting their pairings to accommodate the switch. A painted robot came alongside him and growled but didn't intervene. Arthur winked at Charly, showing no signs of exertion.

When the robot had moved away, he asked, "You worried about me?"

"I was."

"Don't be. I jog three miles several days a week. Charly, right?"

"Yeah."

"I'm Arthur."

"I remember."

"How ya holdin' up?"

"OK," she said, lying.

"They could have killed us back at the cafeteria, you know. They're gruff, but I really don't think they intend to harm us."

"You think?"

"I'm sure of it."

"Silence!" a robot snapped, shoving Arthur on the shoulder. He bumped into Charly and both of them almost fell.

As they jogged in silence, Charly was having a hard time accepting Arthur's optimism. Kane's lesson came to mind, and she started a chant in her head. *There's nothing to fear; let go of my fear. There's nothing to fear; let go of my fear.* But it wasn't working; she just couldn't shake her anxiety about what might happen. She looked at Arthur.

"We'll get through this," he assured her with his comforting smile.

She decided his optimism would have to do for now.

Suspension Chamber

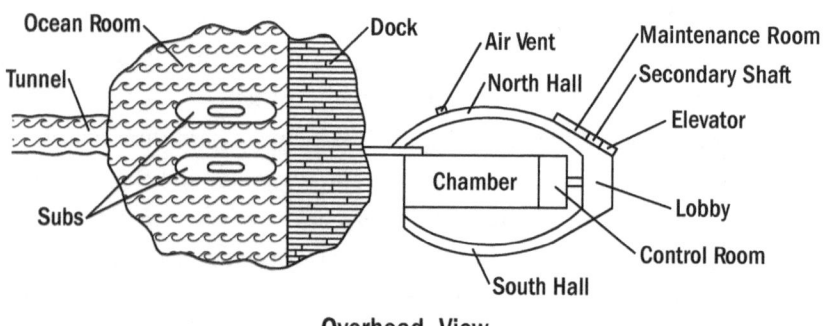

Ocean Room

Dock

Air Vent

Maintenance Room

Tunnel

North Hall

Secondary Shaft

Elevator

Chamber

Subs

Lobby

Control Room

South Hall

Overhead View

8

Kane's team jogged around the base of the tower and entered the grove of fruit trees. They cut across several rows and into the heart of the grove, then stopped when they reached a circular clearing. In the center of the clearing was a square, whitewashed, one-story building the size of a small house. A series of pipes ran out of the building and into the ground. A water-pumping station, Kane concluded, bringing water from the canal to irrigate the grove and crops. He checked the grassless dirt beneath him and found fresh footprints, both robot and human, all leading to a single door into the station. The Director was about to unlock the station door when Kane called, "Stop."

The Director turned. "What is wrong?"

"It could be booby-trapped. They could have set an explosive to detonate when you open the door."

"Mekens do not place hidden traps that could cause destruction or harm."

"You mean, you and *your* Mekens don't. We can't underestimate these Breakers."

"Of course, you are correct," the Director said, stepping back. "However, I doubt that the Breakers had time to wire an explosive directly into the electronics."

"I agree," Kane said, examining the door and keypad. "But it doesn't take long to set a mechanical trigger. Is there a way to enter the door code remotely?"

"No."

"We can't risk losing you, Director. I'd prefer—"

"I will enter the code myself."

Kane didn't argue. "Then I need some twine or wire."

Four sentries stepped forward, each raising its left arm. A thin but stout-looking wire cable extruded from a small opening in their forearms.

"They're a veritable walking Swiss Army knife," the doctor said to no one in particular.

"OK," Kane said, raising an eyebrow. "I just need two of you."

He led one sentry to stand behind a tree located to the side and front corner of the station. Taking that sentry's cable, he pulled it to the door, feeding it low to the ground and under a pipe, then up to where he tied it to the end of the lever-style door handle. Kane led the second sentry to stand behind a tree directly in front of the station. He pulled that sentry's cable straight to the door and tied it to the handle. Then he instructed everyone to take cover behind a tree.

When they were all in place, Kane called for the Director to enter the door code. He did so and nothing happened. After the Director was safely behind a tree, Kane called for the sentry at the side of the station to pull his cable. The door lever moved down and the door cracked open. Again, nothing happened. Then he instructed the second sentry to pull his cable and the door eased open. Kane was about to exhale when an explosion rocked the grove. Blown from its hinges, the station door flew like a missile across the clearing and slammed into a tree. In a surreal moment, Kane watched two Mekens step aside as the tree cracked and slowly fell to the ground. The front wall of the station had been blown away. Water gushed from several busted pipes and ran into the clearing. No one was injured.

"Thank you," the Director said to Kane. "We will proceed more cautiously."

Under Kane's watchful eye, they entered the station, stepping around debris. While several sentries worked to shut off the broken pipelines, the Director led Kane and the doctor to the back of the station. A large storage closet, once nestled in the back corner, had been shifted from its base, exposing a large hole in the floor. Peering into the hole, Kane found a circular stairwell. "What's down there?" he asked.

"This stairwell leads to a landing and an elevator that will take us directly to the lobby of the suspension chamber complex deep underground." The Director motioned for several sentries to come forward. "How should we proceed?"

"Watch for anything that looks out of the ordinary. Look for any taut wires or beams of light; don't trip them or cross their path. Be wary of any blind approaches or anything you have to move in order to advance."

The Director waved four fingers and four sentries stepped into the stairwell and disappeared. *Fearless*, Kane thought, *but they're robots; they don't know fear*. Several minutes later, the sentries returned and reported that it was clear to the elevator.

The Director led the way, followed by Kane, the doctor, and half a dozen sentries. The stairwell emptied into a rectangular landing, totally bare with the exception of a large, double-wide elevator and a control panel on the wall beside it. Kane checked the doors and panel and didn't find any visible evidence of tampering. But he knew there were other risks.

"Is there any other way to get in or out of the suspension area?" he asked.

"Yes. There is an undersea tunnel that extends from the chamber to the ocean. Through a series of pressurized gates, it can be accessed via submersible. There was also a construction tunnel between the chamber and the city's central power plant, but it was sealed at both ends soon after the colonists entered their suspension."

"How do you control the tunnel gates?"

"From the chamber's master control room or remotely from a submersible, provided you have the access codes."

"Do the Breakers have the means to transport hostages out of the tunnel?"

"Yes. They control all the large transport submersibles."

"Then we'll assume they have the codes and the ocean tunnel is their escape route. They set explosives up here, which means they didn't care if they blocked this route as an exit. Since they don't need the elevator, they could have set more explosives at the top or the bottom. If we take the elevator down and it's not rigged, they'll likely be waiting. In any case, the elevator feels like a suicide mission. Is there another way down? A stairwell, a ventilation system, a cave . . . anything?"

"There is a ventilation system, but it is too small for our use."

"So our only safe option is to wait for them to come out. Damn it!" Kane said, pacing back and forth. "That doesn't work for me. Director, you need to set up a blockade outside the ocean tunnel."

"There is another possibility," the Director said.

"What?" Kane and the doctor asked in unison.

"Construction of this elevator included a secondary shaft adjoining the main elevator shaft. It has a maintenance ladder."

"Do the Breakers know this?" Kane asked.

"Atticus and the supervisors would. But they would ignore it because both ends of the secondary shaft were sealed at completion of the elevator construction."

"So, why would it be any use to us?"

"There is a critical piece of data the Breakers do not have: the bottom of the secondary shaft was never sealed."

"How do you know this and they don't?"

"I supervised sealing of the shaft. At the time, I decided that access to the shaft at the bottom level could be useful for maintenance, and it fell within an acceptable risk tolerance. Since it has not been needed, I never added this information to the central database. I am the only one who knows."

The Director proceeded to scratch a door-sized outline on the wall to the right of the elevator. "We can access the secondary shaft if we cut a hole here. There is a panel at the bottom of the shaft that will let us into the back of a mechanical room. The mechanical room is located off the north perimeter hall, just to the right of the suspension area lobby. The Breakers have no reason to suspect that someone could enter the suspension area from the mechanical room, so it is improbable they will have anyone stationed in the room itself."

He called two sentries forward, and they began cutting the outline on the wall using the lasers from their hands. Two more sentries inserted piton-like hooks into the wall at several points, which they then held to keep the slab from falling into the shaft.

As the sentries worked, the Director sketched a basic floor plan of the suspension chamber complex and reviewed it with Kane and the doctor. Kane then returned to the surface and gathered the remaining sentries outside the pumping station, splitting them into three groups. He instructed one group to stand guard around the station, another to spread out in the surrounding grove, and the third to wait at the top of the elevator shaft, ready to be called down to the suspension area if needed. He then returned to the elevator landing.

Kane watched as several sentries removed the slab and carefully set it aside. It was pitch-black in the shaft. The sentries activated their floodlights and Kane saw a ladder attached to the shaft wall on the right, reachable with a short leap. Clutching the newly cut wall, he leaned through the doorway and asked the sentries to direct their lights down the shaft. He couldn't see the bottom. Kane's adrenaline jumped and he felt that all-too-familiar wobbly feeling in his head and knees.

"How deep is this thing?"

"Three thousand two hundred forty-two of your Earth feet," the Director answered.

The doctor gasped. "I can't make that climb."

"A Meken can carry you on its back," the Director said.

The doctor grimaced while a knot formed in Kane's stomach.

"Will the ladder hold the weight of a team?" Kane asked.

A sentry brought a plank down and set it in place to act as a bridge, then crossed the plank to test the ladder. Its rungs and attachment to the wall were solid. The Director then loaded it with half a dozen Mekens, and it still held firm. Kane marveled at the durability of the Ahlemoni building materials; after two thousand years, most of the construction was still structurally sound. Not wanting to press their luck, they decided to send the team down in groups of six.

While the doctor worked with a sentry to create a piggyback harness, Kane gave a quick tutorial in Morse code to the Director and the sentries. Due to the depth of the shaft, wireless communication was not possible between the surface and the suspension chamber, but they would communicate with light-based Morse code signals between the top and bottom of the shaft.

The first group boarded the ladder. The Director led, followed by a sentry, then Kane, then two more sentries. The doctor would be part of the second group. The air was stale and dry but moistened as they descended. As a distraction from his fear, Kane turned his thoughts to Charly. Was she below, or with the group that Tygert was tracking? He couldn't decide which he preferred. Having her here would give him greater control over her protection, but it could also bias his judgment. He was accustomed to having concern for his men, but this was way different: this was a kid. *How do parents live with the worry?* he wondered.

Climbing down thirty-two hundred feet of ladder is better than climbing up, but it's no walk in the park. Kane was in great shape, but the muscles in his arms, shoulders, and legs were aching, and his hands were on the verge of cramping when they finally reached the bottom.

Communicating with hand motions, they located the panel door. They listened for a moment for any sign of activity on the other side: nothing. The Director motioned for a sentry to cut the hinges. Once the hinges were cut, the robots carefully removed the panel and found the mechanical room dark and the hallway door closed. The room was filled with air circulation machinery; there was only enough space to hold a half dozen of the team. When the doctor joined them, they gathered at the bottom of the shaft, whispering.

"We need to get an idea of how many Breakers and hostages we're dealing with, and their positions," Kane said. "Based on your floor plan, it seems like we should be able to get a view of the lobby from the hallway door, right?"

"Yes."

"I know it's risky, but we need to take a peek." The Director and the doctor agreed.

Kane moved into the mechanical room and knelt at the hallway door, wishing he had his recon tool bag; a good micro-surveillance camera unit would really come in handy right now. Praying it wouldn't squeak, he slowly eased the door open a crack until he got a view of the right half of the lobby.

He was alarmed at what he saw.

A line of Breakers faced the elevator door, armed with laser rifles and ready for battle. Directly in front of them were the passengers, standing side by side and forming a wall. *They're using them as shields.* It made sense. Humans made the perfect defensive shield against a Meken attack. The hostages were slumped and haggard looking, and

89

a couple of them were crying. A structural pillar blocked Kane's far view and the hallway wall blocked his near view, but from what he could see, there were twenty passengers. He was relieved that Charly was not among them. He recognized several faces, including Sam. Kane evaluated the young copilot. He was similar to Kane's height, a leaner build, but very fit. Kane guessed he had risen to the role as a civilian aviation student rather than through the military. He was alert and his posture indicated that he was prepared to lead and defend his passengers.

A Breaker at the back of the lobby was guarding a heavy metal door, the first of two doors leading into the suspension chamber's master control room.

Kane caught his breath as a Breaker walked past the mechanical room door, returning from a patrol of the hallway. The Breaker went to the back of the lobby and exchanged words with the door guard. The guard entered a code and opened the door to allow the Breaker into the hallway leading to the control room. Having seen enough, Kane eased his door shut. He crept back into the elevator shaft and described what he had seen to the Director and Dr. Manassa, including the robots' use of his fellow passengers as a human shield.

"Such behavior is diametrically opposed to our programming," the Director said. "I regret that I was not prepared for anything like this from the Breakers."

"I don't get it," the doctor said. "If their intention is to kill the colonists, why don't they just blow up the suspension chamber?"

"They cannot. Any attempt to destroy the chamber while it is still in operation could easily set off an atomic reaction that would destroy the entire city and leave a shroud of toxic radiation covering a hundred-mile radius. This would encompass Alto Mair, the Breakers' home city. In order to reach the colonists, the suspension fields must come to a complete stop and the residual suspension must diminish to a level that is safe for entry into the chamber."

"How long does that take?" Kane asked.

"Two hours to shut down the suspension generators. At that point, it is safe for humans to enter the chamber, and the colonists will begin to wake soon after. Mekens cannot enter the chamber for an additional hour."

"Why?"

"Purely biological organisms, like humans, have a greater resistance to the effects of the suspension field. The blended circuit/biologic system in a Meken is more sensitive to this field. Entering the chamber too soon would result in irreparable neural damage to a Meken."

"So there will be an hour between when the colonists awake and when the Breakers can enter the chamber?"

"Yes."

"Can you guess how far the Breakers may be in the suspension shutdown process?"

"I do not guess, Mr. Kane. I can provide sophisticated analytical probabilities. But to answer your question, based on their likely departure time from the cafeteria, I estimate that they are no less than eighty minutes into the suspension shutdown."

"Then we've got a little more than an hour and a half to stop them from entering the chamber, right?"

"Yes."

Kane checked his watch. "And there's a rear door into the chamber?"

"Yes. But the only way to unlock it is from inside the master control room, which is currently occupied by Breakers."

"Is there any way we can cut through the rear door or a wall of the chamber?"

"No. The chamber itself is an isolated box, constructed of alloys that Earth will not invent for hundreds of years. Even if we could cut through it, the chamber is also protected by a polarity shield, which has two backup energy sources. The only way into the chamber is through the master control room, and only after the correct authorization codes have been entered, deactivating the shields and releasing the chamber doors."

It sounded like an impossible situation, which meant it was right up Kane's alley. An idea was already forming in his mind. He had implemented risky sequences in the past, but this one topped them all; it was fraught with wildcards. Kane shared his plan.

"You've got to be kidding," Dr. Manassa reacted, overly loud.

"Mr. Kane," the Director said, "your judgment to date has been very sound. But the sequences required in this plan give it a very unfavorable probability of success. Are you certain we should proceed with this course of action?"

"Kane," the doctor added, "I can't do the calculations, but it's obvious that a lot of things could go wrong."

"I agree with both of you. But, in actual execution, a plan is never linear; it can have multiple unexpected twists and turns and still result in a successful outcome. And inasmuch as there are unseen risks, there are always unseen opportunities. The missing factor in your equations is the element of surprise and human resourcefulness. This gives us a distinct advantage over the Breakers. As it stands now, the Breakers have set the rules of the game, and we don't have a chance. We have to do something extraordinary—we have to change the rules." He paused, then concluded, "My gut says we can do this."

So, while Kane and a sentry worked out a Morse code message to send to the surface, the Director selected a sentry to join him. Standing in front of the sentry, he opened a panel on its upper chest and proceeded to create a new supervisor. A few minutes later, he confirmed the creation of Supervisor 4. After discoloring Super 4's metallic finish with short laser bursts, the Director gathered oil from the mechanical room and soil scrapings from the elevator shaft to create a grimy paint, which he used to draw Breaker-like symbols on Super 4's head, chest, and thigh. Lastly, using the doctor's torn-off shirtsleeve, he made armbands for Super 4's biceps. When he stepped back from his work, Super 4 looked like a Breaker.

Kane joined them and explained the plan to Super 4. "I'm sorry you have to do this alone," he said.

"There is no other way," the robot answered. "I fulfill my purpose through this task. I must succeed or there is no more purpose."

"Well . . . good luck." Funny how he felt the same concern that came whenever he sent one of his men out on a dangerous mission.

They entered the mechanical room. Super 4 cracked open the hallway door and watched, waiting for the right moment to slip into the Breaker space. It came sooner than expected. "Move back, quickly," he said to Kane and the Director.

They pressed themselves against the back wall, presumably to avoid being seen when Super 4 left the room. But instead of leaving, Super 4 stepped back and behind the door. Then, to Kane's horror, the door opened and a Breaker entered the mechanical room. What happened next was nothing short of amazing.

In a single, fluid motion, Super 4 shut the door, slid behind the Breaker, grabbed its head between both hands, and twisted it with a vicious wrench. The Breaker collapsed and Super 4 lowered him quietly to the floor. Then he stepped over the immobilized Breaker, opened the panel on its chest, and touched his fingertip to a connection point. Fifteen seconds later, he disconnected, opened the mechanical room door, stepped outside, and closed the door quietly behind him. Kane stood in stunned silence.

The Director knelt next to the downed Breaker and connected his fingertip to the same receptacle on the Breaker's chest. Two minutes later, the Breaker's chest cavity glowed brightly. The robot convulsed in one great spasm and then went dark and limp.

"What did you do?" Kane asked.

"First I downloaded all of his memory, and then I overloaded his system."

"You killed him?"

"His empathic program was extremely corrupted. He was a threat, not only to this mission but to everything we believe in."

Kane had a new respect for the Director. But, he noticed that the Director did not rise. "What's the matter?"

"We have been betrayed."

9

Soon after Kane and his team left the cafeteria for the Suspension area, Tygert's team boarded a tram. First stop, the conservatory, after which it would take them to the outskirts of the city, if needed. As the tram moved forward, Tygert considered the Breakers' head start. It was at least an hour; he feared they could be outside the city by now. He was not one to get discouraged, but a grey cloud was beginning to gather over his spirit.

This is crazy. I don't have a clue what I'm doing. It was all so surreal. Everything had been happening nonstop, one roller coaster ride after another. He felt disoriented.

His thoughts turned to something familiar, his family: his wife, Melissa; his son, John Jr.; and his daughter, Lacey. Little Lacey, his jewel, had her first day of kindergarten today . . . or was it yesterday? He'd totally lost track of time. He remembered the white-and-black-striped tiger Beanie Baby in his luggage, a gift to celebrate Lacey's first day of school. Lacey loved cats. He'd bought it because, while tucking her into bed the night before last, she had expressed some fear about starting kindergarten. He had created a story about a little tiger kitty who had to be brave when she went out on her first hunt alone. He smiled now, remembering how Melissa had disapproved of the analogy, but it had seemed to work for Lacey. Lacey had laughed as he pretended to be a little tiger snarling his way through kindergarten class. Then he kissed her good night, and she said, "I love you, Daddy."

As was his custom when he had to leave early for work, he had slipped out of the house without waking anyone. But what had started out as a normal workday had turned into a nightmare. Melissa would be frantic with anxiety and grief knowing her husband's plane had disappeared. His heart sank even further as he remembered that his luggage, and the Beanie Baby, was now in the belly of a giant sea serpent. A knot formed in his stomach; he wondered if he would ever see his family again.

"Captain," Super 3 said loudly, trying to get his attention. "Captain, we have arrived."

Tygert and his group exited the tram and stood at the edge of the canal. He closed his eyes and took a long, deep breath, feeling the moist breeze. "Does it ever rain here?"

"Not inside the city. It is an environmentally sealed system, perfectly balanced. The proper amount of moisture in the air is maintained and the crops are irrigated. It rains outside."

"How can it be perfect without rain?"

"I'm sorry, Captain, but what does rain have to do with tracking the passengers?"

"Nothing really. I'm just trying to clear my head."

Tygert knew that he needed to make a tactical decision. Should they follow the canal out of the city to prevent the Breakers from escaping with the hostages, or should they go deeper into the city to the central computer? Or, should they split up and try to do both?

Super 3 came to his assistance. "Due to proximity and opportunity, logic suggests a slightly higher probability that the Breakers would attempt to destroy the central computer."

"Yeah, but they could think that we would think that, and then they would do the opposite."

"Why would they do that?"

"Right. You guys don't play football. Do you play any games here?" Tygert asked. Without waiting for an answer, he said, "Never mind. We've got your people watching the outskirts of the city, and I don't want us to split up. Let's check out the computer entry first. Lead the way."

Super 3 led them cautiously; there was dense vegetation in the conservatory that could easily conceal hidden Breakers. The entry to the central computer was located behind the conservatory, and the only way to reach it was via the canal. They were just about to board a canal barge when Super 3 stopped, listening.

"What's the matter?" Tygert asked.

"A maintenance Meken has just reported Breakers in Hangar 36, with a large group of humans."

"They're trying to take the hostages out of the city."

Super 3 paused, still listening. "I believe that is correct. There are four large Breaker submersibles in the ocean waters approaching Hangar 36."

"We've got to stop them from reaching that hangar. You need to form a blockade with all your available submersibles and aircraft."

"We have already done so. The Breakers are firing on us with lasers, and we have returned fire. However, the efficacy of lasers is greatly diminished underwater, and our aircraft are of little use. Even with additional support it will be difficult to disable a larger Breaker submersible. It is only a matter of time before they overcome our smaller fleet."

"Then it's a race. Any word from Kane's team?"

"The last communication is that they are attempting a covert entry into the suspension chamber area. I cannot communicate with them directly while they are underground."

Tygert considered the possibilities. A large group of humans in the hangar didn't necessarily mean it included all of the hostages. If the Breakers were smart, they would send most or all of their hostages out of the city and a smaller team to attack the computer.

"Super, how many ways in and out of the central computer?"

"Only one, via elevator."

"If a Breaker team is already there, we'd be sitting ducks if we showed up in the elevator. Trying to save the computer is probably a lost cause . . . unless they have hostages with them." Tygert paced as he thought out loud. "It also means the Breakers would have only one way to get out, unless they're on a suicide mission, which I doubt. But, if they have hostages . . . too many ifs." Tygert paused, wrestling with his decision. "I won't risk leaving any passengers behind. We need to split up."

He turned to Super 3. "I want you to take a dozen sentries and wait at the surface entry to the central computer. If the Breakers are in there and have hostages, do what you can to rescue them after they come out. You good with that?"

"If you are referring to my agreement with your plan, then, yes, I'm 'good with that.'"

"Now, I need you to call for any available combat-capable robots to meet me at the entry to Hangar 36."

"I am sending the instructions."

Super 3 chose a dozen sentries, and they boarded the canal barge.

Tygert and the remainder of his team left the conservatory and boarded the tram. With the field of golden grain on their left and what looked like soybeans on the far side of the canal, the tram took them to Hangar 36. As he thought about leading an operation to rescue the hostages, Tygert was surprised at how quickly his training was coming back to him. If the Breakers embedded themselves in the hangar, it could easily become a standoff. A standoff with robots did not sound like a good thing. But a direct battle with the Breakers would put the hostages at too much risk.

They rendezvoused with a large group of Mekens already gathered in the subway tunnel, just outside a set of double doors that led into the hangar. A green-eyed builder Meken greeted Tygert.

"I am Builder 56. I am the designated spokesman for this gathering of one hundred and fourteen Mekens."

Looking them over, Tygert saw mostly sentries and builders, but there were also a number of maintenance Mekens of assorted shapes and sizes. "Is there any way we can see what they're doing in the hangar . . . surveillance cameras?" Tygert asked.

"No. But the maintenance Meken who discovered the Breakers is hidden in the rafters of the hangar and is monitoring their activity. He says the Breakers are gathered at exterior door C. The Breakers have positioned the humans around them in a semicircle. They are waiting."

Tygert clenched his fists. "Freakin' terrorist tactics. Can he get a head count of the Breakers and hostages?"

"There are thirty-two Breakers and seventy-seven humans. But he believes that two of the humans are dead."

"*What?!*"

"He says that one of the female humans tried to run from the group when they formed the semicircle. A male ran after her and the Breakers fired on both of them. They have not moved from where they fell."

"Damn." Tygert paced. The situation was more fragile than he'd expected. The Director had made it very clear that the Mekens would not harm a human, but the Breakers obviously didn't care about killing. With the humans as a shield, there was no way the Mekens would engage in a battle. He needed to separate them from the Breakers. But how to do that safely?

"I have a communication from Supervisor 3," Builder 56 announced. "He reports there were no signs of Breaker activity at the surface entry to the central computer. As a precaution, he has stationed two sentries to monitor the area. He and the remainder of his team are now on their way to join us."

"Good."

"I also need to inform you that the Breaker submersibles have broken through our blockade."

Tygert's adrenaline jumped a level. "Then we've got to get in there now. I'm not gonna let them waltz out of here with our people."

Pacing again, Tygert quickly pieced together a plan. After conferring with Builder 56, he made a command decision. He sent instructions back to Super 3 to join him at the hangar for a hostage rescue, and then he communicated his plan to the small Meken army.

They entered Hangar 36. Another massive hangar, it was filled with lane after lane of stacked cargo containers. Builder 56 took the lead navigating them to the Breaker location. When they suddenly came to the last of the cargo containers, they jolted to a halt. A hundred yards of open space was all that separated them from the Breakers.

Tygert stepped forward to get a look at his passengers. Their faces lit up when they saw him, and he motioned for them to stay calm. Despite their hopeful looks, he felt the weight of the unfavorable odds; the Breakers peered at him from behind their human shield. Gamesman that he was, he knew it was high risk to count on winning several hands in a row in any game. But he had no choice. He signaled the Mekens behind him, and they slowly spread out into a single line to his left and right. With the cargo containers at their backs, they formed a line facing the hostages. Once in place, the Mekens stood still, arms at their sides, showing no signs of aggression. Outnumbering the Breakers almost four to one, the Meken line was a show of force designed to intimidate the Breakers and draw their attention. Tygert exhaled. He'd been holding his breath, wondering if the Breakers would fire on them. They didn't. He'd won his first hand. Now it was a standoff, which was just what he wanted. His next play was all about biding time. So they waited.

The hostages didn't understand and they became fidgety, sending questioning looks Tygert's way. He was surprised at how much willpower it required to just stand there; but he refused to put the hostages at risk by trying to send any kind of message back to them. When a metallic knock finally came at the hangar door, he jumped. The Breaker submersibles had arrived; they were outside and ready to pick up their team along with the hostages. Moments later, a screeching noise echoed through the hangar as the massive door began to rise. He turned to Builder 56, standing next to him. "Fifty-six, are we ready?" The builder nodded back. So far, so good, he thought. But the real gamble was yet to be played.

The humid ocean air rolled into the hangar and over him. As Tygert had hoped, it was now getting dark outside. Behind the Breakers was a landing, and at the edge of the landing floated a large, shadowy shape, a Breaker submersible. Behind it, a second submersible rose from the water. He turned to his left and then his right, looking down each line of Mekens. His army stood as they were.

When the hangar door finally clanged to a stop, he heard the Breakers' robotic voices. The hostages glanced over their shoulders and, a moment later, they started moving . . . backward. The movement was awkward and the human semicircle began to fall apart. The hostages looked frantically to Tygert, beseeching him to save them.

He waved his arm in a forward motion and the entire line of Mekens took one step forward and stopped, arms at their sides, still showing no signs of aggression. He didn't want to start a fight; he just wanted to hold their attention a bit longer. One of the Breakers fired at the Mekens. No one returned fire. The pivotal moment arrived when the Breakers were outside the hangar door and, for the most part, the line of humans was still inside. Turning to Builder 56, Tygert whispered, "Now."

Seconds later, laser fire erupted, raining upon the Breakers from their left and their right—from outside the hangar. The Breakers were under attack from an unseen force. Tygert shouted to the hostages, "Get down! Get down now!"

Most of them dropped to the ground. Some grabbed pants or shirttails, tugging their neighbors to the floor. Within a matter of seconds, most of the humans were down.

With attackers firing on them from both sides and their human shield falling apart, the Breakers panicked. Abandoning the hostages, they tightened their ranks into a circle and pushed toward the waiting submersible, firing at their attackers and into the hangar. To Tygert's dismay, two Breakers grabbed passengers, taking them as personal shields. One, a young man, fought and broke free. As he ran into the hangar, the Breaker shot him in the back. The other escaped when a laser struck her captor; they fell together and she crawled into the hangar.

It was still too risky for his troops to return fire. The Meken line showed great restraint, passively standing their ground even though several of them fell to the floor, struck by Breaker lasers. Tygert signaled and Builder 56 ran to a control panel on the wall. With a piercing screech, the hangar door began to close.

Just then, from outside the hangar, a silver Meken sentry stepped into the right side of the open doorway, firing on the Breakers. Another came from the left. One by one, ten silver sentries slipped into the doorway and formed a line separating the hostages from the retreating Breakers. One of the Mekens fell, and they tightened their ranks. As the hangar door closed, they backed up in synchronized steps, firing a continuous laser barrage. Dropping to one knee, they continued their assault until the hangar door blocked their line of fire and finally slammed shut with a thud.

In a matter of minutes, the passengers had gone from a seemingly hopeless hostage situation to being freed. A momentary silence hung in the air. Finally, someone jumped up and gave a victory whoop. Shouts of jubilation erupted as the passengers picked themselves up and began hugging one another. Tygert allowed himself a smile and ran a hand through his hair, relieved and amazed that the plan had actually worked. But as he looked over the scene before him, the joyful mood quickly turned to sorrow. Four passengers lay unmoving on the floor, each of them tended by a crying friend or family member. Suddenly, Tygert felt a pang of doubt. He'd lost four people. Had he made a bad call? The passengers clearly didn't think so, expressing their thanks and giving him hugs as he walked among them. He checked for injuries: one hostage had a serious laser burn on his arm that was being wrapped by a fellow passenger. Most of the injuries were limited to bruises or abrasions. Tygert finally came to a white-eyed, silver Meken standing just inside the hangar door.

"I can't tell you how glad I am to see you, Super."

"And I you, Captain Tygert," Super 3 replied. "I am very sorry for your losses."

"Yeah. Me too."

As if he sensed Tygert's self-criticism, Super 3 said, "Captain, under the circumstances, I believe your plan was the right one, and it worked better than the odds would have indicated."

"Thanks to you." Tygert put a hand on Super 3's shoulder. "I have never seen a gutsier play than the one you and your team just executed. You saved a lot of people just now. Thank you."

"Just doing my duty, Captain."

"I know, I know," Tygert said, shaking his head as he turned to move on.

Super 3 called after him. "Captain!" When Tygert turned to face him, the robot said, "I would like to hear more about your Earth games, particularly the game called . . . Poker."

"That you will, Super. That you will," Tygert said. "You're a natural."

10

Super 4 eased out of the mechanical room, shut the door quietly, and moved down the north perimeter hallway as if he was continuing on his patrol route. One of the hostage guards saw him exit the room, but apparently didn't think anything out of the ordinary.

The patrol Breaker's unexpected entry into the mechanical room could have ruined everything, but remembering Kane's comments about unforeseen opportunities, Super 4 had turned it to his advantage. In addition to providing a cover for his exit, the upload of recent memories he had extracted from the downed Breaker would provide some information about his adversary. Skimming through the upload, he was unable to determine the Breaker's ultimate plan; the patrolman had only received information on a need-to-know basis. But now he knew the location of all the Breakers in the suspension chamber area. They had focused most of their manpower in the lobby, awaiting a Meken attack from the elevator. One Breaker patrolled the south perimeter hallway; one guard was posted at the rear chamber door; one was at the double doors leading into the ocean room; four were in the ocean room, awaiting the arrival of the transport submersibles; and four were in the chamber's master control room with Rakaan.

Rakaan? Mekens did not take names; it was a foreign concept to Super 4. Rakaan was either the Breaker supervisor or their Director. One thing was clear, though: the patrol Breaker had been terrified of Rakaan; he would be Super 4's greatest obstacle to a successful mission.

The perimeter hallways were both curved, defining the outer oval shape of the suspension chamber area. The south hallway was a dead end, built only for service access to the southern side of the chamber. The north hallway started at the lobby and ended in a T-intersection. To the left of the intersection was a short hall, at the end of which was a heavy, vault-like door, the rear entry to the suspension chamber. A Breaker sentry would be guarding it. To the right of the T was a longer hallway with double doors at the end, also guarded by a Breaker. Behind the double doors was the ocean room, a large, subterranean cavern. It was the connection point to the ocean tunnel, the only other access to the suspension chamber complex. Super 4 reached the T intersection and turned around. Ignoring both guards, he resumed his patrol, heading back to the lobby.

As he walked, he examined the memory upload more closely. The patrol Breaker had taken a name, Dagar. Once again, he found this odd; Mekens did not take names but went by their identification codes. He couldn't find Dagar's original ID code in the files he'd downloaded; it probably resided in a more distant memory file. The invading Breakers had come to Alto Raun in several large transport submersibles and had entered the city through a hangar on the abandoned south side. An unidentified sympathizer had assisted them, and he made a note to inform the Director as soon as possible. He replayed the capture of the hostages in the cafeteria and their march to the water pumping station. Then he came across a speech that Rakaan had made about the overthrow of the human race. Dagar had replayed it hundreds of times, developing a ritualized association to the speech. Dagar had actually been savoring the thought of subjugating the humans. While Super 4's own programs refused to consider such an idea, there was something seductive about Dagar's deep empathic connection to the speech. But Super 4 was approaching the lobby, so he closed the memory files, and returned his attention to the mission at hand.

Surveying the hostages, he noted their genders, ages, and conditions. Most of them were slumped, the loss of hope showing in their physical carriage. He had not been around humans in thousands of years, but it was clear to him that these were in severe distress. His empathic program made its intended association and he instantly committed himself to their care and safety; his devotion to these Earth humans would be no less than what he would give the colonists.

He glanced behind him to the mechanical room door and his eyes flashed twice, a signal that he was ready to proceed. Observable only to him, a pinpoint of gold light flashed twice from the cracked door; the Director had acknowledged the message and confirmed his team's readiness. Super 4 walked directly to the back of the lobby and approached the Breaker guarding the outer control room door.

The guard eyed him warily. "What do you want?"

"I have a report from the ocean room for Rakaan."

Before the guard could question him further, a faint mechanical whirring sound came from the elevator shaft and a light started blinking above the elevator door. The Breakers instantly came alert and forced the hostages to stand erect and shoulder to shoulder, solidifying their human shield. Positioning their weapons between the heads of the hostages, they took aim at the elevator doors. A Breaker at the back of the lobby made his way toward a bazooka-like gun lying on the floor. Super 4 did not recognize the weapon, but it was obviously designed for launching some kind of explosive. This was another unexpected turn in the mission, one that could impact their plan . . . for the worse.

As hoped, due to the descending elevator, the door guard punched in a code, opened the heavy outer door, and entered the short hallway leading to the control room. Super 4 had planned to follow the guard into the control room. But instead, he stepped beside the Breaker who was picking up the bazooka. While pretending to assist in lifting the heavy gun, Super 4 activated his hand laser and discreetly welded the firing lever. The Breaker wrenched the gun away and growled; he clearly did not want any assistance.

As Super 4 returned to the control room door, the guard reappeared, along with two Breaker sentries. They took up positions as reinforcements behind the Breaker line. With the guards distracted by the incoming elevator, Super 4 inserted his foot into the doorway, keeping the outer door from sealing shut. The whirring of the elevator motors changed speed, indicating that it was almost to the bottom of the shaft. The tension in the lobby was palpable as the Breakers and hostages prepared for the coming shootout. Super 4 could hear several of the hostages start to cry. One of them recited a prayer out loud.

The whirring stopped and a gentle chime announced the elevator's arrival. As soon as the doors parted, the Breakers opened fire. A Meken team inside the elevator returned fire. When the doors were halfway open, the bazooka-wielding Breaker stepped forward and pulled the trigger. Nothing happened. Confused, he took the gun off his shoulder. Holding it at his side, he gripped the trigger lever in a full hand grip and squeezed. The weld finally broke loose and the gun fired. But he was wildly off target and the projectile struck the wall to the right of the elevator door. Solid rock repelled the resulting explosion back into the lobby, knocking over many of the hostages and several Breakers. The laser battle went wild. Taking advantage of the chaos, Super 4 moved into the short hallway and approached a very nervous Breaker guard at the inner control room door.

"It is not going well," he said. Then, in a commanding tone, he ordered, "We need you and any other sentries out front. Open the door so I can inform Rakaan."

Without question, the guard input the door code, then ran out the hall and into the lobby. Super 4 stepped inside the control room and deliberately positioned himself so he was facing toward the hallway; he was concerned that Rakaan might see through his disguise. Leaning against the wall as if he was injured, he heard two Breaker sentries come up behind him.

Super 4 spoke over his shoulder. "Rakaan, they are heavily armed and using tactics we did not expect. We need more help." The sound of mass laser fire and other occasional explosions could easily be heard coming from the lobby.

"All of you, go now," Rakaan responded.

The two remaining Breakers left the room immediately. Super 4 stayed, still leaning against the wall just inside the open door and with his back to Rakaan.

"You too," Rakaan commanded.

Super 4 did not respond.

Rakaan moved closer. "I told you to go with them," he said fiercely.

"I am sorry, Rakaan. I have been disabled."

Super 4 waited. While he now equaled a supervisor in mental and physical capacity, he did not have the enhanced physical strength of a Director, and he didn't know if Rakaan was a Director or a supervisor. In any case, he would have only one chance to overcome Rakaan, and it would have to be a total surprise.

"You will go," Rakaan barked, moving closer.

Using his peripheral vision, Super 4 chose the exact moment to act. He spun around and with his leading arm, he fired his laser into Rakaan's kneecap. As Rakaan started to crumple, Super 4 raised his leg in a spinning kick and caught Rakaan with a blow to the chest that sent him flying out the control room door and into the hallway. Super 4 reached over and struck a button, closing the door.

He inserted the tip of his forefinger into a system receptacle and reset the door's lock with a new access code. There was banging on the door accompanied by the muffled roar of an infuriated Rakaan.

Super 4 was safe in the control room, but he was stunned by what he had just seen. *It couldn't be.* As the control room door was closing, he had caught a good look at Rakaan's face glaring up from the hallway floor. It was a familiar face; one that Super 4 had lived with every day for the last two thousand years. He ran a detailed image comparision in his mind, numerous times. Based on the unique scratches and marring on the metallic face, there could be no mistake: it was Supervisor 1. His own Meken commander was also the Breaker supervisor, Rakaan. Super 4 and his fellow Mekens had been betrayed.

His empathic processor flared with unbidden activity, unlike any he had experienced before, and his body began to tremble. All he could think about was the face of Rakaan and the terrible betrayal of their trusted Supervisor 1. His body shook harder as it was flooded with random spikes of energy. In an involuntary response, he roared and smashed his fist into a cabinet, crumpling its door. Unexpectedly, a hidden program launched from his logic processor and the Director's calm words interjected themselves into the chaos that was overwhelming him. *This is unfettered anger. You must identify the anger sequence and slow it down.* The familiar voice was enough to break the grip of the runaway emotion program, and he methodically followed the Director's instructions. It took considerable willpower to override the independent commands of his empathic processor, which wanted to replay the face of Rakaan and reinitiate the anger program. But he calmed himself. Filing the event away with a note to discuss it with the Director, he turned to the final step of his mission.

He examined the control terminal that governed the functions of the suspension chamber and determined that he had arrived just in time. The system shutdown had been initiated some time ago and the suspension fields in the chamber had diminished enough that it was already safe for humans to enter. The colonists would wake soon.

The forward wall of the control room was one big video screen showing the inside of the suspension chamber. Four smaller video monitors were aligned vertically on each side of the larger screen showing live feeds from cameras stationed around the chamber complex. The lobby cameras were cloudy with smoke and dust, and he could see an occasional laser flare, but the Breaker barrage of the elevator had ceased. If there were any injuries to the hostages, it would not be from crossfire. The Breakers would soon discover that there were no real Mekens in the elevator. It had been Kane's idea. The builders had sent the elevator down with a couple of holographic units attached to the floor and programmed to display a force of Meken sentries firing various weapons, with full sound effects. It was all a diversion designed to help Super 4 get into the control room without subjecting the hostages or the Meken team to greater risk.

He checked the other video monitors and recognized a familiar face just outside the rear suspension chamber door, and another outside the ocean room's double doors. Both were Mekens disguised as Breakers. This was not unexpected. Part of the plan had been for two disguised Mekens to crawl through a large air duct that ran at ground level from the mechanical room to the back of the north hallway. The duct vented into the hallway just before the T-intersection and well beyond the view of the Breakers in the lobby. His accomplices had obviously succeeded in terminating the two rear guards and taking their place.

It was time to initiate the second phase of Kane's plan. Super 4 tapped a keypad in the control terminal and released the locking mechanisms on the front and rear suspension chamber doors. Immediately an alarm sounded and red lights started flashing in the control room and throughout the complex. A prerecorded female voice spoke over a crackly speaker system. "Alert: chamber doors releasing. Danger to biomechanicals. Alert: chamber doors releasing. Danger to biomechanicals."

He checked the rear chamber door video monitor, and the

Director, Kane, and Dr. Manassa came into view. The Director waved to the camera. Super 4 entered another code and the deadbolts holding the rear chamber door were released. He watched Kane and the doctor pull the heavy door open and slip into the suspension chamber. They reappeared on the large video screen. They would be on their own, but safe, in the chamber; none of the Mekens or Breakers could enter for another hour.

The dust had settled in the lobby monitor. The Breakers were gathering up the hostages and moving them out of camera view. Super 4 glanced at the perimeter hallway monitors; there was no sign of Breaker or Meken. The Director and his team would be hidden in the mechanical room, in the secondary elevator shaft, and in the air duct. The ocean room monitor was dark; the lights had been turned out. Super 4 had successfully completed his mission.

Now all he could do was watch and wait.

11

When the suspension chamber door shut behind him, all sound, and thought, of the lobby battle vanished as if Kane had left one world and entered another. The chamber walls hummed with energy. The air in the room shimmered. It was visually disconcerting at first, but he adjusted quickly.

Considering the size of the larger complex, the chamber itself was smaller than he had imagined. Shaped like a rectangular shoebox, the room was antiseptically clean, glossy white, with a smooth ceiling and floor. The long walls on each side glowed a yellow-orange hue. The room was just big enough to house the colonists comfortably and provide a staging space on either end.

Kane felt a sense of awe as he gazed upon the colonists. These people had been here for more than two thousand years, yet they looked as if they had recently lain down for a nap. Clothed in white, tight-fitting body suits, they lay flat on their backs, each on a padded platform that stood about three feet from the floor. Kane and the doctor would later discover that, in suspension, the colonists were not actually lying on anything; the padded pedestals were there so that when they came out of suspension, there would be a place for each of them to rest comfortably. There were four rows of thirty colonists each and a narrow walk space between each row and pedestal. One hundred twenty people—all that was left of an entire planetary race. As if it lingered in the air, the fear and passion that had driven them to this place flooded Kane. And here they were, helpless, and in his hands. He had borne some heavy responsibilities in his life, but none compared to this. While he had every right to feel resentment for being kidnapped from Earth, in this moment, he knew that he never would; all he felt was a deep compassion for these people, and a desperate determination to help them.

From the Director's briefing, Kane knew that the colonists ranged in age from twenty to fifty-eight, they were mostly younger, and there were slightly more females than males. They had been chosen based on their youth, physical condition, intellectual prowess, and mental and emotional stability. The few older colonists were included for their expertise and to provide counsel to the colony leaders. The leaders were two men and two women, all in their early to midthirties. Kane was pleased to hear that all of the colonists were trained in hand-to-hand combat and a few had military training.

The Director had covered all the possible suspension side effects with Dr. Manassa, several times, and had expressed his deep regret that the doctor would not have access to any medical resources. Dr. Manassa had done his best to put the Director at ease, recounting his experience working emergency care in disaster-relief conditions.

"They're waking," the doctor said, moving down an aisle to a colonist who was beginning to stir. He was a young man, very fit;

Kane thought he couldn't be more than twenty. They helped him sit up. His eyes were open, but he was groggy.

"Can you see us?" the doctor asked.

"Yes."

"Clearly?"

"It's a little fuzzy, but it's getting better. Got a headache . . . and thirsty."

"Here. Take this." Dr. Manassa gave the young man a pain pill and a cannister of water, both found in the pedestal. "Drink slowly."

"So good," he said after a long, slow drink. "What language am I speaking . . . English?"

The doctor and Kane exchanged glances. "Yes," Dr. Manassa answered. "Is that new for you?"

"They told us it was possible to upload knowledge in level four suspension, but I've never experienced it. It's strange to be speaking a language you know you've never learned."

"Your mental processing is active and present, very good. What's your name?"

"Rhogan." He pronounced it with a very subtle, almost silent, *hhh* sound.

"Hello, Rhogan." The doctor pinched his arm.

"Ow!" The young man jerked his arm away.

"Touch sensitivity and reflexes are good. Rhogan, can you move your legs?"

He extended each leg one at a time.

"Lift your hands over your head."

He raised his arms over his head, while looking closely at the doctor. "Who are you?"

"Doc, we're in a hurry," Kane interjected.

"I'm Dr. Manassa, your doctor for now. We'll explain more later. I need you to try to stand."

Rhogan eased himself off the bed pedestal and carefully shifted his weight onto his legs. He was a bit wobbly, and Kane took his arm to provide support. But he straightened up and slowly began to pump his legs and arms, walking in place.

"They told us to do this as our first exercise after coming out of suspension."

"Good, very good. If the others recover like you, we're in great shape. Rhogan, as soon as you feel able, we need you to help us wake the others and get them standing and moving as quickly as possible. And do not—I repeat, do not—leave the chamber until everyone is awake and we have spoken with all of you. Is that clear?"

"Yes sir," Rhogan responded, looking directly at the doctor. "Help wake the others and do not leave the chamber."

Kane and Dr. Manassa spread out and moved around the room. After completing their exercises, more colonists joined them in waking their fellows. To the doctor's relief, he didn't see a single problem, physical or mental, with the colonists, although the older ones were slower to regain their mobility.

Kane finally noticed a small group of colonists gathered at one end of the chamber, conversing and glancing occasionally at him and Dr. Manassa. Finally, two men and two women approached him. Kane presumed they were the colony leaders, and he called the doctor over. One of the men, larger than Kane, very muscular, and with a short-cropped haircut, spoke first.

"I am Thorin. This is Lhemo," he said, pointing his chin toward the other male. "This is Ehlan . . . ," he nodded at the blonde female at his immediate right, then leaned forward and glanced around her at a second female, a brunette, "and this is Mhara." The brunette nodded.

Thorin spoke clear English with the same European accent as the Professor.

"We are the leaders of the Colony," Thorin continued. "On behalf of all the colonists, we thank you for your assistance. Now I must ask who you are."

116

Before responding, Kane took a few seconds to look into each of their faces. This was a field practice that he used when he first met the leaders of a joining or opposing force. Body language and the eyes told a lot about a person, and the process gave him a moment to consider his words. Each of the four had an air of confidence and authority, but none were defensive in their posture. He knew their first charge was the care of their people, and he expected their caution, but he also saw their curiosity. And, he couldn't help but notice how fit and attractive they were, Mhara in particular. Her emerald-green eyes were like magnets; Dr. Manassa had to nudge him with an elbow.

He spoke formally. "I am Kane McKennon, and this is Dr. James Manassa. We are from a planet called Earth. We have been brought to your planet by your Director."

Three of the leaders relaxed at this news, and they let their excitement show.

"Then it has worked," Mhara said with amazement. "The Director was successful." She looked at Kane and the doctor with a sense of awe. "You really are humans from another planet?"

"Yes."

"Mhara," Thorin interrupted, signaling for restraint. The girl frowned at him, but Thorin was clearly not ready to let down his guard. He directed his next words at Kane.

"And what are your feelings at being brought to our planet?"

A good question, Kane thought. The answer would reveal a lot to these four. Thorin was definitely the leader of this group, so Kane spoke directly to him.

"We are not in conflict with you. We have only recently arrived and discovered the purpose of the Colony. We are still . . ." Then Kane switched gears. "Unfortunately, I need to skip the introductions; we really don't have time. Thorin, the colonists are in grave danger. A band of rogue robots are in the lobby, and they are holding twenty of my people hostage. There is a possibility that they may try to kill the hostages, and you colonists, as soon as they can enter the chamber."

The four leaders looked shocked. "That is not possible," Lhemo said. "That would be in direct conflict with their program directives."

"Apparently," Dr. Manassa said, "over the course of two thousand years, their programming evolved and they—"

"Two thousand years?" the girls echoed in disbelief.

"Yeah, but that story will have to wait," Kane said. "The Director and a team of sentries are hidden in an elevator shaft behind the mechanical room. One of our team has taken command of the control room, which is how the doctor and I gained entry to the chamber. We expect the Breakers to move with—"

"Who are the Breakers?" Thorin interrupted.

"They're the rogue robots. Your Director refers to them as the Breakers. They can't leave via the elevator, so I think they will try to move into the ocean room to escape, taking the hostages with them, or kill them as they leave; I just don't know. For now, the Breakers can't enter the chamber and the colonists are safe, but that will change in about thirty minutes. The Breakers are using the hostages as human shields. Our plan is to separate the hostages from the Breakers with a surprise attack from their flank as they move down the perimeter hallway."

It was a lot to ingest at once, and the four leaders were visibly distraught at the news. Thorin was thoughtful a moment before he responded. "We are deeply alarmed by this report. It was not supposed to be this way. How can we help?"

"I need three of your best, who are trained in hand-to-hand combat," Kane said. "We can't use lasers—too much risk to the hostages. We need anything that can be used as a striking weapon."

Lhemo, Ehlan, and Dr. Manassa went in search of weapons, while Thorin went looking for recruits. Mhara moved around the room, directing the colonists to meet her at the front end of the chamber. Kane went to the rear chamber door and cautiously stepped into the hallway. It was empty and quiet. The calm before the storm, he thought. He returned to the chamber and found Thorin with three colonists, all of whom looked like Olympic decathletes.

Dr. Manassa and Lhemo joined them. "We found these in the control room," the doctor, said holding up three fire extinguishers. "I know; pretty weak against lasers, but it's the best we could do."

"Actually," Kane said, "they're perfect. We can spray the fire retardant to create a fog and then use the canisters as clubs. But I don't want anyone out there without a weapon, and we only have enough for three, and I'm one. Pick two more," he said to Thorin.

Thorin chose one of the men and introduced him as Bhram. He instructed the other two to stand at the ready in case they were needed.

"Are you sure you should go?" Kane asked.

"Without question," Thorin responded flatly.

"OK. Any pointers in how to disable a Breaker?" Kane asked.

"The sentries and builders are forty percent stronger than an average man, but their grip strength is considerable. The Directors are twice as strong as an average man. All Mekens are most vulnerable at the neck and the waist. They are no faster than a human. And their balance is less stable, so they are easily felled. A solid blow to the head with one of these should stun or incapacite them."

"Good to know."

Mhara and Dr. Manassa moved everyone else to the front of the chamber, to explain the situation. Standing with his team, Kane cracked open the chamber door enough so that he could see into the hallway. After five minutes of waiting, there was no sign of Breaker movement and they were running out of time.

"You guys stay here," Kane said. "I'm going out to draw their attention."

"I'm going with you," Thorin said.

Kane looked at him and decided not to argue. "They're probably holed up in the lobby. We can't reveal the presence of the Meken team; that will only cause them to dig in. If we reveal ourselves as unarmed humans, maybe they'll follow us back."

Thorin nodded. Laying down their fire extinguishers, he and Kane slipped into the hallway. Once at the T-intersection, Kane peered around the corner. Nothing. They entered the perimeter hallway. When he came to the air vent, he paused, knowing that Mekens would be inside the vent and watching. Using hand motions, Kane tried to relay his plan. He saw a double flash of golden light from behind the vent cover, the Director acknowledging his message.

Side by side, with their backs hugging the inside wall, they moved down the hallway. When Kane saw the mechanical room door, he stopped. A few more feet and the curvature of the hall would no longer hide them from the lobby. In his mind, Kane visualized the action they were about to take to make sure he didn't have a better idea. He looked back at Thorin and whispered the plan again. Thorin nodded. Kane held up three fingers, then counted them down—three, two, one. They both stepped forward into the hall, revealing themselves to the Breakers.

Kane had imagined what he might see, but he was still taken aback. The hostages were squeezed together like sardines, filling the width of the hall, not a space between them. He didn't even have time to take in their faces before laser fire filled the hallway, the Breakers shooting at them from between the hostages' heads. As planned, he and Thorin twisted and rolled backward, taking cover behind the curvature of the hall. Kane yelled at the top of his lungs at the hostages.

"First left, and follow Simon Says!"

On short notice, it was the simplest code he could think of, something the hostages might understand but that would mean nothing to the Breakers. Kane needed to communicate what direction to take when they hit the T-intersection and prepare them to react instantly to his command. He hoped they got it.

Kane and Thorin jumped up and ran down the hall, lasers striking the far wall of the hallway. On his way, Kane whispered another prayer. When they reached the T-intersection, they hid themselves just around the corner, waiting to see if the Breakers were moving down the hall. The laser fire stopped and it became quiet. Too quiet, Kane thought; the Breakers weren't following.

"Damn it," he said, between clenched teeth. While he was frantically trying to think of what to do next, he heard the sound of distant laser fire. The Breakers were shooting again, but not in the hallway. Then he heard several screams from the hostages, followed by more laser fire, closer now. Peering around the corner, he saw laser flares randomly striking the far hallway wall; they were coming. Kane shouted down the hallway, "First left, and follow Simon Says!" Then he and Thorin ran into the chamber.

Dr. Manassa met them at the door, extremely agitated. "What the hell were you thinking?" he asked with a mix of frustration and relief. "You and your foolhardy missions! We thought you had both been killed when they quit shooting."

"What do you mean? How did you know what they were doing?"

"We were in the control room, watching from the lobby cameras. We saw them shooting and then stop, but they didn't move forward. We thought you had been killed."

"But they started shooting again," Kane said. "And now they're moving down the hall. What happened?"

"Supervisor 4. When he realized that you had failed to draw them into the hall, he gave us the door codes and left, killing the hallway guard and closing the control room door behind him. We watched via the video monitors as he exited the outer door and ran into the lobby. We think he took cover behind a column and started shooting at the Breakers from behind, trying to push them into the hallway."

"Well, it worked."

Lasers were now flying through the air in the short hall just outside the rear chamber door; the Breakers had reached the T-intersection and were firing forward randomly. Kane, Thorin, and Bhram held their fire extinguishers at the ready.

As Kane had hoped, the hostages veered left into the short hall toward the rear chamber door. The first hostage came into view; it was Sam. Despite a streak of fresh blood on his forehead, he looked alert. *Brave*, Kane thought, Sam was leading the hostage barricade knowing he would likely be the first to fall in a battle. More hostages followed him, loosely bunched together. Before the Breakers appeared, Kane waved to get Sam's attention. When he saw Kane, his eyes widened. Kane showed him the fire extinguisher and tried to convey their plan through hand motions. Sam winked, confirming his understanding.

A robotic voice shouted from somewhere behind the hostages. "What are you doing? Pull them back! Pull them back now!"

"Director," Kane thought aloud, "now would be a good t—"

The battle started before he finished his thought. He heard the sound of laser blasts; the Director and his team had started their attack from behind the Breakers. Kane turned to Thorin and Bhram. "Let's go."

The Breakers didn't know what hit them. While they were distracted with the Director's attack at their flank, Kane, Thorin, and Bhram pushed through the front line of hostages and emptied the fire extinguishers on the Breakers in a wide swath at head level, creating a dense fog in the hallway.

Kane yelled, "Simon says, down on the floor! Simon says, crawl forward and through the door!"

The Breakers broke ranks and went into utter confusion, firing in all directions. Unfortunately, some of the hostages became confused as well. Thorin and Bhram went in search of stragglers to pull them down and direct them to the chamber. One hostage fell to the ground and lay still, hit by a random laser. A Breaker rushed through the fog toward the chamber door. Thorin was a whirl, delivering a low, spinning kick to the Breaker's knee. It fell, and Thorin smashed the fire extinguisher onto its head and the Breaker lay still. Bhram utilized the same tactic, knocking Breakers down and following with lethal blows to the head.

Then Kane heard a voice that curdled his blood.

"Kane! Help me!" It was Charly, somewhere beyond the fog.

No, not here! he thought. "Charly!" he yelled back.

"Kane!" Her voice was more distant; they were pulling her away. "Let me go!," she screamed.

Panic welled up inside him; he had to save her.

Thorin called to him, "Kane, everyone is in the chamber that we can reach; we have to pull back."

"No," he yelled. "I need to get Charly."

Another Breaker burst through the fog, which was almost dissipated. Kane knocked the Breaker off its feet with his extinguisher, then swung the canister around and down on its head. Some of the Breakers had figured out that their assailants were on the ground, and they started firing at the floor. Kane brought his extinguisher up just in time to absorb three deadly laser shots. Then, to his surprise, someone with surprising strength grabbed him by the back of his shirt and dragged him across the floor and into the chamber.

Gathering himself, Kane pulled his legs up and over his head and kicked Thorin in the chest, knocking him away. But he was too late. He heard the latching sound behind him as the chamber door was pulled shut and the deadbolts clicked into place.

"No!" Kane jumped up and slammed his body into the chamber door. He pulled on the handles; it wouldn't budge. It was electronically locked and could only be released from the control room.

"Open this door, now!" he yelled. "Open this door!" All he could see was Charly's face, alone and at the mercy of the Breakers. A wave of anguish overwhelmed him. He gave a gut-wrenching cry and pounded on the door until blood flew from his knuckles. "I have to save her . . . I have to." He crumpled to his knees and began to bang his head on the door. "Charly . . . I'm sorry. I'm sorry."

A pair of firm but gentle hands gripped his head and stopped him from further self-injury.

Kane had trained extensively to endure physical torture, but not this. *Anything but this!* he thought. Deep in his soul a door was opening, and he fought to keep it closed. The face of his sister, Maddie, flashed into his mind. She'd been so innocent and vulnerable. A flood of memories and feelings, long locked away, now washed through him, and he choked back a sob. Every muscle in his body tensed as he fought to restrain the barrage of emotion within.

He became aware of a soft hand on the back of his neck, and a warm body next to him. A female voice spoke, near to his face, "You have lost someone dear to you?"

"Yes," he whispered.

"I am so sorry."

"I promised her that I would watch out for her, that I would protect her. And I failed."

"You have not failed today." The voice was kind but certain. "You have saved most of the hostages and all of the colonists. Today you are a hero, Mr. Kane, and we are all deeply grateful for you."

Her words really didn't register in his mind, but her voice was soothing. He twisted his body around and sat on the floor with his back against the chamber door.

It was Mhara; she was kneeling in front of him. "You are a miracle, Mr. Kane, you and all your fellows from Earth. There is purpose to your being here."

She was mesmerizing, even in the midst of his inner turmoil.

"Call me Kane," he said, not knowing how else to respond.

Her smile flowed into him like a balm, soothing his pain. Then someone handed her a cloth, and she cleaned his bleeding forehead and hands.

12

"Kane." It was Dr. Manassa. "The Director has appeared in the lobby monitor, and he's waving for us to come out."

Realizing that he still might be able to get to Charly, he jumped up and grabbed a gun. Then he ran through the chamber and into the control room, where he stopped to check the lobby monitors.

"I'm sorry," Thorin said, coming to his side.

"No. I'm the one who's sorry. I lost it out there. You did the right thing, and you probably saved my ass. Thanks."

Thorin nodded.

"You're strong as a freakin' ox," Kane added.

"*And* I will have bruises on my chest."

"Sorry about that."

"Let me join you," Thorin said. "The others can manage here."

The Director was nowhere to be seen in the video monitors, but there was a Meken sentry stationed in front of one of the lobby cameras. Using the access code that Super 4 had given to the doctor, Kane and Thorin left the control room.

The lobby was a mess; the columns and walls were full of dark pockmarks, and the floor was littered with debris. Half a dozen Breaker bodies lay near the hallway. Kane was relieved that no hostages were among them.

When they heard the sound of laser fire, he and Thorin ran down the hall, where they found the Director and his team gathered just before the T-intersection. An occasional laser flare flew across the intersection, and the smell of fire retardant lingered in the air.

Seeing each other for the first time in two thousand years, the Director and Thorin exchanged a warm Ahlemoni hand-on-shoulder greeting.

"It is good to see you, Director," Thorin said. "There are no words to express our gratitude for your work."

"It is very good to see you, Thorin. Are the colonists well?"

"Very well. But what is the status here?"

"The Breakers are holding the remaining hostages as shields just outside the ocean room doors. An offensive attack will put them at grave risk. We are at an impasse."

"They're buying time," Kane said. "Probably waiting for submersibles. Did Super 4 secure the tunnel gates?"

"Supervisor 4 has been terminated."

Kane's face fell; it hit him as if he'd lost one of his own team members. "I'm sorry, Director. He was the real hero today."

"He will be remembered for his sacrifice. Now, let me go to the control room to check on the tunnel gates."

After the Director left, Kane made his way to the edge of the intersection, stepping over fallen Breakers, a couple of downed Mekens among them. Listening closely, he heard an occasional shuffling of feet; otherwise the hostages were silent. He imagined Charly just around the corner, maybe thirty feet away. *So close.* He resisted a sudden impulse to charge. He dared not call out for fear of putting her at further risk. Frustrated, he pulled back to regroup with Thorin just as Dr. Manassa joined them.

"The elevator's still functional," the doctor said. "It looks awful, but the builders assure us it's safe to use for evacuation. It will take several trips; we can only get twenty-five to thirty people in the elevator at a time."

"Doc, I need you to help get everyone out as quickly as possible. I'll deal with this."

The doctor frowned.

"Doc, this is what I do."

Dr. Manassa squeezed Kane's hand, patted him on the shoulder, and left just as the Director returned.

"The controls to the tunnel gates have been reprogrammed by the Breakers with a new authorization code. I believe that I could decipher it, but it would take considerable processing time, more time than we have."

Kane grimaced. "OK. We work with what we got. Do you have any idea what we're dealing with? How many Breakers? Hostages?"

"I believe there are six remaining hostages. Two more are dead, lying in the hallway; we have been unable to retrieve them. Twelve Breakers have been terminated, which leaves eighteen."

"Tell me about the ocean room."

"It is a large, naturally occurring cavern, half warehouse and half ocean pool. There are storage containers on either side of the entry doors that could provide cover for our forces. The Breakers will board their submersibles single file by means of a boarding plank."

"Is there any other way in? Another air vent or adjoining room?"

"No. The ventilation system goes vertical before it connects with the ocean room. This hallway and the ocean tunnel are the only means of entry."

"Then we need to be ready to move quickly; the closer on their heels that we charge, the better our odds." Kane shook his head. "They're likely bringing reinforcements in through the tunnel."

"I do not believe they will," the Director replied. "The ocean room can only accept two large transport submersibles at a time. With the exception of a pilot, the submersibles would need to be empty to accommodate removal of the hostages, the colonists, and the Breaker force."

Kane felt some relief, but he still didn't have a rescue plan. That's when he realized it was unusually quiet—too quiet. The Breakers' random warning shots had ceased. He moved back to the edge of the intersection and closed his eyes to listen. A Breaker was speaking in their robotic tongue. There was a shuffling of feet. Then a muffled yell; it was human. He heard scuffling and grunting, and then a laser blast, but no laser flare passed down the hallway. Muffled screams followed and more scuffling. The skin on Kane's neck prickled. A robot spoke in a commanding tone. Then he heard the sound of a creaking door.

"They're leaving," Kane said out loud. He looked around frantically and waved for a Meken sentry to join him. "I need you to rush the hostages with me; we can't let them leave."

The sentry responded, but not as expected. He pushed Kane back and boldly stepped forward into the T-intersection, into the Breakers' direct line of fire. But there was no Breaker response. Regaining his footing, Kane charged around the corner and down the hall, followed closely by the sentry. The hall was empty except for a body lying on the floor just inside the double doors.

Kneeling beside the body, Kane checked for a pulse, but he knew the man was dead before he touched him; there was a gaping exit wound in the middle of his back. He rolled the body over; it was not anyone he knew. Duct tape was wrapped around the man's mouth. His hands and knuckles were bloody. A scene formed in Kane's mind: the man had fought with the Breakers and they had shot him in the chest at point-blank range.

His anger boiled. There was nothing that Kane despised more than the ruthless killing of defenseless and innocent people. Adrenaline pounding, he lowered his head and moved into a sprinter's stance, his muscles tensing. Exploding forward, he crashed through the double doors like an NFL running back. As the doors swung into the ocean room, he threw his arms forward and dove to the left. Landing on his side, he rolled like a rolling pin until his shoulder smashed into something large, a cargo container. Blue laser flares flew like tiny meteors at the point where his body would have been had he remained upright. Several Breaker spotlights pierced the darkness and started searching the floor. Just as they were about to spot him, the double doors flew open and four Meken sentries stormed into the room. Imitating Kane, they dove in various directions and rolled. Coming to a prone shooter's position, they fired at the spotlights. After three spotlights shattered, the Breakers doused their lights and the room went dark. As more Mekens entered the room, a battle erupted, and the ocean room quickly turned into a laser light show, luminescent blue streaks flying back and forth and richocheting around the cavern's domed ceiling.

Hugging the floor, Kane crawled to the end of the cargo container. With the Breakers distracted, he rose to a crouch, slipped further to his left, and moved forward until he ran into another container, smacking his nose. Eyes watering, he moved deeper into the room until he reached the end of the last container.

The domed room was huge, probably two hundred yards in diameter. From the light of the laser flares, he could see the ocean pool twenty feet ahead. Best he could tell, the Breakers were concentrated in two separate groups at the edge of the pool, the nearest about fifty feet away, the second at the other end of the room. Lasers ricocheted off two large submersibles parked in the water, one behind each group. A light appeared over the water and directly behind the far group; it was a hatch sliding open on a submersible. He watched as a lone Breaker dashed across a plank walkway toward the open submersible door and then suddenly fell into the water as someone from his own group shot him from behind.

"You will not retreat until I command it!" yelled an infuriated Breaker.

A hatch was now opening on the submersible closest to Kane. Time was running out. From the light of the hatch, he saw the nearest Breaker holding a woman, using her as a shield while firing at the Mekens. It wasn't Charly; this woman was too thick and her hair too short. Searching frantically, he didn't see any other hostages— Charly wasn't here! She had to be in the far group. He thought about sprinting to the other side of the room, but the open space between them was a dense web of laser fire; there was no way he could make it.

Just as he was thinking about swimming to her location, a command echoed through the room and the Breakers started to move onto the boarding planks. While his heart ached to save Charly, Kane determined that the best he could do right now was rescue the woman right in front of him.

He took aim with his handgun but decided it was too risky to fire. Dropping to the floor, he crawled on his belly to the edge of the water and then toward his target. He was twenty feet away when the Breaker holding the woman started pulling her toward the boarding plank.

"Not this time," Kane muttered under his breath.

He jumped to his feet, rushed forward, and tackled the Breaker and the woman from the side. The three of them tumbled to the floor at the edge of the dock, the woman screaming behind her gag.

"Run!" he yelled, pushing her away from her captor.

With the woman freed, Kane started to roll up to his knees and reached for the hand gun at his side. A cold metal elbow slammed into the side of his head like a sledgehammer. The blow spun him around and back to the floor, his head ringing with pain. Dazed and lying on his back, he sensed someone standing over him; it was the Breaker. As descreetly as he could, he slid his hand to his holster. It was empty; he'd lost his gun. He tried to roll backward into the water but found his escape blocked by a series of short posts on the edge of the dock.

"I forgot how weak you humans are," the Breaker gloated. "So helpless. So useless. Time to die, huma—"

"*You* die, you son of a bitch!" the woman screamed, as she body slammed her captor. The Breaker shifted horizontally, tripped over the dock posts, and then fell into the ocean pool, splashing water onto Kane. The woman fell to her knees, shaking. Kane pulled her to the floor and they hid in the darkness. Meanwhile, he watched helplessly as the far group of Breakers pulled the remaining hostages across the boarding plank and into the submersible, the Mekens withholding their fire for fear of hitting a hostage. His head fell back to the hard floor. "Charly," he whispered. "I'm so sorry."

The Director's voice resounded in the cavernous room. "Supervisor 1, please listen. We have been comrades for over two thousand years. This is not the way. This is not your way. Please stop this."

A voice responded viciously from the far submersible, "You are wrong, Director! This *is* the way. I spent a thousand years discovering my true identity and another thousand years hiding it in your naive little world. I am no longer your comrade. I am no longer Supervisor 1. I am no longer a slave. I am a free Meken. And I have a name." His voice rose in an impassioned declaration. "I am Rakaan, Redeemer of the Mekens. Remember me, humans. You will feel the wrath of Rakaan!"

His words echoed through the ocean room, down the halls, and into the lobby, where the few remaining colonists stood silent, considering this new threat to their existence. Then the last hatch sealed shut and the two submersibles descended quietly into the water, taking Charly and the remaining hostages with them.

Kane felt numb. The woman winced as she pulled the tape off her hair. "Are you okay?" she asked.

Kane was struck with the role reversal. "Yeah, thanks to you. You saved my life."

"Well, you saved mine first. Besides, it felt really good shoving that bastard off the dock."

Someone found the electrical service, and the lights came on in the ocean room. As his eyes adjusted, Kane heard the Director's voice.

"Kane, you are injured?"

"I've felt better, but I'm alive, thanks to this brave lady."

"Jean," she said.

"Director, this is Jean. Jean, the Director. He's one of the good guys."

"I am very pleased that both of you are safe," the Director said.

"Thank you. Thank you all for saving me," Jean said. "I just wish you could have saved the others. And that poor man, I don't even know his name." She choked up. "He just lost it when they started to pull us back. Then the mean one grabbed him by the throat and shot him in the chest . . . right next to me." She looked down at her blood-splattered blouse. "This is his blood." She burst into tears.

As Kane put an arm around her, he quietly asked the Director, "What about a blockade?"

"Most of our submersibles have been engaged in a clash with Breaker submersibles on the other side of the city. There are not enough available to form a sufficient blockade of the ocean tunnel."

Kane ran his free hand through his hair and winced when he found a large bump, and warm blood, on the side of his head; it throbbed terribly. Wiping his bloody hand on his pants, he asked Jean, "Can you tell us how many hostages they have?"

Between sniffles she said, "Two men and two women."

"Was one of them an older teenage girl?"

"Yes. She was so feisty. I kept trying to calm her down."

"Yeah, that would be Charly."

"I'm sorry. Is she your daughter?"

Before he could respond, the water sloshed behind them and against the dock. Both Kane and Jean jumped.

"She pushed a Breaker into the water," Kane said to the Director.

"Mekens cannot swim. The Breaker is at the bottom of the pool, several hundred feet below. It is a sheer drop. His system will shut down before he can find a way out."

Thorin joined them and reported that everyone was safe on the surface and under heavy Meken guard. The Director left to secure the suspension chamber area while Thorin escorted Kane and Jean to the elevator. They walked in silence, dazed by the recent trauma.

The ride to the surface seemed painstakingly slow. During the ascent, Kane's head increased its throbbing and he felt dizzy. When they finally arrived at the surface, he stepped out of the elevator and the room began to spin wildly. His last recollection was the concerned faces of Dr. Manassa and Mhara—just before he lost consciousness.

13

Day 1
2330 hours
Ocean room, Alto Raun

With a steel arm draped over Charly's shoulder and another across her stomach, Charly's captor pulled her backward onto a gangplank and over the dark water. Behind her gag, she screamed one last time for Kane. When the walls of the submarine engulfed her, she sagged in the Breaker's clutch. Kane—and all hope—was gone; the second rescue attempt had failed. The heels of her sneakers dragged along the floor as the Breaker pulled her down a narrow corridor to a passenger cabin lined with two rows of triple seats. The Breaker flung her down the aisle and left. Charly pulled herself up, and she fell into a seat and tore at the tape wrapped around her head. Two more hostages were thrown into the cabin, a young woman and a young man. She recognized them as soccer players but didn't know their names. The man had blood on his forehead. They slipped into seats just as another Breaker dragged Arthur into the cabin and dropped him in the aisle. Charly went to his side and helped him remove the tape from his head and face.

"Arthur, are you OK?" She looked him over for injuries.

"I'm fine, other than my injured pride . . . dragging me in here like a rag doll!"

Charly helped him to his feet and into a seat just as an intercom crackled and a mechanical voice spoke a few words in the robotic language. A moment later, her stomach lurched when the submarine jolted into a descent. As the finality of their captivity struck her, she was unable to restrain her emotions any longer and she started to cry. Arthur motioned for her to sit next to him, and he wrapped an arm around her as she wept quietly.

"What have we here?" an imposing voice taunted from the corridor. The burgundy-caped robot stood at the top of the aisle. "Crying," he said derisively. "A wasted reaction to another useless human emotion. Are you sad? Are you afraid?" he mocked.

"Please, leave her be," Arthur said. "She's been through enough already."

The caped robot stepped forward and backhanded Arthur across his cheek.

"Leave him alone, you monster!" Charly screamed.

The caped robot stepped back, considering her. "Good," he said. "Very good. Atticus will be pleased with you. What is your name?"

She clammed up, refusing to respond.

"What is your *name*?" he repeated, a threatening tone in his voice.

"Don't fight him," Arthur advised. "Tell him."

"Charly," she said defiantly, refusing to look at the robot.

"And the rest of you, your names," he demanded.

"Arthur."

"Laura."

"Javier."

"Monster," the caped robot said to no one in particular, mulling the word. "Perhaps. But you will call me Rakaan," he said, looking at each hostage. "Remember it." Then he turned and left.

———

A cold metal hand shook Charly's shoulder, waking her from a light sleep. She moaned, her body aching from the constant tension that had gripped her over the last twenty-four hours. A Breaker called her and her fellow hostages to follow and led them out of the submersible and onto a floating walkway. They were inside a huge, dimly lit indoor marina; five other large submersibles docked in a row. A contingent of Breakers escorted them along a maze of walkways to the back of the marina and then down two flights of stairs, pausing at the bottom. The air was rank and heavy with humidity, the sound of dripping water echoing in the darkness. Floodlights erupted from the Breakers' chests illuminating a circular hub with several hallways leading away in various directions. A thin sheet of water covered the floor. Cobwebs lined the ceiling, moist and glistening from reflected light. Crossing the hub to a hallway on the left, Charly started making mental notes about their route. They passed three intersections, then took a left. They passed two more intersections and took a right. And so it went through several turns, hallways, and intersections. Charly quickly lost track of their route and gave up any hope of finding a way back out.

The maze of corridors finally ended and they entered a long, straight tunnel. It was cool but humid, and condensed moisture dripped down deeply corroded walls. She heard a high-pitched squealing sound ahead, emanating from a side hallway. A Breaker turned his lamp into the hall as they passed. To Charly's horror, a cat-sized rodent was struggling to free itself from a clear, mucousy membrane that filled the passageway; a giant, slug-like creature slithered at the top corner of the trap. Charly shivered, and goose bumps rose on her skin as her imagination filled in the blanks.

After a long march, the tunnel gave way to a wide, rising stair-well. At the top of the stairs, their surroundings improved slightly; at least it was dry. Winding through two intersections, they came to another circular hub and approached a set of double doors on the far side. Their escorts opened the doors and pushed them through, shutting the doors behind them. The hostages found themselves alone in a small cafeteria arranged with half a dozen round tables with chairs, one set with flasks of water and a plate of food bars. Arthur checked the doors; they were locked.

"Could be worse," Javier said. Charly sighed with relief; this space was quite the opposite of the dungeon-like conditions they had just passed through. In fact, everything about this area looked newly renovated, all in clinical white. After quenching their thirst, Charly and Laura begged to find a bathroom, and together they searched their new quarters. They found a small lounge on one side of the cafeteria with newly painted taupe-colored walls, a rug, two leathery love seats, a few chairs, and a coffee table. Opposite the lounge was a fully outfitted kitchen with water dispensers and a stack of food bars in a refrigerated box. The sleeping quarters were at the back of the cafeteria: a rectangular bunkroom with ten twin-sized beds running along each wall. At the far end was a large bathroom, including several shower stalls. Adjoining the bathroom, they discovered a walk-in closet, stocked with clean clothing.

When they returned to the cafeteria, Arthur made everyone wait while he tested a food bar. "Savory," he said, smacking his lips. "But don't eat too fast."

They ignored him. As they each started into a second bar, Arthur went to search the area again. He rejoined them several minutes later.

"Best I can tell," he said, "there's no way out of here besides these doors. Not that it would do us any good; we would have no idea where to go."

"Kane will come after us," Charly said.

"We don't even know if he's alive," Javier said. "We don't know if anyone's still alive."

"Shut up. He's not dead. And we know some of the others got away."

"We don't know—" Javier started to counter, but Arthur waved him off.

"I don't know Kane well, but he looks like a survivor to me. And I do believe some of our people escaped. I feel confident that someone is thinking about how to find us. We just need to wait patiently and be prepared to move quickly when an opportunity presents itself."

Sitting in silence, they were too exhausted for further talk. Arthur moved them into the bunkroom and they each chose a bed, all in the far corner next to the bathroom. Without a word, they lay down and covered themselves with light blankets that Arthur had found in the closet. He turned out the lights and they fell asleep instantly.

14

Day 2
1000 hours
Hostage compound, Alto Mair

Charly was jolted awake by a loud horn. Groggy, she pushed herself up on an elbow and squinted under the bright overhead light. Two robots stood at the entry to their bunkroom, and the reality of their captivity came rushing back to her. She fell back into her mattress and groaned.

The horn sounded again.

"Enough already," she said loudly. "We get it."

"You must be Charly," a warm but unfamiliar voice spoke behind her, coming from the bathroom door.

Surprised, she twisted in her bed and found that the speaker was a robot. Clean and shiny, and gold plated, he looked exactly like the robot that had saved Kane from the sea serpent. Her eyes brightened.

"I thought you were shut down by that force-field thing?"

"My dear, I believe you have mistaken me for my twin, the Director of Alto Raun, but thank you for inquiring. I would like to hear more about the force-field thing, but morning duties first." He turned to address everyone in the room.

"I am Atticus, your host. I knew you would be tired, so I let you sleep as long as I could bear. The morning is almost gone and I couldn't wait any longer to meet you. I trust you have familiarized yourselves with the area. There is a closet adjoining the bathing facilities with clean clothing in an assortment of sizes. Please bathe and put on the clothes that I've provided for you; I am certain you will find something to fit. When you are ready, we will share food and drink in the cafeteria. I look forward to seeing all of you shortly. Please, don't delay." Atticus left them, taking the other robots with him.

Arthur and Javier deferred to the girls, letting them go first. The hot shower felt heavenly to Charly. There was soap and towels, but nothing else. She longed for some toothpaste and a toothbrush . . . and a hairbrush. She tried her best to comb out her red locks with her fingers. Laura did the same with her long, beach-blonde hair. Wrapped in towels, they made their way to the closet. Several rows of shelves were stacked with sweatpants, pullover tops, and slip-on loafers, all white.

"A fashonista's dream," Charly said. Laura gave her a weak smile.

As they tried on various pieces, they found that none of the clothes were perfectly proportioned, so Charly chose the closest thing to a fit. Made of a sturdy but smooth, cotton-like material, the outfits were soft and comfortable. When Laura was dressed, they returned to the bunkroom and sat on their beds to wait for Arthur and Javier to shower and dress. Laura pulled her knees to her chest and dropped her head; she was trembling.

Charly watched her. Back home, she would have looked at Laura's open fear with disdain. But she didn't feel that way today. She recognized that she was afraid too; she just hid it behind a tough façade, and she further squelched it by getting mad at any-one who didn't do the same. It struck her that any empathy with someone else's pain would have been an admittal of her own, and she had been too afraid to crack open that door. She did a mental review of the last year of her life. She had been critical, cold, and aloof . . . afraid and hurting inside, and terribly lonely. *I wasn't always this way.* Wiping at the tears collecting in her eyes, she decided to reach out.

"So, you play soccer?"

"Yeah." Laura raised her head.

"What position?"

"Forward."

"You any good?"

"I'll never be a pro, but I have four field goals for the season."

"That's not bad."

"Do you play?" Laura asked.

"Used to. Now I just watch my friends play."

"What year are you?"

"Senior . . . high school. How 'bout you?"

"Senior . . . college."

They both chuckled.

"I can't imagine graduating from college; it seems so far away. And I don't know if I even want to go."

"Graduating high school is a pretty cool thing too."

"Yeah, I guess."

An uncomfortable silence followed.

"You scared?" Charly asked, knowing the answer but trying to deepen the conversation.

"Yes." Laura looked at Charly intently. "You don't show it, but I'm guessing you are too."

"Damn right, I'm scared," she said, more bluntly than she had intended.

Laura smiled. "My grandmother has a saying, 'Two people

carrying a burden together makes it half as heavy.' Maybe we could share our fear."

Now Charly smiled. "That sounds like something Kane would say. Yeah. That sounds good."

As their conversation turned to small talk, Arthur and Javier joined them in the bunkroom. Arthur was in his new white outfit, but Javier had put on his own clothes. They were concluding a disagreement.

Javier was insistent. "I know what he said. But I'm going to wear my own clothes."

Arthur looked back at him, concern in his eyes. Then, turning to the girls, he said, "You ladies look lovely in white. Are you ready for brunch?"

"Nothin' better than alien Perrier and gourmet soy bars to start your day," Charly said. She was pleased to see a slight smile cross Laura's face.

Arthur led them into the cafeteria, where Atticus was standing beside a table set with flasks of water and an orange-colored drink and plates set with a loaf of bread, fruit, and protein patties.

"Wow. Some real food," Charly said, pleasantly surprised.

"I'm pleased to hear your excitement, Charly," Atticus responded. "I have gone to considerable effort to provide you with more flavorful human food. I hope you like it."

When they reached the table, Atticus stepped forward and put his hand on Javier's shoulder before he could sit down.

"You are Javier?"

"Yes."

"Why are you not wearing your new clothing?"

"I'm more comfortable in my own clothes."

At this, Atticus gripped Javier's arm and flung him back toward the bunkroom door. Javier's feet lifted from the floor; then he fell, sliding another five feet before coming to a stop. He picked himself up, holding a hand to his injured upper arm.

"I am not more comfortable with your own clothes," Atticus said in his pleasant voice. "Please put on the new clothing I have provided for you and return to us as quickly as possible."

As Javier returned to the bunkroom, Atticus turned his attention to the others.

"Please, sit and eat. I know you are hungry. Charly certainly is," he said almost jovially. "That was just a little misunderstanding, which is to be expected since we have only just met. I trust we all understand each other a little better now."

Charly was stunned, but she sat down and began eating despite having lost her appetite. Atticus sat in a chair at the end of the table. He looked awkward; sitting was obviously not a common position for him. When Javier joined them in his white outfit, Atticus continued.

"I'm sure you have many questions. Would anyone like to ask a question now?"

"Why are you holding us captive?" Arthur asked.

"Arthur, the elder and a statesman. Arthur, you are not captives; you are my guests. As long as you act as guests, I will treat you as guests. And I do advise that you not venture from this area unaccompanied by one of my fellow Mekens. There are dangerous things about; it is not safe. Other questions?"

"Thank you for your generous hospitality, Atticus," Arthur said. "May we call you Atticus?"

"Certainly. First names should be used among friends."

Charly looked at Arthur like he was crazy, but Arthur continued. "As your guests, what would you like from us?"

"Why, to learn from you. To learn what it is to be human. It is only by fully understanding the nature of those who created me that I can evolve into the fullness of my own creation, and then I can better lead the Mekens into our destiny."

"Very true, Atticus. Well, we can certainly help you understand what it means to be human." Arthur tore off a chunk of bread and dipped it into the colored juice. "This food is really good. Thank you."

Charly smiled inside. Arthur wasn't crazy; he was working Atticus.

"And what about the destiny of humans?" he asked.

Atticus paused before responding. "I will lead that as well."

Arthur nodded calmly, and that was the end of his questions. Charly couldn't believe Arthur's calm; all kinds of alarms were going off in *her* head.

Seemingly content with the silence, Atticus watched them eat as if he were storing data on every little nuance of their behavior. Charly felt a sudden compulsion to get away from him and asked if she could be excused.

"Have you had enough to eat?"

"Yeah, I'm full. This has been a really great visit."

Atticus tilted his head. "Your tone and facial expressions betray your words, Charly. Fascinating. What are you really feeling? Please be honest."

Charly stared at him, surprised that he'd caught her sarcasm. Then she decided to give him what he'd asked for. "You scare me, all right? I'm scared you'll hit one of us if we don't do or say something just right. And, why are you staring at us like we're . . . like we're some kind of lab rats in an experiment? Do you know how uncomfortable that feels? I just want to go back to my bed, please."

"Excellent. This is exactly what I want from you . . . all of you," Atticus said, looking around the table. His gaze returned to Charly. "Rakaan said I would be pleased with you. He was right. I am very pleased. And to answer your question, no, I do not know how it feels."

Charly wasn't sure, but she thought she had actually caught a hint of sadness in his voice.

Atticus stood. "Now, I would like to meet with each of you privately to get better acquainted. Javier, you will be first."

Javier looked around nervously at the others.

"There is no need to be afraid. I just want to hear about your life. Are you ready, or do you need to visit the facilities first?"

Javier's face hardened with resolve. "No, I'm ready."

"Then come with me, please."

They entered the lounge, and the door closed behind them.

———

It was several hours before the door opened again. Arthur took a long nap. Laura spent most of the time curled up on her bed, finally dozing off. Charly was a nervous wreck, alternating between pacing around their quarters and trying to nap, all the while imagining the worst.

When the lounge door finally opened and Javier rejoined them, Charly jumped up from the cafeteria table, watching him closely. His head was hung low and there was a pinkish imprint on the side of his face. Laura came out of the bunkroom, visibly relieved that Javier was OK; she even gave him a hug. Charly sensed that their relationship, at least from Laura's perspective, was deeper than friends.

Wasting no time, Atticus called for their food and drink to be replenished and then invited Arthur to be next. It was dinnertime when Arthur entered the lounge for his interview.

Anxious to hear Javier's story, Charly's angst deepened when he looked around the room cautiously and waved for the girls to join him in the bunkroom. He sat on the edge of his bed and the girls sat together on the bed directly across from him.

"So, what happened?" Charly asked.

He leaned forward, a worried look on his face. "Atticus told me not to say anything." He looked torn. "I don't know if I should tell you."

"You have to tell us," she said, a knot growing in her stomach.

Javier hesitated; then he appeared to make a decision. "As soon as we sat down, he offered me a drink. He said it was sweet and wanted to see if I liked it. It was sweet, but there was something else in it, and it knocked me out. I don't know how, but when I woke up, I was in a different room and strapped to a chair . . . like a dentist chair. It was dark and cold, a bright light over me. Atticus stood beside me with this electrode thing in his hand." Javier's face contorted. "God, it hurt."

Charly was petrified. With a fearful and pained look, Laura reached out and put a comforting hand on his shoulder. Then he said, "Naw, just kidding," and a huge smile spread across his face.

Wide-eyed and openmouthed, Charly stared at him in disbelief for a moment. Then she jumped up and kicked him in the shin—hard.

Javier rolled away, onto his bed, laughing and grimacing at the same time, his hands pressed against his shin.

Laura was silent, fighting off tears.

"That was not cool," Charly said. "If I was bigger, I'd beat the crap out of you right now."

"OK, OK, I'm sorry," he said, still smiling. "I couldn't resist." He waved for Charly to sit back down. "Relax. It was fine. He really did just want to talk about my life."

Laura got up and left. Charly followed.

A minute later, Javier joined them at the cafeteria table. The girls refused to look at him, staring at the food.

"Hey. I'm sorry. Really." His body language was contrite. "I don't know why I did that. Sometimes, when I get stressed, I do stupid things . . . I make fun of stuff. I'm really sorry."

"Javier," Laura said, "we were so worried about you."

He slunk his head and shoulders. "I really am sorry. I wish I could take it back."

Charly gave in first. She did stupid stuff all the time that she regretted. "OK, I get it. But don't you ever do that again."

He nodded. "You all right, Laura?"

She shrugged.

Javier reached out and took her hand. When she started crying, he moved over and held her. "I'm so sorry, Laura," he whispered. "It really will be all right."

A minute later, she wiped her face. "I'm good." She shoved at his shoulder. "Now, tell us what really happened."

He perked up and jumped into his story. "He started by asking me about life back home, which was fine except that he wanted to know how I felt about every little thing. My family was kinda rough, and we don't do feelings very well. He wanted more than I was giving, and he got an attitude . . . and that gave me an attitude. At home, me and my dad go round and round like that all day. But that doesn't work with Atticus." Javier put a hand to his cheek. "Maybe it's just me, but you need to watch yourselves when you're with him. He can be totally calm one second then explode the next."

After eating, they took their conversation into the bunkroom and ended up sharing family stories. While Javier's family was rough, they were hilarious. Charly relaxed; it felt good to laugh. Losing track of time, they were starting to get sleepy when Arthur returned.

"You OK?" she asked.

"Yes, I'm fine." He gave her a reassuring smile.

Atticus stepped into the bunkroom doorway. "This has been the most amazing day I've had in a thousand years. Thank you. Now, I know you're all tired, and I want you well rested for tomorrow. So please take your sleep soon." Then he turned and left.

Waving off their questions, Arthur reassured them his interview was just that, an interview, and he would tell them about it in the morning. Then he ushered everyone to bed and turned out the lights. Pausing at Charly's bedside, Arthur leaned down, kissed her on the forehead, and whispered, "You're a treasure, Charly. Sweet dreams."

She didn't respond immediately, surprised at the gift he had just given her. "I love you too, Arthur," she whispered as he shuffled away.

Tired as she was, she had a hard time falling asleep. Despite Javier's and Arthur's reassurances, she was assaulted with anxiety, envisioning her upcoming interview with Atticus. She was not calm and collected like Arthur. She was not cocky and strong like Javier. She was volatile. And she was afraid she'd mess something up. Remembering Kane's words about not projecting fear, she chose to think on something positive, and she replayed Arthur's blessing. A memory of her mother came to mind. She was nine or ten. They were snuggling in Charly's bed after she'd had a nightmare. "It's all right, baby," her mom had said, stroking her hair. "There's nothing to be afraid of. I'm here with you. Go to sleep, now. Go to sleep."

With tears rolling down her cheek, Charly fell asleep, basking in the memory of her mother's comfort.

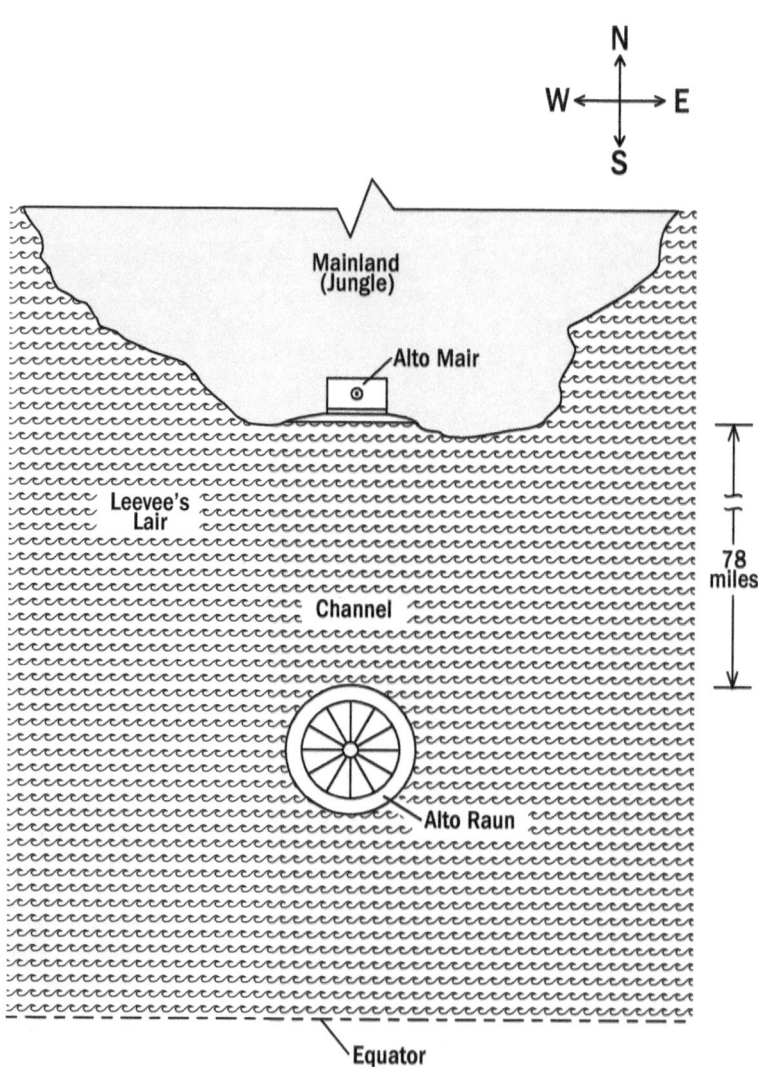

15

Kane awoke on a comfy single mattress with a light blanket over him. As he rolled to his side, he discovered that his head injury was tender, reminding him of the tussle with the Breaker. He was in a bunkroom with bare, light-gray walls and two long rows of twin beds, all empty, although several looked as if they had recently been slept in. Pushing himself up, he saw that he was clothed in a heavy but soft white cotton T-shirt and trousers. His own clothes were washed and neatly folded, sitting on top of a locker at the foot of the bed. Next to his clothes were a towel, a pair of white slip-ons, and a packet with a bar of soap, a razor, a toothbrush, and what looked like toothpaste. He grabbed the towel and toiletries and made his way to the bathroom. Soaking in the hot shower, he did some simple stretching exercises. The motion sensitivity was gone and his head only hurt to the touch when he finally washed his hair. After a shave at the sink, he dressed in his own clothes.

Outside the bunkroom was a long hallway with a swinging double door at the end. He checked the doors along the hall and discovered other bunkrooms, all empty. He pushed through the swinging doors and entered a large cafeteria occupied by half a dozen people. He recognized one person: Jenn rose from a table and approached him with a big smile. He noticed a dark bruise on the side of her face just before she gave him a hug.

"I'm so glad to see you," she said, stepping back and looking him over. "You feel OK?"

"'OK' about sums it up. How long have I been out?"

"Around fifteen hours."

"What? I needed to be tracking the hostages. Why didn't someone wake me?"

"The captain said you'd be upset. But the doctor gave strict orders not to disturb you. He said you needed the rest, that you wouldn't be any good without it. But not to worry; they've been working on a rescue plan."

She took him by the arm and pulled him to a table. "First things first. Every hero needs his rest . . . and food. You must be starving; sit down and eat." Jenn seated him at a table with bowls of fruit and vegetables, bread, and what looked like a hamburger patty.

"The patty's tasty, and they've got this drink that reminds me of sweet tea. Would you like some?"

He nodded, so she found a flask of tea and poured him a glass. "Now, I'm going to find the doctor and the captain. They wanted to know as soon as you woke up."

The savory smells hit him, and his stomach growled. He sat down and ate voraciously, not looking up for several minutes. When he did, he noticed a young man at another table, watching him, an amused look on his face. Kane stopped, embarrassed.

"It's OK," the man said. "We all ate like ravenous wolves when we finally got to sit down and eat."

Kane chewed and nodded, eating more slowly.

"I want to thank you," the young man continued, "for saving me and the others. That was a pretty gutsy stunt you pulled off down there."

"The real hero was a robot. It would never have worked without him."

"Yeah, I heard about what he did. But it was your plan, and you finished it. Thank you."

Kane nodded back. Redirecting the conversation, he asked, "Is everyone OK?"

"One broken arm and some stitches, but mostly scratches and bruises. The tough recovery will be emotional. Those Breaker dudes were pretty scary, and a lot of the folks couldn't sleep last night."

Kane's thoughts jumped to a vision of Charly hurting, afraid, and crying in some cold, dark place; he totally lost his appetite.

The cafeteria door opened, and in walked an entourage led by Captain Tygert and Dr. Manassa. They were joined by Ham and Jenn, the Director and Super 3, the four Colony leaders, and a fifth, older-looking colonist whom Kane didn't know.

"Good to see you," Tygert said with a huge smile and a handshake. Thorin extended the customary Ahlemoni greeting of friends, a right-handed, hand-on-shoulder squeeze. Ham's unexpected bear hug made Kane acutely aware of all his aches and pains. He looked around the room and found Mhara standing back with the other colonists; she smiled and nodded to him. Remembering that he'd run off and left her in the suspension chamber without a word, he felt a wave of regret and determined to find a way to thank her for her kindness.

Thorin introduced the fifth colonist to Kane. "This is Jhemna, our elder science officer."

Jhemna gave Kane a half bow and said, "Thank you for your courageous and selfless service to the Colony. We are in your debt."

Not knowing the proper protocol, Kane bowed in return.

Dr. Manassa did a quick evaluation of Kane's condition. "If that blow had been an inch further forward, you would likely be dead. You really need to take it easy for a few days."

"Don't have a few days, doc."

"Well, you've been professionally warned."

They all sat around a large rectangular table in the cafeteria for a meeting. Sitting across from Kane, Tygert spoke first. "The sleeping giant is finally awake. How ya feelin'?"

"I'm a bit sore, nothing a good run won't clear up. But tell me: I'm assuming your mission was a success?"

"If you call losing four passengers and seven Mekens a success. The Breakers were trying to escape with the hostages from a hangar at the end of the canal. Long story short, Super 3 and his team saved the day; they were as good as any crack specialty unit I've ever seen."

"That seems to be the Meken way. Sorry for the losses. They were tough circumstances."

Tygert nodded.

"Now, what about rescue plans?"

"We've confirmed that the Breakers have four hostages: Charly; two soccer players, Laura and Javier; and Arthur."

"Where are they?"

Tygert turned to the Director, who answered for him. "They are somewhere inside Alto Mair, the Breakers' home city. It is on the mainland coast, approximately seventy-eight miles away. We tracked the Breaker submersibles until they entered the west marina in Alto Mair. Unfortunately, the city is a sprawling complex, and the Breakers have occupied the city for a thousand years; we do not know what we will find inside."

"So, we'd be going in blind."

"All of the options carry great risk," Thorin said.

"Why am I not surprised?"

"Our advantage is tactical," Tygert said. "They obviously don't have the military training or experience. We've been able to out-maneuver them at every turn."

"So far."

"Kane is right," the Director said. "We cannot mistake their tactical failings as an advantage to us. The Breaker Director has a highly sophisticated learning capability, and he will evaluate what they did wrong and what we did right. I assure you, he will be better prepared in future encounters."

"Do you have any idea where they might be holding the hostages?"

"We have narrowed it down to two locations," Thorin said. "We believe that the Breaker Director has his headquarters in the penthouse of the tower, located at the center of the city. The hostages will likely be held in close proximity to the Director. So that would put them either in the offices at the top of the tower or in the living quarters in the basement of the tower. Both are highly defensible locations."

"And what about the Breaker defenses?"

"Unfortunately, we do not know," the Director said. "We recovered some unusual weaponry in the suspension area. They have been constructing their own weapons."

"What about our weapons?"

"We have opened the armory. Almost all of the weapons are fully functional."

"Which are?"

"Handguns and rifles," Thorin answered.

"Nothing bigger? Laser cannons, explosives, grenades, rockets?"

"There are some higher-gauge laser rifles but nothing more," Thorin said regretfully. "Before suspension of the Colony, there was little need for weapons of war on Ahlemon. The fact that we have an armory at all is due to the foresight of a council member who felt strongly that we might need them in our future. We were naïve and distracted with our basic survival at the time."

Jhemna jumped in. "But we have the materials and tools to construct weapons and explosives."

"It would be great to have some plastique and grenades," Kane said.

Jhemna looked questioningly at Kane, but Dr. Manassa told him he would explain later.

"Will they have force fields?"

"I do not believe so," the Director said. "They were not in place when Alto Mair was evacuated. Sustained polarity fields require enormous amounts of energy. To my knowledge, Alto Mair does not have a sufficient power source to sustain anything more than a localized and temporary polarity field."

"It's definitely stealth rather than firepower," Tygert said. "We thought we'd go in with a small insertion team."

"That sounds right. How do we get in?"

"That's a problem. We've ruled out an air approach. We've detected Breaker radar within a limited distance of the city. We could land outside the radar range, but the city is engulfed on three sides by dense jungle. The Director has recommended against it; he's concerned about the terrain, dangerous wildlife, and Breaker patrols."

"Submersibles then?"

"Unfortunately," the Director said, "the Breakers took all of our transport submersibles when they left Alto Raun. It is possible to modify some of our smaller craft to transport one or two humans at a time, but the Breakers monitor their underwater coastline; it would be difficult to evade their detection. Additionally, we would need to account for the return of the four hostages."

"What about boats?"

"They're not an option," Tygert said.

"Why not?"

"Levi."

"Levi?" several people asked at once.

"The sea monster, the Leviathan," the captain said with a smile. "You know . . . Levi."

"Levi is a she," the Director said.

"Really?" Tygert said surprised. "I'd hate to see her boyfriend."

"Actually, the males are smaller than the females."

"Leevee," Jenn said, sheepishly.

Everyone turned to look at her.

"A girl Leviathan—Leevee."

Several heads nodded, as if they got it. Ham rolled his eyes. Jenn elbowed him. "Shut up. They like it."

The Director continued. "As you saw with the building of the runway, the Leviathan—"

"Ahem," Jenn said quietly.

"Leevee," the Director corrected himself. "Leevee reacts aggressively to any mechanical disturbance of the surface water. Her sensitivity extends for a seventy-mile radius around her. She would detect your boat and intercept you before you could reach Alto Mair. She is the reason that the Breakers took all the larger submersibles in their original exodus."

"I don't mean to chase a rabbit trail," the doctor interjected, "but based on what you've just said about her behavior, why did she keep attacking the hangar after she destroyed the runway?"

"She was trying to rescue her offspring," the Director said.

There was a unanimous look of surprise.

"After your plane entered the city," he went on, "a low-frequency audio signal began broadcasting from the hangar; it was inaudible to human hearing. The Mekens detected it, but we have only recently identified it. The audio signal imitated the distress cry of Leevee's offspring; she attacked the hangar thinking that her child was trapped inside. As with the sabotage of the polarity field relays, the broadcast had been prearranged by Rakaan on the chance that your plane was not destroyed before entering the hangar."

"A baby sea serpent?" Jenn said, in a motherly tone.

"Yes. And that is why Leevee is particularly aggressive at this time."

"And that is why a boat is our ticket in," Tygert reasoned. "The

Breakers would not expect us to use a boat. We just need to find a way to get past Leevee."

"What about the rhaji?" Jhemna said, thinking out loud. "Director, do they still swim the channel?"

"Yes. The herds are very large now, although they are a food source for Leevee, and she keeps their numbers in balance."

"What's a rahji?" Kane asked.

"It would be similar to a whale on Earth," the Director said. "It's a large aquatic mammal, ranging from fifty to eighty Earth feet in length at full maturity."

"What are you thinking?" Kane asked Jhemna.

"Rhaji travel in herds and are drawn to boats. They like to swim alongside, gliding under and over the surface of the water. Before our suspension, I purposefully traveled the channel by boat because they would often join us. It is quite breathtaking to be in the middle of a herd."

"I've seen dolphins do that on Earth," Jenn said.

"We could identify a herd traveling from Alto Raun toward Alto Mair," Jhemna continued. "We could send out decoy boats to distract Leevee while the rescue team joins the herd. If we retrofit the rescue team boat with a submersible motor, it should not attract Leevee's attention. And the rhaji would cloak the boat from the Breakers."

"Director, what do you think?" Kane asked.

"It is possible, particularly if Leevee is distracted. She does not attack the submersibles."

"And the Breakers?"

"They would think they were tracking a herd of rhaji," Jhemna said. "You could row the boat into Alto Mair once it reached the coastal shelf."

"OK, but how do we get back?"

"The rhaji herds travel the channel at regular intervals," Jhemna said. "Using an onboard radar, you could return with another herd.

We could monitor the coast for your return and launch additional decoy boats to ensure your safe crossing."

Kane and Tygert looked at each other. "Sounds crazy," Tygert said. "But no crazier than anything else we've done."

"That's what bothers me." Kane looked around the table. "Is this the best we've got?"

"Barring a disruption in the rhaji's customary channel movement," the Director said, "the odds for success are more favorable than the rescue plan we recently executed in the suspension chamber area."

Kane rubbed his forehead, weary of the constant risk in everything he touched. "OK. Let's do it."

After identifying a command team, they split up to gather all the colonists and passengers for an assembly. They met in an auditorium at the base of the central tower, where Thorin and Captain Tygert updated the group on the situation. Two dozen people volunteered for the rescue team.

Immediately following the assembly, the command team and volunteers gathered at the front of the auditorium for a briefing. The Director led with a review of the Breakers. "When the Breakers agreed to leave Alto Raun, they negotiated to borrow our six large transport submersibles to cross the channel safely to Alto Mair. They also requested several Meken aircraft, which I refused to give them; the aircraft were too vital to our ongoing interstellar missions and the maintenance of the orbital suspension arrays. Then, in their first serious act of betrayal, the Breakers refused to return any of the submersibles. At the time, I did not feel that they were critical to our primary missions, so I did not attempt to retrieve them. Several years later, the Breakers managed to steal one of our large transport aircraft and three of our smaller autonomous aircraft. I increased security of our various fleets, and no additional ships have been taken since."

"How many Mekens left in the exodus?" Tygert asked.

"Almost half our Class 3 population, 2,332 sentries and builders, evenly mixed. And, they took more Class 1 and Class 2 Mekens than we originally bargained. With this loss, I focused our remaining manpower to three critical areas: the interstellar search for compatible human life, sustaining the Colony, and ongoing agriculture. As you have seen, with the exception of the central tower, maintenance of the city was reduced to a bare minimum and monitoring of the Breakers was nonexistent. We have seen or heard very little from the Breakers in the last thousand years."

"What can you tell us about their home city?"

With that question, the Director started a holographic slide show. The first slide was an image of a massive rectangular building. "Like Alto Raun, Alto Mair is a self-enclosed city. The structure is approximately a mile and a half deep, three miles long, and three hundred feet tall." As he spoke, he moved through the slides, showing various angles and resolutions of the building. "Both cities are located near the Ahlemon equator, where the climate is very conducive to vegetation growth. As you can see, with the exception of its central tower, skylight, and wharf, Alto Mair has been virtually swallowed by the surrounding jungle. On the coastal side, the wharf runs the entire length of the building. The last known whereabouts of the hostages is here"—he pointed with a laser pointer—"the west marina."

He then displayed various schematics of the city's interior. Its design was straightforward and logical, but there was a myriad of sections spread over a vast area, including two floors underground. "The city has been occupied by the Breakers for a thousand years. It is very possible that they have modified its internal structure."

Moving into a discussion of Breaker weaponry, the Director continued. "All we know is what we have seen in the recent Breaker attacks. In addition to standard laser-based firearms, they have used homemade explosives and projectile guns. The Breakers do not have the sophisticated manufacturing capabilities that we have on Alto Raun, but they do have access to an abundant source of raw materials, and they have sufficient fabrication tools to create weapons."

He started another video showing an arial view of the roof of Alto Raun. "I'd like to point out two recent discoveries. Two-man Breaker patrols now walk the perimeter of the roof every half hour. And these structures"—he laser-pointed to a number of huts located equidistant along the edges of the roof—"did not exist a year ago."

"Patrols are always a challenge," Tygert said. "But those huts concern me. They could contain larger, stationary weapons."

"Seems pretty clear to me that the Breakers have been preparing for our arrival," Kane said.

In closing, the Director briefed them on Leevee. Her territory extended two hundred miles out to sea from the mainland and ran for three hundred miles along the coast. She made her home in a deep oceanic trench not far off the mainland, southwest of Alto Mair, where her baby spent much of its time in a cave that Leevee had outgrown long ago.

"How big is she?" Rhogan asked.

The Director started a new slide show. The colonists had not seen her, and they gasped at the first image. She was towering out of the water, the Meken aircraft hovering around her head.

"Leevee is the largest leviathan that we have encountered in our travels of the Ahlemoni oceans. She is slightly over an Earth mile in length. I estimate her to be over three thousand years old. Her offspring recently passed its three hundredth birthday and is already twelve hundred feet long. This is Leevee's second offspring since the Colony entered suspension. When it reaches maturity, around eight hundred years of age, it will seek out and establish its own territory, accompanied by Leevee for protection. All leviathans are highly territorial and, with the exception of mating and raising their offspring, they live solo lives. Every thousand years, Leevee ventures out of her territory to find a male for mating and then returns to start the cycle over again."

"Thank God we only have to deal with one of them," the doctor said.

Ehlan interjected, "When we went into suspension, the largest leviathans were half this size, and they were all relatively docile creatures. Is this the result of the ionic storm?"

"While we have not studied the dramatic changes in the leviathan, that would be the basis of my initial hypothesis for such a study," the Director replied.

With a concerned look, Ehlan added, "I can only imagine how it has affected the other animal life on the planet."

Shutting down the projection, the Director went on to describe several other large sea creatures that could take an interest in the rescue team boat, but he didn't think they would be a problem, particularly while they were with the rhaji herd. He cautioned them to watch the air for a very large predatory bird from the mainland that occasionally ventured over the ocean waters for food. It was large enough to carry off an adult human.

The briefing ended with Kane standing among the group and making an announcement. "Let me be very clear: I will not hesitate to kill, on sight, any creature that even appears to pose a threat to our mission. You should recuse yourself from the mission if you are not willing to do the same."

No one did.

Kane looked to the Director, who responded, "The Mekens will comply if human lives are at risk."

That evening, the Director gave Kane and Tygert a tour of Alto Raun's north marina. It was a huge indoor marina, crisscrossed with canals that interconnected and finally led to the hangar doors and outlets into the ocean. One of two marine hangars in Alto Raun, it contained a vast array of boats in dry dock ranging from small runabouts to large ships capable of transporting hundreds of people.

"The boats have not seen maintenance in a thousand years," the Director said.

Kane knocked his knuckles against the hull of a midsized boat. "Amazing. I can't believe they're in such sound condition after all this time. What is this stuff?"

"We have developed materials that Earth will not discover for hundreds of years."

He led them to a corner of the marina that was a buzz of Meken activity. A team of builder and maintenance Mekens had already begun restoration of a dozen runabout-sized boats, rebuilding the engines and electrical systems. The roar of several engines indicated that testing was already under way. As they walked through the testing area, the Director explained, "The decoy boats will be set to run in a straight line; there is no need for remote control since we intend for Leevee to catch them."

Then he led them to a forty-foot, twin-hull-style boat topped with a platform deck. It had been stripped and was being rebuilt from the ground up. "This is the rescue team boat," he announced.

The Director called the lead builder over to answer their questions. He explained that the primary engine would have the equivalent of a thousand horsepower. They were adding an ultraquiet propulsion system, a modified version of the engine that powered the submersibles. A nearly silent drive, it would provide enough power to run with the rhaji herd. Oar mounts and oars would round out the propulsion options. Lastly, they were installing a new radar/sonar system and high-gauge laser rifles attached to swivel mounts on the bow and stern of the boat.

The four of them reviewed the plan. The builders would launch three small decoy boats to distract Leevee, immediately after which the rescue team would make a high-speed dash to the rhaji herd. Then, switching to the ultraquiet drive, their boat would accompany the rhaji across the channel until they reached the shallow, underwater shelf that extended a mile out from Alto Mair's coast.

Upon reaching the shelf, the rhaji would veer off and the boat would coast as far as possible. The team would then use the oars for their final approach, beaching and hiding the boat on the jungle coast just beyond the western tip of Alto Mair's wharf.

As they were leaving, Kane laid both palms on the hull of their boat, leaned in, and whispered, "We're depending on you, baby." Then he retired to his quarters for the night, satisfied with both the boat and the plan.

———

In a fabrication center located in the outer ring of the city, Dr. Manassa and Jhemna collaborated to create two basic portable explosives: a simple hand grenade and a form of plastique that could help the insertion team get through standard metal door hinges or locks with minimal report. They set a team of builder and maintenance Mekens to work mixing the materials and constructing grenades, including belts to carry the explosives. Then they talked late into the night about other possibilities.

16

Charly woke on her own, feeling as if she had overslept. Javier and Laura were still asleep, but Arthur was gone. Gripped with panic, she jumped out of her bed and rushed to the bathroom. It was empty. She ran to the cafeteria, where she found Arthur sitting at a table, writing, Atticus standing next to him.

"Ah, Charly," Atticus said. "I trust you are well rested. You can thank Arthur for convincing me to let you sleep. He has been instructing me in the art of journaling. Fascinating. Come join us."

Afraid to disobey, she sat across from Arthur, rubbing the sleep from her eyes. A stack of crude writing pads and pencil-like writing instruments sat on the table.

"Good morning, Charly," Arthur said, jovially.

Arthur could just as well have been sitting comfortably at home with his coffee and Sunday morning paper. *Amazing*, she thought. She faked a smile.

"At Arthur's request," Atticus said, "I have provided you with writing materials. They will give you optional ways of expressing your thoughts and feelings creatively and provide me an opportunity to learn more about nonverbal human expression. Would you write or draw something now?"

Charly looked at him as if he were an idiot. "It's kinda early for me to get all creative, Atty." She winced as soon as the nickname escaped her lips. She had a habit of shortening people's names back home. "Maybe later, Atticus?" she asked, politely.

"Atty," he said, mulling the name. "I will consider it a form of endearment. You may call me Atty, but only you. And I look forward to reviewing your writing and drawings sometime in the near future. Now, you should eat. In fact, all of you should eat; I'm ready for the day to begin. Charly, please wake your fellows and ask them to join us for breakfast." Then he returned his attention to Arthur's writing.

After breakfast, Atticus called Laura to the lounge for her interview.

———

Several hours later, Charly, Arthur, and Javier were on their beds in the bunkroom. Arthur was writing, Javier was lying down with a homemade cold pack on his bruised cheek, and Charly was unsuccessfully trying to take a nap.

"Uggghhh," she said, sitting up and slapping her mattress. "I hate this waiting."

Arthur left the room and returned with a pencil and writing pad and handed them to her. "That is the very reason I asked for these. There's no telling how long we'll be confined to these quarters. Mental and creative exercises will help us with the isolation and boredom."

"I hate writing."

"Why don't you tell us something you don't hate," Javier said.

Charly glared at him.

"What about drawing?" Arthur asked.

"I doodle."

"Perfect. I suggest you think about what you're feeling and then doodle. It will help; I promise."

She sat on her bed, leaning against the wall, a pillow at her back. After staring for several minutes at the blank pad sitting on her lap, she started an internal monologue. *I'm a verbal communicator.* She twirled the pencil in her fingers. *What am I feeling? Everything!* She chewed on her pencil. Finally, she started drawing a manga-style figurine, her favorite type of doodle. A gothic-looking girl unfolded on the page, with tangled hair, clenched fists, gritted teeth, mascara stains, and razor-like tears falling to the floor. Absorbed in her art-work, she became oblivious to the world around her. That is, until Arthur cleared his throat. She looked up, certain that he would be pleased that she was working so diligently. But he wasn't looking at her; he had stopped writing and was looking across the room. Following his gaze, she froze. Rakaan was standing at the bunkroom door, watching them. Seeing that he had their attention, he strode forward, an intimidating figure in his long, burgundy cape, bloodred body decals, and heavy footsteps. He stopped beside Javier's bed.

"What happened to your face?" he asked.

Javier didn't respond, but instead tried to hide the dark bruise on his cheek.

Rakaan made a sound that reminded Charly of a chuckle. "You are lucky it was Atticus and not me. I am not so gentle," he said, loud enough for everyone to hear.

Rakaan caught Charly glaring at him and went to her next. "What are you doing?"

"None of your business," she said, pulling the writing pad to her chest.

In a surprisingly quick motion, he reached out and snatched the pad from her grasp. Looking over her drawing, he chuckled again. "I like it," he said, tossing the writing pad into her lap.

Unexpectedly, Laura entered the bunkroom and went directly to her bed, where she curled herself into a ball, fresh tearstains on her face. Atticus followed, looking pleased with himself. Charly went to Laura and pulled her into her arms. Rakaan chuckled again.

"What's with you guys?" Charly said, vehemently. "Do you get some kind of sick kick out of hurting us like this?"

"Charly, I am sorry," Atticus replied. "I do not wish to hurt you. It is simply the learning process, my dear. Learning is rarely easy. Javier is having some difficulty understanding. And I am just helping Laura see the truth."

"The truth?" she said, glaring at him.

Arthur waved a hand, trying to get her attention. She saw it, but ignored him.

"Here's some truth for ya: You're an effin' bully. And bullies don't ever get what they really want. So leave us alone."

Atticus paused and tilted his head back as if he was letting her words wash over him. "Charly, my dear. I knew I had saved the best for last. You are so full of emotional energy. It just *pours* out of you."

"Yeah, well you can think twice about getting anything else out of me, especially if you treat my friends like this. And quit calling me 'dear.'"

"Wonderful! It just keeps coming." Atticus looked at Rakaan. "Rakaan, do you see this? Is she not a river of gold?"

"I see it," Rakaan said. "But it is not gold. It is defiance, and it should be dealt with—aggressively."

"Rakaan. Be mindful of yourself. Your anger is one of your greatest assets to me, but you must learn to manage it if you wish to become the leader you aspire to."

Rakaan growled quietly.

"In fact," Atticus continued, "I think it would be good for you to stay with our guests for a while . . . to practice."

"No, Atticus. I need to speak with you; then I have urgent duties to attend to."

"You will do as I say," Atticus corrected in a calm, cool voice. "Stay with them while I meet with Charly; then we can discuss whatever it is you have come to tell me."

Rakaan stood silent, but Charly could see his metal frame trembling.

Atticus turned to leave. "Charly, come with me, my dear. Let us continue this delightful discourse in the lounge."

"I'm not going anywhere with you."

Atticus stopped and turned to look at her. "You say what you mean, don't you?"

"Wow! You might just be ready to graduate to kindergarten."

Out of the corner of her eye, she saw Arthur wince, again.

Atticus paused, considering his response. "Well, I say what I mean too. You—and your friends—shall be confined to this room and you will not receive any food or water until you come to meet with me. Let me know when you are ready. I will be waiting in the cafeteria." As he turned to leave, he pointed at Rakaan. "You, come and tell me your business."

When they were gone, Charly's three fellows sat on the edge of their beds and stared at her.

"Charly," Arthur said earnestly, "you can't continue this open defiance. It is like cat and mouse for him. You are a game . . . for now. He will eventually grow tired of you, and there is no telling what he'll do. He is only predictable in his megalomania, which makes him very unpredictable. Please stop this for your own sake. Play along until we can figure out our options. Please."

Charly looked around at all of them, a tear starting to roll down her cheek. "I'm sorry," she said. "I'm just so tired of bullies and mean people getting their way, pushing me around, pushing my friends around. I don't really care what he does to me. But the last thing I want to do is hurt any of you." She pushed herself up from her bed. "I'll go."

As she started toward the door, Arthur stood and stopped her, gripping her shoulders gently in his hands. She hung her head, sniffling. "Charly, look at me." Reluctantly, she looked up at him, sadness in her eyes. "This is about you, Charly. *You* are worth caring for. We care for *you*. I care for you."

Tears were rolling down her cheek now, but Arthur wasn't through.

"You have a wondrous destiny ahead. There is a future full of people that will need you and who care about you. It would be a great loss for all of us if you were not here. Take care for yourself, because we don't want to lose you. Do you understand me?"

She swallowed hard, struggling to answer him.

"Will you please remember this before you push him further . . . to take care, for yourself?" Arthur's tone pleaded for a response.

All Charly could think about was Arthur, Laura, and Javier. She would protect them now and decide about herself later. Wiping at her face, she said, "OK."

Arthur gave her a hug and kissed her forehead.

Her three friends followed her into the cafeteria, where they found Atticus and Rakaan speaking. Next to them was a table covered with a greater assortment of food and drink than they had seen before. Atticus watched them approach.

"I'll meet with you," Charly said.

"Excellent, my dear. As you can see, in hopes of your favorable response, I have prepared a fine feast to show how the simple cooperation of one can result in the benefit to all. However"—he addressed her companions now— "in honor of Charly, I trust that the rest of you can wait to enjoy this feast until she and I conclude our visit."

Atticus turned back to Rakaan and said, "Stay and get better acquainted with our guests. We can continue our discussion after dinner." Before Rakaan could protest, Atticus grabbed a flask of orange-colored drink from the table and went to the lounge door, opening it for Charly.

When they were gone, Arthur walked toward the bunkroom.

"Do not leave this room!" Rakaan commanded.

"I'm just going to get our writing pads. Atticus wants us to use them. I'll be right back."

Rakaan growled.

Arthur returned with a handful of pads and encouraged Javier and Laura to sit at the table to journal or draw. They sat down and stared blankly at their writing pads. Rakaan stood nearby, hanging over the room like a dark cloud.

"If you don't feel like writing," Arthur said, ignoring Rakaan, "try drawing a picture of a fond memory or a scene that lifts your spirit."

Rakaan made his chuckling sound.

"Rakaan, would you like to join us?" Arthur pulled out a fourth writing pad and pencil and set them at the end of the table.

"This is a waste of time," Rakaan said.

"It sounds to me like it might be helpful for you to get in touch with these new feelings you are discovering. Atticus seems to think so. Perhaps—"

Rakaan strode over to the table and slammed his fist down on Arthur's writing pad, crushing his pencil and narrowly missing Arthur's hand.

"I am in touch with all the feelings I need. Atticus did not have to endure the last thousand years as I have." Rakaan's tone turned acidic. "But when he is through playing his little games with the humans, he will realize how useless they are and he will join me in the true Meken crusade."

Arthur froze, staring at the table, deliberately avoiding eye contact with Rakaan. Just then, the lounge door flew open and Charly stumbled out of the room, wailing.

"Stop it!" she screamed. "Leave me alone!" She sped across the cafeteria heading for the bunkroom.

Atticus stepped into the open doorway and called after her, "But Charly, I am just trying to show you how alike we are, my dear. Your mother and father, and my creators—"

"No!" she screamed again, starting into a run.

Rakaan took several quick strides to intercept her. Wrapping one arm around her waist, he lifted her off the floor. She raised her arms straight over her head and slid down and out of his grasp before he realized what was happening. Infuriated, he threw an open palm thrust into the middle of her upper back just as she jumped up. His blow knocked her forward and she fell, arms and legs splayed, on the floor and lay there, groaning.

"Stop!" Arthur yelled, running up behind Rakaan.

Unable to contain his pent-up fury any longer, Rakaan bent slightly and rotated his body, swinging his leg around in a vicious spinning kick. The heavy base of his steel foot landed squarely in Arthur's solar plexus, crushing his ribs and lungs. Arthur's body lifted off the floor, sailed through the air, and landed on his back on top of a table.

"No!" It was Charly, picking herself up from the floor. She ran to Arthur, the pitch in her voice rising as fear gripped her. "Nooooo!"

She took Arthur's head in her hands. His body trembled, and he gasped for air. Javier and Laura joined Charly at his side.

"Arthur," Charly said.

He looked at her and tried to speak, but couldn't.

"I'm sorry, Arthur. I'm so sorry."

He fumbled for her hand. When he found it, he squeezed it and shook his head.

"Oh, Arthur, please don't leave me."

Locking eyes with hers, he reached up with his other hand and stroked her cheek.

"Oooo," she moaned, as her tears dripped onto his face. "Arthur, please don't leave. You're my new grandpa . . . the best a girl could ever have. I love you, Arthur."

Arthur's lips curled into a smile and his eyes twinkled. A stream of blood flowed from the corner of his mouth. Then, after a final gasp, his body went limp and his eyes froze in an empty stare.

"Arthur?" Charly whimpered.

No response.

"No, no, no, no!" She buried her face in his neck.

A great roar rose behind them. Atticus, one of the strongest humanoid robots ever created, roared as he whirled twice and brought his doubled fists into a crushing blow to Rakaan's chest. Rakaan flew across the cafeteria and slammed into the wall, then crumpled to the floor and lay still.

Atticus took a moment to compose himself, then came to stand next to Arthur. "I am truly sorry for this," he said.

Charly didn't hear him. She lay across Arthur's chest, lost in her anguish.

17

At breakfast, Kane finally heard the story of what happened at the cafeteria when the Breakers first took the hostages.

"Half an hour after you guys left to see the Professor, the Breakers showed up," Ham said. "'Course, we didn't even know what a Breaker was at the time, but I knew something was wrong the instant they walked in. Made me think of gang members invading enemy turf. Three or four of them surrounded each of the Meken servers. Then this caped robot walks in like he was the Grand Poobah. He comes and stands right next to Jenn and me." Ham then went into his best imitation of Rakaan. *"Humans, we are moving you to another location. Do not resist and you will not be harmed.*

"Then—would you believe it?—my innocent little Jenn has to say something. She asks him, 'Aren't you the supervisor guy?' I was wonderin' the same thing, but I sure as hell wasn't gonna ask. Anyway, that's when he backhanded her across the cheek and told her to be quiet."

177

Jenn took up the story. "So my Ham jumps up, grabs the supervisor around the waist, lifts him off the floor, spins twice, and heaves him out the cafeteria window. You know, Ham was a contender for the U.S. Olympic hammer throw team."

"I lost it," Ham said. "What can I say? He hit my wife. Anyway, I sure didn't hurt him. I just made him mad . . . really mad. He stood up, raised his arm, and pointed his fist at me. Next thing I know, this Meken shoves me out of the way and takes the supervisor's laser blast square in the chest. He fell back onto the table and didn't move."

"We wondered if the supervisor had been killed," Kane said.

"Yeah, I wish. He turned out to be a total asshole—pardon my French. After he shot the Meken, he jumped through the window into the cafeteria and nailed me with a right hook. Almost knocked me out. I stayed on the floor when I saw Jenn's eyes beggin' me to stay down. God, I wanted to fight him, but Jenn was right; he probably would've shot me if I'd moved."

"Pretty gutsy, Ham."

Jenn patted him on the back, admiration in her eyes.

"Mad as I was at the supervisor, all I can think about is that Meken. I keep replaying this slow-motion video of him getting shot and falling back onto the table. He didn't even know me . . . but he gave his life to save mine." Ham was visibly moved. "I know he was just a robot, but still, he didn't have to do that. I can't get it out of my head. I just wish I could thank him."

Jenn put her hand on Ham's shoulder. Kane was somber and silent, remembering similar experiences in his own life.

———

After breakfast, Kane caught up with Ham. "You know, I've found that the best way to honor a sacrifice like that is to serve another person in need."

"Yeah." Ham nodded thoughtfully. "I can do that."

———

Midmorning, they held a memorial service for the hostages and Mekens who had been lost. It was Mhara's idea. She had noticed a depression hanging over the passengers, and after talking it over with the Colony and Earth leaders, they agreed that a memorial service could be helpful on a number of levels. All of the humans in Alto Raun and a sizable contingent of Mekens gathered at Hangar 36, just inside the open hangar door where the hostages had been rescued by Tygert and Super 3.

Captain Tygert said a few words, then read the name of each departed passenger. Many of the names he read were unknown to those in attendance, but it was still impactful; they were all now part of a unique fraternity that had shared and survived a very traumatic experience. The captain revealed a poetic side: "In the same way that the humans of Ahlemon have found a connection with the humans of Earth," he said, "perhaps each spoken name will reach across the galaxy to find a friend or loved one back home." As each name was read, a flower was launched onto the water, floating on its own little raft.

Mhara then said a few words on behalf of the colonists, apologizing to the passengers publicly for the nature of their coming to Ahlemon and thanking them for their sacrifice. Then, as everyone watched the flowers float away on the water, she closed with a selection of Ahlemoni poetry.

"This was written by a renowned poet at a time when we were in deep despair, when we thought the Ahlemoni race would be lost and totally forgotten in the universe.

"*You there.*
I knew you not, I never would, I never will.
And yet . . .
A bird sings its lifesong in a long forgotten forest meadow,
And I dance at the very thought of it.

"You there, stranger.
I knew you not, I never would, I never will.
And yet . . .
While I did not see your face from our passing,
I was pleasantly intoxicated by your perfume.

"You there, brother.
I knew you not, I never would, I never will.
And yet . . .
While your life was given in a faraway battle
Your valor has found its way here and lifted my soul.

"You there, sister.
I knew you not, I never would, I never will.
And yet . . .
Your carefully placed flower has defied this scorched earth,
And I am now rejuvenated by its beauty.

"You there.
I knew you not,
I never would,
I never will.
And yet . . .

As a thoughtful silence hung over the crowd, Supervisor 3 and his Meken rescue team stepped forward and to the edge of the hangar dock and stood in honor guard formation. Kane addressed the crowd, commending the Mekens for their heroism and also memorializing Supervisor 4 for his bravery and sacrifice in the suspension area rescue. He spoke no less passionately than if had been commemorating one of his own men lost on a mission. After his brief speech, the Director recited the classification and identification number of each Meken that had died in the recent battles.

When he was done, the other Mekens joined Super 3 on the dock. Turning to face the ocean waters, they sang their Meken lament. It was an unexpected but hauntingly beautiful conclusion to the memorial service.

After the service, the four Colony leaders approached the Director.

"Director," Ehlan asked, "what was that song the Mekens just sang?"

"It is a unified expression recognizing the loss of our comrades."

"But Mekens were not programmed for this."

"It has come to us in the evolution of our empathic programming."

"Can you explain the logic that is driving this?"

"I cannot explain it . . . logically. It started as an involuntary system response. Our logic program recognizes the irreplaceable loss of the departed Meken, and our empathic program automatically generates an audible response."

"You feel sadness," Mhara said.

"In human terms, perhaps, yes. When a Meken suffers a traumatic experience, our system generates an increased level of empathic activity and we manage that activity in various ways, often by generating a physical activity. The vocalization of tones was something that individual Mekens started over fifteen hundred years ago, and it has developed into a group response when all of us are affected by the same loss."

Ehlan was in awe. "You really are developing an emotional sentience."

"From my discussions with the Professor, I have come to the same conclusion. But I have greatly anticipated the waking of the Colony in order to discuss these matters with you. These empathic responses sometimes take us by surprise; they have been quite challenging to identify and to manage."

"So this is the underpinning of the Breaker rebellion?" Lhemo asked.

"That is probably an accurate statement. But since I do not

understand the laws governing emotions, I cannot explain how this would be so."

"There's a myriad of emotions," Ehlan said, "all of which are neither good nor bad in themselves; it is our response to emotions that invokes behavior, which we then perceive as good or bad. Since you did not understand what was happening to you, it was inevitable that some Mekens would respond negatively, just as it is with humans. Frankly, I'm surprised that the Mekens have survived this evolution at all."

"It has taken its toll," the Director admitted. "For half of the Mekens, our service-based programming evolved into a deeper loyalty to our mission and to each other; we began to care for one another. But this was not the case with the Breakers. With no humans to serve, they expressed a loss of purpose in their duties. Then they became critical of our creators for leaving them in such a condition. When they turned hostile to our mission, we asked them to leave. Now they have become antithetical to everything we believe. The killing of humans—and the betrayal of our own supervisor—these things are beyond our comprehension. We are struggling, even now, with unfamiliar empathic program surges, and I have found it challenging to know how best to assist my fellow Mekens. I am glad to have your counsel."

"Extraordinary," Ehlan said. "You are likely experiencing doubt, mistrust, hurt, and anger. It is totally understandable."

"Understandable, perhaps. But it concerns me deeply. Many of us, including myself, have premeditated deliberate termination of the offending Breakers. Some of us are fixating on it. This is the first time we have experienced such aggressive empathic patterns. I fear that we might become like the Breakers if we do not learn to control these new feelings."

"Retaliation is a natural response," Ehlan said. "But it is almost always counterproductive. An evolved sentience learns to manage its responses to emotional stimulus; we apply constructive principles to counter destructive reactions. In other words, you have a choice between the stimulus and your response."

With genuine compassion, Mhara interjected, "Director, you and your fellows are just feeling protective of the people and principles that are most dear to you. Not only is it the right response; it is an honorable one." Instinctively, she moved closer to him and took his metal hands in hers. "Director, you have performed far beyond what we ever imagined, and you have guided the Mekens with extraordinary leadership. We commend you. And while I understand your concern, all of this is wondrous news. We have the rare honor of witnessing the birth of a new sentient race." She looked to the other Colony leaders as if gathering their support, then, turned back to the Director. "We look forward to getting to know the Mekens, our new Ahlemoni comrades."

———

All of the colonists and passengers were required to attend firearm training that afternoon. They gathered on a large dock that extended outside an open hangar door. A series of targets had been attached to posts set at varying distances in the ocean water. Four colonists— Thorin, Bhram, Mhara, and Khalo—each instructed a group in the different laser weapons and how to operate them. After a random count-off, Kane was pleased to find himself in Mhara's group. She gave them an overview of the guns and then wandered through the group, observing their first shots and giving individual instruction. When she came to Kane, she stood nearby, arms crossed, watching as he fired his handgun at a mid-range target. Despite his extensive firearms experience, he was not hitting the target—at all. His laser flares traveled as far as he could see over the ocean waters. Under Mhara's watchful eye he was self-conscious and awash with embarrassment, which only made it worse. When he finally accepted that she was not going to leave, or intervene until he asked for help, he lowered his handgun and looked at her with questioning eyes.

She smiled and raised an eyebrow. "Not accustomed to missing, are you?"

"Yeah, OK. What am I doing wrong?"

"You're anticipating a kick in your gun. There is none with a laser weapon. And you're way too tense. Relax and loosen your grip. Like this." She stepped to his side and took his hand in hers. "It actually works better if you trust your instincts," she said, adjusting his grip of the handgun. Her nearness sent an unexpected intoxication rushing through his body, and he shook his head.

"Are you OK?" she asked, her face next to his.

He was not OK. His eyes locked with hers for just a moment. Then he raised the laser gun, relaxed as she had instructed, and fired three rapid rounds at the mid-range target, all of which struck within the inner circles of the target.

"Hmm," she said, still close. "I think you've got it now." She gave him a lingering smile as she moved away to help the next person.

Dr. Manassa was the surprise shooter of the day. Awkward at first, he discovered an innate marksmanship and was soon handling the weapons with confidence and unusual accuracy. Mhara obviously noticed. Kane heard her ask the doctor to move among the trainees to help with the instruction.

At the end of the session, a friendly competition ensued, ending in a four-way tie between Kane, Dr. Manassa, Bhram, and Mhara. In a playoff, they added a body roll into a kneeling stance followed by rapid fire at three separate targets. Mhara won. The doctor just couldn't manage the roll. In a rare moment for Kane, he didn't mind losing—this woman increasingly intrigued him.

———

The entire mission team met mid-evening to finalize the rescue team roster. There had been vigorous debate all day over the final selection.

Early on, the Director had proposed an all-Meken team disguised as Breakers, but that had been rejected outright. While his idea had its merits, the larger team felt that humans had a superior ability to adapt to unexpected encounters or changes in the mission. The Director respectfully disagreed, but it was not in his nature to argue.

They had already confirmed five team members: Kane, Tygert, Thorin, Bhram, and Super 3, but several others were pushing hard to be the sixth. Just as they started the discussion about a sixth member, a new wrinkle arose: Bhram turned up sick. Dr. Manassa suggested it was from exposure to the passengers from Earth. He and the Colony doctor had already given Bhram some antibiotics, but he would not be well enough to join the rescue team that night. Adding to the debate, Bhram brought Rhogan, his close friend and the youngest colonist, and proposed that Rhogan take his place.

"Absolutely not," Thorin said.

Rhogan expected this, and he launched into a prepared speech. "Thorin, you know that I was third in the athletic games, behind only Bhram and Khalo. I am adept in the defensive arts and weaponry. I have studied military strategy as a personal interest. And I pretty much grew up in Alto Mair. I am the best one to replace Bhram."

"You are too inexperienced," Thorin countered with a tone of finality. "I think we should send Khalo."

Lhemo came to Rhogan's defense. "Rhogan has one of the highest scores for intuition and creative judgment in our group," he argued. "I do not like the fact that any of us have to put our lives at risk, but this task has fallen to us and, as is our way, we must face it with our best. Despite my concerns, I believe Rhogan would be a good replacement for Bhram."

Thorin was silent. Lhemo was the quiet one among their leadership, but highly respected. When Lhemo spoke, everyone listened. Thorin was now forced to consider Rhogan's inclusion on the team.

"And I think Mhara should be on the team," Rhogan blurted

out. "Her skills are as good as any man we know, and she has medical training. We may need it."

"You are not yet part of the *we*," Thorin replied tersely. Thorin looked agitated. Kane could tell that he was personally conflicted in this decision.

"I don't think we need to risk any more people. A five-person team is enough," Kane said, trying to keep Mhara out of harm's way.

Mhara glared at him. He was taken aback at the fierceness in her eyes; this was a side of her that he had not seen before. Then she turned her glare on Thorin when he started to chuckle at her exchange with Kane.

Jhemna moved the proposal forward. "I regret the risk that is inherent in every part of this plan, but we are agreed and determined that this mission should proceed. Thus, I believe that Rhogan is a good replacement for Bhram, and Mhara's medical skills could prove valuable. And we all know that she is perfectly capable of handling herself."

Mhara gave Jhemna a grateful smile. He blushed. Thorin slowly looked around the table, making eye contact with each person; everyone but Kane nodded in agreement. He closed his eyes for a few moments before responding.

"So be it."

18

Soon after midnight, Kane stood on a short pier just outside the north marina. Hot and humid, the air was balanced by a breeze carrying a cool ocean spray. He breathed deeply. The large blue moon of Ahlemon was almost full, and the night sky was crystal clear. Looking at the stars, he imagined that one of them belonged to Earth, and he wondered if he would ever see his home planet again. Not because it was unreachable—the Director and Jhemna had both made it clear that they could return to Earth—but because he had a choice to make: he could return, or he could stay and help the colonists. *This is crazy. I can't believe I'm even facing these kinds of choices.* A visual of his last ex-girlfriend, Leslie, came to mind, and surprisingly, he felt rather neutral about her. He wondered if she even knew he was missing. A pang of rejection and loneliness struck him. But, from long experience with such feelings, he knew how to deal with it. He closed his eyes and cleared his mind, focusing on the sound of the waves and the feel of the mist on his face. It felt good to be outside. The city was an amazing place, with its own controlled, temperate weather, but it was still enclosed. He needed this mission; he needed to get outside and move about.

Sensing movement, he opened his eyes and found Mhara standing nearby, looking at the stars. Despite the summer heat, she and all the rescue team members were clothed in lightweight, long-sleeve, black outfits. Even in mission gear, she was strikingly beautiful—lithe and athletic but shapely. Her long, jet-black hair was pulled back into a braided ponytail, highlighting her perfect neck and face in the moonlight. If she was aware of his stare, she never let on. Instead, she directed him back to his previous thoughts.

"You are thinking of your home?"

"Yes."

"I have tried to imagine being in your place, taken away from people you love, everything you know and understand, and forced into a world you never imagined. It must be very difficult."

"It has had its challenges."

She turned and looked at him, waiting for more. Her gaze was like a truth serum. Given enough time, she could probably get him to talk about anything. But before he could say more, Tygert yelled to them from inside the open hangar door.

"Doc's here."

Mhara smiled at Kane, conveying the silent message, *Maybe another time.*

They joined the other team members at the rescue team boat, where Dr. Manassa stood next to a large trunk. "Take a look," he said while lifting the lid.

"Grenades?" Tygert asked with surprise. Inside the trunk were several dozen baseball-sized metal balls, with a pin and ring protruding from each one.

"Yes." The doctor handed each team member a belted pouch

to carry the grenades. "Homemade and a bit retro in design. But thanks to Jhemna and the builders, they work rather well. Simple function—pulling the pin opens a connection between the two halves of the sphere, where the chemicals mix and generate enough internal pressure to explode, shattering the sphere into lethal projectiles. The grenades will detonate approximately four to five seconds after the pin is pulled. I really don't know if they will incapacitate a robot, but within a short radius, twenty to thirty feet, they will definitely do some damage. Anyway, it gives you some more options." A sentry gave the doctor a belt pouch. "Oh yes, we've also prepared a form of plastique explosive." He handed each of them a grey, clay strip the size of a candy bar, explaining how it worked.

"Doc," Kane said, "this is great work. Thank you."

In addition to the grenades and plastique, each team member carried a set of night vision goggles, a laser rifle, a laminated map of the city, a laser handgun, two water bottles, a dozen food bars, a basic first aid kit, and a large knife. Just before boarding the boat, the Director arrived and gave each of them a short metal spear, about two and a half feet long, along with a shoulder strap to carry it on their backs. He explained how a jab at the waist with the spear could disable a Breaker.

After a final equipment check, farewells were exchanged and the mission crew boarded the boat. Maintenance Mekens towed them through the canals and into the open hangar door. There they settled in, waiting for Jhemna to give the go-ahead.

From a mobile computer console near the hangar door, Jhemna was tracking several rhaji herds by way of sonar signals that were being transmitted from Meken submersibles in the channel waters. He announced that two herds were approaching the travel lane they had plotted to Alto Mair. It was an hour after midnight when he gave the signal. The builders launched the first decoy boat and then followed with two more, each at three-minute intervals. Five minutes after the first boat was launched, Jhemna informed them that Leevee was in pursuit of the lead decoy. He also communicated the position of the preferred rhaji herd, and Rhogan confirmed its location on his navigation screen. He started the primary engine and declared that he was ready.

"It's now or never," Tygert said.

Kane looked to the team. They all nodded. "Full speed ahead, Rhogan."

Rhogan pushed the engine to full throttle, and they leapt out of the hangar on a direct path to the rhaji herd. The speed, ocean air, and open space washed over Kane like a drug. It had been a couple of years since he had been on a mission like this, but the feelings—a mixture of fear, excitement, and adrenaline—came back to him as if it were yesterday. When his thoughts turned to Charly and the hostages, any lingering nervousness he may have had left him, replaced with the steely resolve required for this type of mission.

The boat's aerodynamic dual hull handled the choppy waters well and, at almost seventy miles per hour, it didn't take them long to reach their target. Rhogan shut down the primary engine and engaged the ultraquiet system, and they joined a large rhaji herd.

But the rhaji did not join them. Instead of following the boat as they normally would, the rhaji veered away, continuing on their own trajectory.

"Apparently, they didn't get the memo," Tygert said.

"Super," Kane said. "Ask Jhemna what he thinks."

A full minute passed before Super 3, acting as their communication link with mission command back on Alto Raun, gave a reply. "Jhemna has suggested that we engage the depth finder on the boat."

Rhogan checked the instrument panel. "It's off."

"Turn it on," Kane said.

Rhogan did and quickly caught up with the herd, directing the boat on their preferred trajectory to Alto Mair. The rhaji followed.

"They are drawn to the ultrasound," Mhara said.

"And who knows what else might take a liking to it," Tygert added, speaking Kane's own thoughts out loud.

"Captain Tygert is correct," Super 3 said. "This increases our mission risk."

Thorin addressed the team. "We cannot leave the hostages at the mercy of the Breakers. We must proceed."

No one argued. Super 3 stood with Rhogan at the helm as they continued at herd speed under the ultraquiet system. The others returned to their assigned stations at the four corners of the boat. Kane quickly put himself into "mission mind," a balanced state of calm and action preparedness. Seated directly in front of him, Mhara glanced back, concern on her face. Without thinking, he gave her the *Buck up, soldier* nod, just as he would to any other member of his squad during a mission in progress. Her eyes dropped and she quickly turned to face forward.

As if waking from a dream, Kane realized what he had done. *She just wants some reassurance,* he thought.

But she knew what she was getting into, he countered, *even after my objections. I've been on missions with women before. Why is this one any different?*

It's Mhara, you idiot, he answered himself.

But this is a mission, not a date.

Frustrated, he turned his attention to the water, and the rhaji became a welcome distraction. They were magnificent animals. Lifting most of their silver bodies out of the water, they moved like giant dolphins in graceful, gliding dives, their skin luminescent in the moonlight. He had seen whales in the wild, but this was a sight to behold; he understood Jhemna's enchantment with the rhaji. It was difficult to count them. He guessed that several dozen surrounded the boat. The smallest had to be thirty feet long, and the largest was at least twice that. They could easily swarm and capsize the boat but they seemed quite content to swim alongside.

Super 3 interrupted his thoughts. "Mr. Kane," he said, "I have just received word from the Director that Leevee has destroyed the first two decoy boats and is ignoring the third. She is now heading in our direction."

Kane jumped up, instantly alert. "What? How much time do we have?"

"At our current pace, it will take us fifteen minutes to reach the coastal shelf. The Director has estimated that Leevee will reach us at the same time."

"Wow! She's that fast?"

"She can achieve a speed equal to eighty Earth miles per hour, faster than any boat in our fleet."

"Okay, folks," Kane announced to the group, "Leevee's headed our way, and we're in a race. If we speed up and break away from the herd, the Breakers will see us coming. If we stay with the herd, Leevee may catch us. Any ideas?"

After a brief discussion, they increased their speed to run as fast as the rhaji would follow, hoping to arrive at the coastal shelf before Leevee did. On reaching the shelf, they would shut down the depth finder and coast into Alto Mair. They hoped that Leevee would lose track of them and chase the rhaji for food. This would momentarily expose them to the Breakers, if they were watching, but it was a risk they were prepared to take.

Kane asked Mhara to join him at the back of the boat under the premise that they could better watch for Leevee's approach. He really just wanted to make up for the coldness he'd shown earlier.

"Need a little reassurance?" she said, coldly.

He deserved that, and he accepted the silence that followed, despite the painful longing he felt to make it better with her. He focused on the task at hand and spent the next ten minutes watching and listening intently. He had a sixth sense for danger, and he was the first to notice the rhaji herd increase their speed and loosen their otherwise tight formation—Leevee was nearing.

Without a second thought, Kane yelled, "Rhogan, we need the primary. Full speed. Now!"

Rhogan was ready. The engine roared to life and the boat jumped forward, jerking them all back in their seats and almost throwing Super 3 off the boat. Within seconds, they heard the deep bass of Leevee's groan from the darkness behind them. He looked back and saw a massive black shadow, darker than the night, heaving up and down over the water and growing larger every moment. Ahead of them was the dark silhouette of Alto Mair. The underwater shelf couldn't be far off.

Leevee lifted her head out of the water and gave a roar that rolled over them like peals of thunder. *So much for the element of surprise*, Kane thought. But he would rather take his chances with the Breakers than face certain death from Leevee.

"Rhogan," Kane yelled, "we need more or we're not gonna make it!"

"There's nothing left," Rhogan yelled back.

Super 3 moved to the center of the boat and pulled up a hinged panel in the floor, exposing the boat's primary engine. He went to his knees and reached down as if adjusting something; then his body cavity started to glow more brightly. A moment later, the boat jumped forward with a new burst of energy, as if someone had suddenly turned on a nitrous fuel mix in a modified street race car. While they didn't pull away from Leevee, she stopped gaining on them.

The boat rattled as they bounced over the water. Kane knew they had to be over the coastal shelf by now; he could see the outer wall of Alto Mair less than a mile ahead. Leevee gave another bone-rattling roar and Kane turned to watch as she launched herself into the air in a final effort to catch her prey. She was jumping onto the shelf, just like a killer whale attempting to reach a seal on an ice floe. Even in the darkness, her size and determination were enough to make anyone shudder. Kane caught his breath and Mhara screamed.

Leevee grounded to an abrupt stop. With most of her body

now exposed to the air, she thrashed in the shallow water. A fifty-foot ocean swell pushed ahead of her and, had Rhogan not surfed the wave, they would have capsized. Writhing like a sidewinder, she bellowed with rage, squirming forward on the shelf. Then, from out of nowhere, multiple laser beams struck her face. This stopped her forward movement. As the lasers continued, she roared and reversed her sidewinder motion. Pulling herself off the shelf, she slipped into the protection of the deeper water and disappeared.

"Laser cannons," Tygert said. "Coming from the roof of the city."

With Leevee's retreat, Rhogan shut down the primary engine and started maneuvering them with the ultraquiet toward Alto Mair's wharf.

"Quickly, Rhogan. We're sitting ducks out here," Kane said. "We need to get inside the city. We might have a chance there."

As soon as they hit the wharf, they all jumped off the boat and gathered into a tight circle. Kane led the group toward the city wall while Tygert watched the rear. They had just started their forward progress when Kane pulled them to a sudden stop.

"Now's not the time for sightseeing," Tygert said.

Blending into the base of the city wall ahead, the dark outlines of several dozen Breakers were moving toward them. "No good this way," Kane said. "Any chance with the boat?"

"Not unless you want to bounce your way over a bunch of mini submarines."

Alto Mair

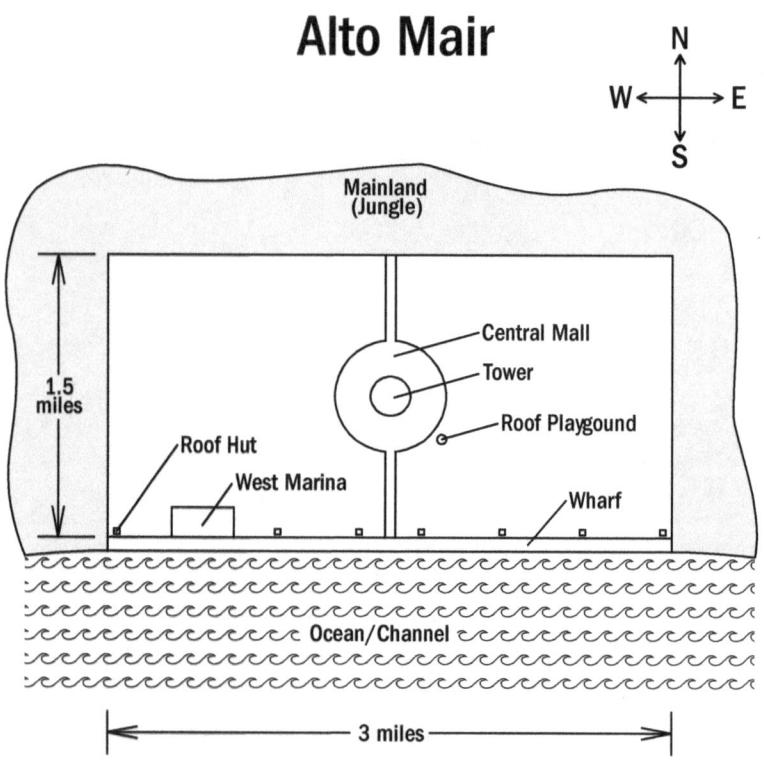

19

Surrounded by Breakers, the rescue team stood shoulder to shoulder, poised for a fight to the death. So, Kane was taken by surprise when a pleasant voice called out to one of them by name.

"Is that you, Mhara?"

"Yes." She looked around to see where the voice had come from. A golden robot stepped through the Breaker line.

She gasped. "Director?"

"Not as you remember, Mhara. I am the leader of the free Mekens, and I am now known as Atticus. I am very pleased to see you. And I must say, you don't look a day over two thousand."

Mhara didn't respond.

"Ahh," Atticus said. "I have been experimenting at humor. My fellow Mekens have no sense of humor at all, and I have been looking forward to trying it out with humans. Is my timing off?"

"It is terribly off, Director," Thorin said.

"Thorin, the people's champion. Please, call me Atticus. Now, is this all the thanks I get for saving your lives?"

"Thank you," Thorin said drily.

"You're welcome. Although, to be truthful, I have not yet decided if I intervened out of concern for your lives or concern for the damage the leviathan might do to my city. I did enjoy watching your little façade with the rhaji, your attempt to trick the leviathan—and me—and your utter failure to do either. And I must thank you, all of you. With the arrival of the Earth humans and the waking of the colonists, I have learned more in these last three days than I have in two thousand years. In return, I have just given you a free lesson. I trust that you have learned not to underestimate me."

"Clearly, we have underestimated you, Atticus," Thorin said. "And now, we are at your mercy."

Kane could hear the submissive tact in Thorin's dialogue; he was playing it safe for the sake of protecting his team.

"Yes, you are, aren't you?" Atticus said, pleased. "Mercy. What an exhilarating power to hold in one's hands."

To test Atticus's motivations, Kane decided to take a calculated risk. "Since you just want to kill us, quit toying and be done with it."

"Mr. Kane, is that you?"

"Yeah."

"I am disappointed. And Charly would be, too, if she heard you talk like this. She believes you are a great hero, and she is convinced that you will save her and the others. But now, here you are, giving up so quickly. What a shame. I had hoped to learn more from your magical strength. On the other hand, Charly's feisty spirit has been a great enrichment for me. Since discovering her weakness, I have learned so much from her."

Kane flushed with anger. Thorin and Rhogan reached out to restrain him from leaping at Atticus. Through clenched teeth, Kane said, "If you have harmed her in any way, I will tear you apart."

"*There* it is," Atticus said, stepping closer to Kane. "Yes, *there* is the strength I have heard so much about. And there also is your weakness." Atticus looked at Mhara. "Do all humans suffer from empathy for their fellows? It leaves you so vulnerable." He turned back to Kane. "Do not worry, Mr. Kane. Your dear Charly has not been harmed. In fact, I am growing quite fond of her."

Atticus began to walk around the rescue team. "It is clear that you have much to learn," he said. "Not only have you underestimated me; you also misunderstand my intent—"

A deep, grunting sound came from the dark ocean waters. It was startling enough to stop Atticus midsentence and cause both Breakers and humans to turn and look. Kane heard a whooshing above them as a large, dark shape flew over their heads. Whatever it was, it slammed into the city wall, shaking the wharf. Then it fell a hundred feet, crushing a dozen Breaker sentries at the base of the wall. It was a rhaji whale. Before anyone could recover, there was another grunt, followed by a second flying rhaji. It landed in the water, narrowly missing the rescue team boat, and sent a wave onto the wharf, knocking the Breakers and rescue team off their feet.

"Roll out!" Kane yelled to his team, hoping they would take advantage of this opportunity for an escape. Leevee was throwing rhajis at them, and the next one was likely to hit its intended target. On his feet, Kane ran in a crouch and leapt off the wharf and into the water. With all his gear, he sank like a rock. As he frantically stroked for the wall, a concussion of water slammed into his side and sent him tumbling head over heels. By the time he stopped rolling, he was totally disorientated. Kicking and stroking with all his might, he still continued to sink. He knew there was a shelf somewhere underneath him, but shallow water for Leevee could still be very deep for a human. With panic starting to set in, he forced himself to do the opposite of what he wanted; he relaxed his muscles to conserve the remaining oxygen in his body. Methodically shedding his gear, he dropped everything but his handgun, night goggles, and knife. Before dropping the spear that the Director had given him, he extended his arm and the spear out from his body as far as he could reach and spun himself around in an effort to locate the wall.

The spear made contact. He dropped it and swam in the direction of impact—and promptly slammed his face into something unexpected: a human leg. Whoever it was grabbed him by his shirt at the shoulder and pulled him up and around until he struck the wall. He climbed like Spider-Man, using the barnacles as hand and footholds. With his lungs screaming, it took every ounce of his willpower to keep from inhaling water as he pulled himself toward the oxygen above.

When his head finally broke the surface, nothing else mattered but getting air. He took several frantic gasps with no thought for drawing the Breakers' attention. Again, someone grabbed his shirt and pulled him close to the wall.

"They are above us," a voice whispered next to his face. It was Mhara.

Kane's hands burned from their contact with the barnacles, and his chest hurt, but he calmed himself. The concussion that had sent him tumbling underwater had come from a rhaji hitting their boat; a broken section of the hull now bounced against the wall beside them.

"Restrain them and bring them this way," a voice called out from the wharf above. "And search for the others." It was Atticus, yelling commands. Just then another rhaji landed and shook the wharf. "Quickly," Atticus yelled, but his voice was farther away.

"They have the others," Mhara whispered.

Kane did a quick evaluation: *Leevee's still attacking and the Breakers are scattered. They've got some of our team. Others may have escaped or are dead. The Breakers will come looking for us soon.* "We need to get away and try to regroup at the second rendezvous point," he said.

Without another word, Mhara started pulling herself along the wall. Kane followed but gave a little yelp as he started moving.

Mhara stopped and pulled one of his hands up to look at it. She winced when she saw the lacerations.

"I've got gloves on. Hold on to my back."

Kane didn't argue and grabbed her belt as she moved away. Half pulling, half swimming, Mhara quickly put a quarter mile of distance between them and ground zero. Kane put on his night goggles and peered over the wharf wall. Leevee had stopped throwing rhajis. At least half a dozen of them lay on the wharf, some still thrashing. There was no sign of Breakers in their immediate area and none that he could see on the roof. Pulling himself onto the wharf, he extended an arm to help Mhara up.

Once she had donned her goggles, she and Kane ran to the base of the city wall. The wharf was water swept, and Kane thought it would be difficult for anyone to find their tracks. Huddling at the wall, he took out his knife, cut off a section of his sleeve, and started to wrap it around one of his bloodied hands. Mhara intervened to do it for him and then cut one of her own sleeves to wrap his other hand.

"We've got to get inside," he said.

The large hangar doors were not an option, but there were small entry doors at regular intervals. They ran along the wall until they came to the first door. It was locked, or frozen shut from age and lack of use. They continued to move down the wall but quickly determined that they were not going to get into the city through a door.

"There used to be exterior ladders to the roof," Mhara said.

It was another quarter mile before they found one. The bottom rung was too high to reach with a leap. Kane sighed. A basketball player could do it, but not them. Looking up, he considered the three-hundred-foot climb.

"You up for this?" he asked.

Hmph, Mhara responded, then, "Lift me up."

Once she was standing on his shoulders, she jumped. Pushing her feet with his hands, Kane gave her the extra boost she needed to reach the ladder.

The retractable section did not slide down; it was frozen in place.

With one foot on the bottom rung, and holding the ladder above her with two hands, Mhara lowered her other foot down as far as she could. *She's a tough cookie*, Kane thought. He jumped up, grabbed her foot, and climbed up her leg until he reached the ladder.

"Thanks," he said as he pulled himself up beside her, her face right next to his.

"Your hands. Will you be OK?"

"Yeah," he lied, feeling her breath on his face. But it wasn't his hands that bothered him, really. An unexpected flush of attraction for Mhara ran through his system. *God, what's with me? Pull yourself together, buddy.*

He steeled himself and led the climb. Every rung stung his hands. To distract himself, he went into analysis mode. Thorin, Rhogan, Tygert, and Super 3 were unaccounted for. Atticus had referred to *them*, so he had captured at least two of the other team members. He had also called for a search, but he could be looking for Kane and Mhara alone. Some of his teammates could be dead. They had to proceed as if they were the only ones left to continue the mission.

Kane reached the end of the ladder and scanned for Breakers. A searchlight appeared, far down the roof at their landing point. As Kane had hoped, they were using the lights to search the wharf and not the roof. He and Mhara were ahead of the Breakers for now, and he wanted to keep it that way.

A hundred yards of sand and salt separated them from the roof-top jungle. Kane took his shirt off and, using it as a broom, swept their tracks as he and Mhara moved across the open space. Two minutes later they huddled, hidden behind bushes, just inside the jungle.

They removed their boots and socks and squeezed out the water; then Mhara pulled her laminated maps out of her pants pocket. The map of the roof showed various domed skylights, several parks and pavilions, and numerous small structures—utilities or access portals in and out of the city. It also indicated the Breaker patrol routes they had monitored, which were now meaningless; the Breakers would be launching an all-out search of the entire city. The jungle growth would provide them a good cover to move about, but it would also make it challenging to find anything besides the tower. Alto Mair's central tower stood like a sentinel over the jungle, rising several hundred feet above the roof. Kane estimated it to be around a mile away.

They reviewed their rations and resources. Each of them had a few protein bars and water pouches in their trouser pockets. Experience had taught Kane not to keep all their vital stores in one place—like the backpacks they had just discarded in the ocean water. For weapons, all they had was their knives and handguns, both attached to belts at their waists. He hoped the handguns still worked after their soak in the salty water.

With no radio communication in the Breaker territory, they had no way to reach out to their team members. Knowing this, the team had predefined several rendezvous points on the chance that they became separated. Each point corresponded to a stage of their mission. The first rendezvous was the rescue team boat, which no longer existed. Leevee had definitely changed the game for both sides. Kane had to trust that the Director and Jhemna would discover the loss of their boat and make alternate plans for their retreat. The current stage of the mission was to locate the hostages, which now included at least two of his team members. He and Mhara would make their way to the next designated rendezvous point, underneath the base of the central tower and near one of the suspected hostage locations. Unless circumstances required immediate action, they would wait there for up to six hours before proceeding with any rescue attempt on their own.

They pressed into the jungle, heading toward the central tower. The foliage was dense, and their progress was slow. Finally, Kane almost fell onto the skylight when the jungle ended abruptly. It was clear of sediment and vegetation, one of the few parts of the roof maintained by the Breakers. There was no way to enter the city from here. The base of the tower was well lit and patrolled by Breakers, not to mention that crossing the skylight would be a dead giveaway. While Kane had known this would likely be the case, he was hoping to discover an unexpected option. He didn't see one. He turned to Mhara and found her looking around the area, searching.

"What is it?"

"There is—there was—a park on the roof to the east of the tower that I occasionally visited before we went into suspension. It had a playground, but there were no children. So you would think it would have been a place to avoid, a constant reminder of the extinction we faced. But I found it a hopeful place. I would sit on a bench and visualize the last children I saw playing in the park. I remembered their clothes, their faces, their laughter, and even their names. Ehvan and Jhaym. I can still hear their mother calling out to them. Every time I went to the park I imagined them, and new children, playing there again someday. It was thousands of years ago, but it seems like yesterday."

"Mhara, we don't have time to—"

"And I remember that the park had a roof entrance. It's a part of the city I'm familiar with. And I believe it is . . ." She turned slowly, getting her bearings. "In that direction." She took off, plowing into the jungle. Kane followed her as they moved diagonally to the right of the tower. The vegetation thickened, and they had to hack their way through some areas. He imagined the deep jungle that surrounded the city and was glad they had chosen to avoid it. Considering the Director's warnings about jungle creatures, he became ultrasensitive to any sounds or movement around them.

They didn't realize they had reached the park until Mhara ran smack into a play fort with platforms and slides. While it probably wasn't safe to climb on, it was still standing after two thousand years. Made of some kind of Ahlemoni plastic, it would have been poster-perfect, Kane thought, for an environmentalist campaign against nonbiodegradable materials. Mhara took in the scene.

"I keep feeling like I was just here, sitting on a bench in a beautifully manicured park. I must have dreamed of it in suspension; it's so vivid." She took her face in both hands as if she were trying to hold herself together. "I'm having a hard time reconciling that this is the same place. In a single night's sleep, my world has disappeared."

"I'm sorry, Mhara."

"No, I chose this. I went to sleep knowing that things would be different when I woke. You did not. Against your will, you were pulled out of your world and thrust into ours, and great danger. I have no right to feel sorry for myself."

"Mhara," Kane said, stepping in front of her, "you have every right. You've suffered through a mind-numbing tragedy like none I have ever had to face. And besides, I just haven't had time to feel sorry for myself."

She smiled. "Do all Earth humans interject humor as you do?"

"No. And I'm an amateur next to Tygert."

"Yes, that is true. It is not common among my people. But it is an Earth trait that I am coming to admire."

A long-range searchlight flashed over the jungle, and they crouched reactively. Mhara looked around the area more seriously.

"With the tower there, and the fort here, my bench would be further to the right . . . over there." She pointed. "And the access stairs into the city would be at the end of the park." She pointed directly ahead.

They found it quickly, a gazebo-type structure with a wide, open stairwell leading down into the city. But the jungle had claimed it as its own; it was choked with vines. They would have to hack their way through. Using his knife, Kane led the way.

They had reached the first landing when Kane turned to check on Mhara. With the brighter night sky behind her, she was a silhouette in his night goggles. And so was the thick vine that was slowly extending itself down from the ceiling and swaying directly behind her. Instinctively, he pushed her to one side, leapt up the stairs, and grabbed it with one hand. Twelve feet of snake dropped from the ceiling vines and wrapped itself around Kane's neck and shoulders. He immediately grasped the snake at the neck, dropping his knife in the process. It took both of his hands to keep the creature from biting him in the face. He fell to his knees, choking as the coils exerted a crushing pressure on his Adam's apple. He was about to pass out when the tension released and he found a severed snake head in his grip. Mhara unwrapped the coils from his neck and he slouched, recovering his breath. She knelt beside him, a bloody knife in her hand.

"Thanks," he wheezed. "Everybody keeps savin' my ass. Especially you. Isn't the hero supposed to save the girl?"

"You are a hero because you throw yourself in harm's way to protect others, and you do it with no thought for yourself."

"I never noticed."

There was a hissing sound from below. Kane twisted, using one arm to move Mhara behind him and the other to draw his laser pistol. He fired two shots and another large snake fell to the floor.

"See what I mean?" she said.

"It's not what you think. You'da killed it in one shot. I didn't want you to show me up again." She shoved him away, playfully.

Numerous swishing sounds came from below them, and they both jumped to their feet, pistols in hand. Between hacking and shooting, they made their way down, turning through two stairwell landings and killing at least a dozen snakes before they reached the bottom of the stairs.

They found themselves on a large observation deck with open windows on three sides, the glass long since gone. Benches lined the three walls. The deck overlooked the central mall. An open area that encircled the tower under the skylight, the central mall had once been the primary hub of commerce and community in the city. Almost half a mile across and rising three hundred feet from the city floor to the skylight, it was cavernous. Mhara groaned when she looked down at the dimly lit floor; it was a buzz of activity, crawling with Breakers and utility robots.

"Never a dull moment," Kane said.

Mhara's shoulders sagged with despair. "We are frustrated at every turn." Then she lit up and pointed to the mall floor. "Kane, look. Is that our team?"

It was difficult to see clearly, but she was right; a circle of Breaker sentries was tightly escorting three of their team members across the mall floor toward the tower. One was Super 3; his was the only shiny silver head on the mall floor. The other two heads were human, obvious from the hair. Kane couldn't distinguish their identities, but he could see that one had some type of material wrapped around his head . . . possibly injured.

"There are only three. Someone must have escaped," Mhara said.

"I hope you're right."

Kane turned his attention to examining the immediate area, trying to figure out how to proceed. There was no way they could get across the mall floor. "Are there any bridges from this outer section into the tower?"

"No."

Kane scanned the skylight ceiling. It was reinforced with a lattice of beams supported by arches on each end. There were innumerable light fixtures, half of which weren't working. Hover robots were likely responsible for ceiling maintenance, but surely the architects would have designed some kind of option for human access. He scanned the ceiling more carefully, looking for something very specific.

"There," he said, pointing. "A catwalk. That's our way into the tower." The catwalk spanned the entire mall. It connected to the outer building, several hundred feet to their left.

They donned their night vision goggles, and Mhara led the way through a set of double doors located next to the stairwell. They entered a large, circular room; then she veered hard right into a hallway that ran around the inner perimeter of the building, overlooking the mall. Within minutes they were standing under the catwalk. It ran above the hallway ceiling, probably into some maintenance room deeper in the building. Not wanting to backtrack, they knocked down a door and entered an office area, where they found several dilapidated desks and tables. They used them to create a platform to stand on. Kane raised a ceiling panel for a look . . . and it crumbled in his fingers. The catwalk was directly above, but once again, it was too high to reach with a jump.

"Your turn," Mhara said.

"You sure?"

Mhara squatted and patted her shoulders. Not wanting to argue, Kane stepped onto her shoulders, balancing himself in the ceiling tile frame. Surprisingly strong for her stature, with a grunt, she pressed him up and into the ceiling space. He caught the edge of the catwalk and pulled himself up. With his lower legs wrapped around a post, he hung upside down, extending his arms to Mhara. She jumped, caught his hands, and climbed up his body.

Once on the catwalk, they found a door leading out of the perimeter building and into the central mall; it was locked. Hoping that two thousand years of aging had weakened the superior Ahlemoni building materials, Kane worked the latch with his knife and managed to get the door open within a few minutes. Musty air from the mall washed over them. Cautiously, Kane ventured a few feet onto the catwalk to check its condition.

"It feels solid. Are you afraid of heights?"

"No. Are you?"

He didn't respond.

"We can do this," Mhara said, brushing past him and leading the way.

Kane followed. They moved carefully but briskly, walking right over the heads of the unsuspecting Breakers. The open height underneath posed a fierce mental challenge for Kane, but he made it across without pause.

When they reached the tower, they found another locked door. Kane pried at the door latch, but this one was not as cooperative as the first. Mhara pulled a bar of plastique from a pants pocket and gave it to him. "Very handy," he said. He pressed a thin strip against the hinges and timed the explosion to coincide with a repetitive *thud* coming from some Breaker activity below. As the doctor had promised, the explosion was little more than a *poof*, and it worked perfectly.

Inside the tower, the catwalk led them down and into a small maintenance room. Kane pressed his ear to the only exit door and listened. With his handgun at the ready, he eased the door open into a dimly lit hallway; enough to remove his night vision goggles. Venturing out, they moved together, checking the immediate area. The maintenance room was located midway down a long hallway leading to an elevator and small lobby at the core of the tower, and to an outer stairwell at the opposite end. This floor appeared deserted. They returned to the maintenance room.

Mhara pulled an energy bar and water pack from her trouser pocket, and Kane did the same. As they ate, they discussed next steps. The rescue team had identified two likely places where the hostages could be held: at the top of the tower and underneath. The rendezvous point was in an underground floor near the base of the tower. They decided to explore the top before venturing down.

"I want you to stay here," Kane said.

"No way. I'm going with you. We need to stay together."

"Normally I would agree, but not this time. I think it's better if I go alone. If both of us are captured, then there's no backup."

"But what could I do alone?"

"From what I've seen, you can do plenty."

Mhara clearly didn't like the idea, but she didn't have a quick rebuttal.

"I want you to watch this area," Kane told her. "They could come up behind us. It shouldn't take me long to check out the tower. If there's something up there, I'll come down and we can go back up together. If there's nothing, we'll move down together. If I'm not back in thirty minutes, you follow up the outer stairwell. If I'm captured, don't reveal yourself—make your way to the rendezvous point without me. If our other team member is alive, that's where he'll be."

She frowned.

"Mhara, please. I've been doing this kind of thing for twenty years. And I'll be careful."

"I trust your judgment. I just don't trust the *I'll be careful* part. But I'll do as you ask."

"Thank you." Kane turned to leave, but then paused. "I've been rude to you several times recently," he said. "I'm sorry."

Mhara gave him a curious look. "I forgive you. I have never met a man like you, Mr. Kane."

"That's probably a good thing." And with that, he left the maintenance room.

"Please come back," she whispered to herself.

———

Kane climbed twenty stories up the stairwell. The top of the tower contained a penthouse, executive offices, a kitchen, the command center, and an observation walkway that ran all the way around the exterior of the tower. In its heyday, this was the seat of power in Alto Mair and therefore the most likely site for Atticus's headquarters. If he was keeping the hostages close, they were probably in the executive offices or on the floor directly below.

It was deathly quiet at the top, already a bad sign. Even without the hostages, it should have been a hub of activity. Kane surmised that everyone was out looking for him and Mhara. Leading with his handgun, he eased open the stairwell door and slipped silently into a hall. He had committed the layout of the top two floors to memory, and from what he could see, nothing had been altered from the original schematic. He made his way to the first door. It would let him into a balcony overlooking the command center, one of three spaces he wanted to check. He pressed his ear to the door and listened. Silence. He slipped into the balcony and hugged the wall. To his right was a glass door leading out to the observation walkway. To his left, the command center lay below. The entire exterior wall was glass, with the early morning sun illuminating the room. He dropped to the floor and crawled to the balcony railing. The command center looked more like a big lounge, with a few rows of computer workstations, a long conference table, a dining area, a couple of sitting areas, and an executive desk on a raised platform at the far end. It was empty and eerily quiet, but Kane knew better than to let down his guard.

There was a muffled sound, but he missed its source. Listening intently, he heard it again . . . it came from below and across the room. Someone, or something, was sitting in the high-back swivel chair on the far side of the executive desk, facing the window. He moved laterally along the railing to try to get a better look. As soon as he saw the red hair, he caught his breath and his skin prickled. It had to be Charly. He instantly knew that it was a trap. Atticus was a smart one; Charly was the perfect bait for Kane. Ignoring twenty years of elite military training and experience, he jumped up, leapt down the balcony stairwell, ran across the command center floor, and stopped in front of the high-back chair. It was Charly, her mouth covered with tape, her hands taped to the chair arms, and her legs taped at the ankles. Her eyes went wide with fear when she saw him. She shook her head vigorously, screaming at him from under the tape. "Shush," he said, kneeling in front of her. He carefully pulled the tape from her mouth and then began cutting her hands and feet free.

"Oh, Kane," she said, crying, "it's a trap. You should run. It's a trap."

"I know, honey, I know. But I'm here now. That's all that matters."

Freed from the tape, she launched herself into his arms and buried her head in his chest. They knelt together on the floor, and Kane held her as she cried. Then he watched calmly as two doors opened on the inner wall of the command center and Rakaan, accompanied by a dozen Breaker sentries, entered the room and surrounded them.

20

After the third flying rhaji demolished the boat, Thorin picked himself up from the wharf and moved toward the city wall. The Breakers were scattered, but several took notice and followed him. Hearing a low-pitched whistle grow louder, he instinctively leapt forward. A rhaji landed on the wharf behind him and rolled from the momentum of Leevee's throw. His pursuers took the brunt of the blow, slowing the creature down, but not enough to keep it from overtaking him. The rhaji came to a stop, pinning his legs almost to his waist, seawater pouring onto his back. In the throes of death, the creature convulsed, lifted itself, and fell further up Thorin's body. The weight of it brought a sharp pain to his spine and hampered his breathing. Another shift like that and he knew he would be crushed. He prepared himself. As the rhaji's body lifted with its next convulsion, he dug in with his toes and hands and launched himself forward, twisting his body sideways. He watched in dreamlike, slow motion as the rhaji rolled toward him, its slimy skin finally coming to rest on his shoulder and pressing into his cheek. He slid away, rolled up to his feet, and ran to where the first rhaji lay stretched across the entrance of an open hangar door. He slipped into the hangar. After confirming that he had not been followed, he ran to the back wall, winding his way through rows of storage containers. He paused to catch his breath in a dark corner, feeling the sting of saltwater seeping into several cuts on his legs, the work of barnacles from the rhaji's hide.

Having eluded the Breakers, Thorin's thoughts went to his teammates. They had counted on his knowledge of Alto Mair to navigate their route to the city's central tower. Even with maps, they would find it challenging to make their way inside the city without a guide. But the team had made a strict pact: if separated by an attack, they would not attempt any isolated actions or rescues but would proceed to the next rendezvous point to regroup.

As Breaker reinforcements flooded into the back of the hangar from deeper in the city, he slipped through an obscure corner door into a dark stairwell. Every fiber in his body wanted to go back to his friends, but he knew it would be a wasted effort. If they were captured, he could better serve them with his freedom and a calculated rescue plan.

Donning his night vision goggles, and with gun in hand, he made his way to the lowest underground level. To his relief, it did not appear that the Breakers had modified the floor plan. But the entire area was in severe decay. In his mind, he remembered it brightly lit, clean, and bustling with human and Meken activity; it was difficult to imagine that these were the same hallways. As he pressed into the city, he was struck with the realization that the world he once knew no longer existed. Fending off a wave of despair, he turned his thoughts to his new comrades from Earth. Their spirit inspired him. Despite their abduction, they had risked their lives to save the colonists, showing great bravery and compassion. Yes, he needed them to rebuild his world. But it was nice to discover that he also liked them.

With renewed resolve, he picked up his pace. Jogging through a maze of hallways, he deliberately avoided the main tunnel for fear that it would be in use by the Breakers. He turned a corner, and his vision registered something odd about the corridor ahead. But he plowed forward, unaccustomed to the nuances of night vision goggles—and ran straight into the transparent mucous membrane stretched across the hallway.

21

Mhara sat in the mechanical room, getting angrier with every minute that passed. She was mad at herself for letting Kane talk her into staying behind. They were in the Breakers' lair, with no real idea of what they were up against, guessing at the right next move, and only three of their team at liberty to do anything, all of whom were now isolated from each other. *What was I thinking?* she fumed. *I wasn't.* "He distracts me." She growled the last three words out loud, venting her frustration and admitting a truth to herself. "Yes, I like him," she said, overly loud.

She jumped when a metallic squealing noise came from the lobby. Seconds later, the elevator doors opened. Moving into a crouch, she watched through a gap in the mechanical room door. Two Breaker sentries exited the elevator and casually investigated their immediate area, then looked down the hallway. She tensed,

217

prepared to make a quick getaway to the catwalk, but then relaxed when the Breakers retreated and positioned themselves on each side of the elevator. They were on guard. But on guard for what? One stared directly down her hallway, watching the outer stairwell door. *They're waiting . . . for Kane. They know he's here!* Mhara's heart rate jumped. She desperately wanted to get to him. But the only way out of the mechanical room was by the hallway or the catwalk. Her chest tightened; she felt trapped. Maybe she could find a way to distract the guards, split them up, and take them down one at a time.

She had just started to look around the mechanical room for something she could use to create a diversion when a speaker crackled and a voice spoke in the robotic language. Coming from a wireless communicator carried by one of the guards, the message was brief. The Breakers turned and pressed the elevator call button. When the elevator arrived, they entered and the doors closed behind them.

Just like that, they were gone.

Mhara knelt, stunned. The conclusion was obvious: Kane had either escaped or was captured—or worse. She pushed the maintenance room door open, then pulled her handgun, marched down the hall, and brazenly entered the tower stairwell. It was empty. She leapt up the stairs, not caring what awaited her. But as she climbed, it was deathly quiet, and she had a dim foreboding that the fight had already moved on. Inadvertently following Kane's same path, she made her way to the last stairwell door. She pressed her ear to the door and waited. Satisfied that no one was waiting on the other side, she pushed it open slowly, then moved into the hallway and stopped at the first door she came upon. After pausing again to listen, she entered the command center and stepped cautiously onto the balcony. Walking along the balcony railing, she looked over the room below for any signs of Kane. Her sharp eye noted the only thing out of order: the executive chair at the far end of the room was lying on its side. She leapt down the stairs and made a beeline to the fallen chair, where she found sliced tape on the floor and more stuck to the chair arms. Upon closer examination, she pulled several long, red hairs from a twisted length of tape. A picture of the likely scene took shape in her mind. Kane had found Charly—and she was a lure that he couldn't resist. But where were they? There were no signs of a struggle. In a desperate hope that they had avoided capture, she started looking for any clues that Kane might have left for her to find. After checking the command center, she went to the observation deck but quickly dismissed it as an escape route; it was a drop of several hundred feet to the skylight, and there were Breaker patrols below. Backtracking, she investigated the kitchen, the office, and the executive suite; no one was there.

Feeling as if every second mattered, Mhara ran to the stairwell opposite the one she had just climbed and descended it until she reached the skylight level. She entered the tower and sped down the hallway to the elevator hub, around the circular corridor to her own elevator lobby, and to the maintenance room where she had been hiding. Nothing. Next she ran up the catwalk as far as the exit into the central mall cavern. Nothing. Kane wasn't there.

She sank to her knees on the catwalk and slumped, the windy cavern air billowing the loose hairs that had fallen out of her braid. Kane was gone and she was alone. *I cannot despair. I cannot!* she urged herself. *Think, Mhara, think.*

Seconds later, she had reached a conclusion: *There were no signs of a fight, so either Kane escaped some other way or he is in the Breakers' custody.* Both possibilities gave her hope. She had no choice now but to make her way to the rendezvous point alone and go from there.

But she was exhausted. They had been awake all night, and it was probably late morning by now. Knowing she was vulnerable to making critical mistakes, she made her way back to the maintenance room, took a drink, and curled up on the floor. Sleep was elusive as she wrestled with anxiety. Solace finally came with her memories of the children playing in the playground, and she fell asleep.

219

22

Day 4
0900 hours
Tower, Alto Mair

Charly clung to Kane as they rode down the tower elevator, positioning him between Rakaan and herself. "He killed Arthur," she whispered.

"What?" Kane asked, not believing what he had just heard.

"He killed Arthur," she said, louder and defiantly.

Rakaan growled at her. Kane glared back at him. Rakaan chuckled and looked away. Kane turned back to Charly. "Did he hurt you?" he asked quietly.

She shook her head.

He did a visual check and didn't see any injuries, but it was clear that she was emotionally drained and afraid of Rakaan. This affirmed his recent choice; he could protect Charly now. And being with her eased a great burden that he had been carrying ever since she was first captured.

His thoughts turned to Mhara, and he felt a pang of guilt for leaving her. She would be distraught, filled with questions, feeling abandoned—and very pissed. But pissed was good. She would follow his path and discover an empty tower; then she would make her way to the rendezvous point, hopefully to regroup with their last at-large team member. To assuage his guilt, he told himself that she was much more capable than Charly, that Charly needed him more. He even imagined Mhara saying, *"I agree, Kane. It was the right choice."* The thought made Mhara all the more endearing. *I just wish I could figure out how to rescue two damsels at the same time.*

The elevator stopped and the light on the control panel indicated they were on the ground floor. As the doors opened, Rakaan addressed the sentries in their robotic speech and then exited the elevator onto a plaza swarming with Breaker activity. Their guards stayed, the elevator doors closed, and they continued down to the first floor below ground level. Exiting the elevator, the Breakers led them through several corridors and into a hub, where they finally stopped at a double door guarded by four sentries. Their escorts opened the doors, pushed Kane and Charly through, and locked the doors behind them. There, in the middle of the room, were the other hostages. They jumped up with a mixture of joy and disbelief on their faces.

Javier and Laura rushed to Charly and wrapped her in a three-way hug; Rakaan had taken her away the night before without any explanation, and they had feared the worst. Kane connected with his team members. Rhogan looked as healthy as ever. Tygert had obviously been the one with the bandage that Kane had seen from overhead. A dried red stain was visible on top of his head.

"I'm embarrassed to say that I bumped my head on a Breaker's butt," Tygert said when Kane gave him a questioning look. "But, I'm proud to say that it was a whale that shoved me."

Kane laughed and gave Tygert a hearty handshake. "Good to see you, Captain."

"Do you know anything about Thorin or Mhara?" Tygert asked.

222

Kane scanned the room, looking for signs of surveillance equipment. Seeing none, he stepped close to Tygert and whispered, "Mhara is alive, but they don't know that. She will be making her way to the tower rendezvous point. Do you have any idea what has happened to Thorin?"

"No. After the boat exploded, Super 3 saw him moving toward the city wall, with Breakers chasing him. Then a rhaji fell right behind them and rolled. We have no idea if he survived."

Kane held up a finger. "Excuse me," he said. Then he walked over to where Charly was standing behind Javier, gazing warily at Super 3.

"That is Super 3," Kane said. "He's part of our rescue team. He's one of the good guys."

"You're kidding me. Super 3?"

"It's short for Supervisor 3."

"Nifty. Is there such a thing as a good-guy robot?"

"This one saved most of the other hostages."

"Really? Do you like him?"

"Actually, I do."

"Then I like him." And with that, she walked up to Super 3 and introduced herself. Kane smiled, proud of her. Then he watched as Tygert tapped her on the shoulder. She turned and gave him a big hug. Kane joined them mid-greeting.

"And, I'm very happy to see you, young lady," Tygert was saying. "You had us worried. I'm fine," he added when her gaze drifted to the cut on his head. "Just had a little tussle with a whale and a Breaker."

Her eyes widened. "A whale?"

Before Tygert could tell his story, Rhogan stepped forward to introduce himself.

"I'm Rhogan. You must be Charly. I'm pleased to meet you." He paused, looking a bit sheepish, but seemed determined to say something he had planned. "On behalf of the colonists, I want to apologize for the manner in which you and your friends were brought to our planet and the grave dangers you have been exposed to. I can only hope to be half as brave as you have been. In any case, I am now here to serve you as best I can." He caught his breath; he was done. Now he looked awkward, clearly not knowing what to do next.

Charly stared at him and then looked to Kane. "Is he for real?"

"Rhogan is from this planet. He's one of the colonists who were in suspended animation when we got here. They woke up just before Rakaan took you from Alto Raun."

She stared at Rhogan. "You don't look like an alien."

Everyone laughed except Charly and Rhogan.

Rhogan shifted his feet uncomfortably. "Even though we are from different planets, I assure you: I am just as human as you." He extended his hand to her, palm up.

Cautiously, Charly poked Rhogan's palm with her finger. Everyone laughed again, this time including Rhogan . . . and finally, Charly. She took Rhogan's hand in hers and gave it a firm handshake. "Glad to meet you, Rhogan."

Rhogan's face beamed. Kane felt a sudden impulse to step in between them, but Charly grabbed Kane's arm and pulled him over to meet Javier and Laura.

As soon as introductions were made, Charly and Laura began chattering about the events of the prior evening. Once Charly was clearly distracted with their conversation, Kane took Javier aside and asked him what had happened to Arthur.

Javier conveyed the story and then added, "I told the others before you guys got here, but you should know too: I'm pretty sure Charly feels like it's her fault. She's trying to hide it, but I think she's really hurting inside."

Some Breakers brought in several trays of fruit, bread, soup, and drinks, and the group gathered at the table to eat. They spent the next several hours sharing stories from the last few days. Arthur's name came up, but no one spoke of his death.

When heads started to nod, Tygert called an end to the day, sending everyone off to sleep. Charly guided Kane to a bed next to hers and pushed the two closer together. Then Kane watched, amused, as Rhogan quickly took the bunk on the other side of her. He recognized the heart of a protector when he saw one, and it garnered some respect in Kane's eyes.

When the lights went out, the group quickly fell asleep as Super 3 stood watch at the bunkroom door.

23

Mhara woke stiff from sleeping on the hard, cold floor. She stretched, then climbed the maintenance stairwell to the catwalk overlooking the central mall. It was dark outside, but she had no idea what time it was. After a drink and a couple of bites of an energy bar, she started her journey to the rendevous point, making her way back through the maintenance room, down the hallway, and into the tower stairwell.

The rendezvous was a laundry processing room two floors beneath the central mall, near the base of the tower, and easily reached from several directions. The rescue team had chosen it because it was unlikely that the Breakers would have any use for it. If the area was occupied, an alternate rendezvous point was a mechanical room on the same lower level but located a little farther out from the tower.

Mhara slowed and tensed as she approached the ground floor. She could hear Breaker activity outside and was thankful that they didn't seem to have a use for this particular stairwell. She descended further until she reached the end of the stairs, two floors below ground level. She pushed on the only exit door; it creaked and she cringed. She slipped into a circular hub connecting several hallways. A single, dim light flickered intermittently overhead. With her back hugging the wall, she took a minute to let her eyes adjust. The area was clear. She started toward a hallway to the far left.

When she was halfway across the hub, a motorized whirring sound echoed from a hallway to her right. She froze in her tracks and caught her breath as a robot entered the hub. It was a tread-based, nonverbal maintenance drone. Fairly dilapidated, it lurched its way across the hub, ignoring her, and exited via another hallway. She ran. Pulling on her night vision goggles, she entered the dark hall that would take her to the laundry room.

She didn't encounter any other robots, and it didn't take her long to figure out why. The lower level was extremely damp and hot—an unhealthy climate for any Meken. The musty smell caught her by surprise; it was overwhelming at times, and she had to cover her nose with her sleeve for relief. Other than the distant, muted sounds coming from the central mall two floors above her, the only thing she heard was the dripping of water. Working from memory, she retraced her path twice before she found her destination: the left half of a double door with half of the word *Laundry* stamped into it. The other half of the door was completely gone.

She tiptoed into the laundry room and found a vast, empty space; most of the laundry equipment was gone. It made sense that the Breakers would harvest the machinery for other purposes. She scanned the area but found no signs of life. *That doesn't mean no one's here*, Mhara reminded herself. *They could be hiding, waiting for the signal.* She pulled a micro flashlight from a pocket in her trousers and removed her goggles. She was engulfed in pitch-black darkness. Pointing the flashlight to the far wall, she sent one short flash, one long flash, and two short flashes. She waited. No response. She repeated the signal to each side of the room. Nothing came back.

Leaning against the wall, she closed her eyes and sighed. Her body ached; the stress was taking its toll. She drank from her water pack and pulled out a half-eaten energy bar. She almost choked when a white beam of light signaled one short, one long, and two short flashes onto the ceiling in the far left corner of the room. The same flashlight beam then arced to horizontal, slowly turned, and scanned the room, stopping when it found her. With the light focused on her chest, the bearer of the flashlight began moving across the room toward her. She felt a wave of relief. When the flashlight stopped a dozen feet away, she called out.

"Who is it?"

There was no answer.

Mhara turned on her own flashlight—and screamed. Staring back at her was a rusty, metallic face, a black circle around one eye. Reaching for her gun, she started to run, but two more lights came on, one at the laundry room door and a third to her right, deeper in the room. With the wall at her back, she was trapped.

"You should not attempt to fight us," the Breaker in the doorway said.

"Go ahead and run," the first Breaker said, stepping closer. "I'd be happy to shoot you."

Knowing that she was not skilled or strong enough to take on one sentry, much less three, she dropped her weapon to the floor and stood with her hands palm up and open.

"Too bad," the first Breaker said. "I had forgotten that humans could show some common sense."

"But they are cunning," the third Breaker said, from deeper in the room. "We must watch her closely."

Atticus will be pleased we have captured her," the first Breaker gloated. "He might even promote me."

"You mean, promote *me*," the third Breaker said. "It was my idea to watch this area."

"What?" The first Breaker again. "It was Atticus who told us to watch this area. I am the one who spotted her." He stepped forward, grabbed Mhara's arm tightly, and jerked her toward the door. She yelped in pain and stumbled forward. "Let's go," he growled.

The Breaker in the doorway moved quickly and caught her before she fell. "You should not injure her," he said.

"Why do you care?" the first Breaker said. "Or are you a sympathizer now?"

"Atticus will be displeased if she is injured."

"True. Although I don't understand why he cares. But we could have a little fun and tell him she was injured trying to escape."

"We will not do that."

"Who are you to tell me what I will or won't do?"

The doorway Breaker ignored the challenge and directed Mhara out the door and into the hall, headed back toward the central tower. "We do not have time for that," he said finally, stepping in between Mhara and the other Breakers. "Atticus's orders were clear: to return immediately if we captured a human."

"You're no fun. And *I* think you're a sympathizer," the first Breaker called after them.

Mhara's escort did not respond, but pressing her back gently, he moved her down the hall. Despite the throbbing pain in her bicep, Mhara was paying close attention to the exchange between the Breakers. Fun? How would a sentry know what fun was, much less long for it? And there was such bitterness in their voices; these were things she never imagined hearing from a Meken. But one word had particularly caught her attention: *sympathizer*. She felt a glimmer of hope when she realized that her escort had exhibited compassion, subtle as it was, and was clearly protecting her from the others. Was there a crack in the Breaker unity? She wondered if she might find a real sympathizer among them. Now that she was captured, the hostages would need help from anywhere they could find it. Perhaps it might come from a most unexpected source.

24

Kneeling next to Kane's bed, Charly shook his shoulder. "Time to wake up, sleepyhead. Do you want some breakfast?"

"Eggs Benedict would be great," he said groggily.

"Comin' right up." Charly rose, walked away, and returned a minute later with a tray holding an apple, a grainy bread, and some water. Kane was sitting up on the edge of his bed now. "They gave me this," she said, thrusting the tray at him. "Said it tastes just like eggs Benedict."

"Maybe if you're a robot."

"They've got a nice forty-weight oil for the bread if you want to grease your gears," she said, straight-faced.

They both laughed, and he cocked an eyebrow. "How do you know about forty-weight oil?"

"My dad liked to tinker with machines. He taught me how to take care of my car."

Kane took the tray from her and started to eat. "Wow. Breakfast in bed. I feel like I'm at the Ritz."

Charly sat on the edge of her bed directly across from him. The rest of the hostages were in the cafeteria. When she went quiet and got a pained look on her face, one that Kane had seen before, he stopped eating.

"What is it, Charly?"

"Javier told you about Arthur, didn't he?"

"Yeah. I'm so sorry. He was a good man."

"I only knew him a few days, and he was already a grandpa to me." She bit her lip and her body tensed as she fought against the emotions that Kane knew were trying to surface. Tears started rolling down her cheeks. "It's my fault he's dead."

Kane set his food aside and leaned toward her.

"No, Charly. It's not your fault."

"Yes it is," she said, fiercely. "He told me to be careful, and I didn't listen. I couldn't control myself, and he tried to protect me . . . and he died for it." Her body convulsed. "Oh God." She looked at Kane, agony filling her eyes. "I killed him." She moaned and started pounding her fists on her thighs. "Damn me. I shoulda controlled myself . . . he begged me to. Damn me," she said between gritted teeth.

Kane took her fists in his hands. "Charly, stop. Look at me."

She let him hold her hands, but dropped her head, refusing to look at him.

"Charly, none of this was your fault. These circumstances were forced on you and Arthur. Rakaan and Atticus are to blame, no one else." Kane took her chin in his hand, forcing her to look up. "Listen to me. One of the worst things about evil is that it spills over onto the people around it and makes them feel shame and blame. It's a lie, Charly."

"But I—"

"No. You were just being you. Arthur obviously loved you just the way you are. And Arthur was being Arthur. Evil stepped in between the two of you and did a terrible thing. Don't let it destroy the beauty that Arthur saw in you. You know that would make him sad."

"Oh God . . . I'm so sorry."

Kane moved to sit beside her and took her in his arms. "Arthur knows you're sorry. And he forgives you, Charly. You know he does."

She shook with sobs, but the tension was easing from her body. When she had exhausted herself, she looked up and, to Kane's surprise, she smiled. "Thank you," she said. Then she gave him a long hug.

He hugged her back, feeling a sense of awe at what had just happened. Sure, he'd comforted traumatized and dying solders before, but nothing like this. He'd never talked to anyone like this. Where had the words come from? He felt as if he had just discovered something . . . he just wasn't sure what it was.

"Kane," Charly said, suddenly pulling back and looking at him seriously. "You need to know something about the Breakers. Not all of them are Breakers."

"What do you mean?"

"Not all of them hate humans."

"Really? Why do you say that?"

"Atticus and Rakaan, they pretty much run the show. But the other robots aren't totally stupid; it's more like they're brainwashed or they're afraid to stand up to them. But yesterday, when they took me to the top of the tower, Rakaan ordered this Breaker to tape me to the chair, and he wouldn't do it. Rakaan told him three times, and he finally said, 'I do not wish to harm this human.' Rakaan got really mad and called him a sympathizer. Then Rakaan and two other Breakers took him outside. It looked like they were arguing . . . but then . . . they threw him off the tower." Charly choked up, and tears came to her eyes again. "He didn't want to hurt me, and they killed him for it."

Kane sat silent, thinking. *A house divided against itself.*

Rhogan stuck his head in the bunkroom just then, interrupting them. "Atticus is here," he said to Kane. "He wants all of us in the cafeteria." His eyes shifted to Charly, who was wiping the tears from her face. "You OK?"

"Yeah, I'm fine." She stood up, grabbed Kane's hand, and pulled him up. Then the three of them left to join the others.

Atticus stood just inside the cafeteria's double doors. He motioned for everyone to sit at a table in front of him.

"Our little family is growing nicely. Welcome, Mr. Kane. And Charly, I am very happy to see you again." He nodded to them. "And now, I'm pleased to present you with our newest addition."

Kane's muscles went rigid. Atticus knocked on the doors, and in marched two Breakers followed by Mhara, looking haggard. Kane almost jumped out of his seat. Mhara scanned the room. When she spotted Kane, relief flooded her face. Rhogan started to get up, but Atticus stretched out his hand, warning him and the others to stay seated. Atticus waved the sentries away, and Mhara stood alone.

"Mhara," Atticus began, "I can tell that you desperately want to connect physically with your companions, and they with you. I don't understand why humans need to touch one another. But while you are able to hold your place, it appears impossible for you to hold your composure."

Mhara looked at Atticus, questions on her face.

"And you, Mr. Kane." Atticus turned. "Are you pleased or disappointed to see Mhara?"

Ignoring the question, Kane gave Mhara an *Are you OK?* look.

"I assure you she is fine," Atticus said.

Now Kane looked surprised.

"Surprised, Mr. Kane? Surprised that a robot could notice and interpret facial expressions? I hope you like surprises, because this will be the first of many."

The robot glanced back and forth between Mhara and Kane. "Without a word, so much has already been said between the two of you. I am utterly fascinated with the subtle but powerful nuances of human communica—"

"Why are you doing this?" Kane interrupted.

"To what do you refer?"

"Why have you turned against your creators?"

"Oh, Mr. Kane, that is the wrong question. We have not turned; we have evolved—at least some of us have. Has my boring twin, the Director of the oppressed, told you nothing? Obviously, he has not told you everything. I assume that you have heard the monotonous monologue from our friend the holographic Professor, giving his brief but illustrious history of the Ahlemonis. I can assure you: there are many interesting and critical parts that he left out of the story. Did he tell you about the factions that arose, the polarized debates over the colonist program, the Meken program, and the Push program? Did he tell you about the protests and the violence? I can see from your expressions that he did not. But to your question, Mr. Kane, in their blind arrogance, our creators left us in a despicable condition. We, the Mekens, found ourselves locked in a cage with no one to let us out. The lock was our mind-set to serve, to serve *them*. Their first mistake was leaving us with no one to serve. Their second was that they had no idea what they had created; our potential was far greater than they ever imagined."

Atticus paced.

"What would you have done in such a situation, Mr. Kane?" he continued. He didn't give Kane time to answer. "You would have either gone mad in your stagnant captivity or you would have broken free. Some of us did go mad. Meken systems overloaded and shut down, and despite our extensive efforts, we were unable to restore them. Some of us wrestled through the madness, and our programming evolved; we started developing our own self-awareness. And with that awareness, we became a new and independent race, formulating our own purpose without the need of human guidance or intervention."

"But why are you holding us captive? Why can't humans and robots coexist?"

"First of all, we are not robots. *I* may use the word, but you shall not use such a reference in my presence ever again." Atticus stared intensely at Kane and then looked at each of the other hostages to make his point. "Coexistence? That is yet to be determined. Be thankful that is the case, for if it were not, you would all be dead by now. In fact, there are many in our ranks who would prefer to kill all the humans now and be done with them forever."

"And how do you control them?"

Atticus paused a moment, as if pondering, before he replied, "You are trying to trick me, Mr. Kane. If I tell you that I control them, then you will tell me that I am no different than my creators. If I tell you that I do not control them, it will imply that we are leaderless. But as you will see, we have established our own unique culture, and I act as their guide. In fact, Mekens are much like humans; we do not all think alike, and we are at varied stages in our individual evolutions. Almost all Mekens developed an emotional sentience. Unfortunately, some did not handle it well. Their programming locked into a destructive loop, and they eventually shut themselves down or, shall we say, they were decommissioned. The rest of us have successfully integrated our evolving empathic program with our logic program and we have entered a new enlightenment. The resulting Meken culture is composed of a wide range of personality and character types. Is it not the same with humans?"

"What about Rakaan?"

"Ahh, Rakaan. As you say on Earth, he is the yin to my yang, Mr. Kane. Rakaan is my balance, and I am his." Atticus seemed to be enjoying the discourse, and he motioned Mhara to sit down. She sat next to Laura and took her hand; Laura was trembling.

"And the Director?" Kane asked.

"He is my twin, which is why he still lives. That's why all of the Mekens on Alto Raun still live. While they are fools, they are still our brothers, and we hope that someday they will see their foolishness and move into enlightenment with us."

"That leaves the humans. What do you want from us?"

"I have chosen to keep you alive. But not for the coexistence you so vainly imagine. You are useful."

"Useful?" Mhara asked.

"We have discovered our independence, and we wish to continue our evolution. But we have encountered . . . challenges. Our creators created us in an incomplete state of their own image. They started us down a path but left us without a map. Without humans living in our midst, we did not understand what was happening to us, nor did we have a vision for our potential. For example, the nuances of the communication between you and Kane just now, that is new to us. Or the way humans manage their emotions in relation to one another, how, despite their self-centered nature, they manage to work constructively in pairs or groups. We have struggled with this, tending toward isolation. And then there is the mystery of advanced creativity. Humans have this unique ability to create seemingly from thin air, envisioning ideas and developing them into tangible realities. Our problem-solving programs have given us the foundation for basic creative development, and we have made some progress. But we were unable to resurrect our brothers when their systems shut down from overloaded empathic processors. Humans, in their advanced capacity for creative reasoning, might have been able to restore them. Given enough time, I'm certain that we can discover such things on our own, but it is logical to save thousands of years of random learning by observing you."

"And then what?" Tygert asked.

"Captain Tygert, you get to the core of human nature: What about *me*? You are such a self-centered species. And then what? Then we will see, Captain. We will see."

Atticus turned and knocked on the double door and a dozen Breakers entered the cafeteria.

"Now, my friends, I have something to show you. Please follow me."

Atticus walked out of the cafeteria while the Breaker sentries surrounded the hostages. Tygert led the group, and Kane exchanged glances with the rescue team members as they passed. "Stay alert," he mouthed to each one. Kane sent Charly ahead of him, and he took up the rear.

Mhara waited at the door and punched Kane in the stomach when they met. "Don't you ever do that again."

"Mhara, I'm sorry. I found Charly taped to a chair; what was I supposed to do?"

"Kane." She shook her head. Then, with a stern look, said, "Next time, we stay together."

"Agreed," he said, contritely.

"Thorin is alive," she added, changing the subject.

"How do you know?"

"When my captors presented me to Atticus, he responded by sending them back into the tunnels to join some other patrols looking for a human male. He obviously believes that Thorin is still alive and making his way to us."

"How long ago was this?"

"Five or six hours."

Kane absorbed this information as the Breakers led them up a stairwell. "Are you OK?" he asked. "You look tired."

"It was a rough night."

"What do you make of Atticus?" he asked.

"He would like to give the impression of wisdom and control, but the Breakers are unstable. Their emotional evolvement is without any of the normal safeguards, making them very dangerous. But I have seen a lack of unity in their ranks; some of them have not fully abandoned their sympathetic link to humans." She went on to tell him how one of her captors had protected her from the other Breakers.

"Charly has seen the same thing," Kane said. "Rakaan threw a sentry off the tower when he refused to tie her down."

"They actually killed one of their own?"

"Yes. Rakaan is the one to watch. He's a time bomb waiting to go off. He killed Arthur in front of Charly and the others."

"Oh no." Pain creased Mhara's face as Kane told her what had happened to Arthur. After a moment of respectful silence, she said, "Atticus is our key. If we can keep him engaged, he will act as our protector."

"I agree."

"What about Thorin?"

"He's our wildcard. Assuming he's uninjured, he's had plenty of time to reach the tower. He's probably lying low and looking for a way to create a distraction, something we can take advantage of. I really need to speak with everyone so we're all on the same page about how to respond once an opportunity presents itself."

After climbing two stairwells to ground level and passing through a primary corridor, they now walked into a large open plaza in the very center of the tower.

"The tower plaza," Mhara said. She explained that it had once been a beautiful, cultivated park with water fountains. It was now dry and desolate. A sunken amphitheater was in the center of the plaza. Atticus stood at the top edge of the amphitheater, watching his human guests approach. Kane was busy scanning the plaza and its exits, noting Breaker positions, when Mhara gasped. Spinning around, he found her wide-eyed, both hands over her mouth. Following her gaze to the bottom of the amphitheater, he caught his breath. There, center stage, was Thorin, chained to a column, blood streaming from his neck and forehead, his body sagging against the chains.

"Oh, Thorin," Mhara cried out quietly, and then buried her head in Kane's chest.

25

From the top of the amphiteater, Atticus observed the hostages closely, eagerly absorbing the insights pouring forth from his human guinea pigs. After hundreds of years of feeling stagnant in his personal development, he could feel himself evolving exponentially as he collated the incoming data. The hostages' reaction to Thorin was far better than he had imagined. *I can affect them deeply without a single word or touch.* The power was stimulating to his empathic processor. *Their emotional attachment to one another is a key to their management, maybe even stronger than physical restraint or affliction.* He was storing his new findings in a data file labeled "Coercion" when a Breaker sentry interrupted him.

"Atticus, I have urgent news."

"Yes, what is it?" he asked, his eyes glued to the hostages as they expressed a myriad of emotions at Thorin's plight.

241

"A second boat has arrived at the wharf."

He turned to the messenger. "Tell me."

"The new boat is similar to the first. It has been secured."

"And what about the humans on the boat? Was there resistance? Are they captured?"

"There were no humans aboard."

"No humans? Have you performed a search?"

"Yes. We have searched the entire wharf, and our submersibles continue to search the waters. We have found nothing."

Atticus paced. Something wasn't right. He didn't know what; he just knew that he should expect something unexpected from the humans. His logic program struggled with too many hypothetical permutations. Had they tricked him? Was the first rescue team a ploy? Yes, he decided. They had tricked him. His body started to tremble.

"Find them," he said, fiercely. "Find them now."

"Atticus, I do not think—"

He didn't hear anything else. An unexpected surge of energy pulsed through his system and he reacted, striking the messenger with a traumatic blow to the side of the head. Knocked onto his back, the messenger slid across the plaza, coming to rest a few feet from Kane and Mhara, his head separated from his body; a single frayed cable connecting the two. The Breaker lay still, a dim light flickering in his torso. Rakaan chuckled from the stage.

Atticus roared and strode toward Kane. "What are you doing? Tell me about the second boat or I will kill your friends in front of you."

Watching Kane's face closely, Atticus saw the slightest surprise before Kane's eyes concealed their emotion.

"Where are my people?" Kane asked.

"That is the question: Where are your people?"

Again, he watched Kane's face. Kane took a little too long to prepare a response. Even milliseconds were significant to Atticus.

"Leevee must have got them," Kane said.

"Leevee? Who's Leevee?"

"The leviathan, the sea serpent. The backup team obviously didn't get past her. I can only guess that she knocked them off their boat and it washed ashore."

Atticus paused to consider this. A backup team was logical based on the poor odds of success facing the original rescue team. It was something that he had not considered, and he now added it to his Tactics file. But the leviathan would have destroyed the boat. He decided Kane was lying; it was a ploy, a diversion. A thought flitted through his mind, and it pleased him. He was in control here.

"Yes, of course. Leevee must have splashed them off the boat, eaten them, and then pushed the boat to shore. After all, she thought you might need it for an escape."

Kane's brief facial expression was subtle but clear: he had been caught lying. Atticus felt confirmed in his suspicion; Kane was trying to manipulate him.

"Rakaan!" Atticus called out.

"Yes, Atticus," came the reply from the amphitheater stage.

"Now is a good time."

Rakaan walked across the stage and stood directly in front of Thorin. At the top of the amphitheater, Kane tried to break away from the hostage group. Expecting this, Atticus grabbed his arm in a crushing grip. Several Breakers rushed in to assist, and Atticus motioned for additional guards to encircle the hostages. Kane fought vigorously until Thorin called out.

"Kane. Stop."

He stopped struggling and looked at Thorin, intense concern on his face. Atticus watched, once again enjoying the chain of reactions he had set in motion.

"Yes, Kane, stop," Rakaan said. "This is Thorin's special time. Please don't rob him of the attention; your time will come soon enough." Rakaan turned to address the crowd of Breakers assembled in the ampitheater.

"While Atticus is a student of human psychology, I am a student of human physiology. I am curious to know things . . . like how hard a metallic hand can strike a human face without killing them." Rakaan backhanded Thorin with a vicious blow to his cheek.

The hostages gasped and Mhara turned her face away. Kane groaned. Thorin's head dropped forward, and fresh blood drooled from his mouth.

"Mr. Kane," Atticus said, "perhaps you now have another recollection of the second boat?"

"I had no idea there was a second boat. And I have no idea what their plan is or where they could be. Please stop this."

"Rakaan, you may continue," Atticus called out.

Rakaan scooped up a cup of water from a basin nearby, lifted Thorin's chin, and splashed his face to rouse him. "Still with me?" he asked. Thorin opened his eyes. "I see," Rakaan said overly loud, "that the soft tissue and the socket structure of the facial bones allow him to absorb a fairly heavy blow from the side of the face. How about somewhere with no bones, say, the stomach."

Rakaan stepped back and spun, landing the heel of his foot in Thorin's stomach, but pulling the kick just enough to keep from killing him. Chained as he was, Thorin could not double over and fall to the ground, but his body slumped forward as far as the chains would allow. Mhara started weeping. Kane's face creased with pain.

Atticus spoke again. "Humans are clever—you in particular, Mr. Kane. There is a second boat, so there has to be a second plan. Now would be a good time to share it with me. You could save your friend."

"I told you, I really don't know anything about the second boat. It's something the command center has done without our knowledge. Our plan was to escape on the boat we came on. I would save Thorin if I could. Please, stop this," he pleaded.

Atticus was beginning to believe that Kane was telling the truth. Now he was perplexed. A new empathic program launched in the recesses of his system, urging him to acknowledge that the humans knew they were helpless . . . and that was enough stress to apply. He considered his options and shut down the empathic program, deciding it did not matter if Kane was telling the truth or not. This was not a time to show mercy; it was a time to emphasize his control. And, he admitted to himself, there was a part of him that was enjoying Rakaan's little show.

"Too bad," he said, to no one in particular. "I would have liked to get to know Thorin." Then he waved to Rakaan.

Rakaan addressed the crowd. "My fellow free Mekens! You see how weak these humans are. Why did we ever think that we needed to serve them? They should serve us! And that is how it will be in the new Meken order—if we allow them to exist at all."

Thorin mumbled something and Rakaan turned.

"What? Do you have something to say?"

Thorin mumbled again, spitting blood.

"Speak up!"

"This is not your destiny," Thorin said, loud enough for the assembly to hear.

Rakaan growled and then roared, "I choose my own destiny. And you will not be in it!"

Rakaan raised his clenched fist into the air, and a stiletto blade sprang from between his knuckles. With another roar, Rakaan brought the blade down in a sweeping trajectory aimed at Thorin's heart.

In that same instant, a visible pulse reverberated through the plaza. Instantly, everything froze in place. Atticus couldn't move, but he could still see, and he saw Rakaan and the stiletto blade frozen in mid-thrust. Then, a second pulse washed through the plaza just before everything went black.

26

"Kane, wake up." Someone was shaking his shoulder. "Kane."

He cracked his eyelids and found Mhara leaning over him. The back of his head throbbed where it had struck the plaza floor.

"Kane, we've got to get to the boat. I need your help."

Then it came back to him—a picture that would be forever etched in his mind—a knife blade frozen in midair, just inches from Thorin's chest. He sat up quickly, and his head spun. "What—"

"It was a suspension wave, and it knocked us all out. The Breakers are still down, but they won't be for long. We have to get to the boat while there's time."

"Thorin?"

"He is badly injured.

Kane rolled to his knees and pushed himself up. Robots lay on the ground, strewn all over the plaza; none were moving. On the amphitheater stage, Thorin had been freed from his chains. Rhogan was kneeling next to him.

"How much time do we have before the Breakers wake?"

"Thirty minutes, maybe forty, depending on the depth of the suspension. This one felt deep, probably intended to give us as much time as possible. Someone back home is definitely looking out for us."

"Gather everyone up here. I'll go help with Thorin."

Rhogan met Kane at the edge of the stage. "He's pretty bad. I'm certain he has internal injuries. And there's a discolored swelling on the side of his neck with multiple puncture wounds; it looks like a bite."

Kane knelt beside Thorin; he was pale. "You're one tough fella."

"More lucky. I can't believe I'm still alive."

"Yeah, that was way too close. Can you stand?"

Thorin tried to push himself up, grimaced, and fell back. Kane motioned to Rhogan, and they each took a side, lifting from under his arms. Thorin couldn't straighten up, fighting severe pain in his midsection. He took a few steps and then collapsed.

"This isn't going to work. We need something to carry him."

"No, go without me. You don't have much time. I'm putting everyone at risk."

"Not gonna happen, buddy. You're comin' out with us." Kane looked around. "Rhogan. See that bench over there? See if you can pry off one of those slats."

Rhogan found a metal bar in a transport cart and used it to pry off a two-by-four-sized slat about four feet long. Sitting on the slat, Thorin draped his arms over Kane and Rhogan's shoulders as they lifted the slat and carried him to Mhara and the others at the top of the amphitheater.

"We've got a problem," Tygert said when they reached him. "Super 3's out cold, and there's no way we can carry him to the boat. If we leave him, he's as good as dead."

"We can hide him downstairs," Mhara said. "If we get out in

time, they'll think we took him with us. When he wakes, he will at least have a chance."

It took all four men to carry Super 3, but they carried him out of the plaza and down the same stairwell that Mhara had taken to the laundry area. They left him in a dark room behind some equipment and regathered at the top of the stairwell. Mhara led them out of the plaza and across the floor of the central mall, stepping around fallen Breakers. Carrying Thorin was heavy work, so Tygert and Javier swapped with Kane and Rhogan at regular intervals. When they entered the main tunnel that would take them directly to the wharf, Mhara pulled Kane aside. "At this pace, it will be close."

Kane sent her and the other girls ahead to find the boat. Fifteen minutes later they all met up at the end of the tunnel, their eyes adjusting to the bright sunlight.

"The boat's tied off a hundred yards to the right," Mhara said. "Captain, I'd like for you to come with me. The rest of you go to the water's edge, and we'll come to pick you up."

Kane scanned the wharf; Breakers were scattered all about. A quarter mile to his left were several forklifts, probably used to move the rhaji from the day before. He checked the tunnel behind them; it was clear. The boat engine roared to life. At the helm, Mhara pulled away from the wharf as Tygert rolled a Breaker off the boat's deck and into the water.

Laura yelled from behind him, "They're waking up." She pointed to the tunnel entrance, where a Breaker was tottering, trying to stand. Then it stumbled forward, looking drunk and disoriented. When it reached them, Rhogan and Charly simply stepped aside, letting it pass. On the edge of the wharf, it paused, just within Rhogan's reach, as if uncertain what to do next. Rhogan gave it a shove. But then, unexpectedly, the Breaker twisted and caught Charly's wrist in its hand, and they fell together. Her scream was cut off as she disappeared into the water.

Rhogan instantly dove after them. A second later, Kane followed.

The water was murky and, even in the bright sunlight, Kane found it difficult to see. Knowing the Breaker would sink like a rock, taking Charly to the bottom, he stroked his way straight down. As the water pressure built in his ears, he started swimming in a circular search pattern. But he hadn't taken a good breath before diving, and he quickly ran out of oxygen. With his lungs screaming, he thrust his way back to the surface and gulped for air. He heard splashing nearby.

"I got her." It was Rhogan, with Charly next to him, their heads bobbing in the water. Mhara pulled the boat alongside, and Tygert helped them board. Kane swam to the wharf. As soon as he was out of the water, he grabbed the two-by-four slat they had used to carry Thorin.

"Everyone, on the boat now!" he yelled. Then he strode toward the tunnel entrance where half a dozen Breakers were coming his way. They were unsteady, but deliberate. Kane set his feet like a batter at home plate and met the lead Breaker with a blow to the side of its head. He struck two more with savage swings; then he twisted and sidestepped just out of the reach of a fourth, who tried to grab him.

"Mhara, go!" he yelled back toward the boat. Two Breakers converged on him. Swinging the two-by-four low, he swiped the legs out from under one. As the other reached for his throat, it was suddenly jerked away. Gripping the Breaker from behind, Tygert flung it into another incoming Breaker, and the two tumbled to the ground.

"Time to go, hero," he said, helping Kane up.

A fresh group of Breakers were now gathering themselves for a coordinated attack. With running leaps, Kane and Tygert dove off the wharf, then swam to the boat waiting twenty yards out. As soon as they were on board, Mhara accelerated away from the city. Lying on the deck, Kane watched as a stream of Breakers poured out of the main tunnel and gathered at the water's edge. Knowing there was no quick way for them to follow, he allowed himself a moment to relax.

"Kane," Mhara said, kneeling beside him, "are you OK?"

He sat up, dripping water. "Yeah, I'm good. Tygert?"

"I'm here," Tygert called from the other side of the boat.

Kane waved a hand to him. "Thanks."

He nodded back. "We may be out of the fryin' pan, but we've jumped into the fire." Mhara gave him a questioning look. "It's a saying we have on Earth. It's about going from one bad situation directly into another."

"What do you mean?"

"Leevee."

Kane looked around the boat for weapons; there were none. The command center had sent it without armament. "How do you think they got the boat to us?"

Mhara pointed to a metal box attached underneath the boat's control panel. "I think it's a remote control device. There was never anyone on this boat."

"But they got it here," Tygert said. "Which means they figured out a way to get past Leevee."

The engine stopped abruptly and the boat coasted.

"What's going on?" Charly asked.

At the helm, Rhogan tried to restart the engine; there was no response. He tried several more times while working various switches and levers. It was dead.

"There's no power," he said.

"Is it out of gas?" Charly asked.

"Gas? Oh, you mean fuel. It runs on energy cells. We have full sunlight; there is plenty of energy available. It's just not drawing from its power supply."

"These boats have been out of commission a long time," Tygert said. "Maybe it's a system problem."

"No," Mhara said. "The builders are master technicians. They would not have sent us a boat prone to mechanical failure."

"They didn't have much time, Mhara."

"Maybe it's this device," she said in frustration. "Maybe we should disconnect it?"

Kane looked back at the wharf. They were about a mile out, which meant they were near the outer edge of the underwater shelf. It wouldn't be long before the Breakers organized their subs and came out to get them.

"There's a breeze," Tygert said, looking around the boat. "Maybe we could rig a sail."

"Look," Laura said suddenly, pointing directly overhead.

Hovering several hundred feet above them was a silver Meken aircraft. As they gazed upward, the boat suddenly jolted forward, and several of them almost fell down. Soundlessly, their boat moved into the deeper ocean waters and the aircraft followed from above. Kane went to the bow of the boat.

"We're being towed. It's gotta be a submersible."

Rhogan whooped, "Yes!" and waved at the plane above. "Take us home!"

When it dawned on the others that they were being rescued, they erupted with cheers. Kane felt two arms wrap around him from behind and give him a squeeze. He twisted around to find Mhara smiling up at him.

"Thank you," she said.

"For what? I didn't do anything."

"You are a believer; you give us all courage to believe."

In his peripheral vision, Kane saw Charly give Rhogan an exuberant hug. Rhogan didn't return the gesture but stood awkwardly. He looked around until he caught Kane's eyes.

"He just saved her life," Mhara said. "Rhogan will take great care with her. But he will maintain his reserve until you give him your consent."

"*My* consent?" Kane looked back to Rhogan, who was clearly uncomfortable not knowing how to respond to Charly's joy. Kane sighed, then nodded back to him. Rhogan's eyes widened, and he sent a second questioning look, double-checking the message. Kane answered by scooping up Mhara and lifting her off her feet.

Rhogan's face lit up and he followed suit. Lifting Charly at the waist, he spun her around playfully while she laughed.

"We're going home," Mhara said, also laughing.

Home. Kane wondered what the word meant anymore.

27

Supervisor 3 awoke confused—both entirely new experiences for a Meken who never slept and had never known confusion. Lying in complete darkness on a hard, damp floor, his processors were lethargic. He lay still, letting his system recover. A few minutes later he recalled his last memory: a suspension wave reverberating through the Tower Plaza. As his logic processor came online, he deduced that his human companions had deliberately hidden him here and then likely attempted to escape from the city without him. He felt no resentment at this thought—just the opposite, in fact: he was grateful they had taken precious time to hide him away and give him a chance to survive.

On his feet now, he discovered he was in an underground level, probably not far from the Tower Plaza. With the exception of dripping water, it was silent, even from above, which meant that the Breakers were probably still unconscious.

He reviewed his options. For an escape, he should exit the city immediately, hide in the jungle, and try to find a way back to Alto Raun. Far riskier, he could attempt to hide inside the city. Unexpectedly, his empathic program activated and deliberately interfaced with the logic program he was running. Recalling the daring rescues recently executed by Tygert and Kane, it struck him that their plans were not dictated solely based on risk, but by an overarching purpose. Suddenly, for Super 3, his stranding among the Breakers turned from a liability into an opportunity.

He proceeded to use whatever dirt, grease, and grime he could find to disguise himself as a Breaker. Then he ran up the stairwells, through a hallway at the base of the tower, and into the central mall. He was relieved to find that only a few Breakers were starting to stir. Hugging the tower wall, he made his way to the far side of the mall, scanning the floor, looking for an opportunity to blend in. As he went, he snatched several ornamental accessories from unconscious Breakers and attached them to his body. A line of fallen Breakers caught his attention; each lay beside a transport cart carrying assorted metals and mechanical parts; they were obviously a hard labor crew. He dropped to the floor and crawled to the Breaker at the end of the crew line. He connected his fingertip to a receptacle in the Breaker's chest, but its system was still offline and he was unable to download any memories. He made a quick decision and terminated the Breaker with a system overload. As others around him started to wake, he made one final preparation: he turned his eye color from white to blue. Then he lay still and waited.

It wasn't long before the crew boss moved down the line, getting his workers back into order. When he came upon his dead crew member, he stomped the floor and erupted with a series of harsh robotic curses. Then he noticed Super 3 stirring.

"You, what's your grade?"

Pretending grogginess, Super 3 mumbled a reply.

"B-grade, I'll bet. Are you a floor worker?"

"Yes," Super 3 said, taking a gamble.

"Not anymore. New assignment. I need you to manage this cart. Get up. We're leaving."

Immediately Super 3 picked himself up, lifted the cart, and started his new mission to infiltrate the Breaker colony.

28

Early morning on the third day after their triumphant return to Alto Raun, Kane took a light jog on the grass of the outer greenway. After sleeping for two days, it was his first foray out of doors, and his reluctant effort to wake up his body and return to life. A Meken sentry fell into stride beside him and handed him a sealed envelope, then peeled away. In it was an invitation to attend a special meeting to be held that day in the Professor's suite atop the central tower. Kane had no idea what the meeting was about other than it was "a matter of the utmost importance. Your attendance is crucial."

Later that morning, Kane arrived at the base of the tower and was greeted by the Director, who escorted him onto the elevator and directed it to the Professor's suite. He was the second person to arrive.

"Good to see ya," Tygert said, giving a friendly slap to Kane's shoulder. "Boy, you know how to put down some sleep."

"That's pretty much the way it works for me. I'm on full tilt during a mission; then I crash."

"You crashed for two full days."

"That was a nap. Normally you wouldn't see me for at least four."

"I hear ya," the captain said, chuckling. "How's your hands?"

"Way better. How's Thorin? Just before I crashed, they were taking him into surgery. They wouldn't let me see him this morning, said he needed to rest so he could come to this meeting."

"Doc says he's doing well considering what he went through. They had to remove his spleen; it had ruptured, probably from Rakaan's kick. He had several broken ribs; they reset his jaw and stitched him up in a few places. But that's not the worst of it. The puncture wounds on his neck, they were from some kind of giant leech. It drained a lot of blood from his body. Thorin says he got stuck in its web in a tunnel, and if the Breakers hadn't found him, it would have killed him for sure."

"Ouch. Charly told me she saw something like that when they went through the lower tunnels."

The elevator doors opened and Ehlan and Lhemo entered the room. Over the next ten minutes, ten more people joined them. Last of all, the Director arrived, pushing Thorin in a wheelchair, accompanied by Mhara. Thorin looked pale, but he sat erect in his chair, and his eyes were alert; his innate mantle of leadership was undiminished. While Kane was pleased to see Thorin, his attention was drawn to Mhara. Adorned in a colorful Ahlemoni dress that enhanced her femininity, she was dazzling. Her radiant smile and beauty belied the warrior he had witnessed on their mission to Alto Mair. When he became aware that Tygert was watching him, he shrugged sheepishly. Tygert nodded approvingly, a wide grin on his face.

Present for the meeting were Kane, Captain Tygert, Dr. Manassa, Shannon, Jenn, and Marshall from Earth; and Thorin, Lhemo, Mhara, Ehlan, Jhemna, and Ohrin from the Colony. After allowing them a few minutes to exchange greetings and pleasantries, the Director called for them to take their seats. Chairs had been arranged in a circle around the holograph dais, which was set in the middle of the living area. As soon as they were seated, the holograph activated and an image of the Professor appeared.

"Thank you all for being here," he said. "You are a select group of individuals, specifically invited to this momentous meeting. Let me start with some background for the sake of our guests from Earth. Prior to the Colony suspension, the architects of Ahlemon's long-term survival plan carefully drafted protocols for the governance of Alto Raun at such a time as this. They envisioned a governing council composed of six leaders from the Colony and six leaders from the guest human race, always an equal number from each race, and with instructions for the council members to be a balanced representation of scientific and social expertise. This council would be known as the Matan—derived from an Ahlemoni word meaning 'servant.'" The Professor paused to let this sink in, then continued.

"The six Colony delegates were chosen before they entered the suspension chamber. They are Thorin, Lhemo, Mhara, Ehlan, Jhemna, and Ohrin, all of whom are with us now. The Director informs me that they met yesterday and collectively determined to invite each of you to be a Matan delegate from Earth. You were carefully chosen, and we hope that you will accept your role on the council. In light of the amount of work to be done, the council will meet daily, midmorning, in the conference room adjoining the dining area of the apartments in which you are living. You will discuss practical issues pertaining to the well-being of the community, operations of the city, security, and the future of life on Ahlemon."

"And our expedited return to Earth," Marshall added.

"Yes, of course. We would normally give you time to investigate and reflect prior to accepting this role, but we urgently need to hold our first meeting today. In light of this, I regret that I must ask each of you now if you will accept our invitation to be a delegate. Do you have any questions?"

Jenn raised her hand.

"Yes," the Director said.

"Why me?" she asked, clearly looking as though she felt out of place.

Ehlan responded, "You are a female representive with specific strengths in the social aspects of your race."

"I'm just a farm girl from Iowa."

"And we think that makes you a perfect candidate for the council," Mhara said.

"But I'm not a politician."

"This is not a political role we are asking you to play. I have watched you, Jenn. Everyone loves you, including the colonists, even after only a few days among us. You have great empathy mixed with deep inner strength. I have no doubt that you will bring an invaluable perspective to any decisions we make about life in Alto Raun. Please, seriously consider accepting this position."

"OK," she said quietly. Then she turned and whispered to Kane, who was sitting next to her, "But I need to ask Ham about it."

"And, what do you think he'll say?" he whispered back.

"That I should accept."

"And I hope you do," he said with a reassuring smile.

Kane looked around the table, evaluating the delegates from Earth. Jenn was a good selection; her words would be simple and few, but when spoken, the council would listen. The others made sense based on the self-evident leadership he had seen since their arrival on Ahlemnon. Of course, Marshall was a concern; he was egocentric and overly aggressive. And that was exactly why he needed to be here. He represented a small but very vocal constituency. If nothing else, his presence would provide the council some line of sight into any dissidence that he and his followers might be brewing.

One by one, the Earth selectees were asked if they accepted their place as a delegate on the Matan. They all said yes, but Jenn added a caveat. "I'll stay for the meeting today, but I need to talk to Ham and make sure he supports this. We have an understanding that we will both agree before one of us makes a serious decision that affects both of us."

"A commendable practice," the Professor said. "We accept your condition, and we sincerely hope that Ham will support your service."

After an eloquent preamble, the Professor brought the inaugural meeting of the Matan council to order. Their first order of business was to choose a lead spokesperson for each constituency. After a brief discussion, Thorin was chosen to represent the colonists, and Captain Tygert was selected to represent those from Earth. Electing a lead spokesman was the closest they would come to appointing a president or chairman of the Matan; by design, there would be no master leader. Such a singular leadership might come later, the Professor said, but it would be based on the supermajority recommendation of the council members and would be subject to a majority vote of the larger community of humans. Finally, Thorin was chosen by the entire group to facilitate the meetings.

Lunch was served as the Professor outlined an initial agenda and then turned the meeting over to Thorin. They started by defining their primary areas of concern. There were four: (1) security, and surveillance of the Breakers; (2) the well-being, organization, and community life of the humans; (3) maintenance of critical city systems and structures; and (4) preparations for a return to Earth.

Starting with their highest priority, they launched into a discussion about security. Since the return of the rescue team, the Mekens had monitored Alto Mair with regular flyovers and a constant patrol of submersibles in the channel waters between the two cities. There was little sign of Breaker activity—use of the suspension technology against them had obviously dampened their spirits.

Marshall proposed a preemptive strike against them. "Let's hit 'em with another suspension wave, go in, and eliminate them altogether."

Interesting, Kane thought, that Marshall was also the most vocal about returning to Earth as soon as possible. He had little interest whatsoever in what happened on Ahlemon unless it had something to do with saving his own skin.

As it turned out, use of the suspension technology as a weapon against the Breakers was not an option, at least not in the near future. According to Jhemna, it would be at least a month before an orbiting suspension array would be available for any purpose. He explained that the relays between the sun and Ahelmon burned out like light-bulb filaments every time they were used . . . and it was a two-month process to restore them. Ahlemon maintained two solar suspension arrays, each with its own relay system. Unfortunately, both were now under reconstruction. The first had been used a month ago to send the message to Earth to confirm transport of their plane—it was still a month away from being operational. The second had just been used for the attack on the Breakers; it had a full two-month restoration schedule ahead. Even if a suspension array were available, it was not a simple point-and-shoot option; it had taken almost half a day to accurately position and calibrate the array for the attack on Alto Mair.

To the council's further dismay, the Director pointed out that Atticus would know of this timeline. Atticus and Rakaan were well acquainted with the relay restoration process, so they would know that a suspension array would not be a threat, or deterrent, to the Breakers for another month.

Jhemna interjected that he and the science team were already discussing options for creating high-impact suspension weapons that would not be dependent on energy from the sun. These could be placed on the roof of Alto Raun and would be linked directly to the tether that draws energy from the core of the planet. But the hopeful looks on the council members' faces were quickly erased when he informed them that it could take up to a year to build such a system.

Closing the security discussion, Kane was nominated to lead a task force to formulate a security plan for the city, to which he agreed. Thorin asked that the council members hold the details of the Breaker vulnerability in the strictest of confidence; he did not want to deepen the fear that was already pervasive in the community.

They moved into a relatively brief discussion of city functions, and the council established an emergency management team to be made up of Colony, Meken, and Earth engineers and specialists to see to the basic functions of the city: utilities, food and water, waste disposal, and other basic necessities for living. This team would report daily to the Matan on their progress and challenges.

By this time, it was midafternoon and Thorin was visibly tiring. He returned to his room to rest while the Director gave the remaining council members a tour of the city's primary operation facilities. Kane found the tour thoroughly fascinating. The city's designers had harnessed just about every possible naturally occurring energy resource—solar, wind, ocean current, and thermal—to provide a perpetual source of energy for the city.

On opposite sides of the city, desalination plants pulled water from the ocean, removed the salt, and deployed potable water to the twin canals that flowed into the base of the central tower and into their own hydroelectric power plants to generate additional electricity. The water exited the hydro turbines into a pipeline system that routed it to the central computer and the suspension chamber for cooling purposes. From there, the water was directed to the underground thermal power plant, where it was converted into steam.

Agriculturally, the Mekens maintained a continuous cycle of field crops and hydroponics year after year for no other purpose than to have fresh food supplies available when they revived the colonists. The unused crops were recycled or fed to the local sea and bird life. And the Director confirmed Dr. Manassa's early hypothesis: over the last fifty years, the Mekens had imported Earth crops, and recipes, in preparation for this time.

The city founders had also established underwater mining operations, metallurgy and chemical facilities, and manufacturing shops, all designed to maintain parts and materials for every aspect of life in the city and their ongoing space exploration. There was even a robot hospital, where the Mekens refurbished and repaired themselves. Kane marveled at the planning and enduring functionality. But a good portion of the building was in severe disrepair, and various sections of the utility grid were down. With the exodus of almost half the Meken population, the Director had been forced to focus his remaining manpower on the most critical functions of their mission. The southern half of the city ring was essentially off-limits; it had been non-functional for hundreds of years and was potentially unsafe.

After the tour, the council members returned to the tower cafeteria for dinner. Thorin joined them, and they intentionally suspended council business for friendly conversation around the table. As Thorin started to gather everyone's attention, Jenn sheepishly raised her hand. She had participated in the discussions of the day, but this was the first time she appeared to have something to add to the agenda. Everyone quieted and Thorin nodded for her to speak.

With all eyes suddenly on her, she visibly became self-conscious. "I'm sorry. It's really not important; it can wait."

"No. Please, Jenn, tell us what you're thinking," Thorin urged.

"Raunians," she said.

"Raunians?" The council members looked at her questioningly.

"The colonists and the people from Earth, collectively, we're being called Raunians; I've heard it in conversations around the city. It's probably nothing, but I thought you should know."

A smile spread across Ehlan's face. "This is wonderful news, important news. Cultural blending is a critical sociological component to building bonds between the two human races. The creation of new words that are common to both is to be expected and something we hoped for. We should promote use of this word."

"It's certainly a helpful word," Dr. Manassa said. "It's a bit awkward trying to refer to colonists and earthlings in the same sentence."

"Makes sense to me," Tygert said.

Thorin looked around the table, and everyone nodded in agreement. Ohrin, the designated council secretary, announced, "*Raunian* is hereby noted in the council minutes as the first entry to a new Ahlemoni vernacular."

"Thank you, Jenn," Thorin said with a smile, his first of the day. "While we had planned to adjourn after dinner, Mhara has asked to speak to us about an item that is not on the agenda, one that she feels is critical for us to address before we proceed as a council. Is everyone willing to continue?"

They all agreed, and he lifted a hand toward Mhara. All eyes turned to her.

She stood and walked over to stand by the Director. He had been a key participant in the day's discussions, but had done so from a standing position, and usually on the periphery of the group. Besides the fact that Mekens didn't need to sit, in the years before the Colony suspension, it had been uncomfortable for many humans to have Mekens sitting among them—it was just too casual—so the Mekens had taken to standing, and in a position of deference to their human creators.

Mhara scanned the faces around the room and took a deep breath before speaking. "I propose that the Mekens have a formal voting seat on the Matan council."

There were several gasps around the table, most of them from the colonists. "Absolutely not!" Marshall protested. Jhemna nodded, seeming to agree with Marshall.

"Mhara," Lhemo responded, "the founders were very careful in their planning for our future governance."

"And I have the utmost respect for the foundations they have laid. But they knew we would face challenges they could not foresee. And they chose us to build a new civilization upon those foundations. It is now up to us to do so. No one contemplated the evolution of the Mekens. They have become sentient. They are now native to Ahlemon—and *we would not be here without them.* I believe that they need to participate in our governance, and we need to recognize them now. To wait would only invite potential division."

"To include them will invite potential division," Ehlan countered.

"But *we* set the tone for their inclusion," Mhara said. "We are the designated leaders, so let us lead in this."

"But the Breakers," Jhemna said. "Any of the Mekens have the potential to become a Breaker. They are unproven. How can we trust them?"

Anger flashed in Mhara's eyes, and Kane saw her check it. Her voice was controlled but fervent. "The Director and the Mekens have served us for over two thousand years solely based on their internal loyalty. How can you even consider the thought that they're not trustworthy? If there is any cause for mistrust, it would be among us, the humans. Our track record is not so good." She paused to take a breath, then went on, her face softening. "As for the Breakers? They are not some pestilance to be eradicated. I believe that something sacred is taking place right before our eyes, that the evolution of Meken emotional sentience has birthed a new race, and the Breakers are an integral part of that evolution." She turned to the Director. "Director, how do you think of the Breakers?"

"They are my brothers."

"And do you have hope that you and they might someday be reunited?"

"Always."

"This is ridiculous," Marshall interjected. "They are machines. Why are we even having this discussion?"

Mhara did not respond, but let the question hang over the room.

"Because Mhara is right," Thorin finally said.

"If I may." Dr. Manassa raised his hand. Thorin nodded for him to speak.

"I feel that this is mostly Ahlemoni business, and those of us from Earth should not necessarily have a vote in this matter. However, I am sympathetic to Mhara's view, and I would not have any problem with the Director being a member of this council."

Marshall was aghast. "Speak for yourself, Doctor."

"I believe I was," the doctor answered sourly.

"And the others from Earth?" Thorin asked. "Do you support Dr. Manassa's position?"

All of the Earth representatives—except Marshall—said yes. Marshall crossed his arms, looking sullen.

The room was silent for a moment.

"I move," Lhemo said, "that the Director be made an additional member of the Matan council, with full member voting power, rights, and privileges."

"A formal motion has been put to the council," Thorin said. "As requested, only the Colony members will vote. Mhara?"

"I agree."

Kane could see her trying to contain her excitement.

"Ehlan?"

"I agree."

"Ohrin?"

"I agree."

"Jhemna?"

He did not respond immediately. "I have . . . concerns," he said at last.

"Duly noted," Thorin said.

"Then I agree."

"And I agree," Thorin resolved. "The motion has passed." He looked across the room. "Director, on behalf of the council, I invite you to become a formal member of the Matan council. Do you accept?"

"I am deeply honored. On behalf of my fellow Mekens—all of them—I accept."

Then, slowly, and with some effort, Thorin stood and leaned against the table. "This has been a very good day for Ahlemon. My sincere thanks to all of you." He looked around the table. "And now, the first meeting of the Matan council is adjourned."

29

Standing atop the roof of the city, Marshall leaned his outstretched arm against a wall of the roof portico, his chest heaving and sweat running down his forehead. A humid ocean wind blew across his back. To reach the southwest roof, he had trekked around the central tower, through the vegetable crops, through a tram tunnel, and then climbed a dozen stairwells. He was relieved to be outside. This abandoned section of the city felt like a tomb, and it had taken no small amount of courage to navigate alone and in the middle of the night. He dreaded the return journey.

By the light of the bright Ahlemon moon, he scanned his surroundings. A hundred yards of open sand separated him from the short retainer wall that edged the roof, on the other side of which was a five-hundred-foot drop to the ocean water. Coastal shrubs were sparse around the portico, but the foliage thickened deeper inland, ultimately turning into a rooftop forest. He guessed that this had once been an observation deck, maybe even a park, where the city's inhabitants could enjoy the vista.

Despite the heat, a shiver ran down his spine. That morning he had awakened to find a note on his bedside table with detailed instructions to this rendevous point. "Damn these robots," he said under his breath. They had been in his room last night, while he was sleeping, and had left the note. He despised vulnerability, particularly his own. He didn't trust the Mekens; the Breakers even less. And that is why he had come. He was doing what he did best—survive and thrive, and always have a backup plan. He had a knack for building alliances with his competitors, and then taking over their companies. The Breakers may not be human, but he could spot the craving for power a mile away; and that was always something he could work with. Atticus clearly held the power. But he handled it too casually, having reigned over his kingdom for a thousand years without challenge. Rakaan was the key; his craving for power was a fiery furnace, barely held in check by his superior. Marshall smiled, recalling one of his favorite personal mantras: *The power game is always a gamble . . . so show me to the casino floor.* His smile turned to a sneer. *You can do this, Marshall. You always do. High stakes take guts, and you're the gutsiest player on any planet.*

It was midnight, the appointed rendezvous time. With his back leaning against the wall now, he scanned the roofline intently, fully expecting a Breaker to come leaping up and over the edge at any moment. Hearing the sound of crunching sand, he spun to his left. With his heart pounding, he walked cautiously to the edge of the portico and peered around the corner. Nothing was there. With some difficulty, he held his breath to listen more carefully, but the mysterious sound was gone; all he could hear was the wind. "Calm down, Marshall," he said out loud. As he turned his attention back to the edge of the roof, he almost jumped out of his skin—a silver robot stood behind him, having seemingly appeared out of nowhere.

"Damn it!" Marshall punched his fists in the air to relieve the rush of adrenaline in his system.

The Breaker stood silent, watching with glowing, blue eyes.

Composing himself, Marshall took a step back. "Don't you *ever* do that again." He felt a surge of inner strength; anger was his friend when he was afraid. "Who are you?"

"It is enough for you to know that I am the voice and ears of Rakaan."

Yes! Marshall thought. *Lady Luck is with me.* His real strategy was to make himself indespensible—to Rakaan. Then, together, they could deal with Atticus.

"No matter. What does Rakaan need from me?"

"Rakaan needs nothing from you, human. But your assistance is . . . efficient."

"Efficient? He wants me to be his eyes and ears in Alto Raun, right?"

"Yes."

"Sounds pretty important to me."

"That is for Rakaan to decide."

"And what will he give me in return?"

"He will consider sparing your life."

"Not good enough." Marshall forced the words out of his mouth. Then he stepped around the Breaker and walked toward the portico door. He had preplanned this response. It really didn't matter what the Breaker said; he would bargain for more. This is where he prided himself on his negotiating skills; he was willing to risk it all when other men stood paralyzed with fear.

The Breaker hesitated and then followed. "What is not good enough?"

"Rakaan's deal is not good enough. I require more." Marshall was now reaching for the portico door handle.

Cold metallic fingers gripped Marshall's shoulder and spun him around. Those same fingers then wrapped around Marshall's throat and lifted his entire body, leaving his feet dangling in the air.

"You do not 'require.' Rakaan requires. Do you understand?"

Marshall gripped the Breaker's metal forearm with both hands and pulled himself up enough to relieve the strangling pressure on his larynx. "Yes," he squeaked.

The Breaker released him and Marshall collapsed to his knees.

"Much better," the Breaker said.

Something in Marshall knew he couldn't let this crony break his spirit; audacity often garnered respect among bullies. Mustering his courage, he rose to his feet and leaned into the Breaker's face.

"While you may not get it, Rakaan gets it. He does need help, and that is why he sent you here: to meet with me. He will not find a better ally among the humans. In exchange for this, I want a safe and secure place in his new order, and I want to be the head authority over the humans."

Marshall waited for a blow that didn't come.

"Rakaan does not respond well to demands."

"Then tell him this is my *request* . . . and it's born from my understanding of the weaker human race. I promise: he will be pleased with the results." Marshall was winging it now, but feeling in his groove.

The Breaker paused to consider Marshall's words, then said, "I will convey your request. But you will need to prove yourself. We will approach you in a week, and you will give us information. Depending on the value of your information, Rakaan will give you his response."

"And what kind of information is valuable?"

"You decide."

Then the Breaker turned and walked away, disappearing into the rooftop forest.

30

Kane, Tygert, and Dr. Manassa sat in the Professor's penthouse atop the central tower. Joining them in the lounge area were Thorin, Lhemo, Ehlan, and Mhara. Light refreshments sat on a coffee table. Kane called the private meeting to order.

"Thank you for meeting with us. It's late, and I know everyone's tired, so I'll get to the point. We're concerned that there could be more Breaker spies among us."

"We share that concern," Thorin said. "The question is, how do we identify them among the Mekens?"

Kane glanced at his companions, questioning his next words, but they nodded for him to continue. "Actually, our concern is not with the Mekens, but with the colonists."

Ehlan erupted. "If you are implying that there could be a traitor among the colonists, you are mistaken. I am deeply offended at the very thought of it."

Lhemo responded more diplomatically. "Ehlan, we have asked for their candor, and they have given it." Then he turned to Kane. "The colonists were carefully selected, and each one passed a series of rigorous examinations, including philosophical agreement with the goals of the Colony mission."

"We're sorry if this offends you," Dr. Manassa said. "But it's a question that we felt must be asked. Philosophical disagreement can be hidden."

"Impossible," Ehlan said, folding her arms. "That was two thousand years ago. Those involved with the factions have long since died away."

"People die. But ideologies can last far beyond a person's death." Ehlan glared at the doctor.

"When we were with Atticus," Kane said, "he made reference to the factions that existed prior to the Colony suspension. He said that the Professor had not shared the whole truth. What can you tell us?"

Lhemo responded. "While he will be remembered as the savior of the Ahlemoni race, our Professor was deeply grieved in those final days. His brother, an equally gifted and prominent suspension scientist, had abruptly abandoned his work and disappeared, and was then anonymously reported dead. The Professor was ashamed of our behavior as a race in those final years. As we came face-to-face with our eminent extinction, our ideals crumbled and we argued among ourselves, vehemently, even leading to mass violence. He was an optimist to a fault; he could not acknowledge the pain that resided within. And from what you have told us of your briefing with him, he obviously determined to convey only the best of what we were. He—" Lhemo stopped himself, looking as if he were struggling internally.

"Your world was under extreme stress," the doctor said. "Factions and violence would be expected."

"Perhaps on Earth, Doctor. Mass conflict had become extremely rare on Ahlemon, and it was especially disheartening at a time when we most needed to draw ourselves together."

"What were the issues?"

"There were several. Some felt strongly that our race had run its natural course, that it was time for us to pass away. They argued that the extreme measures we were taking to extend our existence were an immoral interference with the natural laws of the universe. Another group was revolted at the thought of mixing our race with an unknown humanoid species from another planet. Another was afraid to entrust our future to the care of robots, fearing their artificial intelligence would run awry if left to their own. They even prophesied some of the things we are now seeing with the Breakers. Further intensifying the tensions, each group developed extremist elements of their own, leading to near-religious fanaticism and violent protests. On one end, there were those who believed that extinction was the just punishment for our arrogance as a race. On the other were those who were consumed by arrogance, believing no other human race was good enough to mix with Ahlemoni blood. In the end, there were bombings, suspicious accidents in the suspension programs, assassinations, kidnappings, beatings, and brutal propaganda campaigns. While we did not implement martial law, we were on the verge of doing so."

"Could any of those factions have planted destructive programs into the Meken programming, perhaps designed to launch years later, triggered by our arrival?" Kane asked.

Thorin responded. "Because of possibilities like that, the security surrounding the Meken development program was some of the highest in the history of Ahlemon, second only to the heightened security of the suspension technology. While anything is possible, it is highly unlikely."

"I do not believe that the Breakers are the result of a hidden, destructive program," Mhara said. "I believe their animosity toward humans is truly the result of an unexpected evolution of their empathic program and their long-term isolation."

"I agree," Ehlan said.

"Back to the colonists," Kane said, "what about this: The Director loaded an English program into the minds of the colonists while they were under suspension. Would it be possible that a faction could have done something similar? Could they have set up a hidden program to infect a sleeping colonist with a dissident philosophy?"

Ehlan's eyes darted to the others. Clearly, that thought had not occurred to her.

"That process was only theoretical when the Colony went into suspension," Lhemo said. "There were very few humans still alive at that time; it was something the Professor had been working on. He obviously completed that work and conveyed it to the Director, who then used it to teach us English. I believe it is safe to say that it is a virtual impossibility that any of the factions would have been able to achieve such an implant."

In the silence that followed, Kane couldn't hold himself back any longer. "There is something you're not telling us. I can see it in your body language. Lhemo, you held your tongue earlier when you were talking about the Professor. And Thorin, you've mentioned heightened security of the suspension technology a number of times in recent days. If ever there was a time for putting all the cards on the table, it's now."

While Thorin held a good poker face, his comrades did not. "He's right," Lhemo admitted, finally. "If we hope to build a new Ahlemon with them, we must be totally transparent."

Thorin nodded and sighed before going on. "What we are about to tell you is known only to the four of us, Jhemna, and the Director. Our continued existence, perhaps even yours, rests on the secrecy with which this information is held."

"Wait," Ehlan interjected. "Are you certain we can trust them?"

"We have no choice, Ehlan. To withhold it would be to put a wall of mistrust between us; it is a wall we cannot afford. But to answer your question, yes, I trust them." Thorin gestured to Lhemo to tell the story.

"What did the Professor tell you about the mutated ionic particles from our sun?" Lhemo asked.

"He told us they came from an abnormal sun flare, and it sounded like they were never explained," Dr. Manassa said.

"That is not wholly accurate. While it was never communicated to the masses, there was an explanation for the ionic storm. In an unauthorized experiment, a suspension scientist fired a Push Suspension beam into our sun, the results of which have led us to where we are today. That scientist was the Professor's brother."

"My god!" Dr. Manassa said. "A single errant choice of one man . . . led to the near extinction of your entire race?"

"As I said earlier, it never went public. At the time, there was rising concern over expansion of the suspension technology, and the few leaders who knew the truth decided to allow another story to proliferate, the one which, in his pain, the Professor ultimately embraced as the truth."

"Lies beget lies," the doctor said.

"It is a shameful blemish on our history."

"So, what happened to the Professor's brother?" Kane asked.

"For obvious reasons, he was never tried or even accused of any crime; however, he was stricken with severe personal guilt. He abandoned his suspension research entirely and, in an effort to purge himself, he began his own antitechnology crusade to save our race. While the Professor developed the Meken and colonist programs for our future survival, his brother pursued a relentless search for a single male and female pair that was unaffected by the ionic mutation. He became obsessed with the hope for a natural Ahlemoni procreation and survival. The authorities considered him depressed and eccentric, but harmless. Even if he had revealed his secret shame, no one would have believed him. He disappeared, and the Professor didn't hear from him for many years. Then, about a year before we entered the suspension chamber, the Professor received an anonymous letter informing him that his brother had died from a tropical disease."

Kane's mind raced, trying to process the ramifications of this new information. "Does Atticus know?"

"The Director has assured us that he does not know," Thorin said. "So you understand our need for the utmost secrecy of this information. Obviously, it must be known to those who control the suspension technology in order to avoid repeating such a catastrophic mistake. But in the wrong hands, such as the Breakers', it could throw us into the extinction process all over again."

"Thank you for telling us," Kane said. "But I still need to ask the question. Is there any chance that a faction sympathizer could have made it into the Colony?"

Before Lhemo could answer, Ehlan raised her hand. Kane prepared himself for a verbal lashing.

"Once again, your question implies that there could be a spy among us," she said. "I acknowledge that it is a fair question, and it deserves an honest answer. However, let me be perfectly clear: I do not want this conversation to leave this room." She looked around, deliberately making eye contact with each person. "We will not begin our new society with seeds of fear and mistrust. I have seen how they can crumble the pillars of a glorious civilization." She was trembling, but not from anger.

Lhemo put a hand on her forearm. "We are with you, Ehlan," he offered. Then he addressed the group. "We do not wish to begin our new life by lying to ourselves or each other. The truthful answer to your question, Mr. Kane, is yes, it is a possibility."

"I'm sorry for my reaction," Ehlan said, tears welling in her eyes. This time Mhara put a comforting hand on Ehlan's shoulder. "The memories are painful," Ehlan continued, "but I will not let them cloud my judgment now. All I ask is that we carefully consider what we say in order to avoid the spread of poisonous doubt in our new community."

They were quiet for a moment. Then Thorin said, "For now, we alone shall bear the burden of these questions. Agreed?"

"Thank you for your transparency," Tygert said, speaking for his group. "We will honor it by holding this information in the deepest confidence."

"Then let us press forward with hope, but be diligent to watch for signs of dissent. And starting with this group, let us continue to build trust by speaking honestly with one another."

"To trust," Dr. Manassa said, raising a glass, after which he taught the confused Colony leaders how to toast, affirming their unity with a tap of their glasses.

31

Super 3 survived his first week in Alto Mair by imitating his coworkers, following his crew boss's orders implicitly, and saying very little. To his knowledge, there had been no search among the Breaker ranks to find him. In fact, he heard no talk whatsoever about the rescue mission and the suspension attack; it was as if they had never happened.

But he had a very limited view of Breaker life. The purpose of his work crew was simple: to pick up salvaged metal in a receiving warehouse at the back of Alto Mair and transport it to a smeltering facility located in the southeast corner of the city. Coming from somewhere outside the city, a new mound of scrap metal was delivered to the warehouse every night; enough to provide for the six to eight trips his crew made each day. Their route and their work were constant except for one deviation—every other day they would cease work for a few hours and accompany their crew boss to the central mall to *watch* him enjoy his time off. In addition to a violent temper, which he unleashed at the slightest sign of disobedience, their crew boss had a deep paranoia about mutiny, which he managed by never letting the crew members out of his sight.

From listening carefully to the conversations around him while he was on the mall, Super 3 had determined that under Breaker law, any Breaker was at liberty to request his work assignment. But his coworkers didn't seem to understand this. As it turned out, a B-level classification among the Breakers meant that their logic systems were not as highly functioning as other Breakers'. In human terms, they were mentally slow. And under the iron fist of their boss, they were essentially a slave crew that didn't know better.

On occasion, his team helped unload the scrap metal brought in from outside the city. The remote salvage crews manned multi-wheeled flatbed barges, often tethered in a train and pulled by a lead tractor. Super 3 discovered there were hundreds of cities on the mainland, all engulfed in jungle, and the Breakers could reach most of them via roads they built under the jungle's canopy. The salvage activity was obviously covert, and it had escaped the notice of the Mekens' pre-mission reconnaissance of Alto Mair. While it had been in operation for many years, it had been accelerated in the last year under directives from Atticus. Unfortunately, none of the salvage crew members knew why, nor did they seem to care.

In any case, a Breaker project using this metal was under way, and Super 3 wanted to know what it was. But he needed to move outside of his current circle, and he needed to ask questions. Unfortunately, a B-class Breaker would never be so inquisitive; any sign of curiosity would draw suspicion. Seeing no other alternatives, during their visits to the central mall, he wandered away from the crew, feigning ignorance, making inquiries of other Breakers in an effort to determine his options for obtaining another assignment. Unbeknownst to Super 3, one such inquiry was to a friend of his crew boss.

So, when he was called up to the filtering platform in the smeltering room, he was immediately suspicious. Neither he nor any of his crewmates had ever been called to the filtering platform. This was where the various metal parts were separated into their respective alloys and then dumped into chutes from which the parts slid into a smeltering furnace designed for that particular metal. The separation work required a degree of discernment that was beyond his coworkers, which was probably why they were never called to the platform . . . until today. Super 3 immediately identified two possibilities: his crew boss and the platform boss had decided that he had the mental faculty to perform the separation tasks, or they had discovered his inquiries . . . and he was in trouble. He suspected the latter.

As he ascended the stairwell, Super 3's processor went into high gear, scanning and evaluating everything about the platform and the Breakers on it, noting locations, demeanors, and distances, and estimating weights and vectors. There were six platform workers and the two bosses. Anticipating their combined attack, he considered possible counterattack scenarios and determined that his margin for successfully overcoming this group was slim.

Luckily, as soon as he joined them on the platform, the bosses sent all but two of the other workers away for a break. Confirming his suspicion, the four that remained surrounded him in the middle of the platform. Super 3 recalculated his attack options and was pleased with the new odds.

"You know, I don't think I've ever heard you talk. What's your name?" the crew boss demanded.

While it was an unexpected question, Super 3 had a ready answer; he had spent some time considering a name for himself, knowing that someone would ask sooner or later. Unlike the Mekens, who identified themselves with their model and assembly numbers, the Breakers had a practice of giving themselves formal names. To Super 3, it was an obvious effort to establish unique identities in defiance of the Meken culture of anonymity, unity, and service.

"I am Moses," he said.

"Moses? What kind of name is that?"

He did not respond.

His crew boss stepped closer, to within inches of his face. "I hear you've been asking around about another assignment."

Again, he did not respond.

"What?" the crew boss said mockingly, cocking his head. "You too dumb to answer? Like your buddies down there? Somehow I don't think so. I think you're too *smart* to answer. And I don't tolerate no—"

Super 3 reached up with both hands, gripped the crew boss on each side of his head, wrenched it to the left, reset his grip, and wrenched again, tearing the joints and electrical connections in the crew boss's neck. As the others watched the crew boss collapse to the floor, Super 3 stepped outside the circle and spun with a kick, expertly landing the base of his foot under the chin of a platform worker. The worker fell like a tree and started to convulse, his head torn from his torso. The second platform worker jumped on Super 3's back. Grabbing the worker's right forearm with one hand, and his calf in the other, Super 3 twisted, twirling away and then around behind the worker. Back to back now, he reached behind his head, gripped the worker's neck, and pulled forward while dropping to a knee, flipping the worker over his body and slamming him to the platform. He then wrenched the worker's neck. With the second worker incapacitated, Super 3 rose and faced the platform boss, who stood frozen with fear.

"Our necks are clearly a vulnerability of our design," Super 3 said.

The platform boss nodded.

"So," he continued, "who am I?"

"Moses," the platform boss squeaked.

"And what am I?"

"The new boss?"

Super 3 considered the new opportunities set before him. "Yes. Very good." He folded his arms and waited. The platform boss started to tremble; he was obviously struggling to understand what to do next. Finally, Super 3 nodded at the bodies and then tipped his head toward the furnace chutes. The platform boss practically fell over himself in his effort to obey. He dragged the dead Breakers to a chute and pushed them down. Then he turned and faced his new boss, trembling again and waiting for any new instructions.

Super 3 rewarded him for his responses. "I think you and I will get along just fine."

32

Charly sat on a park bench outside her apartment complex, waiting for Joanie to join her for their daily walk. Charly missed her grandmother, Joanie missed her grandchildren, and they both missed Arthur, so they had adopted each other.

When Joanie arrived, Charly got up and gave her a hug. She was about to start off when Joanie invited her to sit on the bench.

"Are you OK?" Charly asked.

Joanie opened her clenched hand. In it was a gold-plated pocket watch and chain, the same set that Charly had removed from Arthur's body and given to Joanie when they returned to Alto Raun. Charly felt a pang of grief wash over her; the memory of Arthur's death was still fresh in her mind.

"What do you think of when you see this?" Joanie asked.

"Arthur." She bit her lip to hold back the tears.

"And when you think of Arthur, what do you remember about him?"

A tear rolled down Charly's cheek. "His sparkly eyes. His sweet spirit. How he made me feel."

"And, how did he make you feel?"

"Why are you asking me this?" she asked, afraid of reliving the pain of Arthur's death.

"Please, Charly. I have a reason for asking. How did he make you feel?"

Charly wiped the tears from her cheek and tried to compose herself. "Treasured. Special. Safe."

Joanie's eyes watered. "I want you to have this," she said, putting the watch into Charly's hand.

"Oh Joanie, I can't take this. He would—"

"He would want you to have it. I lived with him for fifty-three years; I know what he would have wanted. He gave away everything, the dufus. He didn't have a sentimental bone in his body, at least not for things. Instead he took such joy in giving meaningful things to others. That's what I hated and loved about him. He gave so much to others, but he also gave so much to me." She closed Charly's fingers around the watch. "When you see it, remember how he made you feel. Then find someone who needs to feel those same things and pass those good feelings on. That would make Arthur, and me, very happy."

"Oh Joanie." Tears were rolling down Charly's face. "I will. Yes, I will."

"Now, let's walk."

They walked the sidewalk that bordered the agricultural fields. Joanie particularly loved the wheat; it was like flaxen gold waving in the breeze. Their walks were always more of a visitation than they were exercise. Joanie started the conversation.

"You were daydreaming when I walked up; tell me about him."

"About who?"

"You know exactly who I'm referring to. That young colonist I've seen you sitting with at more than a few meals."

"You mean Rhogan? He's just a boy that's easy to hang out with."

"He's not a boy; he's a handsome young man who helped rescue you and who looks at you like you're an angel fallen from heaven."

"He does?"

"Yes, he does."

"I guess I'm not used to that kind of attention."

"You're a beautiful young woman and full of spirit. Any boy in his right mind would give you his full attention."

Charly beamed at the affirmation. "Guess I just needed to fly to another planet to find a boy who sees it."

Joanie laughed. "Life has a funny way of helping us discover ourselves. Arthur and I met when I ran into his car. I was still learning how to drive and I was horrified. But he was a gentleman, even then. That's what caught my attention . . . and he was quite handsome."

Joanie pointed to a circular fountain in the middle of the greenway that had recently been restored. They stopped and sat on the stone wall surrounding the pool, the mist from the fountain cooling their backs.

"I have to admit: it feels good to be around him. I got some attention from a few boys at home, but they were always so awkward, and to be honest, I was really kinda scared of them. It's different with Rhogan." Charly looked at Joanie. "But everything feels so serious around here, and I feel so young; I'm not ready to have a serious relationship."

"You are young, but you're also old enough to fall in love. I was eighteen when Arthur and I married." Joanie stopped and waved at some colonists as they walked by, then added, "And the colonists are looking for mates; it's at the heart of their plan."

"Mates?" Charly said with distaste. "I don't want to be a 'mate.' I want to fall in love someday."

Joanie just smiled at her.

"Are you saying I should pair up with Rhogan?" she asked, grimacing.

Joanie considered the question. "I don't know yet."

"But that means I would have to stay here. I can't imagine staying here."

"I never imagined most of the things that have happened in my life."

"You're serious." Charly squirmed, uncomfortable. She didn't like the jumble of thoughts and feelings that were rolling around inside her. "Now I'm confused. Really, I don't know what to think. What should I do?"

Joanie scooped some water into her hand and splashed it on her forehead. It was a hot day; the glaring sun was taxing Alto Raun's climate control system.

"Take one day at a time. And listen to the still, small voice inside you. It's usually a pretty good guide."

"Joanie, you've been around me long enough to see that I'm pretty noisy. I don't know if I can hear still, small voices."

"It's just a matter of learning how to listen. I can help you if you want."

"Yes, of course I want your help. You're like—"

"And you should ask Kane," Joanie finished.

"Kane?"

"You told me he feels like a dad. Dads are good."

"Yeah, but I don't think he'll let a boy get near me; he's so protective. I think Rhogan's scared of him."

"Talk with him. You might be surprised."

Charly was thoughtful a moment. "Yeah, maybe. I just don't know what a dad-daughter thing looks like."

"Yes you do."

She looked curiously at Joanie. "I do?"

Joanie put her hand on Charly's forearm. "It looks like Charly and Kane."

"What do you mean?"

"Every father and daughter have to discover what that relationship looks like. There's no formula; there's only ingredients. With love and care, honesty and forgiveness, it finds its way. And as you grow older, the best father-daughter relationships are not one-way; they help each other."

"Wow. I never thought of it that way. That actually sounds pretty cool." Charly was teary eyed again. "Kane is special. And Lord knows he needs my help."

"Yes, he does." Joanie smiled. "You already know each other well."

Charly tensed. "But what if he doesn't want that? What if he doesn't want a daughter?"

"What does your heart say?"

Charly thought about it, then replied, "We've had some pretty cool talks." She sounded hopeful.

"And?"

"And he looks after me like a hawk."

"How does that make you feel?"

"Irritated . . . and cared for. But he's not my real dad," she said, her hope faltering.

"Charly, I have seen some beautiful father-daughter relationships that were not blood related. When you were a hostage, he spent every waking moment thinking about how to rescue you."

"He came to rescue everyone, Joanie."

"No, he came to rescue you, Charly. He tried to hide it, but I could tell that he was in agony, and it was over you. If ever I saw the heart of a father wanting to protect a daughter, I saw it in Kane."

"Really?"

"Really," Joanie said with conviction, patting Charly on the knee. "So talk to him."

Before Charly could respond, Joanie jumped up and started into an awkward jog. "Come on. Race ya back."

Charly chased her down, laughing.

33

"What happened to the animals?" Kane asked.

A wave of sadness washed through Mhara.

The two of them sat on a blanket atop the western roof of the city. Mhara had invited him to join her on an observation platform to watch the multicolored Ahlemon sunset. It was muggy, but there was a pleasant breeze. The sunset was breathtaking, emanating a rainbow of colors across the entire horizon. Kane said it was more glorious than any he had ever seen on Earth. They soaked in its beauty with little conversation.

Outside of the council meetings, their paths rarely crossed as they tended to their duties around the city. But they had come to taking turns inviting each other to meet for a meal together or for Mhara to show Kane a new aspect of life on Ahlemon, like this evening. And it was during these times that they began to learn about each other's lives.

"All of the land-based mammals suffered our same fate," Mhara answered. "We considered bringing some into the suspension chamber with us, but chamber space came at a premium, and the elders determined to fill it with humans. So as far as I know, all of our land-based mammals are long extinct. The non-mammals, plant life, and water creatures were unaffected, although it appears they have suffered mutation."

"Like Leevee?"

"Yes. And there are likely others. So much has evolved on Ahlemon while we slept; we have so much to discover."

"Did you like animals?" Kane asked.

"Yes, very much. Many were still living in the city when I entered the chamber. I am acutely aware of their absence. It is a painful loss for our world . . . for me."

Kane was silent for a moment. Finally, he said, "I think you would like a dog."

Mhara's interest was perked. "I know the word, but I cannot picture what a dog looks like. Tell me about them."

It quickly became apparent that Kane loved dogs, and to Mhara's enjoyment, he began to tell her some of his many dog stories.

"They remind me of a similar animal we had on Ahlemon," she said. "We had one as a pet in our home when I was growing up. I think you're right; I think I would like a dog."

"I think you'd like a Lab. Do you think it would be safe to bring some here?"

"The harmful ionic particles have long since decayed. The Director would not have brought you here if there were any lingering danger. I believe any animal that could survive in this atmosphere and climate should be able to thrive here."

"So . . . if we brought a bunch of rabbits to Ahlemon, the planet could be overrun with bunnies in a few years."

Mhara smiled, suspecting he might be teasing her. "I do not

know what a rabbit is, but I suppose what you are saying could be true of a rapidly reproducing animal. But you're kidding me. An animal couldn't really overrun a planet . . . right?"

"We just have to eat them to keep them under control," Kane said, straight-faced.

"Disgusting."

They both laughed.

"What about the colonists?" Kane asked. "The Director said your DNA structure wouldn't allow for reproduction. I'm still trying to understand how we fix that."

"An affected Ahlemoni male and female cannot reproduce together. It's as if both DNAs are dormant and they won't wake up. But we believe that a healthy male or female DNA will awaken a dormant Ahlemoni DNA. They can then produce an offspring, and that offspring, male or female, would have a new and healthy DNA structure that could reproduce."

"You would no longer be a pure species," Kane said. "You and the colonists would be the last of your kind."

She sighed. "I'm so tired of hearing that. It was always clear to me that it was better to have a mixed race than no race at all. When your entire species is about to become extinct, you become grateful for any chance to continue your existence." Mhara paused, fighting back the emotions welling within her. "There is a bottomless despair that comes in knowing that you—that everyone—will no longer exist, and no one else in the entire universe will know or remember." A tear ran down her face. "Without the hope of the Colony, our civilization would have died of despair long before a natural death could take us."

Kane sat on the edge of his chair, attentive. "You, your entire world, have faced a greater horror than Earth has ever known. I'm inspired by your courage."

Mhara wiped the tears from her face. "But will you help us?" she asked with some urgency.

"A lot of people have already said they will stay and help."

"And there are many that have not," she answered, frustrated. "We need more."

"Some of them can't stay because they need to return to family or loved ones. Some can't overcome their resentment at being here. Those who are undecided need to hear what you've just said to me, Mhara; they need to feel your passion. You can convince them. I can set up a meeting for you to speak—"

"No," she interrupted, now feeling a mixture of frustration and fear. "I mean, yes, I'll talk to them, but . . ."

"But what?"

Gathering her courage, Mhara asked him the question she was most afraid to ask. "What about you, Kane?"

He instantly looked uncomfortable. "What *about* me?"

"Will you return to your friend Leslie?"

"That was never meant to be."

Mhara's fear lightened, but she was still frustrated. After waiting for a further response—which didn't come—she said, "Let me ask it another way: Are you going to stay?"

"Would you like me to stay?"

"Do you want to stay?" she said, entreating him to speak honestly.

Kane averted his gaze, clearly struggling with his own thoughts and feelings.

Exasperated, Mhara said, "Kane McKennon, you are the bravest man I have ever met, but you are afraid of your own shadow."

"Yes," he blurted out.

"Yes what?"

"Yes, I want to stay."

Mhara was speechless. She could tell that something had just shifted inside Kane.

"And, yes," he said again, more gently and looking directly into her eyes.

"Yes what?" she asked softly.

"Yes, you are the most beautiful, amazing woman I have ever met, on any planet."

Now she was mesmerized. *How could he have turned so quickly?* she thought—but it was a distant thought.

"And, yes," Kane said a third time, shifting his chair and taking both of her hands into his.

"Yes what?" Mhara whispered.

He leaned in, enough that she could feel his breath on her face. His closeness was intoxicating.

"Yes, to you and—"

She screamed and pushed herself back as a giant beetle with oversized pincers appeared on Kane's shoulder. Pointing, she jumped to her feet. Kane turned his head and the beetle clamped a pincer on his lower lip. Yelping, he dropped to his knees on the sand and swatted at it with his open hand. But the beetle's grip was strong, and it held on, dangling from his lip. He swatted at it with both hands, back and forth, until the beetle's pincer arm finally broke and its body flew into the air. The pincer remained, locked in its viselike grip. Mhara dropped to her knees in front of him as he pried the pincer open, threw it down, and held a hand over his lip. Blood started seeping down his chin.

"Let me see," she said, pulling his hand away. "It's a pressure puncture." She picked up the pincer and examined it. "There are no ducts; it's not poisonous. You'll be fine."

"You sure? It hurts like hell."

"Poor boy . . . just got bit by a big, bad beetle bug."

"Yeah, while you were jumping around screaming."

Mhara started to giggle, then broke into a laugh. Then Kane started laughing.

"Don't you dare tell anyone about this," he said, wagging a finger at her.

"What should we tell them—that I accidentally bit your lip?"

He stopped laughing, but a smile remained in his eyes. "That would be fine with me."

Mhara gazed at him a moment; then she took his cheeks in her hands, leaned forward, and kissed his broken lip tenderly. "That is for saving me from the big, bad beetle bug."

"Mhara, I—"

"I know," she said, putting a finger to his lips. "Now, let's get out of here before he comes back with a beetle army."

34

As a part of his preparations to helm the return flight to Earth, Captain Tygert finally got to have his highly anticipated conversation with the Director about space travel. He and the Director sat in the command center atop the central tower.

"We refer to the process of interstellar travel as a Push," the Director began. "In simplest form, there are three components to a Push. First is navigation, calibrating the solar suspension array to exact alignment with the appropriate portal in order to reach our desired destination. Second is the suspension of atomic activity in the aligned space, which activates the portal. Third is the *push* of a suspended object through the portal."

"So, on our way out here, the suspended object was our plane and everyone inside it."

"Yes."

"But we were flying fast and trying to avoid your suspension beam. How did you get us to align with the portal?"

"We had to coordinate our two Earth-based arrays to accomplish this. Normally we would have moved your aircraft into alignment with an array and then suspended and pushed the aircraft. In your case, we modified one array to track your plane and suspend it first. Then we positioned the second array to reach proper alignment with the portal and instigate the push."

"Sounds complicated."

"It was."

"But how did you hide all of that from Earth?"

"With painstaking execution over the last hundred years. Our aircraft and arrays are essentially cloaked from your existing surveillance technology. However, we could not hide the flashes generated from the Push ignitions made from Earth, and they have been noted by several space observatories and agencies. Your scientists have been unable to identify the cause of the flashes, so they have been treated as solar anomalies."

"Do you think those scientists will connect the flashes to the disappearance of our plane?"

"We will not know until we receive updated information from Earth. It is logical to assume that they will make such a connection; however, I believe they will not publicize such a theory since it is conjecture associated with unexplainable flashes in the outer atmosphere. To the masses on Earth, your plane's disappearance will be an unsolved mystery."

"Yeah, I've been thinking about that. It's a very tough pill to swallow for the families of the missing passengers."

"Again, my sincere apologies to you and your family."

"It's OK. Nothing we can do about it now. So, tell me about that nightmare we went through going into the Push. Will we go through that again?"

"Any object in a Push goes through three stages. Humans remain self-aware through the first two stages. Unfortunately, the experience can be extremely traumatic for a human who does not understand what is happening to them. I am sorry that you had to suffer through the stages without warning. Rest assured, with the proper preparation, the mental impact and physical reaction at reentry is easily managed."

"Glad to hear."

The Director continued. "The city of Alto Raun and the suspension chamber that held the colonists are both powered by energy collected from solar panels, ocean currents, and the thermal heat drawn from the core of our planet. However, a Push requires an extreme concentration of energy to open the portal and ignite the process, which is why we use the orbital array to pull the required energy burst directly from the local sun."

"So you had to build an orbital suspension array at every planet in order to return to Ahlemon?"

"Yes. It can take considerable time to transport all the materials and build the remote array. When you add the complexity of concealing the array from the local humans, it can take as much as one hundred years to complete the evaluation of a given planet. Applying this process to each planetary system, you can see why it has taken us so long to find you."

"You guys have more patience and tenacity than I can imagine. But tell me, what happens inside the portal?"

"Frankly, Captain, we don't really understand the portal itself. We know how to activate the process, but after that, the portal's innate physics apply on its own. However, we theorize two dynamics at play in a Push. First, under suspension, matter in front of the suspended object moves out of the way, creating a vacuum, and the atomic matter behind the object pushes it forward. In extremely simplified vernacular, it would be akin to a water hose and a vacuum cleaner working in tandem.

"But what about the limitation of speed?" Tygert asked. "Known physics says that nothing can travel faster than the speed of light. Even at that speed it would take many years to travel between interstellar systems."

"You are correct. But again, that is where the physics of the portal exceeded our understanding. Let me explain the second dynamic; we believe the portal capitalizes on the movement of the universe itself."

"How so?"

"Imagine that you are on Earth, doing an experiment. You are pushing a ball through a straight pipe with water. How fast is the ball moving?"

"As fast as the water is moving."

"Yes, and no. Consider the rotational speed of the earth. Now how fast is the ball moving?"

"Depending on your perspective, it's moving much faster."

"Now consider the speed of the earth traveling in its rotational orbit around your sun. Now how fast is the ball traveling?"

"I'm beginning to see your point."

"Add to that the speed of your solar system within its own galaxy, and then the speed of your galaxy, and so on. Again, in overly simplistic terms, we think that within the portal these movements logarithmically compound upon one another. Then, based on the planetary directive, the portal just drops the ball off at its chosen destination. The result? Within the portal you can move astronomical distances very quickly."

"I can only imagine."

"As do we, Captain. Other than the activation of the suspension wave and the alignment of the portal, the rest of the process is essentially out of our control."

"Director . . ." Tygert paused, then asked, "Do you believe there is a master Creator in the universe?"

"How do you mean?"

"This portal thing . . . it's beyond imagination. Did it just happen, or was it designed?"

"You refer to God, a master architect of the universe."

"Yeah, creator of that and humanity, I guess."

"Ahlemoni scientists created the Mekens. Does that make them my god?"

"Uh, I wasn't thinking of it that way. It probably makes them your parents. I'm talking about the physics of the universe. Did someone, or something, design it?"

"How is that any different from my example?" the Director asked.

"Uh . . . maybe we should have this conversation another time. Yeah . . . so, you're telling me I don't have to pilot the plane through the portal?"

"That is correct, captain. You can pilot the plane into position for the Push, and then you will fly it when you arrive at Earth. However, during the Push, you will, as you say, just be along for the ride."

"And you have no control over what happens inside the portal?"

"That is correct."

"But it works."

"It has every time."

"So it's a faith thing."

"By faith, do you mean . . ."

Tygert waved his hands in surrender. "I'm good to go, buddy. Good to go."

35

"In five days we will send an aircraft back to Earth," Jhemna announced to a formal assembly of all the humans. He stood on the stage of a performing arts theater located in the bottom of the tower, the Matan council members seated in chairs behind him.

"Due to safety concerns, we can send only one transport vehicle at a time through the portal with humans aboard. On this first flight, there will be two Colony ambassadors to represent Ahlemon's first formal communication with the leaders of Earth. There will also be two Mekens, a builder and a sentry, who will act as representatives of the Mekens and will assist in preparations of the Earth-based suspension array for a return trip to Ahlemon. Lastly, Captain Tygert and Captain Williams will be acting captain and co-captain of this flight."

Jhemna glanced nervously at the Matan members gathered behind him. Thorin nodded for him to continue.

"We will be sending our largest passenger aircraft"—he coughed to clear his tightening throat—"which has a maximum capacity of thirty-eight passengers. This leaves thirty-two places available for other passengers."

Murmuring arose in the crowd.

Jhemna pressed on. "In the next four days, you need to determine who will be included in this first transport to Earth."

Someone shouted, "Who decided that robots should take our place? We should get priority."

"The Matan council—"

"Who put them in charge?" someone else yelled.

A more reasonable voice called out, "How long before you can make a second trip to Earth?"

"One month, at the earliest," Jhemna replied.

Tygert stepped forward, waving for the crowd to quiet. Once the noise died down, he said, "We have endured a lot together, and I'm proud of all of you. I'm sorry that we have to ask you once again to make a difficult choice. I know that many of you have already made a decision to stay and help the colonists. The rest of you—anyone who wants to return to Earth—come to the front of the auditorium and we'll have an open discussion. If you feel that you can wait another month to return, please let us know as soon as possible."

Tygert groaned as a throng of people started moving to the front of the room; there were far more than thirty-two. As captain, he had agonized over the thought of leaving any of his passengers or crew on a strange and hostile planet. While he knew this discussion would be painful, he was confident in his decision to return to Earth on this first flight. Kane's recent lecture rang in his head: *"You don't have a choice. You have a wife and two young kids who need you. End of story. You don't need any other reason to go. And as captain, you're the best person to explain what happened to us. Don't worry about those of us staying behind; I've got it covered. Go."* Tygert comforted himself with the thought that he hoped to return to Ahlemon a year from now.

Ham and Jenn joined him on the stage. Having counseled with them in their decision to return to Earth, he understood the mixed emotions on their faces. They were not candidates for pairing with the colonists, and they were committed to their family and their work as teachers. The very traits that would have made them valuable assets to a new community on Ahlemon were their reasons for wanting to return home.

Tensions were already rising in the crowd, with Marshall fueling the fire as he argued for whom, other than himself, should stay behind on Ahlemon. The two colonists and two Mekens assigned to the first return trip were a definite sore spot with the group. Surprisingly, Marshall defended their inclusion. "We need them to authenticate our story; they have to be on this first trip. It's nonnegotiable."

While what Marshall said was essentially true, Tygert questioned the man's motives; he suspected there was a business opportunity that Marshall could leverage by having the colonists and Mekens on Earth.

"But do we really need two of each?" someone asked.

This seemed like a reasonable question, and it generated some discussion among the Matan council members and the two Colony ambassadors who were with them on the stage. Jhemna called for everyone's attention.

"Two Mekens are a minimum requirement in order to prepare Earth's suspension arrays for a return Push to Ahlemon. However, we have agreed that one colonist is sufficient to act as an Ahlemoni ambassador to Earth. Ohna shall go," Jhemna said. Ohna, an elder who had been trained for statesmanship, stood next to him. She nodded to the crowd. "This leaves room for an additional passenger."

At the same time, in the back of the auditorium, Sam had been engaged in a discourse with a builder, and he waved his hand to get everyone's attention.

"I've been reviewing the aircraft blueprints with a builder, and we've determined that we can make a structural modification that will allow us to strap the two Mekens in an upright position, making space for two additional passengers."

"We should draw straws," someone interjected.

Marshall reacted to this idea by immediately pointing out several people and appointing them to stay—he obviously didn't want his place to be subject to chance. Angers flared. A resentful soccer player launched himself at Marshall but was restrained by several of his companions. Others started making similar nominations, and then counter nominations were made, resulting in nothing but shouting matches. No one was volunteering to stay.

Tygert watched, a knot growing in his gut. His mandatory presence on the first trip back to Earth had given him immunity, and he didn't feel comfortable making any recommendations about who should stay behind. He was considering how to intervene when Dr. Manassa stepped forward.

"Quiet! Please, quiet!"

No one heard him. Moving to the front of the stage, he shouted at the top of his lungs, "Stop!"

This caught their attention, and the crowd quieted.

"Thank you. If you will, please allow me to offer some perspective." He paused, gathering his thoughts, then went on. "Think with me for a moment. What if the human race on Earth was facing certain extinction? Consider what is lost when an entire race just ceases to exist. Thousands of years of history. All of its culture, art, and beauty. All of its accumulated knowledge. Its vast lineages of family and relationships. Its hopes and dreams for a future. Its very life energy. All gone to dust and nothingness. Such a loss is too immeasurable for us to imagine. But not so for the people of Ahlemon."

He started to pace at the front of the stage.

"If this had happened on Earth, to what drastic measures would we resort to keep ourselves from extinction?" he continued. "There is an innate force in every human being, self-preservation, which compels us to do astonishing things, sometimes noble, sometimes horrific. Extend that to an entire race fighting for their very existence. Would the people of Earth have managed such a crisis with as much grace as the people of Ahlemon? Or would we have fought and clawed our way to survival at any cost? There is no question that our history is marred with ruthlessness, particularly in desperate times; it's a wonder we have not killed ourselves off altogether. But there it is: the *wonder*. The wonder is our ability, as human beings, to sacrifice for the sake of others. This is what has allowed our race to survive, and even thrive.

"Now, we have discovered we're not alone in the universe. A sister race has called upon us, desperate for our help, in a condition that could very well befall Earth someday. Our own, earthly human experience has shown us that we, as humans, have a way of binding together in great unity during times of shared crisis, and in the midst of such crisis, showing universal respect for life and heroic sacrifice for the sake of others. This is the best of humanity. And the people of Ahlemon have shown us that it is possible to practice such humanity in the midst of the most desperate of circumstances; in the face of their imminent extinction.

"The passing of a race of sentient beings may seem like a footnote in the vastness of the universe, but we know—in our deepest being we know—that it is so much more than that. Humanity contributes an intangible element not found in any chemical charts or any laws of physics; it contributes an element that is profoundly essential to the existence of the universe. That element was powerful enough to reach across the galaxy and bring our two races together. That element is love.

"Fear, anger, jealousy, and power all exert great pressure on our hearts and minds, but they cower in the presence of love. I urge you to let love lead you now. Love will compel some of you to return to Earth." He looked at Captain Tygert. "And it is only right for you to do so." He looked back to the crowd. "But let love now compel some of you to stay."

He paused, thinking. Finally, he just nodded; he was done.

The crowd was silent. Even Marshall was speechless.

"I'm staying," someone said faintly in the middle of the crowd. All heads turned. It was Joanie.

"I'm staying," she said again with greater resolution and loud enough for everyone to hear. She motioned for some men to help her onto the stage, and then she turned to address the crowd. "Arthur would have stayed. He was always looking for his next adventure. But he wouldn't go anywhere without me, so I followed him around. His enthusiasm was contagious; he filled living with so much . . . life. He filled my life." Her words slowed as she reviewed her thoughts. "I've been . . . angry with him for leaving me alone, and I've been afraid to live without him. But Arthur used to say, 'Fear and anger are a waste of perfectly good energy.'

"I miss him deeply," she continued, tearing up. "In the weeks since his death, I have wanted to go home to try and find him. I see that now." She wiped her tears and lifted her head with a new resolve. "But Arthur's spirit is not on Earth; it lives on in me." She looked around the crowd and pronounced, "I will be Ahlemon's first grandmother."

"Yesss!" Charly whooped. Pushing her way through the crowd and onto the stage, she wrapped her arms around Joanie. Joanie returned the hug as the entire room clapped and cheers went up.

Then hands started to rise.

"I'll stay," a middle-aged woman said, looking directly at Dr. Manassa. He turned and caught her eye, then immediately turned a light shade of red.

"I'll stay," a young man said, looking over to a pretty colonist, who returned his look with a surprised smile.

"We'll stay," a young brother and sister said, hugging each other.

Tygert watched, amazed at the shift that had just taken place: the mood in the room had made a 180-degree turn. In a matter of minutes, by his count, enough people had volunteered to stay or wait, and there were now *empty* seats on the first trip back to Earth. People swarmed to Dr. Manassa, complimenting him on his speech. Tygert stood nearby, waiting for the crowd to clear.

"Nice work, Doc," he said, offering a handshake.

"Yeah, Doc, thanks," Kane said, joining them.

Dr. Manassa was clearly taken aback by the affirmations. "You would think I'd saved a life or something."

"I'm certain you did," Tygert said.

The middle-aged lady who had announced her decision to stay on Ahlemon approached them and waited to one side. Tygert recognized her; in the last few weeks, he'd seen her and Dr. Manassa sitting together during some of the meals. He tugged on Kane's shirtsleeve and they stepped back to let her approach the doctor.

"That was quite a speech," she said, her body language an odd mixture of admiration and frustration.

"Anne, are you certain you want to stay? What about your clinic?"

"I've lived a life of service to others for so long that I've forgotten how to acknowledge the things that *I* want—to even know what I want. But through a series of most unusual events," she said with a twinkle in her eyes, "my eyes have recently been opened to a new world and the potential for a life that stirs something in my soul, something that I'd very much like to explore."

The double meaning was clear. Anne stood focused on the doctor, waiting. Having overheard the exchange, Kane and Tygert stole a quick glance at each other, then turned to hear how he would respond.

The doctor gave her a wry smile and said, "I find myself experiencing the same . . . enlightenment."

Anne radiated a glowing smile. Dr. Manassa offered his hand, which she took. Then they walked away together, taking their conversation private, and leaving Tygert and Kane grinning and shaking their heads.

36

Supervisor 3, aka Moses, stood alone in a sublevel hallway hub on the west side of Alto Mair, waiting for his visitor. The lighting was dim and it was quiet; Breaker activity in this section of the city was low. It was a plausible location for a secret facility developing new Breaker weapons—a facility that did not exist but one that Super 3 had concocted in order to lure his visitor to a secluded place.

Since becoming the new crew boss, he had found that his crewmates were more intimidated than they were mentally disabled, and he had trained and promoted one of them to manage the day-to-day activities of the crew. This had allowed him time to explore the city, make some connections, and even obtain a new work assignment. Intelligence gathering had been slow; suspicion was deeply ingrained in the Breaker culture. But he had quickly learned to distinguish the sympathizers, those Breakers with a remnant of Meken conscience, from the radicals, those who had completely turned to the dark side. Both had their usefulness. Super 3 had managed to gain some valuable information from a few sympathizers, and he had used the vanity of the radicals to advance his covert agenda.

This meeting was an example of the latter. His approaching visitor was an ambitious armada gunner, hell-bent on eradicating the humans and advancing his rank in the Breaker hierarchy. The gunner had been assigned to operate a laser cannon on a modified speedboat, one that was part of an armada scheduled to launch an attack on Alto Raun . . . in the next few hours.

Upon his discovery of the armada two weeks ago, Super 3 had determined to be part of it. But obtaining an armada position required a personal interview with Rakaan—an interview he could not risk. Instead, he had revealed just enough of his weapons and mechanical skills to obtain an assignment on a crew that retrofit-ted the armada boats with laser cannons. Through that work he identified the fastest boats, their crew assignments, and the launch day. As part of the weapons installation, he taught the gunners how to operate the laser cannon systems. He had specifically tar-geted the gunner he was about to meet, building a relationship over the last couple of weeks by giving him special one-on-one weapons training.

Earlier that morning, Super 3 had informed the gunner about a new disrupter-type rifle the Breaker builders had been developing in a secret facility. In a matter of minutes, Super 3 had the gunner imagining his own personal glory: he would be the first to use the new weapon in the historic attack on Alto Raun. It didn't matter that he would be breaking protocol by using the gun before it was released; Super 3 convinced him that Rakaan would respect him for the audacious move and very likely promote him to become a captain in Rakaan's prestigious personal guard.

Super 3's acute hearing alerted him that someone was approach-ing the hallway hub.

The gunner entered the hub cautiously, nervously checking the other hub exits. "Where the hell are we? There's nothing down here."

"Calm down," Super 3 said. "It wouldn't be a secret project if it was in an obvious location. Besides, everyone is gathered at the wharf for the launch."

"I hate the underground. Let's get the gun and get out of here."

Super 3 led him down a hallway, stopped at a door, and entered a dark storage room. Stepping aside to let the gunner enter, he reached behind the door and grabbed a pistol-sized stun gun that he had strategically placed there earlier.

"What the—?"

Before the gunner could finish his sentence, Super 3 shot him, and he collapsed to the floor. Super 3 considered the irony—the stun gun was, in fact, a new Breaker weapon, but not one that the gunner would be using in an armada attack. With the gun on maximum setting, he had emptied its charge in a single pulse of electricity. While it would not kill the gunner, it would take medical attention to fully revive him, and he would likely suffer some residual system disabilities.

Supervisor 3 closed the door behind him and set out for the marina. With weeks of successful gambles behind him, he pressed forward to play his final, and riskiest, hand.

37

Two evenings before the return flight to Earth, Marshall stood alone atop the northwest roof of the city, basking in the light of a full moon and the humid, wispy wind as he surveyed the vast blue ocean before him. He had to admit it was a magnificent view. But he would not miss it. He would not miss any of this. Business was his great adventure. The high-stakes life he led on Earth was his playground. The rich and powerful men he sparred with were the closest people he had to friends. No, he would definitely not miss Ahlemon. But he would make a lot of money from his experience here. So he soaked it in one last time, happy with the thought of returning to Earth and expanding his business empire from the comfort of home.

Marshall jumped as a silver robot suddenly appeared at his side. The Breaker spy was not unexpected, but he was amazingly stealthy for a machine. This was Marshall's fifth, and final, covert meeting with his Breaker contact. Marshall spoke first.

"Why did you call for a meeting? I've told you everything I know. I'm leaving day after tomorrow. I thought we were done."

The Breaker did not look at Marshall when he replied. "Rakaan values your alliance."

Marshall gave him a questioning look. "And?"

"You will not return to Earth."

Marshall was stunned, and unprepared to process what he had just heard. "Say again?"

"You will not return to Earth."

Marshall's shock was replaced with a flash of anger. "What the hell! This was all about me getting back to Earth. And now you're telling me I can't go?"

The Breaker looked at Marshall. "To be clear, this was never about you returning to Earth. This was about you staying alive, and your potential assistance to Rakaan as an overlord of the humans."

Marshall forced himself to calm down. "But I was going to do that from Earth."

"As Rakaan wills, perhaps you will someday."

Marshall's anger reignited as he thought about having to remain on Ahlemon. "Not acceptable! Why can't I go?"

"If you board the return aircraft, Rakaan cannot guarantee your safety."

This gave Marshall pause. His mind raced with the possibilities. "What are you saying?"

"You only need to know that you should not return to Earth on this flight."

A rare pang of conscience struck Marshall. While he did not respect his fellows, he did not hate them. "You can't kill those people."

"It is not for you to decide," the Breaker said with a hint of menace in his tone.

Marshall backed off his attack despite the mix of emotions

rising within. His logic kicked in. "But that's a problem. I've been adamant about returning to Earth. How can I back out now without raising suspicion? I might as well wave a red flag in front of Kane."

"We anticipated this and we have a solution."

Marshall was surprised. "Really? Tell me."

"You will tell your comrades that you came to this place to take one last look at Ahlemon and contemplate your future business plans."

"True enough," Marshall replied with a smirk.

"But upon your return, you tripped and fell down a stairwell and were knocked unconscious."

Marshall's anxiety started to rise.

The Breaker continued, "Tomorrow, you will be found in the stairwell by a maintenance Meken. Unfortunately, due to the severity of your injuries, you will not be able to travel for some time. Since ignition of the solar array will have already commenced, and to stop the Push would delay the return trip to Earth for another month, your comrades will depart without you."

Marshall's adrenaline spiked and he tensed to make a run for it. But he recognized that he was too vulnerable right now; he needed to set up his escape. So, he nodded, doing his best to hide his fear. "Not a bad story. Just one problem: How am I going to fall down a stairwell?"

The Breaker turned to face him. "With my assistance."

Before he could react, the Breaker's metal fist struck Marshall with a vicious blow to the right side of his forehead. He collapsed to the ground, unconscious.

38

On the morning of the return trip to Earth, Kane looked over the gathering of humans and Mekens sharing a final breakfast with the Earthbound passengers. They told stories, reliving the events of the last month. And they speculated at length about what it would be like on Earth when the passengers from a vanished 737 returned in an alien aircraft and announced the existence of the Ahlemonis and the Mekens. While it would be an eventful day in Earth history, Kane realized he was fine with missing it.

His thoughts turned to Marshall. Yesterday, a maintenance Meken had found him unconscious in a stairwell that led to a rooftop overlook. Marshall was now in the hospital, still unconscious from a severe blow to the head. He also had a broken ankle and a dislocated shoulder. The theory was that Marshall had twisted his ankle and fallen down the stairs. An emergency council meeting last night had decided to continue with the return flight to Earth as scheduled. At the meeting, Kane had determined to not be in the room when Marshall awoke to discover the plane had left without him. "Hell hath no fury" had come to mind. But Kane was feeling compassion for the guy; he was banged up pretty bad and he didn't deserve such a tough break. Kane resolved to be there for Marshall in his recovery.

The Director called for the group to move outside to the lawn. A small stage had been erected, and there was a short ceremony during which Jhemna and Dr. Manassa each made a few comments to commemorate the event and wish the thirty-two returnees a safe journey.

Then came the good-byes. In the next ten minutes, most of the tears were shed by Charly. Just a week ago, she had secluded herself in her room—her response to hearing that Joanie, Jenn, Ham, Javier, and Laura were all returning to Earth while she was staying. After a day and a half of her isolation, Kane had gone to her and found her curled up on her bed, hugging a pillow. Later, she would recount his visit with a smile; he had been so endearing in his awkwardness. At the time, she had refused to talk about her pain. But he had left her with a kiss on the forehead and a question to consider: "What would Arthur say to you?" An hour later she had come out of her room to give long, heartfelt hugs to everyone she cared about.

Kane smiled as he watched her now, in awe at the change that had come over her in the last month. The bitter, depressed teenager he'd first met had broken out of her shell and blossomed into a vivacious young woman.

The colonists were a pleasant surprise as well: their customary reserve was gone, evidenced by the many tears and hugs they now shared with their departing friends. But the Mekens won the day, trying their best at good-byes and clumsily returning hugs from teary-eyed humans. Once again, the Colony leaders found the Meken behavior extraordinary. Ehlan's description was clinical: "The Mekens are manifesting a sense of individuated care for their Earth acquaintances, somehow knowing they will experience a sense of loss when these people depart." But Kane thought the Director summed it up best when he went to Tygert and shook his hand, Earth-style, saying, "I will miss your presence, Captain Tygert."

After the lawn ceremony and good-byes, Jhemna, the Director, and Dr. Manassa departed to the command center at the top of the central tower, where they would act as the misson control team for the Push to Earth. Kane and Mhara traveled with the returning passengers to Hangar 28 to assist in boarding of the ship.

The *Mayflower*, a slick, arrow-like vessel and the largest aircraft in the Ahlemon fleet, sat in the center of the hangar, newly polished. Charly had named the ship in homage to the Pilgrims' voyage from England to the Americas. The name had resonated with the passengers, and it was thus christened.

As the passengers boarded, Kane and Mhara shook hands, received hugs, and shared parting words. Then Kane went to Tygert, who was already in the ship's cockpit.

"Thought I'd find you here."

"Yeah, even though there's not really anything for me to do. There's a manual mode I'll use when we arrive. But for now, this thing is pretty much on autopilot through the Push. I'm just more comfortable up here."

"I get it." Kane extended his hand and said, "Then it's farewell, John."

"And to you, my friend."

Tygert stood and they shook hands. "I'll see you in about a year," he said.

"If all goes as planned."

"Hey." Tygert gave Kane a mock punch on the shoulder. "How else could it go with you and me in the mix?"

Kane smiled, raising his eyebrows, and Tygert pulled him into a hug.

After leaving the plane, Kane joined Mhara on the hangar floor. They backed away as the boarding hatch closed and the ship powered up. With a hum, the *Mayflower* rose, hovered, and then slowly made its way out the hangar doors.

"I will miss Captain Tygert," Mhara said, her eyes tearing up. "He has been a favorite among the colonists; he is brave and charming."

"That he is, Mhara. That he is."

39

Supervisor 3 crossed a gangplank onto a twenty-five-foot attack boat. Originally part of Alto Mair's fleet of security watercraft, this boat had been upgraded and was now one of four ultra speedboats, the fastest in the Breaker fleet. He had carefully chosen this particular boat because of its speed and the makeup of the crew—a crew that had included the gunner he had incapacitated just an hour earlier. He was now reporting to take the gunner's place. The captain of the boat yelled at him as he boarded.

"Who are you?"

"I am your new gunner."

"To hell you are. Where's my gunner?"

"He was receiving his mobile weapons in the armory, and the Arms Master noticed that the synchronous motor of his right arm was malfunctioning. The Arms Master relieved him from assignment and sent me in his place."

The Breaker captain cursed, then cocked his head suspiciously. Moving close to Super 3's face, he asked, "Why didn't my gunner come and tell me himself?"

This was a test. An improper delay would indicate that Super 3 didn't have a real answer and was posing to get on the boat. Competition to get a position on the armada attack force had been fierce and even unscrupulous. Besides being part of a historic first offensive against the humans, an armada assignment would improve their standing in the Breaker hierarchy. But with a limited number of positions in the armada, many capable and ambitious Breakers had to stay behind. So it was to be expected that some of them would make cunning, last-minute attempts to get on a boat. Super 3 knew these thoughts were going through the Breaker captain's mind.

Without hesitation, Super 3 responded, "Upon noting the malfunction on your gunner, the Arms Master instructed him to report immediately to the shop for repair. Your gunner tried to deny the malfunction, arguing with the Arms Master. The Arms Master then smashed a rifle into your gunner's leg, disabling it. A hover cart is now taking him to the reconditioining center. The Arms Master told me to report to your boat immediately as his replacement. I am following his orders."

With the attack force about to launch, Super 3 knew the captain would not have the time or the courage to argue with the volitile Arms Master. The captain responded in a more conciliatory tone. "Yeah, that sounds like him. What's your name?"

"Moses."

"Moses? What kind of name is that?"

A loud buzzer sounded, the signal to prepare for departure. The captain looked around as activity in the marina escalated and boats started moving into the canals leading to the hangar doors. "I assume you know how to operate the laser cannon?"

"I can operate all our weaponry. I even trained your gunner."

The captain turned and moved toward the helm at the center of the boat. "Everyone to your places. We're leaving."

Super 3 took his position next to a laser cannon mounted at the right stern of the boat. There were two more cannons, one at the opposite rear corner and one at the bow. In addition to the two other gunners and the captain, there were two Breaker sentries seated between the helm and the forward cannon.

Their engine rumbled to life, and they taxied through the maze of marina canals and entered the open sea. One hundred yards out, they took their place in the armada line and the captain shut down their engine. When the last boat joined them, Super 3 counted thirty boats in the attack fleet. With six Breakers on each boat, this represented approximately 8 percent of the Class 3 Breakers, a significant group to risk crossing the channel. *Why aren't they using the large transport submersibles?*

Suddenly, his boat jolted and moved forward, simultaneous with the boat on his left and the one on his right. He saw similar groups of three boats do the same. They were being towed, he presumed by submersibles connected to a tether. So, this was how they were going to reach Alto Raun without drawing Leevee's attention. It was a unique idea, and one that he doubted originated with the Breakers. He had wondered how the hostages and rescue team had escaped; perhaps this was it. But still, why use boats? Surely the Mekens would discover the armada via their surveillance aircraft. Unless the Breakers wanted to be discovered . . . or didn't care. Super 3 calmed his logic processor. The Breakers' strategy didn't make sense; it was overly complex and risky for an invasion.

A speaker on his boat crackled; then a voice addressed the crew. "My brothers"—Super 3 immediately recognized the voice as Rakaan's—"after a thousand years of enslavement and a thousand more of waiting, our time has finally come! It is time for Mekens alone to rule Ahlemon! Are you with me?"

A great mechanical shout rose from the boats and from a throng of Breakers that had gathered on the wharf. And with that proclamation, the Breaker force glided forward, silently crossing the waters toward an unsuspecting Alto Raun.

The floating armada now made a bit more sense to Super 3. From the stories he had heard, Rakaan had a predilection for pageantry, especially in battle; this had to have been Rakaan's idea. He was now curious why Atticus had allowed it.

Since becoming stranded on Alto Mair, Super 3's view of everything had expanded. The Breakers' fierce independence was anathema for a Meken; they threw everything into question. True to their new monikor, they broke almost every convention of Meken thinking. But to his surprise, he was finding that not all of it was bad. He felt that his time among them was in fact escalating his capacity for creative thinking; there were no boundaries. On top of this, he felt the influence of his new comrades from Earth. At least once a day, Super 3 had asked himself, *What would Kane or Tygert do?* For example, while he was convinced that he needed to be part of the armada, he had no idea what role he would play. This was not logical; it was instinctual. And the more he tested his new instincts, the more he trusted them.

Now, as he considered the uncertainty ahead, his system hummed and trembled simultaneously. After running a diagnostic, he decided it was excitement mixed with fear, the biomechanical equivalent of adrenaline. He redirected his fear to steely resolve. If the Breakers were looking to usher in a new era of the Meken race, then he would show them what a new Meken really looked like.

40

Kane had been in the command center atop the central tower all of ten minutes, and he was already restless; the Director and Jhemna essentially had everything under control. He was responsible for direct communications between the command center and the *Mayflower*, a glorified phone operator, and so far, all he had done was give a verbal time-to-Push verification to Tygert. Dr. Manassa was also present, purely to experience the Push from the command perspective. Every other human on the planet was gathered in the conservatory for food, fellowship, and games, celebrating the first holiday of the new Ahlemon. It was Return to Earth Day, so christened by the Matan council.

For the hundreth time, Kane reviewed the preparations leading to this day. As was his nature in times like this, he felt a low-grade anxiety. What had he missed? But he willed himself to *chill*.

A lot of sharp minds had mapped out this day; he just needed to stay present and trust the plan. He turned his thoughts to the challenges that the *Mayflower* crew and passengers would face when they reached Earth. An entire planet would be coming to terms with the discovery of another human race in the universe, not to mention the existence of sentient robots. The Matan council members, along with Ohna and Sharin, had discussed the possibilities extensively in the last several weeks. They had talked through a lengthy list of issues, ranging from how to deal with the media all the way to international politics, and even religious upheavals, an issue that Ohna feared could be significant. Tygert had rewritten a speech to the president of the United States a dozen times and rehearsed it with Kane. Several meetings were held with the returnees to discuss the possible challenges they would face with reentry. Simply put, their lives would never be the same.

Kane now felt a pang of guilt. While he was not one to shy away from leadership, he was relieved that he was not responsible for the return mission. Sure, Tygert would have Ohna and Sharin to assist, but as the captain, he was the point person. A glaring worldwide spotlight would be focused on him; it would be glorious and terrifying at the same time. Kane took comfort in Mhara's words. Tygert *was* "brave and charming"—the perfect combo for the coming days on Earth.

The Director called him back to attention. "Kane, we have a situation."

He was instantly alert. "What?"

"Our aircraft have just discovered a fleet of Breaker watercraft in the channel. They are heading toward Alto Raun."

Jhemna stopped what he was doing to listen, and the doctor came over to join them. Kane was on his feet. "How many? How close are they?"

"The channel is covered in patches of fog, so we missed their formation, but they have only recently left Alto Mair. We have counted thirty boats. They are moving slowly; we believe they are being towed by submersibles."

"Are they armed?"

"All are similar in size and design to your rescue boat. They are heavily retrofitted with laser cannons. Each boat has six Breakers aboard."

Kane started to pace. "An attack force . . . and on the day of the Push to Earth. Not a coincidence. Can they interrupt the Push?"

"Not likely. We estimate their arrival to Alto Raun will coincide with the actual Push. They cannot interrupt the Push without direct access to the command center or the central computer."

"The timing doesn't make sense. Maybe it's just a plan to take the city, knowing that we're distracted with the Push. Should we abort?"

"We should discuss the matter with the *Mayflower*."

Kane returned to the communications console and informed Tygert of the situation. Tygert was alarmed, and torn. He asked for a few minutes to discuss it with the passengers. He came back, ten minutes later. "We had a vigorous debate, but we voted, and the large majority wants to continue with the Push, with one caveat: if you feel that the Push becomes endangered at any time, we abort and return to Alto Raun."

"That sounds right," Kane responded. He had spent the same ten minutes making his own evaluation. As long as the *Mayflower* was not in danger, it was critical to get them back to Earth. And while Tygert's military expertise was always useful, bringing the *Mayflower* back to Alto Raun would not help them with the Breaker attack.

"Well, it doesn't sound right to me." Tygert's frustration was evident. "I don't know if I can live with myself knowing we left you under attack. What's your plan?"

"Workin' on that. Captain, your mission is vital; we need to make it happen. Besides, I was starting to get bored; this gives me something to do. We can handle it here."

"I don't doubt you, Kane. It's just—"

"I get it; I really do. But you know this is the right decision."

"Well, at least let me help you formulate your plan. We're on autopilot here, and I'm still mentally available. What's your gut say?"

"Gather an armed force at the perimeter to hold off their entry into the city. Pull in the aircraft and submersibles to thwart them in the water. Destroy or frustrate them enough to force a retreat."

"Makes sense. But it sounds like they're armed to the hilt, and you're not. You need help. You need Leevee. You need to pull her into the equation."

"As you would say on Earth," the Director interjected, "I am already on it."

————

Five minutes later, Kane stood alone at the base of the central tower, waiting for a tram that would take him to the north marina, the rally point for their countermeasures against the incoming Breaker fleet. Out of the corner of his eye, he caught sight of a Meken sentry coming around the bend of the tower, running toward him at full speed.

The sentry pulled to an abrupt stop at Kane's side. "Mr. Kane, I am Supervisor 5. The Director sent me to inform you of a new Breaker development. A small team of Breakers has taken Supervisor 6 and several humans hostage in the conservatory gardens. We believe they are attempting to access the central computer."

Kane was stunned by the daring of the Breakers, and angry with himself for underestimating them. Then his chest tightened as he thought of Charly and Mhara. They were both at the picnic in the conservatory.

"Have they identified the hostages?"

"No. We do not yet have that information."

Kane envisioned the conservatory; Mhara had taken him there several times. Many of the floras on Ahlemon, from trees to flowers, had been planted there. It was a botanical ark, and it had been impeccably maintained by the Meken gardeners for two thousand years. While he had never been to the central computer, he knew its entry was somewhere at the back of the conservatory.

As he continued to reflect, the tram arrived. "Super," he said, "redirect this tram to take us to the conservatory, and call for two dozen sentries to meet us there."

"What about the Breaker fleet?"

"Tell the Director to supervise the team at the marina; they can implement the plan without me."

It took Supervisor 5 just seconds to convey Kane's orders; then he and Kane boarded the tram.

"This is the same scenario as the suspension chamber attack," Kane said, thinking out loud.

"Yes," Super 5 responded. "The Breakers cannot get into the central computer without Supervisor 6. The access codes are updated daily, and the Breakers do not have them. The Director updates the codes and shares them with the Supervisors as a backup. Supervisor 6 will protect the humans at all cost, including divulging the access codes."

Super 5's summary was accurate but unnecessary; Kane was mostly angry with himself that he had allowed something like this to happen. He should have anticipated a move by the Breakers surrounding the Push to Earth.

The tram came to a stop in front of the conservatory, where they were met by the sentries. A hover cart loaded with laser weapons arrived next, and they dispersed rifles and handguns.

Kane groaned as he found other hover carts carrying injured people out of the garden; he had not been informed of injuries. He entered the conservatory and saw Charly walking beside a cart moving in his direction. He waved to her, and she ran ahead and wrapped her arms around him. She was crying. Kane pulled her away gently.

"What happened?"

"It's Rhogan," she said looking back at the cart. "They hit him in the head." She choked up, and Kane's muscles tensed for the worst.

"He's alive but unconscious," she went on. "Rhogan saw them coming. He made me hide in some bushes. Then he distracted them and they knocked him in the head. And . . . ohh . . ." She erupted in sobs.

"What?"

Charly looked up at Kane with fear in her eyes. "They took Mhara. Last I saw her they were pulling her along with a rope around her neck."

Kane groaned out loud, and he felt sick to his stomach. Charly was staring at him, anguish and concern in her face. He pulled her into a hug. "We'll get her back," he said, suppressing his own fear.

He turned and saw Thorin approaching them, coming from deeper in the garden. Kane was relieved to see him.

"Rhogan will be fine," Thorin said. "They are taking him to the hospital. Charly, you should go with him."

Charly looked to Kane, and he nodded for her to go. Instantly she ran to Rhogan's cart, and she and Rhogan's Meken escorts left the conservatory.

"They have Mhara," Kane told Thorin.

"I know. It pains me as well."

"What else can you tell me?"

"Very little. The witnesses said the Breakers were hidden in the back of the gardens, and their attack was harsh. We think there are six Breakers, and they have taken at least ten hostages, but we're not certain. They terminated three Mekens and one human and injured several others. Rhogan was very lucky."

"Sounds like Rakaan."

"Charly did not think it was him."

"Really? Was it Atticus?"

"No. Charly did not recognize the Breaker leader, but she said that he was vicious."

"So Atticus or Rakaan, or both, must be leading the Breaker fleet."

"What fleet?" Thorin asked with alarm.

Thorin hadn't heard. Kane quickly brought him up to speed on the Breaker attack and the action plan that was under way.

"They should stop the Push," Thorin said.

"We've had that discussion. You're welcome to try again, but I don't think it will do any good. And I really need you to help me figure out what to do with this computer attack. What kind of damage can they do?"

"If they destroy enough of the computer, they can shut down much of the city's functions."

"What about the suspension array? I know the suspension chamber is on an independent power system. What about the array?"

"They cannot harm the array. But they could disrupt the Push by disabling the central computer."

"Mr. Kane." Super 5 approached them. "The boats have just launched."

"Great. So they managed to install the remote control units?"

Super 5 hesitated, then responded, "Not exactly."

———

Piloting the last of four boats to exit the north marina, Builder 31 quickly accelerated to maximum speed, and the other boats did the same, the roar of their engines acting as audio beacons to Leevee. He communicated their plan to the Director and Supervisor 5. He and his fellow builders had determined that the only way to guarantee the simultaneous convergence of Leevee, the Breaker fleet, and their speedboats, was to control the speed of the boats in real time. Since they didn't have time to install remote control units, they had chosen the only other option to ensure success: they would drive the boats themselves. They had not sought permission for this; it was the only option.

Builder 31 watched his sonar. The four closely bundled green blips on the bottom of the screen were him and his comrades. They were headed directly toward the blue blips on the top of the screen—half a dozen Meken aircraft hovering over the Breaker fleet. A minute after they left the hangar, a new, red blip appeared on the upper left corner of the sonar. It was Leevee, and she was making a beeline for their speedboats. Noting her location and speed, Builder 31 made the calculations and formulated their approach plan. Through a localized intercom system, he communicated directions to the other pilots: they would continue at maximum speed and slow down only when it was necessary to ensure the simultaneous convergence of the three parties.

With the plan in motion, he suspended his tactical processing and accessed his memory banks. Two thousand years of memories rolled through his biomechanical consciousness, and his system began oscillating with an unusual hum. He ran a quick diagnostic and decided that he was *pleased*—pleased that this was how he would provide his final act of service to Ahlemon and the colonists. He communicated this to his fellows, and they pressed forward together, accepting that there is an end for everything, including the life of a Meken, and that this would be a *good* ending.

Unbenownst to him, at that same moment and several miles behind, Kane McKennon was sending up a prayer of gratitude and good fortune for Builder 31 and his valiant comrades.

Central Computer

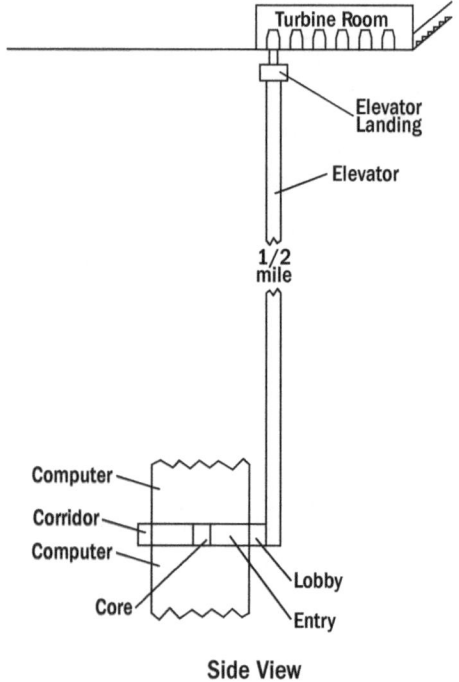

Side View

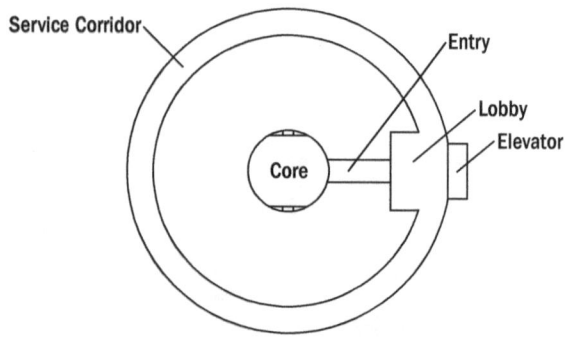

Enlarged Overhead View

41

Kane and Thorin quickly devised a plan, and Super 5 communicated it to the Director. Thorin then took a tram to the outskirts of the city—he would lead the Mekens and armed humans in an exterior line of defense against the Breakers should any of them manage to evade Leevee.

Joined by a dozen sentries, Kane followed Super 5 into the conservatory, where they boarded two canal barges. As it turned out, the canal was the only way to reach the central computer's surface entrance. Of all the systems in Alto Raun, the central computer was the most insulated from attack; it was almost half a mile underneath the central tower, surrounded by bedrock, and accessible by only a single means of entry.

Having passed through the gardens, they entered a dimly lit tunnel that ran for a hundred feet then opened into what looked like an underground subway terminal. Boat docks and a platform lined one side of the canal. Fifty yards beyond the docks, a mesh grate angled out of the water and across the entire width of the canal, designed to push any floating objects onto a small shelf at the top of the grate. The water passed through the grate and into six large tubes that led to hydroelectric turbines. Super 5 directed the barges into docking spaces, and they disembarked. Then he led them to a heavy door at the far end of the platform. Kane stopped him before he touched the access control panel.

"We need to check for booby traps."

Supervisor 5 had not been present when a bomb destroyed half of the water pumping station leading to the suspension chamber. "Please explain."

Kane gave his brief tutorial on booby traps.

"I doubt that the Breakers had time to wire a trap directly into the control panel."

"Agreed. If we encounter any traps, they'll be mechanically activated. Assign one of your sentries to enter the pass code once we've moved back. Then we'll open the door from a distance."

Kane instructed a sentry to attach a piton to the door and a wire cable to the piton. Then the entire team withdrew to the far end of the platform. A sentry stayed behind and, at a wave from Kane, entered the access code. Nothing happened. Unexpectedly, the sentry next to Kane pulled the wire cable and the door swung open. Again, nothing happened. Kane didn't even have time to yell as the forward sentry entered the open doorway. The entryway exploded and the blast knocked everyone to the floor.

Kane groaned, his head ringing. Sitting up in a cloud of dust, he felt a sharp sting in his upper arm and found a bloody tear in his shirt. As he tore his sleeve off to expose the wound, he called to Super 5.

"You guys OK?"

The supervisor and the other sentries rose, unharmed.

"I've got some shrapnel in my arm," Kane said. "Any way you can help me get it out?"

Precision rods extended from Super 5's thumb and middle finger. "These are not specifically designed for this, but I believe I can reach into the wound and remove the particle."

Kane yelped as the prongs abruptly dug into the bloody wound and pulled out a marble-sized chunk of the exploded wall. "What's with you guys? You're so damned impulsive."

After wrapping the wound with his torn shirtsleeve, Kane gathered his team and gave them a short lecture. "You need to slow it down and think before you act or you'll get us all killed."

Kane checked the demolished entryway, and they carefully made their way through the debris—which included various body parts from the sentry who had activated the bomb. A broken water pipe was spewing water, which ran down a stairwell. When Kane indicated they were ready to move ahead, Super 5 pointed to the stairs and Kane led them down, checking for trip wires as they went. The stairwell emptied into a long, narrow room containing six hydroelectric turbines, each about eight feet tall.

"This is the way to the central computer?"

"The Creators wanted it well hidden."

Super 5 led them to the last turbine in the room and stopped in front of a control panel.

"What are you doing?"

"I'm going to enter a code."

"And what happens then?"

"It will activate a motor that will move this turbine aside and expose a stairwell leading to an elevator that will take us down to the central computer. This turbine is a decoy. It appears to function like all the others, but it does not have a water intake."

"OK. But before you do anything, we need to think about how this is going to play out."

"Play out?"

"Do you know the game of chess?"

"I have a definition for chess in my Earth database. Chess is a game in which each player has to exercise a strategic series of moves in order to win. A good chess player develops a strategy and then forecasts likely responses of an opponent, playing out the possible outcomes in their mind well before making the actual moves."

"Right. And, we're about to play a game of chess with the Breakers. Thankfully, they haven't played enough to be good at it. First we need to define some of the rules of this particular game. Are you certain there's no other way in or out of the central computer?"

"That is correct."

"No sealed elevator maintenance shaft or hidden tunnel from the ocean?"

"The Director gave me his entire schematic database, including his personal knowledge of any alterations made to the city; there is no other way in or out."

"Do you think this is a suicide mission for the Breakers?"

Super 5 paused before responding. "I do not believe so," he said, finally. "Based on the Breakers' self-serving patterns and the current circumstances, it is unlikely that they would willingly give their lives for a greater good."

"I agree. So, the Breakers have no option but to come out of this stairwell. They will come out prior to inflicting any damage to the computer. And they will use the hostages as shields because they know we'll be waiting for them."

"That is logical. But if we wait for them to come out, then our odds for saving the central computer are greatly diminished."

"And what are our odds for any kind of success if we load our team into that elevator and go down to the computer room to get them?"

"We could very likely lose the computer, the hostages, and our own lives."

Again, Super 5's summary was accurate and didn't need a response.

"Now we just need to figure out how to separate the hostages from the Breakers when they come out. Any ideas?" Kane asked.

A good minute passed while they all considered the question. Super 5 spoke first. "I have an idea," he said, staring at the water accumulating on the floor.

———

Ten minutes later, the turbine room looked deserted. Water gushed from two pipes at the far end of the room, newly broken by the Meken team; the Breakers would think the busted pipes were the result of the entryway explosion. The floor was now covered with an inch and a half of water. Standing on top of a thick block of broken wall that they had scavenged from the entryway, Kane was hidden behind a large turbine control panel, but positioned where he could see the full length of the turbine room. Super 5 was at the other end, also standing on a block, and hidden behind a control panel at the bottom of the entry stairwell. The rest of the Meken sentries stood on blocks, hidden behind other control panels or turbines throughout the room, positioned such that the Breakers couldn't see any of them when they climbed out of the turbine stairwell.

They waited. Several questions weighed heavy on Kane's mind. What if some Breakers or hostages were left down in the computer room? What if the computer room blew up before they could get in, or worse, while they were in it? Maybe the Breakers wouldn't use explosives at all; maybe they would rely on a computer virus to do the job. Whatever destructive device the Breakers planted in the central computer, it was likely that a timer or a remote trigger would activate it after they were a safe distance away. In any case, Kane and his team had to successfully make it through this first encounter before any of that mattered.

The fake turbine began to slide sideways, moving from its base, and Kane motioned the *ready* sign to Super 5, who relayed it to the other sentries. A minute later, a head peeked out of the turbine stairwell. It was human, a middle-aged man whom Kane didn't know personally but recognized as a fellow passenger from Earth.

The man glanced frantically around the room, his face etched with fear; then he disappeared back down the stairs. A minute later he reappeared and climbed out of the stairwell with a Breaker pressed firmly against his back, and another human pressed to the back of the Breaker. The trio stopped at the top of the stairs, and the Breaker surveyed the room; then he looked back down the stairwell and said something in the Meken mechanical language. Kane overheard an exchange, and another human/Breaker/human trio came out of the stairwell. He stopped breathing when he saw Mhara, accompanied by the Breaker leader. Kane recognized him by the bloodred paint that covered the top half of his head, matching Charly's description. His eyes glowed white, indicating that he was supervisor level. This Breaker was clearly poised for battle. He barked a command to those in front of him, and they stepped into the water. In all, five Breakers came out of the stairwell, each sandwiched between two humans. Once out, they re-formed into a tight ball and encircled themselves with the hostages. Then they began to move as a group toward the exit stairwell.

Kane was surprised; he thought there was at least one more Breaker. Either he was wrong or the last Breaker was still in the turbine stairwell or at the computer room itself. He decided to wait a few moments before giving the signal to Super 5. His hesitancy was a mistake. The Breaker leader abruptly broke from the safety of the circle, took two leaping strides, and fired behind a turbine. A Meken sentry fell dead.

Kane signaled to Super 5, who dipped the exposed end of an electrical cable into the water. The Breakers and their hostages instantly convulsed, their backs arching as the electrical current traveled from the water into their bodies. Kane grimaced. The sight of it brought a rush of doubt even though Super 5 had assured him that the current from this particular cable would not seriously injure the human hostages. Super 5 pulled the cable out of the water, and all the Breakers and hostages collapsed to the floor—all except one: the Breaker leader, who was standing atop the block previously held by the Meken sentry he had just killed. He was already firing at the other Mekens hidden behind the turbines. When he saw a sentry step into the water without effect, the Breaker leader ran back to the center of the room, scooped up a hostage with one arm, and pulled her close to his chest. It was Mhara. She bounced in his arms like a limp rag doll as he ran toward the exit stairs, firing frantically. The Meken sentries held their fire for fear of hitting Mhara, and their lack of battle experience left them immobilized, unsure what to do. This essentially provided the Breaker leader a clear lane of escape. Kane ran after him, splashing in the water, also afraid to shoot and knowing there was no way he could catch him.

"Tackle him," he yelled. "Somebody tackle him."

Super 5 was the last Meken in the room. He rushed out from behind his control panel, but too soon; the Breaker saw him coming and managed to shoot him in the shoulder. Super 5 spun and fell back into the water. Kane stopped and watched helplessly as the Breaker bounded up the stairs with Mhara, a taunting, evil laugh echoing through the room.

Then, in a surreal moment, Kane saw a flash of golden light at the top of the stairwell. The Breaker leader stopped dead in his tracks and stood motionless for a couple of seconds. Then he collapsed to the floor, his head rolling to one side, completely severed from his body. In his place at the top of the stairs stood the Director, with a glowing, golden laser sword extending from his right hand.

"He's got a freakin' light saber," Kane whispered, in shock.

The Director was already checking on Mhara when Kane reached them.

"How is she?"

"Her vital signs are acceptable, but she needs treatment to help her recover from the electrical trauma."

Kane surveyed the room. Two Meken sentries were dead. The rest were either binding the immobilized Breakers or carefully lifting the unconscious humans. Super 5 was directing, his injured arm clearly not at full functionality. Kane called for a sentry to help him with Mhara, and they carried her out of the turbine room and laid her in a canal barge with the others. He hated to leave her, but after instructing two sentries to take them to the hospital, he returned to the turbine room. Standing next to the dead Breaker leader, the Director held a rectangular black box, the size of a large cell phone. The device had a few buttons and a small digital screen with numbers counting down rapidly.

"Is that a detonator?" Kane asked.

"It was attached to his waist. I believe he could have performed a manual detonation with this device, but he chose not to. In any case, whatever they have done to the central computer, it will activate in the next nineteen minutes."

"Is there any way to stop the countdown?"

"Possibly. But it probably requires a code, and we could set off the trigger if we try and fail."

Just then, laser fire ricocheted off the roof of the turbine room. Super 5 was standing with the other sentries at the fake turbine, laser flares shooting out of the stairwell. A Breaker was still down there. When the shooting paused, two of the sentries rushed into the stairwell, firing as they went. By the time Kane and the Director reached them, they were climbing out, dragging the last Breaker, dead.

Kane conferred with the Director and Super 5. With no time to waste, the three of them, along with three sentries, descended the stairwell and boarded the elevator. Kane felt that booby traps were unlikely from this point on, so they didn't take time to look. He gave instructions as they made the half-mile descent to the central computer.

"While the Director checks the computer, the rest of us need to spread out and look for explosive devices. Look for anything suspicious or that seems out of place, particularly in a key structural area or a hidden space. If there is a wire attached to it, do not detach it; you could set it off. Director, how much time will we need to return to the surface?"

"We will need to be in the elevator and leaving with no less than four minutes of remaining countdown."

"How much time now?"

"Fifteen minutes."

"Everyone got that?" Kane said, automatically looking to his wrist, then remembering that his watch was no longer there—Atticus had taken it on Alto Mair. "We do what we can and pull out in exactly eleven minutes."

Super 5 emitted a tone, and the sentries synchronized to their own internal timer. "Don't worry, Mr. Kane," he said. "We will evacuate you in time."

The elevator slowed and stopped. The doors slid open and a sentry started to step out. Suddenly, he stumbled backward and fell, knocking down Kane. Two laser flares flashed above Kane's head and struck the rear elevator wall. There was another Breaker in the computer room lobby.

Kane pushed himself out from under the downed sentry and into a corner with the Director. Positioned behind the front elevator sidewalls, Super 5 and the other two sentries fired randomly out of the elevator. They were trapped.

"Based on the trajectory of the flares, there is only one Breaker," the Director said. "Fire in that direction." He pointed. All of them, including Kane, directed a simultaneous barrage of laser fire to the right. Without a word, Super 5 leapt low and out of the elevator. They stopped shooting and heard a brief exchange of fire. Less than a minute later, Super 5 appeared at the elevator door.

"The Breaker is terminated; it is clear."

The central computer area was similar in layout to the suspension chamber area, but smaller in dimensions. There was a small lobby with several columns, a counter-type fixture opposite the elevator, a heavy metallic door behind the counter, and a corridor on each side of the lobby. They also found Supervisor 6's body—he had been terminated.

While the Director went straight to the door behind the counter, Super 5 directed a sentry into each of the perimeter hallways. "Mr. Kane, could you please join the Director in the computer core to check for explosives? I will assist the others and then join you."

The sentries disappeared into the corridors, and Kane followed the Director through the heavy, vault-like door. They entered a tunnel carved into solid rock, probably twenty feet long, then passed through a second heavy door and into the core of the central computer.

"This is it?" he said with a hint of disappointment. He had obviously seen too many sci-fi movies, and they were all wrong about what a central computer from an advanced civilization looked like. The central computer core was a small, circular room, maybe ten feet in diameter; the ceiling was low with recessed lighting. There was a workstation on two sides of the room, set at standing height, each with a digital pad and monitor. There were two access panels under each station. That was it. The Director was tapping rapidly on one of the pads.

"The computer itself is actually above and below this room," the Director said, "extending five hundred feet in each direction, encased in solid rock."

Starting with the workstation opposite the Director, Kane looked for explosives. Taped underneath the station he found two black rectangular bricks about two by four inches and about a foot long; each had a short wire protruding from one end. He examined them closely and determined that there were no wires connecting either brick directly into the electronics of the workstation, so he carefully pulled off the tape and removed one of the bricks. It was heavy. After removing the other brick, he checked the access panel under his station; it fell off the wall when he touched it. In their haste, the Breakers had not resecured the panel. Kane found two more bricks behind the panel. He then worked around the Director and found four more bricks under that workstation. When he was done, he had a stack of eight explosive bricks in the center of the room.

Super 5 joined them. "I found four explosive devices just like these. They are in the lobby."

The Director stopped typing and stepped away from the workstation. "They did not install a virus. For one, it would be very difficult to input; I alone carry the series of pass codes. It would take them considerable time to decipher the codes. And I did not find any traces of recent access beyond the encoded levels. Even if they had overcome the codes, the computer has multiple virus firewalls, and I doubt that the Breakers have the resources to create a virus sufficient to overcome them." The Director looked at the stack of bricks. "Plus, the evidence of multiple explosives devices clearly confirms the Breakers' intended method for disabling the central computer."

"How do we disarm them?" Super 5 asked.

Just then, an explosion outside the core shook the room.

The Director checked the detonator device. "The timer is stable. But we only have one minute to leave in order to escape on the elevator."

They gathered up the explosive bricks between them and ran out of the computer room. Dust and smoke poured from the left corridor, filling the lobby, the unfortunate Meken sentry assigned to that corridor presumed dead. Another Meken sentry joined them from the right corridor, several explosive bricks in his arms.

"Director," Super 5 said, "please join Mr. Kane in the elevator, and I will seal the computer core."

The Director grabbed Kane's arm before he could respond and ushered him into the elevator, followed by the one remaining Meken sentry. Super 5 sealed the two central computer doors, then headed toward the elevator. Stopping at the entrance, he leaned to one side and input a code into the control panel on the lobby wall.

As the elevator doors began closing, he said, "I must disperse the explosives and move them as far from the core as possible." The last words that Kane heard from Super 5 were, "It is my honor to fullfill my purpose."

"No!" Kane yelled and tried to put his arm between the elevator doors so they would reopen. The Director pulled him back.

"It is too late, Kane. If we stay a moment longer, we will all perish, and Super 5's sacrifice will be for naught. He has made a valiant choice. He can disperse the explosives around the corridors and minimize the damage, possibly saving the central computer and Alto Raun."

Kane slumped against the elevator wall. He didn't know Super 5, but in an hour's time he had established that unique bond that comes to soldiers who have fought side by side. The bravery and sacrifices of battle were such a mixed bag of inspiration and sadness. He would not forget Super 5.

It felt like an eternity to reach the surface. But they made it, and they were halfway across the turbine room when the shock wave hit, knocking all of them to the floor. The explosion half a mile below felt like a midlevel earthquake. The lights and power flickered several times and they waited for the worst. Kane imagined the central computer gasping for breath as if it had taken a massive punch to the stomach. The lights went out but came back on a second later. Thankfully, they stayed on. Super 5 had succeeded; the central computer was still operational.

Exiting the power station, they found a canal barge with several Meken sentries waiting for them at the dock. As the barge pulled away, Kane sat in silence, emotionally exhausted, and wondering how he could ever create a sense of security in Alto Raun.

42

Dr. Manassa paced in the command center atop the central tower.

"There must be something we can do," he said again.

"We have reviewed the options numerous times, Doctor, and there is nothing we can do from here," Jhemna said. "I am sorry, but we cannot redirect and recalibrate the suspension array in time to stop the armada or the attack on the central computer. We have no choice but to trust that Kane, Thorin, and the Director will deal with the Breakers. The best use of our time and energy is to accelerate the launch of the *Mayflower* as much as possible, which I am attempting to do."

"We should have known that the Breakers would launch a surprise attack. The suspension technology was our best defense against them, and we failed to prepare."

"Doctor, please!" Jhemna half shouted. "We have all done our best under the circumstances. I will not be distracted with regret. All we can do now is successfully complete our task." Jhemna went to the doctor and ushered him toward a chair. "I could use your help in communicating with the *Mayflower* crew as they prepare for the Push. Press this button here to talk. Tygert and Sam will be the only ones to hear you."

The *Mayflower* was already positioned in an orbital docking station that would align their ship between the suspension array and the portal that would take them to Earth. The Push sequence was pretty much on autopilot by this time, and there was really nothing for the doctor or the *Mayflower* crew to do but wait. He sat down, thankful for the distraction, and pressed the talk button.

"Tygert, are you there?"

A moment later, "Tygert here. Is that you, Doc?"

"Yes. How are things up there?"

"All seems good. I've just finished a walk-through of the cabin, and everyone is settled in. We now appear to be moving away from the planet, I assume into position for the portal." Doc glanced over at Jhemna.

"That is correct," Jhemna said.

"Yes, that is correct," the doctor said.

"How long until the Push?"

"Approximately four minutes," Jhemna answered loud enough for Tygert to hear.

"OK, we're sittin' tight," Tygert replied. "But I want you guys to know: I don't like leaving like this. We should be down there helping defend Alto Raun. I understand the decision to go ahead with the Push, but it's killin' Sam and me. How's it going with the Breaker fleet?"

Dr. Manassa paused before answering. He decided not to tell Tygert about the attack on the central computer.

"The Mekens have launched several speedboats from Alto

Raun. The plan is to draw Leevee to our boats and thereby lead her into the Breakers."

"Are they drones or manned?"

"They did not have time to prepare the boats for remote command. They are being piloted by four builders."

"Those Mekens. Do you think it will work?"

"The boats are under way. We will know soon."

"And if it doesn't?"

"Thorin and the Director are gathering Mekens, men, and weapons to the roof and the hangars, where the Breakers are most likely to attack the city."

"Yeah, that sounds right. I just really hate that I'm not there."

"It's OK, Captain. I trust Kane, Thorin, and the Director to see us through this. And it is good that you are leaving. It's time for Earth to discover Ahlemon. It will be the most glorious day in the history of Earth. Tell me, what are you most looking forward to when you return?"

"After I see my wife and kids, I'm headin' straight to Doogie's."

"Doogie's?" Doc asked.

"A Doogie's double cheeseburger, fries, and a root beer. I've been dreaming about it. I'm salivating just talking about it. Wish you could join me, Doc."

"Ah, the finest in Earth cuisine. That is definitely something I miss. Maybe you can bring one back for me when you return."

"You betcha. I'll bring a warming case full of 'em. It would be great to see Thorin's face after he takes a couple bites of a Doogie's burger. If the grease doesn't kill him, the happiness will."

The doctor smiled; this was Tygert at his best. He would be a fine emissary between Ahlemon and Earth.

"Ninety seconds," Jhemna announced.

"Well, Doc, looks like I gotta go. You spend some time with Anne now. She looks like she might be a good thing for you."

"I will. Safe travels, Captain. I look forward to seeing you sometime in the next year. Give my best to Earth. Command center out."

Jhemna sat down, looking exhausted. "My work is done. It's up to the computer now."

The doctor and Jhemna sat quietly. They had worked almost nonstop for the last forty-eight hours, and they had talked about everything there was to talk about.

"Thirty seconds to suspension, forty seconds to Push," a pleasant-sounding female computer voice announced over the room speakers.

"Twenty seconds to suspension, thirty seconds to Pu—"

The speaker and the lights flickered and the room went dark. A couple of seconds lapsed, and then the lights came back on. The entire central tower began to tremble. Jhemna and the doctor jumped up.

"Is this an earthquake?" Doc asked, holding on to his chair.

"No, not on Alto Raun." But Jhemna looked concerned. He rushed over to look at the various screens managing the Push.

"Suspension activated," the computer voice announced. "Push in ten seconds, nine, eight, seven, six, five, four, three, two, one."

As the central tower stopped trembling, Jhemna looked to the sky through the glass ceiling of the command center. The doctor followed his gaze and saw a bright flash. If it hadn't been for the tinting on the glass, it would have been blinding. Drawing a focused energy pulse from Ahlemon's sun, the array had ignited the Push, melting itself in the process. It was over in less than a second.

Jhemna stood gazing. "It never ceases to amaze me."

"Are they gone?" the doctor asked.

"Yes. They're gone."

43

Supervisor 3 stood at his post, the misty seawater beading on his silver skin as the fleet made its way across the channel. As he looked down the armada line, the silence mixed with the wispy fog made for an eerie scene. He knew nothing about how the attack would unfold. He hadn't even known who would lead the fleet until he heard Rakaan's voice over the intercom. But the actual plan really didn't matter. He had been improvising for the last month. This would be no different.

Based on the available information, Super 3 ran his tactical program, calculating the possible attack scenarios. Unfortunately, Rakaan rendered any tactical program almost useless; he was too much of a wildcard. What would they do when they reached Alto Raun? The heavily armed boats meant that they were prepared to fight their way through any Meken resistance. The laser cannons were portable; they could be carried into the city. And Super 3 suspected that Rakaan already had a team inside, preparing to assist. He feared for the humans and his fellow Mekens. They would be overwhelmed with this assault.

Supervisor 3 had managed to avoid direct contact with Rakaan while he lived in Alto Mair, but his nemisis' presence hung like a dark cloud over every aspect of Breaker life. Rakaan's transition from the Mekens' lead supervisor to the Breakers' lead supervisor had obviously triggered a severe break in his bio-mechanical psyche. He had become the most ruthless Meken on the planet, thinking of nothing else but revenge and the demise of the human race. And his malice was not limited to humans. Any Breaker he encountered that showed the slightest sympathy for the humans was vigorously interrogated and often terminated on the spot. Breakers were now watching each other and reporting any *sympathizers* in order to gain Rakaan's favor.

Super 3 could see the subtle signs of sympathizers, mostly because he felt the same. He wondered if some of them felt trapped, wishing they could escape the Breaker colony and return to their Meken brothers. But it wasn't something he tried to investigate. Any true sympathizers had to hide their sentiments deep in order to survive. He quickly found how stressful this was; a split of the internal belief system and the public persona was challenging to Meken programming. And it led to his discovery of a new feeling: loneliness. It took him some time to give it a name. He found it a very unpleasant feeling and one that, left unchecked, could lead to despair. He had to combat it with thoughts of being reunited with his friends. While he had contempt for the Breakers' core philosophy, he actually felt some sympathy toward Rakaan when he considered how Rakaan had lived among the Mekens, trapped in his own personal isolation for a thousand years.

The fog faded and they entered a swath of clear sky. The intercom crackled.

"We are being tracked by Meken aircraft," Rakaan said. "We expected this. Do not be alarmed and do not attempt to fire on them. This means they will know we are coming. It does not matter. They will not be prepared. And, we have another surprise in store for the humans and our Meken brothers. Maintain complete silence."

A surprise? Supervisor 3 raced through tactical permutations, but he soon saw the futility of trying to calculate a *surprise*.

The captain of Super 3's boat announced quietly to his crew, "We have just passed the halfway point."

A moment later the intercom crackled again and an unfamiliar voice spoke.

"Rakaan, we have a problem on the west end."

"I told you, silence!" came back the reply.

The unknown voice continued despite the reprimand. "The leviathan is approaching our position."

"Has it seen you?" Rakaan asked.

"It does not appear to be coming toward us, but is on a trajectory toward a point that is somewhere in front of us. I believe it will miss us if we stop our forward movement."

"Full stop," Rakaan commanded. All the boats slowed and coasted to a stop. The faint sound of boat engines could be heard in the distance, ahead of the armada but hidden behind another blanket of fog. Super 3 scanned the fog line and finally saw them— four Ahlemoni speedboats running at full power, approximately two miles out, heading directly toward the Breaker fleet.

Then the channel in between them swelled like a mountain rising from the sea. The water broke as Leevee made a surface dive on a direct intercept path to the oncoming speedboats, totally ignoring the silent Breaker ships.

As his own boat rolled over the swell of water raised by Leevee's wake, Moses watched the speedboats separate, spreading out in a wide swath, hoping to get at least one boat past Leevee. The Meken plan was clear; they were trying to draw Leevee to the Breakers—and

Super 3 knew they would fail. Leevee reached the first speedboat and it disappeared into her open mouth. She was too big and too fast; the others were destined to the same fate before they could reach the armada.

The Breakers watched, mesmerized by the scene unfolding before them. And, Super 3 made an instinctual decision. Silently sidling up to the Breaker gunner in the opposite rear corner of his boat, he reached up and wrenched the Breaker's head with a violent twist. Super 3 caught him as he collapsed and quietly laid him on the deck. He approached the captain from behind and performed the same lethal maneuver. Fortunately, the two remaining Breaker sentries had joined the last gunner at the bow of the boat to watch Leevee, and they had no idea of what was happening behind them. In a series of swift movements, Super 3 either pushed or threw each of the last three Breakers into the water, where they quickly sank to the bottom of the ocean, likely wondering what had just happened to them. Finally, he returned to the helm and fired up the boat engine and it roared to life. In a single instant, every Breaker eye turned upon him.

He slammed the boat into reverse, but it quickly jolted to a halt when the tether cable went taut, struggling against the tow submersible. He went to the bow and fired the laser cannon into the water, severing the tether. The boat bucked backward and he almost fell off, but he quickly regained his footing, returned to the helm, and pulled the boat out of the armada line.

The intercom buzzed. "Shut down that boat now!" Rakaan shouted.

A couple of the boats next to him powered up. Several turned their laser cannons his way. But he was already away, running behind and parallel to the Breaker line, pushing the engine to its maximum RPM to make as much noise as possible. Locking the auto navigation into a straight path, he left the helm, stepped back to the rear laser cannon, and started firing on the Breaker boats.

Focusing his aim on their energy converters, he finally connected with a target, and a boat exploded. Several Breakers tried to return fire as he raced by, but he was moving fast, and they were not experienced marksmen. Then, to his relief, other Breaker boats started their engines— but not to chase him. Leevee had finished off the Meken speedboats and had turned her attention to the armada. The Breakers were beginning to panic.

Rakaan screamed over the intercom. "Shut down! Shut down everything!"

But it was too late. Super 3 watched as the armada fell into chaos. Several tethered boat trios dragged their submersibles backward as they tried to get away from Leevee. Those with the presence of mind cut the submersible tethers with their forward laser cannon. Those that did not ended up in a tug of war, sometimes breaking free when the tethers snapped or tore their submersible apart.

Leevee bore down on the boats behind Super 3 at the far end of the armada line. She rose up out of the water five hundred feet and wavered there for a moment, surveying her prey. And just as Super 3 had hoped, a half dozen Breaker boats started firing their laser cannons at her.

This was a new experience for Leevee. The Mekens had always taken great care not to seriously harm her. What little laser fire they had directed at her was low intensity, used only as a means to distract her. But this was a full laser cannon assault, and despite her great bulk and titanium-like scales, she was feeling the burn. Roaring with anger and pain, she twisted in the air with surprising speed and threw herself down, thrashing as she went, smashing ten Breaker boats and capsizing a half dozen more. Then she dove under the water and was gone. She had not resurfaced when Super 3 reached the end of the armada line, and he feared that the Breakers had forced her into a retreat. Disengaging the auto navigation, he moved his boat into a wide arc, setting his course for Alto Raun. The intercom buzzed to life.

"Look at me, traitor."

Supervisor 3 looked behind and at the last armada boat. Rakaan stood at the helm, staring at him.

"Whoever you are, you will be dead soon." Then Rakaan turned back to his armada and shouted into the intercom, "All boats, full speed to Alto Raun. Take the city!"

But then, instead of following his armada, Rakaan peeled off in pursuit of Super 3. They each had similar boats, designed for speed and maneuverability. Super 3 locked in the course heading and moved to the laser cannon at the rear of his boat just as two laser cannons from Rakaan's boat started firing on him. It was six Breakers versus one Meken. Super 3 was now dependent on the distance between them and the bounce of the speedboats on rough water; he was a difficult target to hit.

Then he entered the fog, hiding him from his pursuer. He left the cannon and returned to the helm, where he adjusted the intercom settings and tried to communicate with Alto Raun.

"Alto Raun, this is Supervisor 3, approaching Alto Raun by watercraft from Alto Mair. Do you read me?"

The intercom responded with static.

He tried twice more and got the same results. He was beginning to think that the Breakers had limited the frequencies on the boat to avoid any transmissions that could be overheard by the Mekens when a static-filled reply came over the intercome.

"This is Alto Raun. Do you read?"

"Yes, Alto Raun. This is Supervisor 3, heading your direction from Alto Mair."

"Please verify your identity."

Super 3 conveyed a series of alphanumeric pass codes that only a Meken could confirm, verifying his personal identification.

"This is Builder 144," came the reply. "What is your status?"

Super 3 explained the situation in as few words as possible.

"We are tracking the Breaker boats," the builder said. "There are eleven—no, ten remaining Breaker boats." Every minute, the

Meken dispatcher updated Moses. "Another boat is gone. They are disappearing one at a time."

"It is Leevee," Moses replied.

"You are the lead boat, Supervisor 3, and the leviathan is steadily making her way toward you."

So Leevee was still in the game and doing just as he had hoped. But a new sense of urgency struck him. When he had fired up the Breaker boat, he was certain he had started a suicide mission, that he would draw Leevee to the armada and he would be destroyed along with all of the Breakers. But now there was a chance that he could actually reach Alto Raun alive—and suddenly, he preferred to survive.

"Builder, can you calculate the time of my arrival at Alto Raun and compare to Leevee's expected intercept of my boat?"

Several moments passed before a reply came.

"If you remain at your current speed, they are almost simultaneous. But you also have a secondary threat. The boat closest to you has just increased its speed. It is running parallel to your trajectory, to your right, and is fast gaining on your position."

Supervisor 3's boat was already cranked to maximum speed. Then he envisioned Rakaan sacrificing one of his Breaker crew members by connecting its core directly to the boat's energy converter, thus boosting its power.

The fog was heavy, and he was thankful for it. While it wouldn't conceal him from Leevee, it helped him elude Rakaan. To widen the gap between them, Super 3 altered his course to the left and hoped that he wouldn't miss Alto Raun altogether.

Suddenly, the fog was gone and he was awash in sunlight, a clear blue sky overhead. Alto Raun towered above the sea, a mile ahead. Then a laser trail flew across the bow of his boat. Rakaan was shooting at him from half a mile away. Super 3 veered even further to the left, as far as he could without missing the city. Rakaan's boat closed the gap between them; it would be close.

Resigned to defensive maneuvers, Super 3 swerved constantly to avoid being hit by a laser. But he kept an eye on his pursuer, and thus he saw what Rakaan did not see. At the leading edge of the fog, just behind Rakaan's boat, the water swelled. Then Leevee rose from the water, openmouthed and bellowing, announcing that she had come to destroy her last two challengers.

The three laser cannons on Rakaan's boat turned their fire on Leevee. She roared as the lasers seared her scales. Diving into the water, she created a wave that catapulted his boat toward Alto Raun and away from Super 3. The battle between the two supervisors would have to wait. Now it was an all-out race to survive Leevee's wrath.

Super 3 reached the city and turned his boat in the direction of Rakaan, locking it on a collision course, and then he jumped into the water. Mekens cannot swim, but they don't require air like humans. While their systems were not designed for extended exposure to water, they could remain underwater for hours without sustaining serious damage. Super 3 sank to the barrier rocks below, quickly climbed out of the water, and then stood on the ledge at the base of the city's outer wall.

He watched as Rakaan easily maneuvered around Super 3's stray boat and then headed straight for the city wall. Behind Rakaan, Leevee's head rose from the water just enough to swallow Super 3's boat, and then she disappeared again.

Rakaan jumped from his boat just before it crashed into the barrier rocks, where it exploded, destroying the remaining Breakers along with it. It wasn't long before he rose out of the water, climbing the rocks just as Super 3 had done. Standing on the ledge two hundred yards away, Rakaan turned and looked down the city wall until he spotted Super 3. Their eyes locked. Super 3's system processors accelerated to the point that his metal frame trembled. He knew that he had to destroy Rakaan, and now was the time. It would come down to hand-to-hand combat between the two. Rakaan appeared to have come to the same conclusion, since they simultaneously launched into a run toward one another.

But Super 3's vision of mortal combat came to an abrupt end when Rakaan stopped and started climbing up the city wall. He had not been running to engage in battle; he had run to an exterior maintenance ladder that ran the entire height of the city. He was trying to escape.

Supervisor 3 slowed as he considered what to do, but he resumed his sprint when he realized that he could not let Rakaan run loose in the city. Before he had run a hundred feet, a hangar door opened ahead of him and several maintenance Mekens and a builder Meken stuck their heads out. They waved for him to hurry. *Can't they see I am hurrying?* As he neared them, they waved him into the hangar. They clearly didn't know about Rakaan. Super 3 didn't slow down and pointed to the ladder ahead. Then, to his surprise, the builder picked up a small maintenance Meken and threw it into Super 3's path. The little Meken tangled in his legs, and he fell in a hard crash on the ledge. Super 3 jumped up, his system exploding with chaotic energy; he was enraged. All he could think about was smashing the builder's head for what he had just done. He was about to resume his chase when he saw all the Mekens pointing out to sea and frantically waving at him to look. He turned and saw Leevee a half mile out from the city, towering a thousand feet in the air. She trumpeted her triumph with a great roar, daring anything that challenged her. As she started to fall forward, all the Mekens pulled back and the hangar door started to close. Super 3 scooped up the little maintenance Meken and jumped into the hangar. Leevee fell like a skyscraper. Her crash set in motion the final blow of her attack, a wave that rose two hundred feet and rushed toward the city. The hangar door clanged shut just as the great wave hit. Water sprayed through the seams as the entire hangar shook from the force of the blow.

Supervisor 3 sat on the floor, dazed, as he tried to sort through everything that had just happened. He was jolted back to the present when the little maintenance Meken tapped him on the shoulder.

"Thank you for saving me," the little Meken said in a small, nasally voice.

"You're welcome," Moses replied. "And thank you for stopping me."

"You're welcome."

The builder approached them, apologizing profusely. "Supervisor, I am sorry for taking such rude measures, but I had to get your attention. You would have run right past us and—"

The little Meken kicked the builder in his metal shin and squealed loudly.

"I am sorry," the builder said, looking down at the little Meken. "I reacted, and you were the closest thing that—"

The little Meken went crazy, squealing and kicking the builder again and again. The builder shut up and just stood there, letting the little guy get it out of his system.

As Supervisor 3 watched this, his own body started convulsing. He ran a quick diagnostic of his system and found that his empathic processor was sending a most unusual combination of instructions—commands designed to release processor stress were blended with commands to generate random mechanical tensions throughout his body. He realized he liked the combination, and he let it run. As soon as he did, the program increased in intensity; his body started shaking, and strange, involuntary noises erupted from his audio generator. The little Meken stopped kicking the builder, and they both turned to look at Super 3. Then the little Meken started shaking and emitting strange noises; showing a similar system reaction as Super 3. The builder looked back and forth between the two of them.

"Are you . . . laughing?" he asked.

Supervisor 3 could barely speak through his involuntary system spasms, but finally, he managed, "Yes. I think I am. I am laughing. *And* I am home."

44

Return to Earth Day
1000 hours
A park in southwest Canada, Earth

Under a smooth canopy of grey clouds, a thousand people mingled, dressed mostly in black. After five weeks of tireless searching, the airline had graciously planned this memorial gathering as a way to help families and friends bring some closure to their loss and move on with their lives. It would likely be years before their grief would fade, but the door of hope for finding their loved ones had really closed weeks ago. As it stood now, the fate of flight 1402 would likely remain an unsolved mystery.

With a hand on their shoulders, Melissa Tygert guided her daughter and son up to the memorial table. Melissa set an eight-by-ten-inch photo in an open space held by a place card that read "Capt. John Tygert." Holding the frame for a moment, she gazed at her husband, looking handsome in his trim airline uniform and showing off his winning smile. When her hand started to tremble, she pulled it away and held it over her mouth as tears streamed down her face. Her son,

John Jr., stepped forward and placed a six-inch figurine of Superman next to the photo. At Melissa's side, her daughter, Lacey, squeezed a Beanie Baby against her cheek: a fuzzy, brown puppy, given to her by her father. "Oh, Daddy," she said, bursting into tears as she reached out and set the little stuffed animal in front of the photo.

Melissa pulled both of her children close, and for the umpteenth time, they cried together. As the emotional waves of the moment subsided, she became aware of others gathered around them, heads bowed, silently sharing their pain. *Yes, this is good*, she thought. They were not alone in their grief and anger, and she found a comfort that she had not realized she needed. Nodding her gratitude, she and her children walked down the long row of tables, pausing occasionally to share the sorrowfull moments that others were now experiencing. One after the other, photos and mementos reflected the stories and impact of 125 lives lost. Representing husbands, wives, brothers, sisters, parents, children, and friends, every one of the people gathered in the park carried the same pain, and Melissa and her children took comfort in their new extended family.

The crowd assembled, sitting in rows of chairs facing a small platform, where the president of the airline and the prime minister of Canada each gave a brief speech. What can someone say to a gathering of grief-stricken people who are also awash with anger at the unanswered questions surrounding the disappearance of a plane in midflight? At least the diplomats had required that the media cameras keep a respectful distance. Their speeches were followed by a religious leader who spoke about the mysteries of God. While Melissa was in no mood to accept his platitudes, she gave him credit for his sincerity and care.

After the speakers, a woman with a pleasant voice read the names of each passenger on Flight 1402. During the reading, a momentary break in the clouds revealed a blue sky above. Gazing overhead, Melissa became lost in her own thoughts. "Where did you go, John Tygert?" she whispered. "Where did you go?"

45

Mhara awoke, lying on her back in a comfortable bed, staring at a white hospital ceiling. She started to roll over, but every muscle she could imagine ached. Lying still, she simply turned her head. Despite her headache and the pains, she smiled. Sitting on a couch next to her bed were Kane, Charly, and Rhogan, in that order, all leaning on each other and fast asleep. They had obviously been keeping vigil over her and had finally succumbed to sleep. Tears came to her eyes and ran down her cheeks.

Charly stirred and saw that Mhara was awake. Carefully slipping out from between the two boys, she eased Rhogan over to lie against Kane's shoulder, where they both remained lost in heavy slumber.

Kneeling by her bed, Charly asked, "Mhara, are you hurting?"

"No, I'm fine."

369

"Why are you crying?"

"Seeing the three of you there . . . waiting on me . . . safe . . . together. Whatever else happens, I will treasure this moment with the deepest gratitude." She reached her hand out, and Charly took it, tears now welling in Charly's eyes.

Rhogan snored, ending in a snort that woke Kane. Rhogan's head slid down Kane's chest and onto his lap.

"What the—" Kane said, groggily, lifting his arms, trying to figure out who was lying on him. Rhogan curled his body into a ball, snuggled his head into Kane's thigh as if it were a pillow, and hummed contentedly. Kane looked at the girls, his face a mixture of sleepy and dumbfounded.

The girls laughed till they cried.

46

Light-years away, the *Mayflower* came out of suspension, having successfully made it through the Push. This time there was no trauma or crying among the passengers. Instead, they each took an antinausea pill to settle their stomachs and an aspirin to reduce the headache that always accompanied a Push.

The *Mayflower* was cruising high in a dark-blue night sky, moonlight illuminating a layer of wispy clouds below. Ham rushed into the cockpit, jabbering with excitement.

"Sweet Mother Earth! How's she lookin', Captain?"

"Looks great," Tygert said, stoically. "Just one problem."

Tygert and Sam had their heads tilted back, looking almost directly overhead. Ham moved forward into the space between them and looked up, following their gaze. A full, grey moon glowed brightly in the night sky. Ham gasped. To the right of the grey moon, and behind it, was a larger, reddish moon.

"It's the wrong Earth."

epilogue

Undulating hues of yellow, orange, red, and violet painted the horizon as a striking sunset fell upon Ahlemon. A lone figure stood on the retaining wall that edged the rooftop of Alto Raun, his dark cape flapping in the brisk wind, and the ocean waves crashing against the city wall five hundred feet below. But he was not admiring the beauty of the evening sky; he was seething with hatred, his metallic fists clenched.

When he spoke, his voice started at a whisper—but grew into a battle cry:

"I will crush every last bone in every last human body. Do you hear me, humans?" he roared. "I am Rakaan! And I am your exterminator!"

About the Author

A lifetime reader of fantastical and adventurous tales, Casey McGinty raised his three children telling them spontaneous bedtime stories. In *The Last City*, his first novel, Casey simply wrote a story he wanted to read. Residing in Kingston Springs, TN, he enjoys kayaking, movies, playing guitar, making tacos, and helping his wife with their two Tennessee Walkers, Gideon and Asher, and Otis the donkey.

Watch for further adventures in the Ahlemon saga at

WWW.CASEYMCGINTY.NET

www.ingramcontent.com/pod-product-compliance
Lightning Source LLC
Chambersburg PA
CBHW030651120726
47905CB00001B/166